TERROR TALES
OF CORNWALL

TERROR TALES
OF CORNWALL

Edited by
PAUL FINCH

First Published in 2017 by Telos Publishing Ltd,
5A Church Road, Shortlands, Bromley, Kent BR2 0HP, UK.

www.telos.co.uk

Telos Publishing Ltd values feedback. Please e-mail us with any
comments you may have about this book to: feedback@telos.co.uk

ISBN: 978-1-84583-121-9

Terror Tales of Cornwall © 2017 Paul Finch
Cover Design @ Neil Williams

Copyright Details

CONTENTS

WE WHO SING BENEATH THE GROUND

Mark Morris

The village school was not quite at the highest point of the steep main street, but it was elevated and isolated enough for Stacy to see the sea through the chain-link fence that bordered the far side of the playground. She could smell the sea from here too, crisp and salty, especially on a day like today, when a brisk November wind bowled up and over the hill, unimpeded by the buildings and patches of woodland that proliferated further inland.

She'd always wanted to live in Cornwall. She'd been in love with the place since spending family holidays here as a kid with her parents and her elder brother Paul. She had such happy memories of Fowey – Daphne du Maurier's house, and the annual regatta with its carnival procession and its hilarious pasty-eating contest, Looe Beach, where the seagulls would steal the food right out of your hand if you didn't remain vigilant at all times, and beautiful fishing villages like Mousehole and Polperro, which to her had seemed deliciously mysterious with their tales of smugglers and pirates.

Carl hadn't been keen on moving so far south, but after their divorce two years ago she'd thought: *What's to stop me?* They had no children to complicate matters – when things had initially started going wrong between them she'd blamed her own inability to conceive, but with hindsight she realised that Carl's increasing lack of consideration and reliability had been far more pertinent factors – and so she had started looking for teaching jobs in the area.

It had taken nine months, but eventually she'd been offered the deputy headship of the little primary school in Porthfarrow (only thirty-eight pupils and five members of staff). Accepting the job had entailed her biting the bullet and taking a twenty per cent wage drop, but in her opinion the positives of her new life far outweighed the negatives. Life was slower here, and less stressful, and more community-minded, all of which suited her down to the ground. She could walk to and from work instead of having to negotiate the nerve-shredding hassle of the Manchester rush hour, which meant she not only saved on petrol but was fitter than she'd been since she was a teenager.

Okay, so she might not have the dating opportunities here that Manchester offered, but that was something that bothered Stacy's mum more than Stacy herself. And small though the village was, it wasn't as if she hadn't turned a few heads since buying her little white cottage just a couple of turns off the High Street. Cliff Monroe, who owned the hardware store, had taken her out to dinner a couple of times, and although he hadn't exactly set her pulse a-fluttering, he was a nice guy with a nice smile – and interesting too. Although he'd been born in the village, and had confessed to her that he'd probably die in it, he'd travelled the world a bit before putting down his roots. Plus he owned a boat. Not that she was particularly materialistic. In fact, she'd become far less so since leaving the city – and Carl – behind.

The little yellow bus, with its daily contingent of more than half the school's pupil population, crept into view at the bottom of the winding, leaf-strewn hill. There had been a couple of days last winter when the icy roads had proved too treacherous for the ancient vehicle, as a result of which those pupils who relied on it – most of whom lived in isolated farmhouses and remote cottages out in the sticks – had had to stay home.

As the bus wheezed to a halt and disgorged its twenty or so passengers, Stacy crossed the playground and opened the little iron gate to admit the chattering hordes. On Friday she had announced that today would be Show and Tell day, and so she was pleased to see that most of the children were carrying something other than their school bags. Richard Charlton had a skateboard, Maisie Flynn had a photo album, and Kylie Kendall, who was crazy about gymnastics and often had to be stopped from cartwheeling about the playground in case she did somebody a mischief, had a large plastic wallet stuffed with certificates and rosettes. Little Adam North, whose black and permanently tousled hair was like an ink dab above his pale, secretive, mole-like face, was clutching something long and curved, wrapped in newspaper.

'What have you got there, Adam?' Stacy asked. 'I hope it's not a Samurai sword?'

She had made it an ambition to get Adam to smile – he was a solitary soul who barely spoke unless spoken to, and who hardly ever showed emotion, be it anger, unhappiness, mirth or joy. If she had been a betting woman, Stacy would have put money on Adam turning up today with nothing to show the class, and so she was secretly delighted that her idea, although not a particularly original one, had at least motivated him to make an effort.

As always he responded to her flippant comment with deadly seriousness. 'No, miss.'

'Well, that's good,' she said, and laughed more heartily than the occasion merited. 'We wouldn't want you to …'

She'd been about to say 'slice off any heads', but at the last second it occurred to her that the phrase was inappropriate, given the terrorist atrocities that turned the news into a rolling account of seemingly ceaseless depravity and horror every day. She hesitated a little too long, glanced again at the sea as if seeking inspiration, and in the end muttered lamely, '… do any damage, would we?'

Adam regarded her with a deadpan expression. 'No, miss,' he said again, and followed his fellow pupils into the school.

Show and Tell, which took place between morning break and lunchtime, turned out, on the whole, to be a great success. Most of the children were loquacious and enthusiastic, and Daniel Roberts' account of his recently departed grandfather's heroism during the Second World War, as he held up the old man's medals, was so poignant that Stacy felt tears pricking at the backs of her eyes.

As each child finished his or her turn in the spotlight, a mass of increasingly fewer hands would shoot up and a chorus of 'Please, miss! Me next!' would fill the classroom.

Perhaps inevitably, the only child who didn't stick up his hand was Adam. He sat near the back, his face expressionless, the strange, curved, newspaper-wrapped object held protectively against his body. Stacy thought he might have remained there all day, if, with six or seven children still to take their turn, she hadn't said, 'What about you, Adam? Do you want to go next?'

He blinked. Shrugged. Made no move to rise from his seat.

'Come on,' she said gently, beckoning him forward. 'Show us what you've brought.'

The other children turned to look at Adam as if they'd only just noticed he was among them. Looking neither intimidated nor resigned, he rose slowly from his seat and ambled to the front of the class. He turned to face his fellow pupils and for a moment just stood there, holding his newspaper-wrapped bundle. They stared back at him silently.

'Do you want me to help you unwrap it? Is it fragile?' Stacy coaxed.

Adam glanced at her, then unceremoniously pulled away the sheets of newspaper and dropped them on the floor.

Revealed beneath was a curved half-moon of what appeared to be a pearly, shell-like substance. It was smooth on one side and serrated, or ragged, on the other. It was perhaps a metre long, and Stacy's first thought was that it was a large boomerang, her second that it was something organic – part of the exoskeleton of some sea creature, perhaps. The children craned forward, their faces puzzled. Stacy held out her hand.

'May I see?'

Adam hesitated for just a second, then handed the object over.

It was lighter than she had expected, and there was a rime of what appeared to be dirt on one side of it.

'What is it, miss?' Caroline Fairley asked.

Stacy had no idea. She turned to Adam with a smile. 'Perhaps Adam can tell us?'

He looked at her blankly.

'Don't you know?' one of the boys – it might have been Luke Cooke – sneered.

'You shouldn't have brought it in if you don't know,' another boy, who was yet to be summoned to the front of the class, piped up sulkily.

'Shhh,' Stacy said. 'Don't interrupt when it's not your turn to speak. It's rude.' The class quietened down. She glanced again at Adam. 'If you can't tell us what it is, Adam, can you tell us where it's from?'

Quietly Adam said, 'Found it.'

'You found it?' Stacy repeated it loudly, for the benefit of those who hadn't heard. 'Where did you find it? On the beach?'

He shook his head. 'Farm.'

'The farm where you live, you mean?'

He nodded.

'And whereabouts on the farm did you find it?'

His eyes narrowed, as though he was wondering how much he ought to reveal. 'Field.'

'I see. And was it lying in the field?'

He hesitated, then shook his head. 'Was buried.'

'And you dug it up?'

So quietly she wasn't sure she'd heard him correctly, he said, 'Came up by itself.'

'What did he say, miss?' one of the girls chirruped, and Stacy was about to reply that the buried object had worked its way to the surface of the soil, before realising she wasn't sure entirely how that process would work. To avoid having to explain it she held up the object and said, 'So what do we think this is, class? Hands up. No shouting out.'

The hands went up, and Stacy pointed to each in turn.

'An alien sword!'

'A shark's jaw!'

'A dinosaur bone!'

'A hockey stick for a caveman!'

Some of the suggestions made the children hoot with laughter, and Stacy laughed along with them. At one point she glanced at Adam, who was still standing silently beside her, and saw that he wasn't joining in with the laughter. He was gazing at his classmates, or at least gave the impression that he was doing so. Looking at his unfocused eyes, though, Stacy couldn't help wondering whether he was staring at something else entirely.

The next day, Tuesday, Adam didn't turn up for school. Between registration and morning assembly, Stacy popped her head into the office.

'Have Adam North's parents rung to explain why he's absent today?'

Moira, the school secretary, a blowsy, middle-aged woman who wore a lot of orange, scowled as if Stacy was accusing her of not doing her job.

'Not yet. I was about to call them. It's on my list.'

'I'll do it,' said Stacy.

'You don't have to.'

'No, but I want to. So could you please give me the number?'

She didn't know why she felt compelled to take personal action. Was it because the boy was such an enigma? She told herself it might be useful to speak to Adam's parents anyway, regardless of his absenteeism, perhaps call them in for a chat. She tried to remember whether she'd met them at any of the three Parents' Evenings she'd attended since arriving in Porthfarrow, and couldn't recall. Not that that was entirely unusual. Some parents were simply too busy.

Moira gave her the number with a disapproving huff, and Stacy punched it in. The phone rang out at the other end. She let it ring fifteen times before replacing the receiver.

Moira looked almost triumphant. 'The Norths are farmers. They'll be busy during the day.'

Out in the fields, digging up alien swords, Stacy thought, and said, 'They're bound to be in at some point. Keep trying, will you?'

Moira sniffed.

Next day was the same story. Adam was a no-show; his parents didn't call; their phone rang out, unanswered.

'Shall I write them a letter?' Moira offered, albeit in a tone that suggested she thought the action onerous and unnecessary.

Stacy shook her head. 'No, I'll take a drive out there after school, see what's what.'

Moira pulled a face. 'Are you sure? It's a long way.'

'It's fifteen miles at the most.'

'Like I said, a long way. Pardon me for saying so, but don't you think you're making a fuss?'

'No I don't. I happen to be worried about Adam.'

'He's only one boy.'

'And he's the one who's currently causing me worry. I'm his teacher and he's not attending school. It's my job to be concerned.'

Moira sighed. She conveyed an awful lot in that sigh. 'They won't thank you for it.'

'Who won't?'

'The Norths. They're a funny lot. Keep themselves to themselves.

14

Always have. The only reason Adam's not in school is because John North'll have him helping out on the farm. They've never been big on education, that lot.'

'Well, I'll just have to point out the error of their ways to them then, won't I?' Stacy said.

Moira rolled her eyes. 'Rather you than me.'

At 4:15 that afternoon, Stacy found herself driving along a narrow country road between high hedges that her sat nav was trying to convince her didn't exist. The wind had picked up considerably in the past few hours, and was making a high-pitched whining sound as it attempted to squeeze through the doorframe gaps of her little Ford Fiesta. The sky was deepening to a muddy blue blotched with muddier clouds, and leaves which had been red and gold when she had set off, but which now looked black, swirled in mad flocks through the twin beams of her headlights.

'Make a U-turn when necessary,' her sat nav instructed her.

'Shut the fuck up!' Stacy retorted and jabbed at the button to silence it as savagely as if it was the speaker's eye. Distracted, she only registered the dark opening on her left, and the lopsided sign beside it, after she had passed them by. She hit the brakes, and then, hoping that nothing was beetling along the narrow, winding lane behind her, put the car into reverse.

And there it was. An opening in the hedge marked by a pair of rotting gateposts. Sagging from the left-hand post, the paint faded, was the sign she'd seen: *North Field Farm*.

'Hallelujah,' she muttered, and manouevred the car around in the lane until it was in a position to nose its way between the posts and on to the dirt track beyond. Flanking the track were huge, flat, muddy fields, bordered in the distance by stunted trees. After the narrow confines of the country lanes the sudden space was almost bewildering. Ahead of her, perhaps five hundred metres away at the far end of the track, she spied her destination: a huddle of buildings that were little more than silhouettes in the encroaching twilight.

Wondering whether the Norths had gone away for a while (*Do farmers go away? If so, who looked after their livestock?*) she began to meander along the track. It was muddy and rutted, and she took it slowly, keeping the car in second gear. Above the grumble of the engine and the whistling of the wind, she could hear the sustained screeching of what sounded like crows coming from somewhere on her left and glanced in that direction. Jutting from the centre of the field, perhaps a hundred and fifty metres away, she saw five lopsided standing stones, above and around which were indeed a flock of crows, flapping and cawing.

Her eyes were swiveling to face front again when one of the stones moved. Or at least, she thought it did; in truth, the impression was both slight and fleeting. It was enough, though, to make Stacy stamp on the brake and bring the car to a jolting halt. As the seatbelt locked across her chest she gasped. By the time she had settled back into her seat she was aware her heart was beating rapidly.

She turned to look again at the stones. Stared at them for a full ten seconds. They were motionless. Yet one of them had seemed to … what? Lean over? Bend in the middle? The idea was ludicrous. It must have been a trick of the fading light, perhaps exacerbated by the constant whirlwind of swirling leaves and circling crows.

She shuddered, as though sloughing off the vagaries of her own imagination, faced front again, and put the car into gear. The dark buildings loomed larger as she approached them, until eventually they filled enough of her windscreen to mostly blot out a sky that was now the colour of slightly faded denim. She passed through another set of equally rotten gateposts and in to a yard of slick, uneven cobbles, across which was strewn a combination of rubble, muddy straw and sizeable clumps of either mud or manure.

Peering at the farmhouse bathed in the glow of her headlights, and at the shadowy buildings set back on either side of it – the most prominent of which appeared to be a barn on the right, which was twice the height of the house itself – Stacy found herself hoping, for the first time, that the Norths *wouldn't* be home, after all. The farm where Adam lived with his parents was a *dismal* place. Not just run-down, but squalid enough to be unsettling. There were tiles missing from the farmhouse roof, the windows were filthy, and the stonework was black and crumbling. Against the side of the house were stacked rotting planks, rusting machinery, stone slabs and large, white plastic bags, many of which were split and leaking what might have been grain or sand or rubble.

For a good minute, Stacy sat in her car, the engine running and the heater on, her hands gripping the steering wheel so tightly that

make turning over in its sleep, albeit amplified a hundredfold. Yet although it was loud, the sound was fleeting, and tangled up in the still-howling wind, and therefore impossible to identify. It was disquieting enough, though, to set off a jittering in her belly, to make her feel suddenly claustrophobic, trapped by the dark. All at once the urge to see what was in front of her overwhelmed her natural caution, her desire to remain undetected. With a trembling hand she snatched her phone from her pocket and switched on the 'Torch' app, shining it in front of her.

She couldn't help it – she let out a gasp that was sharp enough to emerge as a breathy scream. No more than two metres away was a circular pit that, as far as she could tell, stretched from one wall of the barn to the other. She thought of animal traps, in the bottom of which might be sharpened stakes designed to pierce the animal's body as it fell. *Oh God, oh God.* Was that what this was? She tilted her phone down, shining it into the hole.

It wasn't black down there, as she had expected. It was red.

Blood red.

And she could see something moving. Something huge and glistening and slug-like.

She jerked back so quickly she stumbled and almost fell. Her fingers sprang open, an involuntary defence mechanism, and her phone flew out of her hand and into the hole. She watched in horror as it dropped out of reach, briefly illuminating the wet red walls of the pit, before bouncing on the glistening, slowly uncoiling thing at the bottom and winking out.

Now she was in darkness, and she could smell the thing, its meaty, burpy stench, as it rose towards her. At least, she *imagined* it was rising towards her. Imagined it adhering to the walls, hauling its bulk upwards, extruding tentacles to coil around her limbs to ensnare her, pull her down.

'Won't hurt you,' said a voice.

She whirled round with a scream. Squatting in the corner of the barn to the right of the door, just out of the reach of the lamplight, was a small figure. Her heart thumping, she stared at it, and then in a flinty voice she said, 'Adam?'

The figure rose and stepped forward. Now the lamplight illuminated it from below, transforming its small, pale face into a skull-like mask. Stacy saw that Adam's hands were red. Blood red.

Like the colour of the pit.

'It's old, but it's just a baby,' he said. 'Got no teeth. Likes meat, though.'

Disjointed and staccato though his words were, Stacy thought this was the most she had ever heard him speak in one go. She glanced behind her, in the direction of the pit.

'What is it?' she asked.

'Told you. Just a baby.'

'That thing in the pit is a *baby*?'

She saw shadows rushing into the creases his frown made.

'Ain't a pit,' he said. 'That's its mouth.'

For a moment she couldn't make sense of his words. Then all at once she was hit by a revelation. The glistening thing in the red pit wasn't a creature. It was a *tongue*.

'Its mouth,' she breathed. 'You mean ... there's more of it?'

'Lots more. Found its hand first. Came up through the soil. Then it started singing to me. In my head. Told me where to find its mouth, where to dig. Told me how to feed it.'

Its hand... came up through the soil... Stacy thought of the standing stones in the field, how she could have sworn one of them had moved. She thought of the curved, shell-like object Adam had brought to school.

'Oh my God,' she said. 'Show and tell. That was one of its fingernails, wasn't it?'

He shrugged.

Her mind was whirling. 'How big ...' she breathed. 'How big is this thing?'

'Big,' he said, and frowned again. 'Ain't a thing. It's a giant.'

A giant. Cornish folklore was full of tales of giants. But none of them could possibly be true, could they?

A hysterical giggle bubbled its way into her throat. But she thought if she let it loose, if she gave rein to it, it might become something else. Might become terrified, helpless sobbing. She had to hold it together. Had to get back to her car and inform the authorities. Let them deal with this.

Sliding a glance from Adam's motionless figure to the barn door, she asked, 'Where are your parents, Adam? Your mum and dad?'

For a moment Adam looked anguished. Then his face cleared. 'He sang to me. He was hungry. I couldn't say no. It was quick. I used poison. Lots of it. On the animals too. But he's still hungry.'

Oh God, oh God. Her mind kept repeating it, two panicked syllables, over and over. The jittering in her belly had extended to her limbs and she was shaking badly. Her mouth had gone so dry she couldn't even lick her lips.

She made a mighty effort. Unpeeled her tongue from the bottom of her mouth. Forced herself to swallow. When she spoke her voice was a rasp.

'I'm going now,' she said. 'Are you going to stop me?'

His expression was bland. His red hands, his bloody hands, hung by his sides. 'No, miss.'

She nodded and edged towards the door, her eyes never leaving him. He was only a ten-year-old kid, and a smaller than average one at that, but what if he had a knife? Or even a gun? Farmers owned guns, didn't they? If he made a sudden move she'd jump him. She wouldn't hesitate. He might only be a child, but she'd do all she could to get away.

She reached the door. Still he hadn't moved.

At the threshold she paused. 'What are you going to do?'

He shrugged. 'He'll be hungry again soon. He's always hungry.'

She nodded, as if she understood, and slipped out of the door. As soon as she was outside she started running.

The wind howled around her, buffeting her body as though trying to stop her from leaving. She slithered in the mud, went down on one knee, then picked herself up and stumbled on. She glanced back at the barn, expecting to see Adam coming after her, a shotgun in his hands, but there was no sign of him. She started to shake again. To shake so badly she could barely stand. Then she realised it wasn't her who was shaking. It was the ground.

She staggered from one side of the track to the other. She fell. What was this? An earthquake?

The land was wrapped in a deep, dusky grey, but it wasn't quite dark yet. The sun was still hovering on the horizon, providing just enough light to see by.

But all at once a huge shadow raced across the ground, smothering the farmhouse and the yard where her car was parked, blotting out what little light there was. She saw it coming, a tide of black. She looked up.

The shape was vast, vaster than vast, against the darkening sky.

She thought of what Adam had said about the creature in the ground, the creature whose open, wailing mouth was in the barn, and whose fingers were jutting from the soil of a farmer's field.

Won't hurt you, he had said. *It's just a baby.*

The ground shook again. The shadow passed over her like a vast tide.

Only one word filled Stacy's mind.

Mummy.

GOLDEN DAYS OF TERROR

Cornwall is England's most stylish and popular holiday destination. It has the warmest climate in the United Kingdom, the best-kept beaches, the most scenic cliffs, and inland the most sumptuous rolling countryside. Its villages and harbour towns are strictly of the 'chocolate box' variety: quaint, colourful, and filled with local characters and lively entertainments. The accommodation – whether it be hotels, cottages, or wayside inns – bespeaks the 'olde worlde' in a way other tourist haunts in Britain can only dream of.

But Cornwall would not be Cornwall without its multiplicity of spooky tales, its thousands of ghost stories, its legends of monsters, faeries, demons, witches, smugglers and mermaids. And yet somehow, neither of these Cornish essentials – the holiday idyll and/or the spooky underbelly – are mutually exclusive. The mysterious traditions of Cornwall serve to underpin its status as a pretty but ancient landscape, a former kingdom in its own right and a region of deep historical and cultural significance, while the warm welcome provided by the county today is the cosy prism through which some truly fiendish tales can safely be assessed.

The pantheon of scary Cornish mythology is almost without end, and yet England's picturesque southwest tip was firmly and forever pinned onto the horror story map by two seminal works of fiction courtesy of one of the county's most celebrated residents.

World-famous novelist and playwright, Daphne du Maurier (1907–1989), was besotted with Cornwall from her earliest days and spent much of her life there. A mistress of suspense, she saw absolutely no contradiction in setting many of her stories in the land she loved, no matter how horrific the subject-matter. In fact, one often gets the impression that du Maurier actively enjoying this fusion of loveliness and malevolence.

The two most Cornish of her tales and at the same time most sinister date from 1938 and 1952, and are a novel and a novella respectively, and both – while not exactly inspired by eerie events – are traceable to mysterious experiences that du Maurier had while exploring the Cornish peninsula as a teenager.

The first of these, Rebecca, *tells the story of a young wife's attempts to fit into the life of her rich but solemn husband in an immense coastal mansion, Manderley, where he once dwelled with his beautiful and* charming first wife, the titular Rebecca, a now-deceased socialite who all but lives again through the presence of malicious housekeeper, Mrs Danvers. Rebecca is not a ghost story; it is not even, strictly, a thriller. If anything, it is a darkly gothic romance, which became a best-seller in its own right but drew the attention of the whole world when filmed by Alfred Hitchcock in 1940. That said, all the trappings of ghostliness are there – the deep, intangible mystery, the history of vicious deeds, the brooding atmosphere, and of course the magnificent but isolated house pervaded by a sense of evil.

Readers loved it at the time and later were fascinated to learn that Manderley actually existed, though in real life it was called Menabilly and was located near Fowey on Cornwall's verdant southeast coast. In the years following the novel's publication, du Maurier captivated her audience with tales of girlhood summertime ramblings along the Fowey shoreline – through sun-dappled clifftop woods and along sandy paths, the distant sigh of the sea and occasional glint of aqua-blue waves reaching her through a mesh of leafy branches. Surely the quintessential Cornish experience, this was made all the more dramatic when one day she came unexpectedly upon a grand but dilapidated seaside manor house which had all the appearance of having been forgotten. At the time Menabilly belonged to the aristocratic Rashleigh family, but it was unoccupied and going badly to seed. Du Maurier herself, who would be inexplicably haunted throughout her formative years by thoughts of the decayed and overgrown structure – almost as if it was calling to her – eventually took residence there, but only several years after she had immortalised it through the publication of Rebecca and restored it to its former glory.

The second most famous du Maurier tale to utilise a traditional Cornish setting was much more overtly terrifying, and in terms of its apocalyptic concept, far ahead of its time.

Her spellbinding novella The Birds, which first appeared in the author's short story collection, The Apple Tree, follows what we can only assume are the last few days of Nat Hocken, a damaged war veteran, and his family as they seek refuge in Cornwall from flocks of deadly seagulls. The gulls, whose behaviour is never explained, are initially just a nuisance, but become ever more numerous and aggressive, until they actually start killing people. Soon they are bringing unparalleled horror to all corners of Britain, but the focus remains on Cornwall, where Hocken and his loved ones attempt to hole up in a small cottage. What could on the face of it be a ludicrous idea becomes a shudder-inducing nightmare in the hands of du Maurier. The transformation of nature's most graceful and innocent creatures into deranged harpies is shocking enough, but so is the hopeless situation in *which our heroes find themselves – you can sense from the outset that there'll be no happy ending here.*

Of course, most students of the genre are familiar with The Birds *because again Alfred Hitchcock adapted it for film, this time in 1963. Even though, to take advantage of a recent rash of weird bird activity in Santa Cruz due to shellfish poisoning, he transposed the action from Cornwall to California, it is much the same story and incredibly well visualised given the limitations of the period. According to her notes, du Maurier was first inspired to write this tale when she witnessed a Cornish ploughman having trouble with swirling seagulls, which finally began assaulting him in order to get at the grubs he was overturning with his blade. This unexpected scene badly alarmed her at the time, though natives of Cornwall would no doubt regard it with a degree of wry amusement, as the gulls along the Cornish coast are notoriously the largest and most aggressive in the British Isles.*

Neither Rebecca *nor* The Birds *set the standard tone for Cornish terror tales, because these are as many and varied as can be imagined. But they nicely illustrate the nature of the place. Cornwall is a land steeped in fantasy, where fiction, fact and folklore blend together perfectly to create a mist of spooky superstition that cannot easily be penetrated.*

IN THE LIGHT OF ST IVES

Ray Cluley

As Emily walks the darkness, flashing her torchlight into each vacant room, she realises that, yes, a house can be haunted. Not just the old, neglected buildings, the ones with overgrown gardens and broken windows, but also neat, well-maintained, detached holiday homes like this one. She'd never given it much thought before. Now, sneaking around in the dark, she can't *stop* thinking about it. She feels like a child again, a child on a dare, though she's gone further than creep up to touch the front door: she's let herself inside. Not so much a child on a dare, then, but a burglar, making her way around the house by torchlight, treading carefully as if the neighbours are right in the next room. Not that she'll take anything, she's just looking. And not that she'd broken in. Not technically. The door was already broken.

In the living room, cast over the sofa, is the tatty throw her sister has owned since university. A patchwork of primary colours stitched with felt animals, bright silhouettes of camels, elephants, lizards. On the coffee table, a scattering of open books and the candle holder Claire made years ago when sculpture was her thing. Lumpy lines of dribbled wax have hardened, running down to smooth puddles set as sickly yellow circles. On the walls, prints Claire has possessed since her teens. The Lady of Shalott drifting away from the quiet Nighthawks diner towards Dali's long-legged beasts in the desert. Familiar favourites. There are newer pictures too, of course, just as there are ornaments and cushions and hanging displays Emily hasn't seen before, but the room is certainly Claire's. She can feel her presence as if she'd only left moments ago, a trace of her left lingering like perfume.

From the living room, into the kitchen. Again, signs of Claire in a brass plate clock, a comedy coffee mug, an array of crystals arranged at the window. By day the crystals would probably catch and cast the light around in bright sparkles but now the window is a large rectangle of night's darkness. A sweep of the torch shows Emily her own reflection there, ghostlike itself in the room, a non-presence quickly gone as she directs the beam at other things. A row of empty wine bottles by the recycling, but nothing excessive. An ashtray that needs emptying but isn't overflowing. Dishes waiting to be washed.

'At least you're eating properly,' Emily says to what there is of Claire in the room. 'That's good.'

A brief gust of wind rattles the window in its frame. Emily can hear the faint hush of the sea below as it sweeps ashore, retreats, and repeats the process. There's no traffic noise. She doubts there's much even at a more conventional hour. And none of the drunken ruckus Emily associates with two o'clock in the morning, either. Little wonder Claire liked it here. Never mind the wonderful light: the peace and quiet must've been a tremendously welcome relief. Artists need that as much as light, don't they?

Emily's phone buzzes in her pocket, startling her in the quiet she'd been appreciating. She'd left her bag at the hotel but the phone went everywhere with her, even late night trespassing.

It's a message from Tom. *U still awake?*

She tucks the torch into her armpit and thumbs back a reply. *Yeah, went to Claire's.*

How is it?

Haunted, she wants to say, but types: *It's fine.* After a moment's thought she adds: *It's nice.*

She had texted Tom earlier, unable to sleep. She misses him and their comfortable bed and their comfortable life, even the humdrum noise of the city. He'd been awake as well, and after some messages back and forth about Claire they'd exchanged a few dirty texts but Emily couldn't focus and so they'd said their goodnights again. And now here she is, sneaking around Claire's place at two in the morning and wondering where it all went wrong for her little sister.

Another buzz: *Badly damaged?*

Nothing so far, she taps back, *but most of the damage is upstairs I think. I can smell the petrol though.*

There's been a tinge of it in the air since she'd first come in but now, heading away from the kitchen towards the conservatory extension, the smell has become more potent. Sharp, but not unpleasant. Until you consider why it's there.

The conservatory was one of the reasons Claire had taken the house in the first place. The conservatory and the bedroom upstairs, because they both caught so much of the famous St Ives light. 'The house floods with it,' Claire had written in one of her letters (never a text or even an email, oh no, Claire didn't do technology), 'and those two rooms become bright suntraps for endless hours. I should have moved here years ago.'

Years ago you weren't interested in painting. It was acting, or poetry, or learning some faraway foreign language. Or all of the above, all at the same time.

Her phone buzzes and flashes to show Tom asking, *Is it safe?*

Yes, don't worry.

She tells him she loves him and sends a kiss as well. Sincere, but also an indication she's done texting for now. Tom understands. He loves her too, *kiss kiss*.

Emily opens the door onto the conservatory and the overpowering smell of petrol wafts into the kitchen. The windows have been left open in here, just the small ones at the top of each pane, but a lot of the smell has still been contained. It'll be quite a while before it goes away, Emily thinks, though she's no expert. She covers her nose and mouth with one hand and steps inside.

A folding table has been collapsed and it leans against one of the walls, draped with a paint-stained sheet that doesn't quite cover it. Rows of tabletop flowerbeds have been covered with boards to make temporary shelves for pots and jars and canvases. The wood has absorbed much of the petrol. They'll probably need replacing, Emily thinks, wondering if they're still dangerously flammable – the conservatory no doubt gets very warm in the day. The floor is stone, but right now it looks as though the beach has invaded, a carpet of sand covering most of the slabs. Soaking up petrol puddles, she supposes.

This was where Claire had been seen by the neighbours, 'acting peculiar'. Although the house is detached, it still presses close to the neighbouring properties. Mr or Mrs Neighbour had already called for help by then. They were also the ones to call the fire service, which was about as much as Emily had been told over the phone.

She looks at a few of the canvases to see if any can be saved but each is a mess of solvent-washed colours running in ruined lines. Unless they're *meant* to look that way. One looks like it had been a person once, maybe two figures entwined and blurring together, but now it twists and melts, slipping down the canvas in streaks of yellow and green.

'Claire, honey,' Emily says to the empty room. 'What happened?'

Emily had arrived in St Ives in the late afternoon, the light bright but beginning to fade. Her first impression was that it was prettier than many seaside towns but she wasn't as impressed by its beauty as others had been over the years. She suspected her reason for being there had sullied the view. Plus her journey down had been an ordeal. Four beaches and an oceanic climate made St Ives a very popular town in the summer and it seemed all of its visitors were using the same roads as Emily to get there. Finding a place to stay had been difficult, too. Using Claire's house was out of the question and all of the quaint places in St Ives were fully booked, so after a drive of nearly seven hours, most of that on the M4, Emily checked into a bland chain hotel just off the A30. She stayed long enough to dump her bag and splash her face, then headed into town, wanting to see the place that had drawn Claire so many miles from home.

She walked the narrow streets, all shops and galleries, and then each of the beaches where St Ives was dazzling blue sky, bright sands, and a sparkling clean green sea. Cornwall, almost entirely surrounded by coastline, belonged more to the sea than it did the rest of the country. Britain's tentative foot dipping its toe towards the North Atlantic. Perhaps *that* was what had had drawn Claire, ever the rolling stone. The idea of escape. Breaking free from whatever binds you. Maybe that was what she liked about painting.

Emily had arrived late but still she saw many artists at work around the town. St Ives was an international cultural centre and even had its own Tate but she wouldn't have time to visit. It would have seemed too much like a holiday anyway if she'd done that, though she did treat herself to fish and chips. She ate her early dinner leaning against the rails at the lifeboat slipway, paper warm in her hands as she looked at the lighthouse on the end of Smeaton's Pier. She wondered if it was a working lighthouse or simply one of history's leftovers. Claire would know. She'd have looked it up in the local library, visited the museum, all of that. She'd have swum in the sea and strolled the beaches and walked each and every one of the coastal paths by now, storing the views away to paint later in some abstract fashion of hers, all of which was very well, good for her, until six months or so later when she gave it all up to move somewhere new, *do* something new, follow her latest artistic passion.

Fifteen. Emily had counted *fifteen* artists on her walk around town, sketching in pads or sitting at easels near or on the beach. They recreated that beach and the bay and the boats, everything, over and over again with sweeping strokes of their pastels or brushes, sketching bright lines or spreading vibrant water colours. It was a pretty place, of course it was, but so was all of Cornwall, wasn't it? Weren't most coastal places? She didn't understand why Claire needed to come all this way, to this particular town. But then when was the last time she'd really understood her little sister?

One time, when they were children, they had been playing on one of the broken swings in the park. The rubber seat had been split, both halves dangling from the chains, so they'd pretended to be lady-Tarzans, jungle-calling to and fro. Claire, though, at the highest point of one of her swings, decided to let go. For a moment she had been a beautiful gliding figure, hair streaming, body straight, and then she'd landed with a crack that broke her leg. Later, after the cast had been put on, Emily had asked why she'd done it. Why she'd let go. Claire had shrugged and said, 'Seemed like a good idea at the time.' Their parents had blamed Emily because Emily was the oldest and was supposed to look after her little sister. Claire got away with a lot back then. Got a lot of attention, too, and with a cast on her leg she'd got even more. Emily hated that cast more than Claire did.

There were too many chips for Emily to finish so she wrapped what was left and pushed the paper deep into a nearby bin so the gulls couldn't get at them. Claire would have fed the birds, probably. Would have ignored the sign that urged otherwise and thrown chips at her feet, laughing at the feathered chaos.

With the smell of the sea in her hair and clothes, the sharp tang of salt and vinegar on her lips and fingers, Emily checked her watch and saw there was still an hour to go before visiting

hair,' drew a muffled response from Claire.

'What was that?'

Claire leaned away and wiped her eyes. 'Naples yellow?' she said. 'Or misty grey green?'

'I don't –'

'*Fucking yellow or green?*'

Emily was quick to try hushing her. The other patients were looking over and Emily tried to smile them away.

'They seep into *every*thing, Em, *everything*. Seeping colours. Fucking *seeping* colours, *everywhere!*'

'Claire –'

Claire began clawing at the coverings on her arms and a bandage around her chest. 'Look!'

By this time a nurse was in the room, either alerted by Claire's outburst or summoned by one of the others. He hurried to Claire, taking Emily's side of the bed. The police officer came in as well. Emily had to step back to free some space.

'Now Claire, we need you to stay calm, remember?' the nurse said. 'We talked about this.'

Emily watched as Claire fought against even gentle restraint. 'What's wrong with her?'

The nurse only glanced at her, a brief turn of the head, before returning his attention to Claire.

'What's *wrong* with her?'

The policeman said, 'Come on,' and placed a hand on Emily's back to guide her from the room but she shrugged herself away. Claire was crying.

'They seep,' she said. 'They *seep*.' She held eye contact with her sister. 'Naples yellow,' she said. 'Misty grey green.'

Another nurse had arrived and the police officer again urged Emily to wait outside, steering her more firmly this time.

'You'll see,' Claire said. 'Yellow and – Emily? *Emily?*'

'I'm here.'

'Yellow and green. *Seeping.*'

The main bedroom is black with smoke damage. Colourless. An absence in the house like a cavity. The carpet, where any remains, is the sodden black of trampled ash. Beneath, blackened boards. Emily wonders if it's safe. The walls wear permanent shadows. Blackened paper peels away from them in scabby curls or rises in blistered lumps yet to split. The window is a glassless opening taped over with a sheet of plastic that flutters at one corner where it's come unstuck. Whatever curtains or blinds had been there are gone. The ceiling is a single night-cloud of soot except where a light fitting droops in a malformed melted shape. The bed had been stood upon its side to allow more room for canvases and a vague shape of it remains, though the wooden slats are charred stumps and the mattress has slumped away from them, a collapsed heap little more than fused and twisted springs. Easels have been reduced to charcoal. Canvases are blackened square frames, if that. Emily's torch only seems to emphasise all the darkness in trying to sweep it away. The room is a black box, recording what had been done to it and speaking it back in a language of ash.

'Shit, Claire. Good job.'

Where had Claire stood? Did she watch from the doorway as smoke fattened and rolled in the room? Did she stand in the middle of it all, flames licking the walls around her? Would there have been a blast, like in the movies, throwing her out into the hall? She'd been found unconscious but surely she would have had more serious injuries if that were the case? And besides, she'd only used a bottle of white spirit to get the fire started, only downstairs got the full petrol treatment. Emily imagines her sister standing with her arms open, proud of her latest work, fire burning, bathing her with its heat and colour. Flickering reds, oranges, yellows. Naples yellow? Emily imagines her glistening with sweat and reflected light, arms afire from where she'd splashed herself from the bottle, shadows dancing over her body as the flames flickered and licked everything it was to devour. What was that term for light and shadow in art? Chiaroscuro? Claire would have been a chiaroscuro sculpture of flesh, watching her conflagration as it destroyed everything else she had made.

Emily bends and picks up an angle of wooden frame, intending … she doesn't know what. To tidy? She drops the charred wood and dusts the ash from her fingers, wiping them on her jeans.

Did all artists go mad? Was that like an occupational hazard, the price paid for creativity? Or was the crazy artist thing just a cliché?

Emily doesn't have a fucking clue.

'Oh, Claire-bear.'

Her voice is little more than a sigh. Her sister had always been a bit crazy but not *crazy* crazy. Emily decides she'll talk to Tom about letting Claire stay with them again for a while. If the doctors say she can, and if the police allow it. Emily will take care of her little sister. It's what Mum and Dad would have wanted.

A sudden gust of wind tears against the plastic at the window, a loud abrupt sound and then a series of them, like a flock of startled birds flying away in haste. Emily makes her way carefully to where the window used to be. Patches of carpet squelch underfoot, still wet from the efforts of the fire brigade. She holds the thrumming plastic, stills it, and looks out from a torn corner at the night coast. She thinks of the sand down in the conservatory, spread across the stone floor, and the way the ashy carpet here puddles under her feet. The seaside of St Ives expanding into the house. She stands in a burnt dark sea over a petrol-soaked shore.

Emily returns to the spare room. She picks up the photo of her and Claire, wanting it for when she goes back to the hospital. Her fingers are black, and her palm. Soot, she realises. Ash. Not paint. But she's thinking of what the doctor told her when she wipes it off her hand.

'Self portrait,' she says, shaking her head.

While the nurse calmed Claire, one of the doctors spoke to Emily in the visitor's room. This is the room where they break the bad news, she thought, and waited for it.

'As I said on the phone, her burns aren't *too* serious. She'll have scars, but we can do something about minimising those.'

Emily nodded, waiting for him to get to it, and here it was, the awkward pause. The 'but'. And then …

'Considering the *reason* for her burns, and some of her *behaviour* since, I'm recommending a psychiatric assessment.' He raised his hands against a protest that didn't come. 'Just to see where we stand. To decide the next steps in whatever *treatment* your sister needs to get *better.*'

Emily nodded. This was okay. She could deal with this. 'I understand she was quite distressed when she was admitted?'

Ah, the formal tones of her coping mechanisms.

The doctor seemed to relax a little hearing it, Emily noticed. The gulf between her and Claire widened just a little bit more, but in this situation it was useful.

'Well there were the burns. She would have been in quite some pain. And the duress of a house fire,' the doctor explained. 'But I believe there may have been some concerns *prior* to this. *Leading* to this, in fact.'

'I see.'

'When Claire was admitted to us, she ... When she first came in, her ... Some of the staff thought her burns were far worse than they really were. It was quite a shock to them. She was almost entirely black, you see.'

'I don't understand.'

He nodded.

'Before she came to us, before the fire, your sister painted herself.'

'What, like a self portrait?'

'No. I mean she'd painted her body. Black paint, all over herself from head to toe. Her skin, but not her clothes. Her hair as well.'

Emily nodded. She didn't know what to say, so she nodded. Like it was a perfectly acceptable thing for the doctor to say. Painted herself? Must have been for a creative project or something, some new expressive art.

'When can I go back in to see her?'

'She's just being moved to a more private room. For her comfort.'

'And so she won't disturb the other patients.'

The doctor gave her a tight-lipped smile and stood. Emily copied him so he wouldn't be standing over her. 'She's been sedated but you can see her for a few minutes.'

Sedated, definitely, Emily thought, seeing how Claire fumbled with a pillow. She was slowly plumping it into a more comfortable shape, or trying to. When she saw Emily she said, '*Heyyyy*,' long and drawn out, then slurred three syllables into two with, 'Em*ly*.'

'Looking good, sis.' Emily smiled and said, 'The room, I mean. Nice upgrade. No other patients to cough their germs all over you. Even got a picture on the wall. What is that, Picasso?'

'Van Gogh.'

'Yeah, Van Gogh. Picasso did that weird woman one, didn't he? Weeping into her hanky with both eyes on one side of her face.'

Claire's eyes were trying to close but she kept blinking them and

crossed their minds to stick together? Why did they need to decide who got the bus fare when they could've just walked, *together*? *Share* the fucking bananas?

Emily nods. 'Yes,' she says. 'Yes, of course I'll help you.'

Claire sweeps aside canvases, flips them over, until she finds what she's looking for. Some sort of pallet knife or paint-spreader tool. She sets one of the cans upright and levers its lid. Emily picks up the other can and stands it beside her sister's. Both are large cans from a DIY shop. Black emulsion. Well, whatever. If it helps Claire she'll happily take up a brush, paint the whole house. Paint herself as well if she has to, slap on coat after coat of the stuff. Do like The Rolling Stones said and paint it black, paint it all black, if that's what she wants.

'With you here it'll be better,' Claire says. 'You're *sensible* and –'

The lid pops free from the first can.

'Oh no.'

'What is it?'

Claire leans over it to reach the other one.

'What's wrong, sis?'

Claire gets the other lid off as well – '*No!*' – and slaps the can away. It falls before Emily's able to catch it and spills its contents over the floor. Not black, but yellow. *Naples* yellow, Emily assumes. The paint is thick and slow to spill so Emily reaches to turn the can upright but Claire strikes her hands away from it and knocks the other one over as well, grey-green paint glooping free to mix with the yellow.

They watch the spreading puddle of colours seep into the carpet. Seep into their clothes.

Seep into everything.

MORGAWR RISING

Cornwall's oceanic monster tales are legion, and for very good reason. As a peninsula on the southwest tip of England, it juts 75 miles into the Atlantic and is surrounded by sea on three sides, boasting over 200 miles of coastline, much of it uninhabited, which allows for all kinds of mysterious maritime tales that can neither be proved nor disproved.

Sea serpent sightings are a natural staple of this folklore, but over the centuries there have been many terrifying variations on this straightforward theme. For example, a belief still lingers in certain fishing communities that a gigantic octopus dwells beneath the waves off the north Cornish coast, constantly trawling the undersea region between Portreath and Godrevy. Though no photographic evidence exists, numerous disappearances of fishing vessels and their crews have been unofficially attributed to this diabolical entity.

More traditional monster tales emanate from further along the coast, though these vary considerably. Long-necked plesiosaur-type apparitions, humped and horned beasts, one sporting an enormous beak, one covered with thick, brown, kelp-matted hair, and one that was armoured and supposedly seen crawling over the waterline rocks on four jointed legs – 'like a brontosaurus' – have been reported at numerous points on the Cornish shore, under the collective name of 'Morgawr'.

Though this name officially only applies to a serpentine sea creature sighted sporadically in Falmouth Bay off Cornwall's southwest coast, it has now spread all around the county – possibly thanks to Peter Tremayne's classic, Cornish folklore-riddled monster epic of 1982, The Morgow Rises *– and is apparently applicable to a vast range of huge and bizarre aquatic beasts. The sightings are countless, dating between 1876 and 1999, and come to us from locations as far apart as St Mary's Sound in the Isles of Scilly (1944) to Devil's Point, east of the River Tamar in Devon (1987), from Praa Sands in southwest Cornwall (1933) to Port Isaac in the northeast (1935). They have been made from both land and sea, and more often than not come from persons one might normally associate with reliability: fishermen for the most part, local folk who ought to be very familiar with these waters and their usual flora and fauna, but also military naval personnel, harbour masters, lighthouse keepers, and high-status* visitors to Cornwall such as doctors, dentists, lawyers and university professors, whose reputations might have been put at risk by going public.

Three of the eeriest stories – the three perhaps most deserving of the appellation 'Terror Tales' – date from 1933, 1949 and 1970 respectively.

In the first, a small boatload of lobster-men were gathering their pots just off the coast of Annet, one of the most westerly and uninhabited of the Scilly Isles, when a towering, sinuous neck broke the surface close to their boat, with a ghastly head on top and 'eyes like saucers'. Terrified, the men fled, but the belligerent beast pursued them at speed almost the whole distance to shore.

In the second instance, thriller writer Harold Wilkins claimed to have seen 'two remarkable saurians', almost 20 feet long, racing one behind the other up the tidal creek of East Looe in southeast Cornwall, chasing a shoal of fish. Wilkins described their 'dorsal parts: ridged, serrated, like the old Chinese pictures of dragons'. He concluded with: 'These monsters – and two of us saw them – resembled the plesiosaurus of Mesozoic times'.

More unnerving still was the third incident, which involved members of the Salcombe Shark Angling Society. During a deep dive, a bunch of frogmen plunging 80 feet beneath the waves off the south Devon coast, heard what later became known as the 'Lannacombe bark' – a deep and thunderous roar, which repeated itself over and over again like a gigantic undersea dog barking in the depths. The same group also later reported that baited shark-hooks had been bitten clean through, something they had never known before and could not attribute to any species commonly reported around the British Isles.

Of course, these are spoken-word witness statements with little if any other kind of evidence to back them up. Photographs have supposedly been taken of several Cornish sea-creatures, but all have mysteriously failed to materialise. One particular instance of fakery did massive damage to the legend, when in 1976, Tony 'Doc' Shiels, a noted artist and stage magician, reported seeing a monster near Mawnan just north of the Lizard peninsula, and later made a well-publicised attempt to summon Morgawr having recruited a coven of nude witches to work an invocation spell. In 1991, Strange magazine published transcripts from a tape in which a voice alleged to be Shiels implied that the whole thing had been a big hoax.

It is the usual situation that until an unidentified carcass or some other solid evidence is discovered, Morgawr and his many alleged cousins will remain mysteries of the cerulean seas that roll and foam around the rugged Cornish headlands. They may be real, they may be a myth. Just pray you aren't the lone bather who one day discovers the truth.

TROUBLE AT BOTATHAN

Reggie Oliver

It was the breathless summer of 1976 and all of England swam in the unaccustomed heat. That brilliant August afternoon Julian Steadman, Sarath Rajasinha and I, with David Randall, the college chaplain, had set out on a walk together. The other three were keen, industrious walkers; I am a natural dawdler. I like to stop and waste my time by staring at birds and flowers, or the view. As a result they soon began to leave me behind. Once or twice, from the kindness of their hearts, they waited for me to catch up with them, but it was no good. I told them that I could find my own way back if necessary. I had a good bump of direction, or so I thought.

It was strange, wild, choppy countryside. We were not far from Bodmin Moor and the small fields were ringed by irregular dry stone walls, mostly inhabited by sheep. I tried to follow the designated track but the heat and the sheer wild beauty of the place halted me. At last, when it became obvious that I would never catch up with the others, I decided to make my own way back to the house where we were staying, The Place, as it was called.

I don't quite remember where I deviated from the path by which we had come, but it was a considerable time before I realised that a wrong turning had been taken. My young mind had been inhabiting a maze of dreams and hopes; I had not been paying attention. Even when I understood that I was lost, I was convinced that I was moving in roughly the right direction. The sun seemed to be in the correct place, so I was not worried; I even thought that I was making pleasant discoveries with which I could regale my companions when I got back to The Place.

I found myself walking along the edge of a meadow with a stream running beside it to my right. Ahead of me was a dry stone wall and a gate within it on the stream side which led into a wood. Given the torrid heat of that day, the shade looked inviting and I made towards the gate. Flanking the gate in a rough half circle were a number of stones. They were made of the local granite that fangs the neighbourhood of Bodmin Moor, emerging no more than a few feet from the rough tussocky grass, but looking as if they had been deliberately placed there, long, long ago. I made a note of them, as I take an interest in such things, and passed through to enter the gate into the wood.

The gate was weathered and stiff to open as though it was not often used. Once I was through and into the trees I noticed an abrupt change of atmosphere. It was not any cooler; in fact the heat was greater under the canopy of leaves than in the open, and certainly more oppressive. There was a kind of stillness in there as if the air had not moved at all for centuries. To my right the stream was reduced to an exhausted trickle, threading its way over reddish brown loam into which the trees dipped the dark fibrous hair of their roots. The path beside the stream was deliberate and of beaten earth with little vegetation breaking through. I began to wonder if I had come the wrong way, but the straightness of the path gave me hope of an exit on the other side of the wood through another gate, though as yet I could not see it.

The breeze which had offered some relief in the open field was gone and had been replaced by an intense, probing humidity that stuck the shirt to my back. I looked up and a faint glitter in the leaf canopy reassured me that far above me a wind was stirring the trees. I began to be short of breath, so I stopped, and it was then that I noticed the curious birdless silence of the place, free even from the drone of a single insect. The motionless warmth was like a furred hand on my ears, so that I had to click my fingers several times to reassure myself that I had not gone deaf. I also had to suppress a strong desire to sit down somewhere with my back to a tree and sleep. I set off once again along the path, but I had not gone a few more yards before I found my way blocked.

There were no obstacles on the track; nevertheless, I had been stopped. I say no obstacles, by which I mean physical obstacles, but something was standing in my way. It seemed at first like a purely mental inhibition, and yet it was as strong as if I had come up against a wall. I became irritated, angry even with myself. I was quite capable of putting one foot in front of the other, and yet I could not. I stared ahead of me and began to feel the fear that comes not so much from a sense of danger as from an encounter with something utterly inexplicable. My mind had been prevented somehow from telling my body to move forward.

I could see quite clearly ahead of me the path beside the stream wandering away into the trees. And yet the disturbance I felt was not completely internal. A presence was in front of me and my eyes were beginning to sense it. At first it was no more than a slight blurring of the visual field ahead, but the blur had a form. It stood about five feet three inches above the ground and was roughly human in shape. A sensation beyond these visual adumbrations told me it was female, but that was all. I found that if I stared directly at it, I could make no sense of the thing and my eyes began to sting and fill with water; but if I concentrated on some other object within my field of vision, a tree perhaps, I could, perversely, see it more clearly out of the corner of my eye. Then it appeared to be like a semi-transparent shadow and it had a more defined contour, but the form had no recognisable features.

For a long time we stood there, locked in a kind of mutual repulsion, but neither of us moving. I could not say that the entity I had come up against was exactly hostile, but I sensed a stubbornness, a refusal to give place to anyone or anything, and an unknown grievance that fuelled that recalcitrance. I became aware that the thing had been in that place for some time and yet was not in itself at all old.

Putting forth all my mental and physical strength I tried to move my foot forward, but I was repulsed. I am not sure if rage or fear were stronger in me at that moment. I tried stepping off the path and proceeding onward through the trees, but again I was checked. The only way was back. Then it seemed as if the thing were stretching something out of itself towards me, as if it were a limb. I was now being deliberately pushed along the path, out of the wood. I felt myself weakening in mind and body. At last I gave up. I turned round and went back the way I came.

As soon as I was in the field beyond the gate I stopped. There I was suddenly and completely relieved of all mental and physical inhibition. It made me feel quite light-headed, almost exhilarated, but I was not tempted to re-enter the wood. I knew that as soon as I stepped into it the struggle would begin again and I would be defeated. I retraced my steps and found the place where I had deviated from the path and so came back to The Place. As I returned I could just see, away to my right, the wood where I had been turned back, standing in a slight dip in the land, surrounded by a high dry stone wall, very still in the heat except for the tops of the trees which shivered slightly.

As I walked I began to try to analyse my experience. It defied all explanation, of course, but of one thing I was sure: it had changed me. In what way? No. That too was an unanswerable question; all I knew was that I returned to Botathan Place from my walk that day a different person.

As soon as I stepped into the hall I encountered Steadman and Rajasinha. They had evidently been back from their walk for a while.

'Ah, there you are, Roger!' Rajasinha said. 'We were beginning to get worried. Search parties were being proposed.'

'I took a slightly wrong turning, that's all,' I said.

'Ah, well,' said Rajasinha, 'to err is human.' He had a slightly hieratic turn of phrase at times, half mocking, half serious. 'After supper in the library tonight young Steadman here is going to give us a little lecture about Beethoven. That should put you on the right track again.'

Steadman gave a little mock bow, an insincere gesture of self-deprecation, and then the two of them left me there, their curiosity evidently sated. I was disappointed. Something momentous – albeit obscurely momentous – had just happened to me: couldn't they see that? I glanced at myself in the mirror, expecting to see a pale face with something deep and intense about the eyes, but I saw nothing of the sort. My face was, if anything, rather pink from exposure to the sun and the eyes were as they had always been, not, as I had hoped, shining with a new inner light.

The invitation to spend a few weeks at Botathan Place had come as a surprise. I knew about Dr Soper's reading parties in the summer vacation but had always understood that the students he selected to join him there for the month of August were either aristocratic, or good-looking or brilliantly gifted, preferably all three; and I was none of the above. Dr Soper, the Dean of my college, St Saviour's Oxford, was not exactly a snob, but he was an elitist, and he chose to cultivate what he liked to call 'coming men,' those with obviously shining prospects. Coming women were less to his taste, I suspect, and, in any case, St Saviour's was still, at that time, an all-male preserve. Perhaps I was selected because during some drinks party in college at which Dr Soper was present I had let fall something about my Cornish ancestry, my surname being Tregillis. Perhaps my friend Rajasinha had recommended me. At any rate, when Soper approached me in that confidential way of his, as if he were entrusting you with a great secret, and proffered the invitation, I accepted immediately. Despite my family's origins, my parents lived in London, and the prospect of pursuing my vacation studies in the stifling heat of the city did not appeal.

You will read a fair description of 'The Place' in a story written by The Rev R S Hawker for Dickens's magazine *All the Year Round* in May 1867. It is, as he says, 'a low-roofed gabled manor-house of the fifteenth century [I think he means sixteenth], walled and mullioned, and with clustered chimneys of dark-grey stone from the neighbouring quarries of Ventor-gan.' It had been owned by a family called Bligh, the last of whom had been a mathematics don at St Saviour's. When Professor Bligh died in 1973, childless and with no close living relatives, he bequeathed The Place to his college, 'for the benefit of undergraduates in the vacations.'

'Vacations' plural was a little optimistic. Botathan Place was barely habitable, except in high summer. There was, of course, no central heating, not even much hot water to speak of. The arrangements were distinctly Spartan, as the college authorities were disinclined to spend money on it, considering their recent legacy something of a liability. It was situated not far from Launceston, but in wild countryside and up a long dirt road which must have become in winter impassable except by tractor or Landrover. There was electricity, but the cooking was conducted on a stove fed by gas bottles. In some of the rooms on the ground floors there were large stone fireplaces which looked splendid when logs blazed in them, but emitted surprisingly little heat. Apart from Dr Soper's room which was well furnished with electric fires and other home comforts, the bedrooms were sparely furnished with two or three beds to a room. They were primitive things with iron bedsteads and horsehair mattresses.

All that sounds grim, but, of course, it wasn't. The dozen or so of us who accompanied Dr Soper and David Randall to Botathan were young, lively, and largely indifferent to the lack of luxury in our surroundings. We revelled in our remoteness, not only from the comparative civilisation of Launceston, but from contacts with the outer world such as telephones, televisions and radios. This was in the days before mobiles.

The regime was simple, almost monastic in its outlines. After an early breakfast you read until lunch at one. Silence prevailed throughout the house. After lunch the company divided into groups which either went on walks or on shopping and other excursions into Launceston and beyond. From four until about eight we read again in silence, then there was supper. Cooking was Randall's province and washing up was done by us students on a rotation basis, Dr Soper presiding. After supper, we would gather in the main room of the house, called 'the library' and chatted, or put on the record player (classical music only), or played absurd paper games.

It was a long room, this library, with a low plastered ceiling, coffered and pargetted with seventeenth century decoration. The Bligh arms adorned the central panel, but around it in low relief were crude representations of mermaids, sea serpents and other strange beasts. One wall was panelled in oak but the rest were lined to the ceiling with shelves filled with an untidy array of books. The chairs and sofas in the room were of ancient leather, their seats hollowed out from long use. Cushions which had been placed in them to hide their collapse were often worn through or had been flattened and lay on the seating like the geological strata of some ancient landscape. A few lamps were dotted about, but most of us read for as long as we could by the light of the wide mullioned bays that formed one side of the room and faced the great stone fireplace. We all loved this room. The others on the ground floor were impressive but rather gloomy and their neglect was even more obvious.

I loved the room too for its books which crammed the shelves in no particular order. They were a wild selection, and I was the only one of the party who investigated them. Perhaps it was because I was less diligent in my studies than the rest, but I have always had a natural curiosity about other people's books. At a party in a strange house I am often to be found, rather to my own and others' embarrassment, compulsively studying my host's or hostess's bookshelves.

There were, of course, scores of academic and mathematical

treatises belonging to the late Professor Bligh, but the there was also much fiction and other works from the Victorian era, many of them relating to Cornwall. Here was The Reverend Sabine Baring-Gould's *Cornish Characters and Strange Events,* and some of his novels. There was plenty of Hawker of Morwenstow too, that other Cornish clergyman-author, including a volume of his poems:

Young men whom no-one knew went in and out,
With a far look in their eternal eyes!

This is from his *The Quest for the Sangraal,* an uneven poem with some wonderful things in it. That description of the Grail Temple sounded a distant chord inside me and has been with me ever since. I will now spare you any further demonstrations of my enthusiasm for forgotten literature, and go straight to my discovery.

It was on the evening after that momentous walk. Once supper and the washing up was over Steadman duly gave his talk on Beethoven with musical examples played on the library record player. Steadman was one of those sturdily, unimaginatively clever people who acquire first class degrees and successful careers almost as a matter of course. He is now a high ranking civil servant with the standard issue OBE and knighthood. In those days he fancied himself as a classical music buff and I still occasionally run across him at Covent Garden or the Festival Hall when I can afford a ticket. I can vaguely remember him holding forth that night on the relative merits of Karajan's and Klemperer's Beethoven, in between playing movements from symphonies and concertos.

The rest of the company listened to him attentively, though I noticed that there was a smile of indulgent amusement on Dr Soper's face. He was used to undergraduates showing off their extracurricular expertise, and, to some extent, approved of it. I am one of those Englishmen whom Thomas Beecham characterised as knowing nothing about classical music but liking the noise it makes. I soon got tired of Steadman's prosing and wandered, I hoped unobtrusively, to the bookshelves.

In amongst the scholarly and topographical works and the ranks of nineteenth century novels, I noticed a small selection of battered but fairly modern paperbacks. It included several Mickey Spillanes and a well-thumbed Penguin copy of *Lady Chatterley's Lover.* Here was *The Dolly Dolly Spy* by Adam Diment – 'Read Adam Diment – Love him!' I can remember the advertisements saying – *Valley of the*

Dolls by Jaqueline Susann, and Xaviera Hollander's *The Happy Hooker*, works that were already beginning to lose the lustre of their brief vogue. They seemed an odd collection to be found in the library of an Oxford professor. Of course, they could have been placed there by previous undergraduates on a reading party, but I doubted that for several reasons. One of them was that in all of them were scrawled two initials DD together with dates, none later than 1972. Someone called DD who had stayed in the house before it became a venue for college reading parties had left these books on Professor Bligh's shelves.

I was so absorbed in this little mystery that Beethoven's music and Steadman's lecture had by now become no more than pleasant blur of background noise. But even that vanished from my consciousness when I discovered the notebook. It was tucked in between *The Dolly Dolly Spy* and *The Happy Hooker*, a dingy, dark blue thing, only noticeable for the fact that there was no lettering on its spine. It could well have been overlooked from the day it had been placed there until I found it; yet – and I don't think this is hindsight – I had a feeling even then that it was meant to be found.

The pages were lined and filled with handwriting in coloured biro, usually red or green. Was this by the DD of the books? It was probable: the capital Ds were similar, as was the coloured biro ink. It was a journal of some kind, but there were few dates. Occasionally the writer would put the day of the week – 'Wednesday', or 'Friday' – but never the month or the year.

Was the writer male or female? From the first entries it was hard to tell, but I gathered from the later ones that it was a young woman, probably in her early twenties.

The first entry read: 'Saturday: Mum's funeral.' It was written in black biro and after it several lines had been written and scored out so heavily that I could not read them. The second entry was in green Biro and headed 'Wednesday.' I had the feeling that some time – weeks, months perhaps – had elapsed between the first and second entries.

The entry for Wednesday opened with the words 'Christ what is happening to me?' What followed did not provide an easy explanation. The unknown woman recorded dreams and parties, drinking and drug taking, bouts of depression, illnesses, days spent lying in bed and doing nothing, all with the same frenetic wildness.

Fantasies and real events merged. Sentences stopped suddenly in the middle of a description of some happening and then resumed, this time in a dream world. Very few concrete facts could be gleaned. She appeared to be doing some kind of postgraduate research at London University and it was clear from the way she expressed herself that, in spite of the chaos, she had a good mind. I was struck in particular by the absence of other people in the diary. Occasionally a name emerged but the person to whom that name belonged was never described. Usually it was 'a gang of us' or 'the usual crowd' that was described going to a party or simply wandering around London. She equally disregarded herself as a person. There was no self-analysis such as one might expect from a diarist, only random descriptions. The only time when she did have a moment of self-awareness, it was to recognise how lacking in self-awareness she was. After a long description of a party at 'someone's house' heavy with the scent of Marijuana, she wrote: 'It's like everything that goes on is not really happening to me, but I'm watching it, as if I'm sitting in the dark of some huge theatre watching a film or something.' There was mention of a 'bin party' – in an asylum, perhaps? – on New Year's Eve which is not as good as other 'bin parties' that she had been to before. Progressively the writing became more fragmentary. There were more references to depression, and once to some sort of treatment she was receiving for it – 'saw the shrink. Useless as usual' – then a hiatus prefaced by a number of scribbles, curving lines and tangled drawings of half human shapes, interwoven with the odd sentence, such as: 'What the hell is going on?' 'What am I doing?' 'Why are they hassling me?'

After a blank page the writing was resumed in blue biro this time and slightly neater handwriting; but the script was deeply indented into the page, suggesting a suppressed tension.

I had reached this point in the diary when I became aware of a silence surrounding me. I looked up and found that the rest of the company in the library were staring in my direction. Without my having being conscious of it the talk on Beethoven had finished. Most were amused by my oblivion; only Steadman appeared disconcerted.

'Interesting reading?' Steadman asked. There was barely concealed annoyance behind the mild sarcasm. I shut the notebook quickly and concealed it down the back of my chair.

'Not particularly,' I said. 'Excellent little talk, by the way, Julian. I very much agree with you about Klemperer. His tempi can be on the slow side.'

Steadman now looked even more irritated for being balked of a justified disapproval. The company dispersed, but I stayed on in the library reading.

I went back over what I had just read in the blue book, looking for clues that I might have missed as to the writer's identity, but could find none. I was struck even more by a feeling of fragmentation in the writer, as if she were not a person in the sense that we recognise it, but more a random accumulation of impressions and moods. The philosopher Hume would have been unsurprised, since we are, according to him just 'a bundle of sensations.' That was true of the writer, certainly, but of the rest of us? I knew I should go to bed, but I went on reading because my eye had chanced upon a name in the text:

'Sunday. I have been dumped here miles from anywhere at a place called Botathan.' Yes! She was here! 'My Uncle Max (Mum's brother) offered to take me in. There was no-one else. I don't remember all this, but apparently I was found half dead on a park bench in Soho Square or something. They put me in a bin but I couldn't stay there. My whole world has gone dead. I had been walking in a city of the dead. Someone thought the country would help, but the country's dead too. It's all stones and trees. I hardly know my Uncle Max. Oxford Don. No wife. This place has a million books and no hot water. It's miles from a town and they won't let me drive or anything. They want me to go for walks. I hate walks. This house is like a stone tomb. Wood panelled ... coffined. The only half decent room is the library. Uncle Max keeps looking in on me, like he's checking. It's his 'summer vac', as he calls it. He looks at me in a funny way. I wish I could get out. I can't get out. I've got to get my head together.'

'Shouldn't you be in bed, young Tregillis?'

I looked up and saw Dr Soper staring at me quizzically through his gold-rimmed spectacles. He was dressed, with his usual staid correctness, in slippers and pyjamas over which he wore a Paisley dressing gown, its cord neatly tied in the middle with a bow. He was carrying a hot water bottle and a steaming mug of Horlicks: Dr Soper was a man devoted to conventional creature comforts.

'I saw the light on in the library as I was passing,' he said, as if some explanation were required for his intrusion. I too felt that an excuse, however feeble, was in order, so I looked at my watch and feigned astonishment.

'I'm terribly sorry. I didn't notice the time.'

'No apologies needed, Roger. What is the book that has so absorbed you all evening that you failed to pay due attention to Julian's admirable discourse on Beethoven?' His tone contained just the right amount of irony to convey amusement, but not malice.

'Oh, just something I found on the shelves here.'

'I see. Would you care to elaborate?'

'How well did you know Professor Bligh – the chap who bequeathed this place to St Saviour's?'

'Yes, I know whom you mean, Roger,' said Dr Soper: again the gentle irony. 'Hmm. I knew him, of course, as a colleague, well. But then again as a person I hardly knew him at all. He was not an easy man to get to know. A mathematician, you see. Mathematicians are an odd lot: like biochemists, but without their occasional flashes of humanity.'

'Did he die suddenly?'

'Very. But nothing suspicious, if that's what you're after. A brain aneurysm, I believe. Though I gather that prior to that there had been some sort of tragedy in his family, hence his admirable bequest to us.'

'His name was Max, wasn't it?'

'That's right, though even the Master hesitated to call him anything other than Professor. Why? Have you discovered something about him?'

'I don't know yet.'

'How very enigmatic. Very well, I'll let you go to your well-earned rest.'

Without further discussion I followed Dr Soper up the stairs and went to my own bedroom.

The following morning was, if anything, even brighter and hotter and more cloudless than the day before. The windows of the library were open and many of my fellow student readers were sitting with their books on the stone terrace outside it. I, not being an enthusiast for prolonged direct sunlight, stayed in the library. It was exquisitely cool there and I felt I could spend all morning just watching the dust motes turning lazily in the shafts of sunlight that thrust themselves aggressively through the open windows. The book I was meant to be studying was Hume's *A Treatise of Human Nature*, an admirable work, but not the right accompaniment for the perfect summer day on which we were embarked.

The constant conjunction of our resembling perceptions, is a convincing proof, that the one are the causes of the other; and this priority of the impressions is an equal proof, that our impressions are the causes of our ideas, not our ideas of our impressions.

I thought I had once understood what that meant, but not this morning. I read the sentence several times, and still it made no sense. Something in the air seemed to contradict it, or rather to turn it from brilliant rationality into decayed verbal rubbish, like sunlight hitting the undead corpse of a vampire. Finally, I gave up and went up to my room. There I retrieved the dark blue notebook from its hiding place under a pile of socks in a drawer and took it down to the library. Then I began to read.

'Tuesday. I have been outside. My eyes hurt. It is all green, far too green. The trees are like torches of green fire. There was a wind blowing so I went back in. I had been out there for about ten minutes. Uncle Max seemed to be very nice about it. He says I must take things easy. He has a horrible housekeeper called Mrs Gorran who comes in and cooks and cleans for him. She hates me. I sometimes catch her looking at me with eyes like live coals. If I sleep late she just barges into my bedroom and asks if I am getting up. Uncle Max says pay no attention, but what am I supposed to do? He says you're here to get better. Oh, yeah?

'Wednesday. I came down to breakfast in only my shirt and Mrs Gorran said I should watch myself. And I asked her what she meant and she just stared at me with that boiled owl look of hers. Uncle Max didn't seem to notice at all when he came down but later on I caught him looking at me and he said I should get out and enjoy the sunshine. Well I did go in the end. I chose a path; I walked in a field full of unfriendly flowers, and then I found a wood by a stream. I fell asleep and when I woke up there was something with me holding me down. I wasn't afraid because I knew it was part of me, and it was happening again. It was like I was someone else and I was watching myself and what had happened to me had happened to someone else and what was going to happen to me had already happened and I was stuck. It was hot in the wood and it was like there were hands all over me but in the end I crawled out. It was saying to me stop, don't go on. And I don't want to go on, but that means having to die, but I don't want to die exactly, so I suppose that means I have to go on. When I got back apparently I had been out for ages and Uncle Max asked me where I'd been, but I didn't tell him and only mumbled. And he said get some rest and he would bring up something to my room when I was in bed. I wanted to say no but he almost pushed me upstairs to bed, but it was only about eight or nine and not late. And then I got into bed because there seemed nothing else to do and he came in with a cup of tinned tomato soup and when I spilled some on my arm he said he'd lick it off and he actually did and I'm actually writing this down. And then his hands were all over me like spiders in the dark and when I screamed he put a piece of bread in my mouth so I nearly choked and then again and again – and I'm still writing this down after he's gone and I'm bleeding and the blood is sticky on my legs and he's locked the door so I won't get out till morning. The whole world is burning in my ears. And when he lets me I'll go back to the wood, but before that I'll leave this so that some day, he may find it, or someone will…. And then he'll be in hell like I am. Hell will be fire and ice for him but not for me; hell will be warm and hold me close and I will sleep in hell and stay still and quiet and alone for all time, like in that wood …'

There was a blank page opposite this final paragraph and then on the next page she had scrawled in huge capitals across both pages:

THE END

That was it. I put down the book and began to hear in the background the pleasant, trivial sounds of lunch being prepared. Everything was as it had been except myself. I had changed again.

I think I behaved fairly normally at lunch, though I felt like an actor in a play, saying my lines in the appropriate place but not belonging there. The Place felt like a stage on which countless dramas had been played and then forgotten. We were there and soon would be gone and forgotten, and a new drama would be enacted, just as senseless, just as forgotten as the last. I thought that David Randall had looked at me for a moment with concern across the lunch table, but I could not be sure.

That afternoon I turned down all offers of company for my walk.

That was unusual and excited some unfavourable comment. Solitary walks were not deemed to be in the spirit of The Place, but I could not help that. I made sure that no-one was following me and I made tracks for the wood. I do not now remember which way I went, but I found it easily, as if guided by some instinct. Now I was on the path beside the stream again; I was in the silence, and the oppressive, closed-in heat of the wood. As I walked on I was waiting for the moment when I would be stopped; I was actually wanting it to happen, but it did not. Several times I stopped of my own accord, as if to anticipate the unseen resistance, but I encountered nothing so I went on. It was beginning to look as if I would get to the other side of the wood unscathed. And yet I felt enclosed, shut in, as if progress might be made but would lead nowhere. I looked down at the stream a mere trickle of clear water over red brown soil and fibrous tree root. It was then that I saw that I was not, as I had thought, following the rill downstream, but up. I looked behind me and the way I had come had no familiarity. Around me there were trees, above me the tree tops rustled like a distant restless sea, but no other sounds intruded. Then I knew fear.

I turned round and followed the water downstream again, but it was all wrong. I had been walking with the water to my right, now it was on my left. I must, at some point have crossed the stream and turned round. That was the only explanation that made sense, and yet I knew I hadn't. My heart began to thump until it drowned out all other sounds.

Let me make it clear: I did not feel that I was in a hostile environment. There was no sense of malevolence or evil. That, I think, I might have understood. It was the absence of all presence that disconcerted me. Up till that point I had not searched very much for meaning in life, and religion had meant less than nothing to me from a very early age. Now, for the first time, I felt – if 'felt' is the word I am looking for – its absence. I was in a wood thick with trees and heat, and yet it was empty, as hell is empty.

Then, as I followed the stream down, I found that it widened into a shallow pool, no more than a large puddle in the soil that was now black. It looked like a mirror of black glass except that it was stirred by a faint rippling where the stream entered it, and there seemed no exit. Perhaps from then onwards the water went underground and was lost to the sight of man, and travelled into the underworld.

Something lay in the pool, and yet it was not solid because the pool was too shallow to hold anything beneath its surface fatter than a mouse. It was like a reflection where no reflection should have been. At first it was pale and without definition until I saw that it was the shape of a young girl in stone washed jeans and a T shirt that barely covered her midriff. Her face was white, her eyes black and the auburn hair stretched out to the farthest extremities of the pond like the red-brown fibrous roots of trees. It was when this flat image began to raise itself from the water, rivulets streaming from it as if from a razor thin shard of mirror glass, that I began to run.

Somewhere at the edge of the wood I ran into David Randall.

'Ah, there you are,' he said as if he had been expecting me.

I had never had much time for the Reverend David Randall, Chaplain of St Saviour's. He was a gregarious little man with a soft, doughy, sensual face and a passion for opera which he indulged by trips to Covent Garden and Glyndebourne whenever possible. I was disposed to regard him as something of a joke. At the same time, I knew nothing against him.

'I was worried about you going for a walk alone,' said Randall.

This irritated me. 'Why?'

'You've been into Botathan wood?' I nodded. 'I suppose I should have warned you.'

'Why didn't you? What's wrong with the wood?'

'Nothing for the vast majority of people, but for some ... Well, so they say ... Evidently you are one of those.'

I was becoming angrier. Randall was full of mystification and nonsense, pretending to a knowledge and authority which I simply did not recognise.

Then he asked me: 'What happened in there?'

I felt in that moment that I was facing another crisis. I could either hold my experiences to myself and remain silent or let it out. The risks of that were great, not least of being disbelieved, but the tension I felt could not be borne. I told him about the notebook, everything. At the end of it all Randall looked as baffled as I felt. I was expecting some pious and facile explanation, but got none.

After a long silence he said: 'You haven't been reading Baring-Gould, have you? Or Hawker of Morwenstow. About Botathan?' I shook my head. I hadn't. At the time they were little more to me than dead names on a library shelf.

Randall said: 'All right. Only all this has happened before, you know, but a long time ago.'

I asked him for an explanation but he shook his head. We were walking back to the Place in bright sunshine, but its brilliance and warmth were nothing to us.

'Did you know Professor Bligh?' I asked.

'Briefly. I only arrived at St Saviour's in his last year there. The Professor was a very militant atheist, you know, so he didn't have much time for me. In fact his contempt for me was almost personal but I can't say I felt very put out by it. Perhaps I despised him back; I hope not; I can't remember. But very shortly before he died, he came and told me something about himself. I'm still baffled why he chose me, and I won't tell you what he said because the seal of the confessional sort of applies. Not that he believed in that sort of thing, officially of course, but there are times when we act as if we believe in something even when we don't. You may be able to guess at some of what he said.'

'And the niece? DD?'

'Yes. Her name was Dorothy Daniels. Drowned, I believe. Death by water. In this place. Open verdict.'

That evening there was a barbecue on the terrace, organised, as always, with great gusto by David Randall. After it was over, when Randall and I were clearing up, we put the blue notebook on the still smouldering charcoal embers. It made a lot of smoke but was eventually consumed by the fire.

And very early the following morning I happened to look out of the window of my bedroom to see Randall wearing a cassock on the lawn in front of Botathan Place. He was carrying a small black book. Mist still wreathed the ground, hiding Randall's lower extremities so that he seemed almost to be floating over the grass which was showing the first sparkle of dew in the nascent sunlight. I saw him stand there for a while, perhaps a little indecisively, until he began to walk slowly in the direction of Botathan Wood. I felt no inclination to get up and follow him.

That is all really. There is no dramatic conclusion to the story. I started to read Hume again after breakfast and found I made a little more sense of him than I had done the day before. On the other hand I agreed with him less.

The rest is unimportant except that those events, the trouble at

Botathan, as I call it, have brought me here. Here, among spirits in bondage, I have my place. They call it, with unintended irony, a 'secure institution', but there is nowhere less secure. The other men barely notice me most of the time, but they know me and I know them, though I hardly know myself. I even wonder occasionally what, if anything, I believe in. But there are times on Sunday mornings in our hideous little brown chapel when, as I stand behind the altar and lift the host for its consecration, I feel closer to those people than I do to myself.

FROM THE LADY DOWNS

There is much to interest antiquarians in the far west of Cornwall. Archaeologists and prehistorians abound on the open moors above St Ives, Towednack and Penzance, in particular on the picturesque Lady Downs, where a range of Bronze Age artefacts have been uncovered over the years, and cairns, barrows and ancient stones, some arranged in enigmatic patterns, others standing cold and aloof, hint at the former existence of human settlements whose names and occupants have long passed from memory.

If there is any place where the formidable power of the faeries could believably manifest, it is here. And indeed, the Lady Downs provide the backdrop to one of the eeriest and yet more well attested tales of human/faerie interaction in modern times.

The whole of southwest England was long known as 'the Summer Land', largely in reflection of its benign climate. Cornwall in particular, which sits at a southerly latitude in the heart of the Gulf Stream, is famous for its warm summers and amazingly mild winters – in some areas it even boasts evergreen oak trees. This creates a magical aura, which, in a less educated age, was easy to attribute to the presence of mysterious beings. The pixies (or piskies) are a famous Cornish variant on the more traditional faeries and sprites of homespun mythology, but Cornish legend mentions all kinds of little folk, mainly in those areas where there are barrows, ring-forts and dolmens – like the Lady Downs.

In the late 18th century, a certain young woman, whose name is given variously as Cherry of Zennor or Jenny Permuen, and whose age was said to be 16, was found wandering on the Downs in a dazed state, with her left eye 'curious' – either changed in colour, unable to swivel, or simply and inexplicably blinded. She had apparently gone missing several weeks earlier, having left her home to go looking for work.

After much coaxing, the girl, who remained in a confused state, told an astonishing story. She claimed that she was on the road from Zennor to Gulval, which took her across the Lady Downs. Half way over, at a remote crossroads, she met a handsome gentleman dressed in the manner of a country squire. He appeared to know before she even spoke that she was seeking employment, as he promptly told her that he was a recently-

made widower who was in need of a housekeeper and nanny for his son. The payment he offered was good, so the girl agreed to accompany him. He led her along a series of moorland paths, ever downward, through a network of deep valleys and gullies, until they reached a place where no sunshine penetrated. Here, there was a beautiful house surrounded by handsome gardens, which bloomed magnificently despite the permanent shade.

The boy she was introduced to was very quiet and polite, and once the girl had commenced her job, seemed happy to be left to his own devices. However, one very important duty of the new nanny's was to anoint his eyes each morning with a mysterious salve, though his father asserted that on no account was she to use this substance on herself. For long periods each day, the widower and his son would disappear from the house. The girl subsequently found that she didn't have much to do, and so she became bored and inquisitive. Nothing in the house was out of the ordinary, but she'd long noted that the ointment she used on the boy seemed to make his eyes shine. One particularly tedious afternoon, unable to resist temptation, she applied a dab of it to her own left eye.

Immediately, the eye began to burn. In agony, she ran outside to a nearby pool, wherein she attempted to wash the ointment away – only to realise that she could now see bizarre things. Firstly, half men/half fish creatures swam below the surface. But then other beings appeared, dancing on all sides of her: men and women who seemed to have adopted hybrid forms, melding their own features into those of animals and insects. Among these terrifying creatures, she spotted her master and his son. The girl fled back to the house, before fainting onto her bed. In the morning, her master – now restored to his normal human shape – informed her that she was dismissed, and offering no explanation why or for what she thought she had seen the day before, he led her away from his home by various, complex paths, finally leaving her dazed and alone on the Lady Downs.

The weird tale was taken seriously by the girl's family, who demanded to be introduced to this strange widower. However, try though she may, the girl was unable to find any path leading down into a permanently sunless valley, on one occasion taking a track which she was sure she recognised, only for it to end at an overgrown tumulus. In due course, the story was written off as fantasy. It was proposed that the girl might have been injured in some other way, maybe even had poisoned herself eating berries or other ill-advised fruits of the moor, and had dreamed the whole thing.

But Cherry or Jenny, whatever her name actually was, maintained to the end of her days that these things had happened, and was often to be found wandering the Lady Downs on moonlit nights, calling for her former employer in a hopeless, despairing voice.

'*MEBYON* VERSUS *SUNA*'

John Whitbourn

I could have just *stepped* across. A single stride. Without stretching. No danger of getting my feet wet. But I couldn't. Because I mustn't. So I didn't.

I knew only reddened eyes awaited me there. And I don't just mean my own, swollen with tears. Even leaning slightly over, straightaway searing heat in the head arrived. A first stage leading inexorably to brain-boil and death. If I wasn't sliced into slivers first.

It was more tolerable where the Tamar was wide and raced to the sea. Seeing the unobtainable far side wasn't so bad with a real stretch of water before you. I could delude myself there was good excuse to stay put.

Here though, near its north-coast source, the combined river-and-border narrowed to a trickle. Crossing from Cornwall into Welcombe in Devon was just *'one small step for a man'*. But at the same time also a *'giant leap'* beyond what was wise.

Also, there were legal niceties. A tenth century king decreed Cornwall extended to the east bank. Whereas later bureaucrats said *'centre of watercourse'*. Which interpretation prevailed? Testing that out might involve 'the trip of a lifetime'. As in never coming back ...

So, the Wife and I surveyed England stretching away before us. A mere four or five hour drive and then you got to London. She liked London – in moderation. Not to live in, God forbid, but good for an occasional shopping expedition followed by a show. The first step towards which was but a yard away. And doubly desirable now it was forbidden.

England's Capital held no appeal to me – never had – but Welcombe's *Olde Smithy Inn* looked extra tempting today. At its garden tables some combined families were enjoying a pub lunch.

One man was making heavy weather out of a Cumberland sausage casserole, trying to unfurl the uncooperative serpentine coil with his fork and getting gravy specked in the process. His companions made out he was snake-handling and supplied a *sssss*-ing soundtrack. Another 'friend' pretended to play a snake-charmer's pipe.

Much merriment ensued; even their toddlers joining in without fully comprehending. Children instinctively know not to look gift-horse happiness in the mouth.

All this normality occurring a mere stone's throw away! And yet also an astronomical distance. It wasn't these folks' fault, I realised, but that stone chucking option still held appeal. The selfish swine! Sitting there laughing and enjoying themselves? An outrage! Plus the *Butcombe Bitter* thing too! I saw several pints of it before them, on tap for supping *anywhen they liked* ...

I liked Butcombe bitter. Once upon a time I could have strolled over and imbibed lovely Butcombe to my heart's content. *Once*. Alas, for some inexplicable reason it wasn't often available in Cornwall. Not that I was bitter ...

The Wife read my face.

'There's more tears shed over *answered* prayers ...' she said. Not exactly *'I told you so'*, but definitely biscuit crumbs strewn in the marital bedsheets.

I knew why. Yesterday there'd been a hen-debrief on her girlfriends' outing to that *Mamma Mia* musical. The ankle-chain-gang had reviewed it as *'miles* of fun!' Although they still thought it 'funny' she'd refused to join them, even for the mere skip-and-jump to Bideford. Saying she'd become an 'old stick-in-the-mud' who never left Cornwall. 'They don't *eat* people over in Devon, you know ...'

Actually, we *did* know. And know differently.

There ensued what the Wife calls *'one of our silences'*. Of which there were more and more these days; our relationship descending into frigid Polar peace. Which I suspect she could well live with. Silence was an improvement on (and I quote): 'Banging on about bloody Celts and Kernow and Logres. And reciting the *Armes Prydein* – whatever *that* is when it's at home!'

The Wife would never have attended a bullfight – out of compassion and principle. But standing there on the edge of

Kernow, staring into *Logres*, she revealed herself as no mean matador.

It didn't *have* to be said. It was better left *un*said. Yet apparently I'd asked for it. '*It*' being all I'd ever wished for, other than her hand in marriage. And now I'd (we'd) got it. Wherefore *I* now *got it* from her: both barrels. Because it would have been nice to go up to Town and see a show. Just one more time before she died.

The matador-missus waggled her metaphorical cape. Behind it hid a sword-sharp *coup de grâce*.

'It serves you right!' she said. 'I've *no* sympathy ...'

I turned to her. It was to her I'd always turned for sympathy. Where else was I going to get it now?

'Oh, get *you*, *Dr* Clever-clogs!' she went on. 'PhD from *Truro College*: couldn't be anywhere else, oh *no*. Cornwall, Cornwall, *Cornwall*: got to be. But someone's not so clever as they thought, are they? *You* thought *your* dad was bigger than *his* dad ...'

Across the Tamar-trickle imagination made red eyes flare in England's every shadow.

If only it *were* imagination ...

'Hello there! Welcome! Welcome aboard ...'

I was taking inventory of my new garden at the time. Nice flowerbeds and so on, but too high maintenance was my judgement. They'd be going under concrete *toot sweet*.

Neighbourly greetings suggested an even more urgent task for my list. Such as raising the fence above chit-chat level. To exorcise the spectre of *Hail fellow well met* every time I showed my face.

Pending that pressing reform, some reply, sadly, seemed obligatory.

'Meea navidna cowza Sawzneck.'

That did him. As always. A very *handy* phrase. It puts proper distance between me and them every time.

The elderly man's homely face furrowed. 'Er ... pardon?'

More missionary work was required, to enlighten the pagans. Which never ceased to be a pleasure.

'It's *Kernowek*. The Cornish language, in case you didn't know. For 'I won't speak English'. But I see that to you I shall have to.'

'Oh ... right ... Um, well, welcome anyway ...'

He had to hoist himself up to get his handshake over the panels. Meaning he must be a short-arse. Which was a bonus. The natives need not be feared.

I shook the proffered paw anyway. No point in prematurely insulting people. The Wife had warned me about that in no uncertain terms: especially after 'last time'. I still deployed my famed bone-crusher grip though – only to find a surprising steely core awaiting. Unlike most recipients my new neighbour merely winced a bit. Which was disappointing.

'I'm Alfred,' he said, when his pain abated. 'Alfred Ayling. Her indoors is Amy. Lived here for donkey's years – man and boy. Well, it suits us. I only hope you and your lady wife will be as happy as we've been and ...'

I took a step back, pointedly terminating the tsunami of trivia.

'Yeah, well, maybe,' I replied. 'But I don't *want* to be here. Never wanted to live abroad – in England. *If* you can call that living. I wanted to stay in *Kernow*.'

Which bamboozled Ayling again. Which gave me a warm glow. Two-nil up already, only minutes into our acquaintance!

'More *Kernowek*,' I informed him. ''It's our name for Cornwall. Don't you know anything?'

Apparently not. Ayling pointed over my head, across the broad estuary of the Exe towards my longed-for homeland.

'But you're not all *that* far away now,' he said. 'From Cornwall, I mean. Fifty miles or so ...'

'Fifty-one point two-four. I've checked.'

'Oh, right. Well, there you are then. On a clear day you might even see it from here ...'

'I don't want to *see* it. Especially not from *Logres*.'

Bemusement squared. This wasn't going anything like he'd hoped.

'Pardon?'

'You call it England.' I didn't add 'dimwit' – but it was implied. 'We Celts call it *Logres*. In other words, occupied *Prydain* – i.e. the island you lot stole from us. Both places as rendered in the original *Kernowek* – oldest language in the land. Which, as I've said, is what I speak for preference.'

Ayling's face fell.

'Oh, I see,' he said – when he plainly didn't. 'Hence the ... um, *'me a navvy ...'* thing I suppose. Only it's just that, um ... unfortunately, Amy and I don't really spea...'

'*Quelle surprise,*' I countered. 'Don't worry, mate, I wasn't expecting much. Not in this dump. We won't be here long anyway. Soon as the Wife gets a transfer and Kernow job then back we go, pronto. Won't see us for dust!'

Ayling abandoned tippy-toes and sank behind the fence, down to only upper-features-showing level. The 'Chad' analogies made me smile. He mistook that for affability.

'Oh well,' he said, bright and breezy again, 'whilst you *are* here, should you ever need anything – the proverbial 'cup of sugar' and so on – you know where to come. Please don't hesitate to ask ...'

'Neither of us take sugar. Anything else?' I was pre-turned to go.

'Um, well, no, I don't suppose so, Mr ... um, Mr ... you didn't mention your name ...'

Given how he walked into that one I could see how Ayling's punchbag innocence might make him my perfect 'straight-man'. A handy human-amusement-park parked next-door to lighten my English internment. Allowing one's sentence to pass more mischievously.

'That's right,' I replied, heading back indoors. 'I didn't ...'

The Wife disapproved. Women can be so ... *sensible*.

Having heard edited highlights of the over-fence sparring match and my knockout victory, she invited the Aylings round for tea. 'To mend bridges'.

The only bridge I was interested in was the one over the Tamar, Kernow-wards. Speed the day! So, when the 'tea' ordeal arrived I wore an appropriately sour face.

Whereas *La Ayling* and the Wife hit it off, despite age and racial differences. It transpired they had things in common. One retired nurse and another still combatant paired off to exchange NHS war-stories. Leaving me to face Alfred Ayling.

It turned out he'd prepared a conversational gambit to get us going.

'After you mentioned you spoke Cornish,' he said, 'I took the opportunity to look it up. In the library, on their interweb thingy. *Very* interesting. Though it must make things difficult there being three different versions. And their speakers not getting on. Like with that European grant to do a dictionary business. Death threats even, so I read ...'

The ... complex issue of parallel 'Unified', 'Common' and 'Modern' revived Cornish wasn't something I cared to air at the best of times. And never *ever* in the face of the enemy.

'Irrelevant,' I bristled. 'Concentrate on the mere fact it *is* revived. You English had better get over it.'

Did I detect a slight stiffening of Ayling shoulders? I think so, but nothing came of it. *'Nice'* people are pretty plastic, ever agile to switch topic rather than give or take offence.

'I'm retired now,' he volunteered, as yet another uncomfortable silence stretched, finding there was only so much diversion to be had from teacup stirring. 'But I used to have a hardware shop down in the city. In Exeter I mean. Till it got bit a much and you had to go computerised. So we sold up.'

'No! Tell me more. More *detail* ...'

Sarcasm bounced off the Ayling amiability-armour.

'Um, okay. Um ... I had it nigh forty years, bar two months. Inherited it from my Uncle Egbert – and he'd run it a half century himself, so ...'

'Hellfire! I'm hanging on your every *word* here, Alfred! It must be a pain getting pestered with autobiography offers all the time! Not to mention the film rights ...'

He didn't know how to 'take' me. But someone else did. I caught a warning look from the Wife.

'No ...' answered Ayling. 'Not really. Not at all, actually.'

'You *do* surprise me ...'

He took another sip of tepid (appropriately enough) brew. The English think tea the sovereign cure for all ills.

'But enough about me,' he said, rallying for another go. 'What do *you* do?'

A straight answer to that seemed harmless enough. So long as I kept it terse.

'Proofreading: publishers, academic work, local press; the lot. Freelance. Which means I can work anywhere I want. Which isn't *here*, dammit.'

Ayling frowned. Not angrily, but merely concerned for poor little me. Although he found my words hard to credit. Who *wouldn't* want to abide in an identikit English end-terrace box in an identikit English city suburb?

Eventually his puzzlement emerged as: 'No?'

'*No.*'

'May I ask *why* not?'

'You may.'

He really was the perfect foil for fun. It took *ages* of pregnant pause for him to twig.

'*Why* not?' he asked.

I can't recall the specifics now – it being a well and oft-rehearsed recital of mine. However, despite this foreign-fool not meriting excess ammunition, I still ensured he received a proper broadside.

It definitely started off with 'This hole? Pah! Here's just where I park my car ...' And developed into 'Kernow: the proud and ancient nation oppressed by *your* nation'. And how no self-respecting *Mebyon Kernow* – which I kindly translated as 'Sons of Cornwall' lest he not get it – would choose to hang out in hostile territory unless they were conscripted. Or kidnapped by love, as in my case. Courtesy of the Wife's 'promotion' to Exeter.

'Lost capital of now *occupied* Kernow,' I concluded.

After that I wouldn't say Ayling was exactly chilly. More lukewarm. Like all his race.

He set down his cup, straightened his cake fork and checked his watch.

'Really?' he said, not meeting my eye. Which is one of those slippery Swiss-Army-penknife English words where meaning depends entirely on inflection. I decided to take it as the interrogative mode and excuse to further enlighten the *Sawzneck*.

'Yeah, *really*. Because *your* King Aethelstan – *Black Aethelstan* we call him – expelled the Cornish from here. In 927. Out of Exeter, out of our ancestral *Dumnonia*. All of us: ethnically cleansed beyond the Tamar. To stay there on pain of death. Forever. In 936 he even passed a law enshrining it. Which I *spit* upon. Because here I am, loud and proud, part of the Celtic vanguard returned to claim what's rightfully ours. And what are you going to do about it, eh?'

Ayling wouldn't acknowledge the flung gauntlet. A being made of milk-and-water, he pretended not to even notice.

'Oh well,' he said. 'That was all long ago. Water under the bridge ...'

Alas, at that point the Wife re-tuned to our frequency and picked up on the vibes. Being both a nurse and married to me she was a dab hand at applying soothing ointment. In this case the conversational kind.

'Oh no, he hasn't got you onto history has he, Mr Ayling?'

'Alfred, please ... Well, yes, I suppose he has. Not that I know much about it. But it's all ... jolly interesting. I'm getting quite an education here ...'

Whereas I was getting bathed in Wifely gamma rays, singeing the side of my head. Although Cornish to her Celtic corkscrew ringlets, and despite the graveyards near Land's End heaving with memorials bearing her maiden name, the Wife didn't share my born-again nationalism. Strange to relate, she preferred getting on with her neighbours, no matter who.

I don't think Alfred's words carried any subtext. Even though passive aggression is his kind's weapon of choice. Yet the Wife chose to take it so. Meaning I now knew what was on the menu for supper: tongue-pie and cold-shoulder.

But I wasn't that hungry anyway. It had been worth it. Another evening up of the 936 AD score.

The Wife consulted the nurse's watch gracing her front.

'Gracious!' she said. 'Doesn't time *fly*? And here's me nattering on when I've got an early shift tomorrow! Sorry, Alfred and Amy: we *love* your company but not your hours. Lots of things I must do before bedtime, I'm afraid. Why, it's almost ... six o'clock ...'

Multiply satisfactory skirmishes such as that by ... however many it took, and Ayling finally got the message. Thereafter, aside from an unfailing 'good morning' on first sighting and bookend 'good night' should our paths cross, he left me alone.

Whereas I wasn't so stand-offish and unneigbourly. On sunny days, when windows were open or they were in their garden (and

my Wife out), I graciously decided to teach Ayling *The Armes Prydein*
– or *Prophecy of Britain* in usurper-speak. Which is something he and
his nation 'jolly' well ought to know. To broaden their outlook.

I usually started off with that bit where the tenth century bard
says:

> *The warriors will scatter the foreigners as far as Durham,*
> *They will rejoice after the devastation,*
> *And there will be reconciliation between the Welsh and the men*
> *of Dublin,*
> *The Irish of Ireland and Anglesey and Scotland,*
> *The men of Cornwall and of Strathclyde will be made welcome*
> *among us,*
> *The Britons will rise again …*

Though I say so myself, I have a good declamatory voice, well
able to penetrate Castle Ayling even after they'd retreated indoors
and raised the drawbridge. *And*, for my favourite bit, about how the
Celts reunite and chuck out all bloody foreigners, I found it in myself
to step up a decibel or ten.

> *There will be widows and riderless horses,*
> *There will be woeful wailing before the rush of warriors,*
> *And many a wounded hand before the scattering of armies.*
> *The messengers of death will gather*
> *When corpses stand one by another.*

As Arthur's people reclaim Britain from *Manaw Gododdin*
(southern Scotland to you) *to Brittany, from Dyfed to Thanet.*
Whereafter:

> *Let them be as exiles,*
> *For the English there will be no returning.*
> *The Gaels will return to their comrades.*
> *The Welsh will arise in a mighty fellowship –*
> *Armies around the ale, and a throng of warriors –*
> *And chosen Kings who kept their faith.*
> *The English race will be called warriors no more …*

And so on and on, for many more fine lines. More prophecy than poetry, I concede, and not exactly in the Philip Larkin league; but any lack in rhythm and rhyme is more than made up for by its moral.

Wherefore I spoke loud and hearty to do the vision of delayed justice justice.

Although, being a reasonable man, I did occasionally vary the program. Say, with a rendition of *Song of the Western Men*: Cornwall's unofficial national anthem. Even though it was written by an Englishman – which proves I'm not prejudiced.

> *A good sword and a trusty hand!*
> *A merry heart and true!*
> *King James's men shall understand*
> *What Cornish lads can do!*
> *And have they fixed the where and when?*
> *And shall Trelawny die?*
> *Here's twenty thousand Cornish men*
> *Will know the reason why!*

There's myriad verses to it, so no one could complain I was being monotonous. Not to mention a really rousing chorus.

> *And shall Trelawny live?*
> *And shall Trelawny die?*
> *Here's twenty thousand Cornish men*
> *Will know the reason why!*

On the umpteenth occasion (after less than half an hour!) Ayling did his Chad act. First residual locks, then creased brow followed by appealing (as in begging) eyes appeared over my fence.

'Um ...' he said, as he always prefaced everything, doubtless many years before even saying '*Um ... will you marry me?*'. 'Um, I wonder if I could ask you to keep your voice down?'

And I replied: 'Well, you could *ask* ...'

'And change the tune!' shouted Mrs Ayling, unseen from off-stage. Me and she 'no longer spoke' in any other way.

'It's just that our Rose, our youngest granddaughter, is staying,' Ayling went on. 'Revising for her A levels. Next week. Because it's a bit hectic at home, what with all her brothers and sisters. We thought it would help her to have a bit of peace ...'

I dare say it would: doubly so in such a good cause. Ayling made a compelling case. My apparent acquiescence – or leastways pause – emboldened him to demand more. Give some people an inch …

'And, whilst I mention it,' he said, 'your flag – it's very nice and all that …'

'It is, isn't it?' I answered, happy to have something we could agree on. 'Cost a bomb too, including the pukka flagpole and everything. But worth it. About time St Piran's black and silver was flown this side of the Tamar again! Makes a point, don't you think?'

'And a ruddy racket too!' chipped in invisible Mrs Ayling.

'Um, well, yes, because it's so *big* you see,' said Ayling, pouring dilute balm on his wife's whinge. '*Huge*. Plus right up against our house. Which blocks the light. And smacks the spare bedroom window all the time. Where Rose is. *Flap, slap, flap, slap* … Never stops. Due to the wind off the estuary …'

I smiled reassuringly at him.

'Leave it with me,' I said. 'I'll see what I can do.'

Ayling heaved a sigh of relief. He plainly hated confrontation, let alone 'scenes'.

A conundrum: how did his kind ever carve out an Empire?

'Oh good, *thank* you, thank you,' said Chad-Ayling, and quit the field of battle.

'I'll see,' I continued, to myself and for my benefit only, 'what I can do about turning down the wind …'

Meanwhile:

> *The warriors will scatter the foreigners as far as Durham,*
> *They will rejoice after the devastation,*
> *And there will be reconciliation between …*

We have tried our best to be friendly and good neighbours, but you…
… We are very sorry but you leave us with no option to make formal complaint to the proper authorities …

> *Yours sincerely and in sorrow.*
> *Alfred Ayling.*

I didn't show the Wife that note, and happily her shift patterns made it easy for me to intercept any 'letter from the council' or whatever feeble English apocalypse Ayling intended. So I felt pretty sanguine about the prospect of race-war. In fact, the outbreak of active hostilities would enliven things here until my nagging bore fruit and the Wife got a new, better, job back over the border. Concerning which, as I've said, speed the day. Especially since my own employment was starting to go septic. Then gangrenous. Then drop off.

I blamed overwork. And over-taxed eyes. Even though *siestas* and stronger specs failed to cure things. Extraneous full stops – always in double-vision pairs and strained-vision angry red – continued to burn up from every page I proofread. The avoidance of which caused my gaze to skip lines and produce ... lapses.

At first, minor mistakes went unmentioned: not worth a phone-call or amended invoice. But then the slip-ups and solecisms grew so as to be 'brought to my attention'. In e-mails growing ever more peevish. Leading to penal deductions from my bill. And finally the phone call no proofreader wants.

The *Exeter Herald*'s Editor was *incandescent*. He could hardly speak. Up to then I had contracted-out oversight of many of his pages, including the vital-there-be-no-blunders death notices. Now he gave me to understand – in staccato sentences peppered with Anglo-Saxon – that that gig was gone. Plus I was on final notice for the rest.

'*No,*' went his parting worlds to me. '*You* get on the phone and apologise to them. And explain. *If* you can ...'

So I did. But I couldn't. It is no easy thing to convey to a grieving family how their tragically-taken-from-them and beloved *son* came to be called:

'*A TRUE SOD*'

in twenty-three-point-title-font in cold print to hundreds of thousands of readers. My 'sorry' and offer of a free second insertion didn't really cut it. So I even proposed coming round to grovel in person. They said they couldn't guarantee my safety.

After which trauma I took extra-special, burning the midnight oil, burning my eyes red-raw, painstaking care. But by then there were reinforcement red dots too; multiple other *eyes* than mine. Whose stare up at me I found strangely hard to meet. A series of opticians, costing me a packet I could no longer afford, were unable to either account for or dispel them.

Which must be how, in their expensive, full-page, full colour, advert, Exeter's prestigious two Michelin star (till then) Swiss Restaurant came to be dubbed:

'*THE SWILL RESTAURANT*'

throughout.

The owner told the Editor that howlers like that took decades to be forgotten by long-memoried local wags. And that trade was already down. And that henceforth he'd be taking his business elsewhere. *And* suing. Not that that was any concern of mine, because by then I'd been sacked.

My academic work took longer to die, since publishing schedules are stately and errors only filter through at spaced intervals. Like delayed detonations. Yet I suspected they were there and en route, although powerless to prevent arrival. Like some submariner hunkering down in the deep dark silence, awaiting depth charges, the tenterhooks anticipation was exquisite agony.

Then *BOOM!*

Oh, *how* reviewers leapt like salmon to find my half-cocked amendments and allowed-past blunders in their colleagues' works! Or better still, someone's life-work *magnum opus* or *festschrift*. The trumpeted and ill-concealed joy they took in university internecine bitchiness should not have surprised me – but still did.

The concluding gaffe that killed my career dodo-dead went national. '*Among the remarkable revelations to be found in distinguished Professor X's "A New History of England",*' said the *Times Literary Supplement, 'is the bombshell that the Battle of Hastings was won by one "Norman the Conqueror" (sic). And in 1666 – which is somewhat later than hitherto conventionally thought ...*'

I'm told that mortified Professor X actually came to fisticuffs with his publisher about it. Not that that was any concern of mine, because by then ...

Within a short space I perforce became a 'kept man'. The Wife was good about it: didn't say anything. She didn't need to. I was still meeting the mail to head off any complaint from Ayling. A by-product of which was that I got first sight of all the bills. The rapidly reddening bills ...

And thus coincidentally akin in colour to the *eyes* now ever sparkling before me. For I could no longer pretend they were any mere impairment of mine. Liberated from my proofreading pages they now flew solo and stared at me from mid-air, from the TV screen: from the very headboard of my bed. Meaning I must assume they even kept watch as I slept.

Once, in the fitful early hours and 'in my cups' (the Devil finding work for idle, workless, hands), I tried to reason with them. I confess to an edge of desperation entering my voice.

'What do you *want* of me?' I asked the *eyes*. 'What do you want me to *do*?'

And a voice from no mouth I could see replied:

'Die!'

Anxiety has the motivational *oomph* to make you do things you'd prefer not. Things you'd almost rather *'die'* than do. Like talk to despised neighbours.

From upstairs I saw Ayling pottering round his garden. Out of nowhere, I suddenly knew what was needful, no matter how humiliating. I had to ask if he'd ever heard our house was haunted. Or the abode of unclean spirits. Or perched atop a Hell-mouth. Or some such Dark Age balls. For that's how embarrassing things had got: I'd lost all sense of embarrassment.

As I issued into the garden all composure went too. The neighbourhood dogs started barking: from silence to *Hound of the Baskervilles* choir in seconds, synchronised round my scent. All of them wanting to *meet* me – and not for wags or walkies either.

Then a roof tile saw fit to desert its post and crown me.

Bop!

Bull's-eye: centre pate. It was *hard*, edge on. Knees buckled and blood was shed. Nevertheless, my main hurt was to dignity. Even though none but accompanying *eyes* saw.

Being robust I recovered and strode on. Likewise, being of blacksmith-build, I didn't have Ayling's Chad-act problem. I showed up over the fence without stretching.

He'd heard my *'ouch!'* and was heading indoors rather than converse.

'Wait, Alfred! Please!'

Despite all the bad omens, my instinct proved spot-on. Straightaway, I could see I'd selected the right man. Ayling's guilty face told all without need for words. He *knew*.

He also somehow knew what I was going to say.

'Sorry,' he said, setting down his secateurs. 'I'm *so* sorry! But there's nothing I can do. I *can't*. I would if I could. Really I would ...'

It was easily within my powers to have the fence down and be wringing his neck within seconds. Yet Ayling's confession hinted at some useful influence. Which constrained me – that and a tree branch swooping.

Sock!

Right hook! Full face! Over I go!

The windpower behind it was bespoke: tailor-made. No other foliage stirred. Ditto only an extremity getting involved. Enough to down a man and imprint a temporary twig-and-leaf tattoo, but nowhere near lethal force. Not this time. Just a personalised present from an English oak.

Then the rest of my face coloured up to match that arboreal kiss. Because Ayling's *fizzog* appeared over the fence to see me spread-eagled: gracing my lawn like some day-time drunk.

When I say 'lawn' I actually mean gravel. Given my gainful employment pickle, funds hadn't stretched to the original concreting-over plans. Bear with me – it *is* relevant.

'Are you alright?' Ayling looked genuinely concerned. 'Shall I come round?'

I was only just coming round myself. Was I at all 'right', let alone 'alright'? I couldn't say. Literally. Other matters intruded.

In the ordinary course of things, say after a game of Cornish rugby or Celtic wrestling match, I like a massage. Yet the one I was now 'enjoying' from my gravel failed to please. Mother Earth and her stony shroud were both breathing heavily and mobile beneath my back. Not in any attempt to soothe, but rather to *reject*. As in heaving and retching, pre *'parking the tiger'* and a *'technicolour yawn'*. Or 'vomit' to you non-rugby-playing types.

I was inspired to spring to my feet in a single bound. No mean feat for a desk-bound computer-jockey no longer in his prime. Ayling backed away. Not out of fear but guilt.

'Sorry ...' he repeated. Again, in my estimation, sincerely so. 'I did directly think better of it, honestly. I tried to cancel. *Pleaded.* Too late. I'd made the call, you see: blown the horn. Said the *'Ut! Ut! Ut! ...'*

'Said the *what?'*

'Doesn't matter.' Ayling was discomfited: had disclosed more than he should. 'Just something in the *Old Tongue.* But the point *is* that once... certain matters are set in motion ... Well, you know what *families* are like...'

Did I? I didn't have time to think. For just then a gull messed on me. Copiously, *abundantly.* A precision *stuka*-style dive-bomb and then *splat!* One off-white direct-hit to the middle of my mullet. Where it mixed but not matched with the bloodstains already present to make (a mirror later revealed) a sort of Mardi Gras-style raspberry-ripple hair-do

Then another bird emptied its bomb-bay bum on me, then another; then another: a sequence that felt *ad infinitum.* And also *ad nauseum.* With a squadron that size overhead Ayling should have got his proper portion too. But no. This was pinpoint precision bombing solely on and for me.

Needlessly, in words as redundant as I currently was, Ayling pointed out my *guanoed* state. I suppose he was, as ever, in search of something positive to say.

'Um, I think a bird's messed in your hair,' he said. Then: 'Some people say that's good luck ...'

A DICTIONARY OF ENGLISH SURNAMES. Lady Caroline Callipyge Gale. Pevensey Castle Press. 1897.

AYLING: Anglo-Saxon origin. First attested in the *Rotuli Litterarum Clausarum,* (ed. T D Hardy, 2 vols. Record Commission, London 1833-44) c. 937 AD. Signifying the *'SUNA'* or sons or otherwise descendent (*'-ing'*) of Aelle (*floruit* 477- 514? AD), king of the South Saxons and also inaugural 'BRETWALDA' or pre-eminent ruler of the early English Heptarchy.

Initially acquired solely by right of claim in the Darwinian Dark Age struggle for supremacy, the Bretwalda honorific was later adopted by legitimate and recognised monarchs such as Alfred the Great and Aethelstan and their lines. Accordingly, bearers of the

Ayling nomenclature were once attributed quasi-royal status and legal privileges ...

So that was that. It came down to who-you-knew and family connections. I might well be *Mebyon Kernow*, but Alfred Alying was *Suna* Aelle. And *Suna* Aethelstan and *Suna* Alfred *et al* (or *et Aelle*). Which here, on this soil, in this place, was trumps.

Lady Caroline's dusty labour of love, dredged up from Exeter University Library's reference section, was the first book I'd cracked in weeks. Nevertheless, the *eyes* awaited me within. Their peering out from every page made the exercise a misery, costing me dear. Consulting the 'A' section alone was almost too much to take. Plus the whimpering and wincing noises any attempt at reading wrenched from me nowadays nearly got me chucked out. A librarian loudly accused me of indulging in furtive self-abuse. '*Our books are here for consultation,*' she said. '*Not for unnatural intercourse!*'

As if I didn't have enough on my plate. There simply wasn't room for public humiliation too. Not with my mind being perpetually fugged: incubated to fever pitch by the Old-Folks-Home-style heatwave I carried round with me. Such that milk curdled and food corrupted in my proximity. Leaving me *persona non grata* in every shop that sold perishables. And so starving.

Likewise, people shunned sharing my personal portable sauna. Granted, the guaranteed seat to myself on buses and trains was nice, but the Wife said it was like being in bed beside a barbeque. So, no more joint sleeping arrangements ...

I'd gone to the University in search of work but my fame or infamy preceded me. I saw a photocopy of my 'Norman the Conqueror' masterpiece pinned to a departmental noticeboard. Proving I was already well known: but not in any work-recommending way. Therefore I didn't even ask. Derisory laughter often offends.

Exiting via the foyer I stumbled over what felt like an invisible stuck out foot. Flailing for support to stay upright, I brought down to destruction a displayed Grayson Perry vase – or '*objet d'art céramique sadomasochiste*', as per its proud placard.

Bought by the University for 'a five-figure sum', I thus

acquired its shards for the same amount – or so a swarm of security guards and University big-wigs assured me. Prior to the police arriving to 'take my details'. The boys in blue said I might get off with a caution. Maybe.

Exeter is a bumpy place and its University sits atop what students call 'Cardiac Hill'. So, my way home, of necessity, involved descent. Which seemed appropriate and in keeping with my career. The alternative was laying down to die. Which had its attractions too, but felt a tad defeatist. Not the sort of thing a stout *Mebyon Kernow* should do.

So off I set, on foot. Even if we hadn't had to sell my car I no longer trusted myself behind the wheel. Several times recently unseen hands had sought to seize control. That, plus the notion of my shot-nerves propelling a ton-plus weight capable of ton-plus speed ruled motoring RIGHT OUT. Botched books, ruined restaurants, offensive obituaries, even obliterated 'five-figure' *objet d'art*, were bad enough, but bus queue massacres were a quantum leap I wasn't willing to risk. Yet.

Externally, intrinsically, it was a lovely day. Morning dew still laced the grass in places and flights of daddy-longlegs lifted off from the lawns around student accommodation bunkers. The sun shone down impartially on all – or almost all. For it was definitely dimmer wherever I went. In the face of my designer *Jonah-field* the laws of physics faltered and light meant for me instead slowed and then stalled.

As did I upon beholding red eyes at head height blocking my path.

I shifted left. So did they. I moved right and – well, guess what …

This pair were exceptional(!), glittering with fanatic intent. And, I saw, every intention of acting upon it. *Right now.*

I'd arrived at the climactic. Appropriately enough, my private micro-climate stepped up a notch in recognition. Sweat – implausibly both hot *and* cold – poured off me. I was, as the somewhat basic English saying says: 'flooding my boots' …

And yet, irate orbs aside, all around still looked so prosaic. Passers-by passed by, not noticing. Across the road the *Red Cow,* famous for its 'Wally's Special' cider (*'No Patron Shall Be Served In Excess Of A Quart'*), was open for business. Awaiting my order for a gallon.

And looming high above all was the Cathedral. Where I (an ardent atheist until a moment ago) wanted to seek sanctuary. However, all that alluring loveliness, including my house, lay *before* me. In-between, angry *eyes* interposed.

Whereas behind lay a clear – and left-clear – escape route to *Kernow*. Where I should be, apparently. Where all present thought I *really* should be.

I'd had my warnings – a plethora of warnings *way* beyond what was reasonable – and chosen to ignore them. So, a senior figure was now here to insist.

Whoever it was shifted position, suggesting the hefting of an unseen sword held in ditto hands.

I proved less fearless than I thought and always said I was. Which, down the line, would provoke major self-image revision and distress. But back then I merely feared a sharp edge I couldn't see. Survival instincts surfaced and demanded – *demanded* – I address one threat-to-life at a time…

'Can't I go home to pack?' I asked. 'And let the Wife know? Please?'

It sounded even more pathetic than it reads. Perhaps I should have appealed to Aethelstan and co.'s better nature. '*I mean,*' I might have said, had my usual eloquence not failed me, '*when all's said and done, that law of yours is ancient history. And so surely doesn't apply to modern me …*' I could also have dwelled on how the English were supposedly keen on '*fair play*'. Weak, weasel words along those lines …

Too late for words. The eyes slitted. A line of lightning from another universe slashed into mine. Slicing off my right ear. Kindly cauterising the wound at the same time.

I suppose I should have been thankful – over and above the agony. I *was* a wilful law breaker after all, and my offence a capital crime. Strictly speaking, it should have been my throat that was severed, not merely a single *shell-like*. So, maybe fair play and moderation *had* saved me …

Oddly enough, once again gratitude 'no-showed'.

Instead, *I* departed. As in about-turning and conquering Cardiac Hill in surely Exeter University all-time 'best' beating style. Directly away from my aural-amender in any old direction, before settling on the shortest route to Cornwall.

All the way there my shoulders were hunched, any second expecting a *coup de grâce* bisecting blow. Leaving me conveniently autopsy-ready beside the *A30*. A transitory Police and Press puzzle. Then a 'still open' file. Finally an 'unsolved case'.

The doctor I saw at Launceston General said he'd never in all his career encountered such knotted neck and back muscles. Even months of physiotherapy failed to fully unclench them. So they're still much that way today, giving me a hunched, haunted look. As does the unpaid physio's bailiffs-and-bankruptcy debt-collection *jihad*. Just yet another souvenir from my stay in England. Alongside fifty-percent shortfall in the standard ear quotient and consequent keeping-hats-and-sunglasses-on issues.

In short, hardly the 'see the conquering hero come!' triumphal return to Kernow I'd envisaged ...

Still, all that was like a lover's kiss compared to the necessary 'phone call to the Wife'.

She didn't slam the phone down. She listened attentively whilst I was as honest as possible. Yet at confession's end only ominous silence ensued. Concluding in a *click*.

I'd no confidence she'd follow in my footsteps. Wherefore I became single again for a spell; embracing all the associated sad freedoms. Wherein I consoled myself.

Bottles mostly. And other curvaceous items.

Yet eventually she came. Packed up her job, packed up the house and then drove to my – now our – pokey Cornish bedsit.

Fortunately, belief in my tale and her consequent decision had been helped along. Not by my silver-tongued Celtic blarney but by the 'law' now proceeding against her too. Albeit mildly and mercifully: not enforced with the full rigour I'd felt. Her England-quitting car was reportedly buffeted all the way by a customised evil weather-front just a bumper-span behind. Whose wicked winds cried not *'Mary'* but assurance of awaiting her at storm-strength should she ever darken east-of-the-Tamar doors again.

And guess who got the blame for that? Correct: yours truly! Which was *so* unfair! The eviction and expulsion, her crocked career and missed shopping-and-a-show trips? Apparently all *my* fault!

Some reunion! For days I barely got a kind word out of her as she did the laundry and binned empties.

So, welcome back to right now and us at *Welcombe*. The Wife and I studying the lost prospect.

From our permanent-exile-perspective England looked idyllic. A lost *Lyonesse*. Which was a thought I never thought I'd think.

At the *Olde Smithy Inn* the inept pub-luncher had finally acquired sufficient Cumberland-sausage-control to tuck in. He and his gaggle hadn't even noticed us two nosey-parker passers-by not actually passing by but lingering longer and looking more longingly than was polite.

Not so the sentinel eyes, red and vigilant. *They* noticed. Unseen save by us, they watched over these oblivious Englishfolk. Whilst watching us. Like hawks. Waiting, wanting, *ravenous*.

One cross-Tamar step was all it would take. Then these post-human, pre-human-rights-era, immigration officers would step in to do their Dark Age stuff. Or, as they doubtless saw it, simply enforce the Law. Aethelstan's never-repealed law.

Nothing personal.

Unlike the Wife's verdict on all this and me. She turned to (and on) me. To say:

'You *stupid* Celt …'

At least I think that's what she said.

Yet, as *I've* said, she's generally soft-hearted. Many's the time she's said I'd have to leave *her* before she ever left *me*.

Which must account for her snapping. And snap decision. And shoving me into England.

THE SERPENT OF PENGERSICK

In 1966, Hammer Film Productions released their 14th horror feature. As was their trademark in that era, it was another quick, low budget production, and it would go on to be a huge success both at the Box Office and among the critics. But what many of the fans who flocked to the cinemas to watch didn't know was that this latest lurid tale – set in Cornwall, of all England's most tranquil counties – was drawing on a local legend that had terrified rural Cornish folk for many generations.

By the mid-60s, having built a solid reputation for repackaging classic Gothic horror wrapped up in modern sex and violence, Hammer had begun to venture a little beyond their usual remit, producing The Gorgon *and* Plague of the Zombies *in 1964 and 1965 respectively. But the real slammer came the following year, with the aforementioned 14th Hammer horror film,* The Reptile. *It told the tale of a small coastal community terrorised by a very exotic monster, a snake/woman hybrid, which had come to dwell there as a result of Britain's colonial adventures, having been created by a tribal curse in darkest Borneo. Whether the film was actually influenced by the real story of the Cornish snake/woman, a ghastly monster that supposedly lived in Pengersick Castle in the county's southwest corner during the early 16th century, is uncertain, but there are distinct similarities.*

The legend takes place near the modern town of Germoe, which is close to the famous seaside resort of Praa Sands, and it tells how John Milton, High Sheriff of Cornwall, who first built the castle in 1500, was widowed a decade into his marriage and so took a second wife – a scheming witch who had learned her talents in 'far off lands' and was particularly adept with poisons, the effects of which she enhanced with the use of spells and incantations. By all accounts, this witch kept her most toxic potions in a room at the top of the castle's highest tower, and allowed nobody else in there. When her young step-son became curious, and maybe even had begun to experiment with potions himself, she persuaded her husband to sell the lad into slavery. Afterwards, Milton so regretted this deed that he slumped into a state of permanent fret. Seeing no further use in him, his wife poisoned him – one of many such victims according to 17th century pamphlets. She then sacked all the staff, and locked herself away in the otherwise empty castle, which slowly crumbled around her. Eventually, one of her experiments backfired, and she was transformed into a hideous monster, a snake/woman, which began to prowl the district at night, though at length, either through despair at her condition or fear of vengeance from the local populace, she dragged her scaly form to the shore and threw herself into the sea, never to be seen again.

But the eerie story does not end there.

Allegedly, the monster's ghost remained in the ruin for years afterwards, ensuring that local folk continued to steer clear. The castle thus remained shunned and dilapidated until several decades had passed, at which point the son who had been sold abroad finally returned and proclaimed himself the new Lord of Pengersick. Somehow or other, he had acquired freedom during his travels, along with wealth, a beautiful eastern wife and much arcane knowledge. He eagerly continued his step-mother's researches, again concentrating his rituals in the main tower. Many dark spirits were allegedly summoned, among them the monstrous mist-form of the snake/woman, granting it even more power and substance than it had enjoyed previously, and a huge devilish horse on which the new master would ride proudly across his domain, the peasantry fleeing before him.

However, this latest reign of terror also ended abruptly, one stormy night in fact, when a mysterious burned man, who had allegedly been watching the castle for several days from a stone at the entrance to Pengersick Valley, forced his way in, and flames exploded all over the aged structure. When the conflagration had died down, only the main tower remained. There was no trace of either Pengersick, his wife or the scorched stranger, though local folk claimed to have seen three winged shapes ascending from the fire amid streaks of lightning.

Even by the usual sensational standards, these tales are dramatic, yet it seems odd that the legend of the snake/woman is the most persistent, her hissing, misshapen spectre still reported in the gutted ruin as late as the early 20th century. Folklorists often try to connect these stories with the true historical figure of Henry de Pengersick, a brutal knight who occupied a manor on the site in the early 14th century and was notorious for his quarrels with local religious houses, apparently laying violent hands on the monks, and even, supposedly, killing and burying two of them in secret graves. This may explain why later chroniclers demonised both the man and his bloodline, though Henry de Pengersick is never mentioned specifically as a warlock – rather those who came after him were, which seems strange. Likewise, there is no obvious propaganda link between the violent and blasphemous Henry and the serpent/woman who emerged a whole century later.

These days, Pengersick Castle has been fully restored and is in private hands. However, its reputation has gone before it. It regularly hosts ghost-hunting vigils and psychic evenings, and the results are often, or so we are told, spectacular.

THE UNSEEN

Paul Edwards

1

The man behind the stall was short and rotund, with a mop of curly hair and a rounded, pockmarked face. He turned toward Lee, and Lee immediately dropped his gaze to the DVDs on display. *Jeepers Creepers. See No Evil. Saw II. Hostel.*

'Looking for anything in particular, mate?'

Lee looked up, and Curly-Top grinned enigmatically at him. 'Not really.' Lee offered a brief, cagy smile. 'Just browsing, thanks.'

'You into horror movies?'

Lee paused as a gust of wind snatched at his hair. 'Yeah. Got anything else? Most of these don't interest me at all.'

The man gestured with his thumb toward a white transit parked up behind him. 'Got the obscure stuff in there, mate. Wanna look?'

The man rummaged through his pockets before Lee could reply, pulling out his van keys as he shuffled toward the vehicle. He opened the back doors and then stepped aside, allowing Lee to stick his head in.

Laid out on polythene sheets were rows and rows of DVDs, laserdiscs and videocassettes. 'Got a few specialist and collector's editions in there,' the man said, smiling and rubbing his hands together. 'Blue Underground. Anchor Bay. Alpha Video. Something Weird Video. Directors like Fulci, D'Amato, Lenzi, Mattei...'

Lee didn't hear, was too busy examining the videocassettes on display to listen. *Torture Dungeon* and *Bloodthirsty Butchers* caught his eye, and leaning forward he quickly snatched them up. 'How much for these?'

The man took them from him, then stared at the back of the boxes for a while. 'These are ultra-rare. Thirty quid for the pair, say?'

Lee frowned. Could he afford to spend the rest of his Job Seeker's on a couple of videocassettes?

The man saw Lee was reticent, so said, quickly, 'I'll tell you what. Thirty quid, and I'll chuck in a free DVD. Can't say fairer than that, right?'

Lee carefully studied the DVD section. *Zombie Flesh Eaters. Naked Blood. Crazy Desires of a Murderer. Guinea Pig: Flower of Flesh and Blood.* Then he caught sight of himself, and flinched.

'What's this?' he asked, grabbing hold of the DVD, staring into its mirror-effect case at a ghostly caricature of himself. 'There's nothing written on the back. Not even a distribution company or anything. Looks to me like an independent feature, or home movie, maybe.'

Lee pulled the disc out of its case and saw the words *The Black Remote* scrawled across it in black marker. 'Never heard of it.' He puffed out his cheeks with a deflated sigh. 'Got most of the others. Guess I'll have to give this a go, then.'

The man licked his lips, then passed the videocassettes to Lee and closed the van behind them. 'You come to Standerwick much?' Lee asked as he tensed against the wind.

The man smiled and then slowly shook his head. 'First time, mate. Come from Perranporth, Cornwall.' Suddenly the man's smile faltered, and he quickly rubbed his eye with a fist. 'The ending's unspeakable,' he mumbled, the muscles in his face twitching. 'The offerings. The Cult of the Infernal Abyss. *Synchronicity.*' He chuckled and whispered harshly into the wind. 'A gate must open.'

Lee felt the hairs on the back of his neck stand on end. 'Eh?'

'Thirty quid,' the man said, spinning, sticking out his hand and smiling stiffly at him. 'Come on, come on. Haven't got all day.'

Tia sat hunched on the sofa, watching *Hollyoaks* on their beat-up TV. Lee closed the door behind him and she looked up and around with dark, accusing eyes. 'Where have you been?'

He placed his bag down on the floor by the coffee table and shrugged at her as he straightened. 'Nowhere. Just to the market at Standerwick.'

'Buy anything?'

He sucked in a breath. 'Only a DVD for a couple of quid.' He felt the colour rush to his cheeks. 'I'm sticking the kettle on. Want a cuppa?' She shook her head, then muttered something under her breath. 'What's the matter?' he asked. 'What have I done this time?'

She stormed to her feet, shot over to the video cabinet and snatched open the door. 'I want to show you something,' she said, pulling out a videocassette. 'Remember this?' She waved a black and white sleeved Sony videotape labelled *Wedding Day 2007* at him.

A thread of bile rose from the pit of his stomach, and from somewhere far off he thought he could hear screaming.

'I put it on earlier. To show Liam. You know what I got instead of images from our wedding day?' She waited futilely for an answer, then folded her arms across her chest and hissed: 'Some *crap* with a girl getting gang-raped and then shot.'

'*Last House on the Left,*' he managed, feebly. 'It was showing uncut on cable a few months back. I-I couldn't watch it at the time because we were off out to your sister's, remember? There'd been no blank videocassettes, so I'd ...'

'Can't believe I'm hearing this.' She stamped her foot and bared small, stained teeth at him. '*That* was our wedding video, Lee. We had footage of Liam taking his first steps on it, too.'

She switched the TV off, barged past him and slammed the door on her way out.

Deathly silence descended.

He woke with a gasp, his face greased with sweat.

He'd fallen asleep on the sofa, and the only light came from the flickering TV in the corner.

He rubbed at his eyes. Got to his feet and shuffled toward the plastic bag full of goodies by the coffee table.

Time for a midnight movie, he thought with a grin.

He'd seen *Torture Dungeon* and *Bloodthirsty Butchers* before, so he decided on the other film, the amateurish-looking one.

He stuck the DVD in, slumped on the sofa and set it playing with the remote control.

No credits, just a decrepit-looking house on a cliff overlooking a beach.

The sandy coves and wildflower-peppered grasslands hinted at Cornwall, which fleetingly made him think of Curly-Top back on his stall. The camera drifted upwards, where seagulls wheeled above that crumbling manse.

It cut to a darkened room.

A man in a black mask was whispering conspiratorially into the camera. Lee couldn't quite hear what it was he was saying, despite how hard he listened. Slowly the camera panned through the rest of the house, revealing long, spiralling corridors and rooms thick with shadows and rot.

Lee discerned little in way of plot. When the narrative actually began to run, he bore witness to a series of murders, perpetrated by that guy in the black paper mask.

Characters were despatched moments after being introduced – a blonde girl had her throat cut; some skinny guy and his girlfriend were jabbed repeatedly with a spear; a woman with kohl-streaked eyes had her hands and feet bound by cable-wire and a plastic bag thrust over her head; a girl wearing a combat jacket was stabbed in the stomach repeatedly with a machete; finally, a middle-aged man with spectacles was disembowelled with a butterfly knife. There were no gore effects; the camera always panned away or the screen blacked out before it could get interesting.

Though tired, Lee found himself drawn into the film. The macabre atmosphere sang to him, and the acting was of a much higher calibre than usual for this type of movie.

The Black Remote (if that was what it was called – there were no credits or title sequences at the beginning or end) had no dénouement; it finished abruptly, right after the bloodless disembowelling, and snow filled the screen.

Lee's gaze snagged on the DVD timer: fifty-nine minutes had elapsed. It felt frustratingly incomplete.

Hands clasped on his knees, he sat there motionless, trying to take in what he'd seen. It had been amateurish, certainly, and he hadn't felt *scared*. Yet, on some level, the film had disturbed him … although he couldn't think why.

He rose from the sofa, made himself a cup of tea and then switched on his computer. No trace of *The Black Remote* on IMDB. He did a Google search, and as he trawled through endless results pages he couldn't find any mention of the film at all.

The faces of the actors and actresses remained branded in his brain. Their contorted expressions, the panic in their screams …

His brow creased and he chewed his lip. Of course he didn't

think the film was 'real', but he typed in '*The Black Remote* snuff movie' anyway into an obscure search engine, then scrolled meticulously through the results.

This time, on the second page, he found what he thought could be a lead: the title to a thread called *The Black Remote.*

The link took him straight to a horror movie forum named *Let Them Die Slowly*. The forum wasn't active, had only a handful of members. But the thread was definitely entitled *The Black Remote* and there was a single entry from a poster called 'Jan' on it:

Anyone seen a low-budget movie called THE BLACK REMOTE? It's a slasher set in a dilapidated Cornish mansion. Only the heavily-butchered version's available, which can be found in the usual black markets across the net.

Lee pondered this for a moment or two, then signed up to the forum. He had to wait an hour for the activation email to come through, but killed the time by surfing other forums as he waited.

Once the mail pinged into his inbox, he logged in and posted on *The Black Remote* thread.

I've seen it. The quality of the DVD was poor, and the movie was disjointed and amateurish. I liked the atmosphere though, and some of the acting was well above average. Unfortunately the killings occur off-camera, and so the film suffered from a lack of gore. The absence of an ending really disappointed, too.

The decayed mansion served as a memorable setting though, and I'm intrigued by the prospect of an uncut THE BLACK REMOTE – where can I find a copy?

He finished typing, then stared at the screen.

Tia surfaced in his mind abruptly, suddenly.

You know what I got instead of images from our wedding day?

He wondered if she knew he was still down here. She hated him being up so late. Quickly he dispelled the thought with a fierce shake of his head and took his empty teacup into the kitchen. His thoughts had already moved on from his wife and were now centring on the prospect of an uncensored version of *The Black Remote*. Some gore and a satisfactory ending would elevate the movie massively, he realised.

When he sat at his computer again, he saw 'Jan' had responded to his post already.

PM me.

From the post tally next to their avatar (a faceless shadow pointing a video camera at the eye of the beholder), it was only 'Jan's' second post. Yet 'Jan' had responded straight away ... which Lee thought really strange.

He clicked out the thread and brought up the members list. Selected 'Jan' and 'Send Private Message.'

Hi. PM as requested.

Lee didn't have to wait long for a reply; moments later, he received this:

The most complete version of THE BLACK REMOTE is rare and hard to obtain. However, it does tend to seek out those who are suitable – those who are *worthy*, shall we say.

'Huh?' Lee shook his head from side-to-side. 'What's that supposed to mean?'

Glancing at the time on his computer, he saw it was gone five in the morning. 'Christ,' he said, knuckling his eyes. 'Tia'll be up in an hour.'

He had to get to bed. And fast.

2

He woke to the sound of rain clattering against rooftiles.

His thoughts were scrambled, drowned in static, like snow at the end of a beaten videocassette.

He stretched and flung out an arm. Tia's side of the bed was empty. He sat up, glared blearily around the room. By the digital clock on the dresser, it was a quarter to one in the afternoon. *'Shit.'* He threw back the duvet and rolled clumsily out of bed. Tia would be at work and was due to finish at four, which meant he had three hours on his own – Tia's mum was having Liam after school so Lee could job-search.

Tia had left him out a note, and a newspaper cutting advertising for fork-lift truck operators in Westbury, on the kitchen table next to his cigarettes and mobile. *Saw this and thought of you. Can you pick up bread, teabags and milk at the shop. T.*

Application forms would be going out this afternoon, then the recruitment line would be closed. The job didn't interest him in the slightest, although he knew he had to find work soon – Tia's wage was barely covering the bills, and their debts were mounting at a seemingly astronomical rate.

I'll ring the number, he promised, but later – he needed coffee and something to eat first.

He thought back to that message from 'Jan' as he shook out some cornflakes into a bowl. *The most complete version of The Black Remote is rare and hard to obtain.*

He froze and stared glassy-eyed at the wall, mulling over those words for a moment. Didn't he have a reference book somewhere on obscure movies? Placing the cereal box down, he dashed upstairs and entered the spare bedroom.

There was a box under the bed filled with old film and horror magazines: *Fangoria. Shock Xpress. Headpress. The Dark Side. Fear.* He rummaged through them, but the book was missing. He opened the cupboard where there were books and magazines stacked up inside, and immediately a book landed with a *thud* by his feet.

He stooped, picked it up.

Suddenly the search for the reference book fled his mind, and sitting on the carpet he flicked idly through that freshly rediscovered photograph album.

There were polaroids of Lee and Tia at parties; on holidays he could scarcely remember; of the two of them at hazily-recollected social events.

In each picture he didn't recognise himself – he was smiling, his young face so fresh and alive. There were pictures of their first house together: a three-bedroomed terrace situated in the centre of Trowbridge. He saw faded photographs of Liam crawling; of his son in a high chair with chocolate smeared around his mouth; of his boy resting upright in the crook of Tia's arm.

Suddenly the book dropped into his lap, and he quickly covered his face with his hands. Tears slid warm and silent through his fingers, spattering the leaves of his photograph album. 'I'm sorry,' he whispered to no one in particular. 'So, *so* sorry.'

Tia came home after five, tired, cranky, and wet. Liam trudged into the house behind her, dropping his lunchbox and bag to the floor, not even bothering to acknowledge Lee as he stomped upstairs to his room.

Lee switched the TV off, then hid *The Black Remote* DVD behind the sofa. 'How was your day?'

She dumped her bags on the carpet, then said with a grimace: 'Kids were a nightmare. The weather meant there was no outdoor play, so they've been cooped up inside all day, driving me to distraction.' Tia was a teaching assistant at a local primary school, a job she disliked immensely. She found each day a struggle, and never failed to return home drained. 'Honestly thought I was going to lose it with them.' She draped her coat over the arm of a chair before drifting silently into the kitchen.

Outside, the unrelenting rain crackled against the window.

'What about the shopping?' she shouted, a short while later.

Lee squirmed in his seat. 'Shit. I ...'

'Bet you didn't ring about that job, either.'

He chewed the inside of his mouth.

'Fuck's sake, Lee.'

He got up, gritted his teeth and gingerly entered the kitchen. 'Sorry,' he said, and shrugged uselessly.

'Don't want to hear it. Fuck off.' She was seated at the table, smoking one of his cigarettes.

He couldn't think of anything else to say, so stood staring gormlessly at her for a moment or two. Around him the kitchen darkened as a bare, coffin-shaped room began to superimpose itself over his surroundings ...

Tia coughed, snapping him back into the moment. 'Have you been dipping your fingers into Liam's savings again?'

'*What* ...?' He jumped slightly, mouth gaping open and shut as he retreated toward the door.

Her cigarette was smouldering, her thumb and forefinger almost touching as she lifted her left hand. 'I'm *this* close to leaving you right now.'

Panicked screams filled his skull and he shook his head to still them. Walk away, he thought. *Just walk the fuck away.*

'You're trying to distance yourself,' he said quickly, not really thinking about what it was he was saying. 'It's been going on for a while now. You've been turning Liam against me, too.'

'How *dare* you!' Tears welled up in her eyes. 'The patience I've shown, the chances I've given you!'

He whirled, grabbed his coat from the hook in the hall and stormed outside.

He wandered aimlessly into the dusk, hands shoved into his pockets, face painted with rain. He didn't want to go back, not until he'd made sense of a few things first.

He roamed around the estate, pausing occasionally in his street to survey the house. Hours dragged by, the rain intensified. Tia's shadow flitted intermittently past the living-room window.

Eventually the downstairs lights winked out, and Lee counted to one hundred before making his move. He slipped his key from his pocket, unlocked the front door and stood dripping in the hall, listening to the rain seethe around him. It was obvious that Tia and Liam had gone up to bed, and so with a sigh he hung his coat on a radiator and sneaked off to the living-room to switch on his computer.

He sat at his desk, logged on to the *Let Them Die Slowly* website.

No new messages.

His shoulders sagged.

Just as he was about to log-off again, a message from 'Jan' popped up on screen, throwing him completely.

THE BLACK REMOTE is sufficiently interested in you — you have shown promise, my friend. Keep us in your thoughts, and perhaps it shall reveal itself to you soon.

Lee stared long and hard at the message, then dropped his hands into his lap and hissed, '… the fuck?'

Too tired to respond, too exhausted to think up a reply, he switched off the computer and rose wearily to his feet.

He caught sight of *The Black Remote* sticking out from behind the sofa, and instantly froze.

I should go to bed. Catch up on some sleep.

Instead, he crouched down and scooped it up.

Snapped open the case and fed the DVD player the disc.

Darkness reigned.

It was so thick that Lee could scarcely see his hand in front of his face.

Slowly, minutely, his eyes grew accustomed to the gloom. 'I recognise this place,' he whispered.

He was in a coffin-shaped room with stained walls and a grey, splintered door.

He snatched the door open and stepped out on to his own upstairs landing. He looked back to see that the room had changed; was now furnished with a familiar bed, cupboard, dresser and rug.

He gripped the stair rail. Crept hesitantly down into the hall where a bluish light seeped underneath the living-room door. Tentatively he approached it, reached out and froze as he heard hoof falls and the creaking of floorboards behind him.

He wheeled.

Darkness – nothing there.

'Christ.' Sweating, panting, he grasped the handle and turned it until he heard the *click*. He toed the door open and entered the room.

Positioned at various points around the living-room were wax candles, flames sputtering and hissing in the darkness. They were set upon the mantelpiece, the coffee table, around the TV and stereo system. The curtains had been pulled back from the window, and the pane was an empty square of impenetrable blackness.

Sat in an armchair in front of Lee was Tia, her blood-streaked countenance fixed and unmoving, her eyes missing from her face. Those round ragged holes glistened obscenely, and the smile she wore was the smile of a lunatic.

Liam, clad in a black paper mask, stood to her left, his head slightly bowed, his arms hanging limply by his sides.

Lee stepped into the room, and the boy's head snapped up.

'Bywa,' Liam whispered.

Lee's eyes flashed open.

'Fuck,' he gasped, straightening, wiping a thread of drool from his chin. '*Fuck!*' His heart thudded and thundered, cold sweat beaded his brow.

The TV was humming and flickering in the corner. He stood up, disorientated, then realised he'd fallen asleep on the sofa again.

'Dad?'

Lee twitched and whirled toward the voice. Liam, dressed in his Superman pyjamas and cape, was lingering in the living-room doorway. Something like relief flowered inside him when he saw that his boy was unmasked, and that his eyeballs were definitely intact. 'Liam, hi. Hi. What…?'

'You were dreaming.' Liam tilted his head to one side as he regarded his father with an expression drained of emotion. 'Talking and shouting in your sleep again.'

'Was I?' Lee laughed a brittle, nervous-sounding laugh. 'You okay? Where's mum?'

'She's out, remember? Visiting Aunt Trudie. She left early. Didn't want to disturb you.'

They were silent for a moment. Then, softly, Liam said, 'Mum said to wake you at nine. I've got football practice, remember?'

'I remember.'

Liam nodded once, then turned and hurried upstairs to his room.

They left for football practice a short while later.

They scurried through teeming rain, their hoods wrenched up, their coats zipped to their throats. Lee knew it was selfish, but all he wanted was to curl up somewhere and watch movies all day. He tried not to show his resentment, even tried to seem interested in the early stages of the training session.

During a five-a-side match, Lee lingered on the side lines as the other fathers screamed and gesticulated wildly at their sons. He stood hunched and grim-faced, the rain hammering down all around him.

In his head, Lee was inside a coffin-shaped room in a dark and decayed mansion …

He rubbed his eyes quickly.

Overhead, apocalyptic clouds gathered into shapes, figures, faces. He felt wheezy and out of breath, had to turn away from the other fathers so that they wouldn't notice.

Was he having a heart attack?

He stumbled into the Sports Hall to get himself some water. He found the fountain in the hall and quickly drank his fill. When he re-emerged, moments later, the referee blew for full-time, and the two teams trudged off the field toward their waiting parents. Some of the kids went to the hall to shower, but Liam wanted to go home and change.

'Did you see me?' Liam asked, clapping his hands, his mud-spattered face projecting the most incredible grin. 'Did you see me score the winner, Dad?'

Lee, unsettled and disturbed, stared blankly at him.

They walked home, neither speaking.

Liam hitched his bag over his shoulder, eyes not leaving the ground. The grin was gone, his metal studs scraping the pavement as he walked. Lee, desperately trying to think of something to say, clutched at his coat and stared long and hard into the middle distance.

They arrived at the house a short while later. Liam took his boots off outside, then ran wordlessly upstairs to shower. Tia – back early from Trudie's – looked up and around at Lee from her chair in the corner as he came skulking into the room. 'How was it?' she asked.

Liam slammed the bathroom door, and Lee winced.

'Is he okay?' Tia's eyes were hard, wide and unblinking. 'What happened, Lee?'

'Nothing. It went well. He scored the winner.' Lee purposely changed the subject. 'How's Trudie?'

'Fine.' Her slender shoulders dropped a fraction. 'She's invited us over for dinner tomorrow.'

'I can't do that,' he said, surprising himself.

Her expression crumpled and she turned away from him with an offended look in her eyes. 'Why?'

'I-I can't be around people at the moment, Tia. I'm ... struggling. Sorry.'

For some reason Curly-Top flashed into his mind, grinning that odd, enigmatic grin at him. Then he was back in the moment when she said, softly, 'I don't know what's got into you, I really don't. It's like I don't know you anymore.'

Without warning she shot up and left the room, leaving him exposed to a stark and uneasy silence.

'I'm standing on the edge of something.' The words spewed from his lips like bile. 'This is *mine*. Something for me.'

He fell to his knees and switched on the TV. Fed the DVD

player *The Black Remote.*

That decrepit house loomed. The camera panned down long, eerie corridors.

Shadows moved indelibly in corners.

Curved blades glinted and fell.

During the scene where the first victim – the blonde girl – descends into a subterranean chamber, Lee thought he saw a shape in the corner of the screen, a hunched figure with horns sprouting from its head.

Now he was beginning to understand what he liked about the film – you could never trust what it was you were seeing …

The killer stepped out of the darkness with the mask over his face, and whispered something – two words – into the camera.

Lee patted around for the controller, grabbed it. Rewound and re-played it.

Coaxed the killer out of the shadows again.

'Asterion House.'

There. That was it.

He left the video frozen on that black-masked face, hurried across to his computer and switched it on.

It took searching through endless results pages to find mention of the house, and then that link took him straight to a website on derelict buildings and abandoned places.

A grainy photograph of *Asterion House* appeared – the same house that had featured in *The Black Remote*, there could be no doubting it.

There were a few words written about the house underneath the picture:

This dilapidated mansion on the East Pentire headland overlooks Crantock Beach and the Gannel Estuary, which runs from the river mouth in Crantock Bay along the edge of Newquay.

Abandoned during the nineteenth century, little is known about its previous inhabitants, although they were believed to have been a family of influence and high social standing. The last in line was a recluse, who rarely left …

Lee scrolled down to see photographs of some of the interior rooms … and recognised them immediately.

One of the photographs depicted the coffin-shaped room where most of the characters had met their demises, and he stared at it until his eyes grew sore and dry. *So they actually shot the film inside the house,* Lee thought with a shudder.

There was something chalked on the floor in the coffin-shaped room, and pressing his face close to the monitor he discerned a five-pointed star inside a circle.

His window closed down suddenly, and he was left staring at his desktop. He tried to retrieve the page, but was met with the error message: 'This website is currently not available'.

Muttering obscenities under his breath, he logged on to *Let Them Die Slowly* and found a message from 'Jan' in his inbox.

He clicked on it, frowned.

Re-read it with a curious mixture of excitement and disbelief:

You have been invited to a special screening of the most complete version of THE BLACK REMOTE at Asterion House tomorrow evening. I shall meet you outside Newquay Railway Station at precisely 6pm.

I sincerely look forward to meeting you in person. You are very lucky to have been chosen, my friend.

3

Lee feigned sleep while Tia got herself and Liam dressed. He didn't stir until he heard the front door slam. Then he got himself dressed, took £25 out of Liam's piggy bank, and made the long walk to the train station on the other side of town.

He carefully planned his route by the timetable in the ticket office, and boarded his first train shortly before noon. There was just one change at Bristol Parkway, then after that it was a straight run, getting him to Newquay at a quarter to six in the evening.

Throughout his journey, his thoughts alternated wildly between Tia and *The Black Remote.* He was excited by the prospect of watching the most-complete version of a movie few had seen before, but that was tempered by the guilt of embarking on the journey in the first place. He'd left a note for Tia explaining all, yet he knew she wouldn't understand; this was something for *him*, something he could finally call his own. Once it was over, he would turn his sole and undivided attention to his family again.

I'll be a better man, he thought. *Like the me in those photographs that I'd found the other day.*

He arrived in Newquay dead on time.

He stepped off the train, then lingered by the taxi rank outside the station for a while. He pulled his mobile from his jacket, scanned it for messages or missed calls. There were none. Why hadn't Tia been in contact? She must have seen his note by now. He put the phone away just as a hand gripped his arm and turned him.

'You're him, aren't you?' He stood facing a man in a shabby grey suit and tie. The man's mouth twitched inside a dishevelled beard. 'You've come for *The Black Remote,* right?'

Lee nodded.

'Jan.' The man offered Lee his hand, and Lee shook it. 'Nice to meet you. This way please.' Jan turned smartly toward a silver Mercedes parked close to the taxi rank, and opened the passenger door for Lee to sidle inside.

Jan slipped into the vehicle, pulled on his seatbelt and started the engine. 'We haven't far to go. Strap yourself in, please.'

Jan pulled away and soon they were easing along a quiet coastal road, headlights lancing through the darkness. The night smothered the scenery; there was nothing to be seen beyond the twisting, winding surface of the road.

'I'm glad you liked the film.' Jan's deep voice resonated throughout the car, untangling Lee from his thoughts. 'It's been such a long and arduous shoot.'

Lee frowned and glared at Jan's reflection hovering in the darkness of the windscreen. 'Where are we?'

'Crantock.' Jan's fingers visibly tightened around the wheel. 'We're almost there. The house has stood on the cliff overlooking the estuary for hundreds of years. Used to overlook Langarrow, too.'

'Langarrow?' Lee was only half-listening; a remote part of him was desperately trying to make itself heard, instructing him to turn back, to return to Tia and Liam and flee this madness immediately.

'Langarrow used to exist between Crantock and Perran,' Jan said with a stiff nod of his head. 'Until the sands buried it, of course. Wrath of God, they said.' He laughed humourlessly, then with a smirk added: 'Some great men lived in Langarrow. Before the storm it was a city of vice, populated by convicts shipped in or trucked across from less … *tolerant* places. My Master's followers built the house on the cliff overlooking the city, and that's how it's survived to this very day. My fellow brethren and I have been ensconced beneath the house for a good many years, working tirelessly to bring our Master's vision to life …'

They were slowing down, pulling up in front of some wrought-iron gates.

Jan cranked the handbrake, then operated the electric window. It slid down smoothly and he reached out a veiny hand to press a button on the gatepost.

With the car idling, Lee gazed at distant lights shimmering like an alien constellation on the horizon. 'Holiday parks,' Jan sniffed, noticing his interest. 'A travesty really, considering what once was there.'

The gates shuddered and opened, and Jan released the handbrake and eased the vehicle through the gap. Lee's nose wrinkled as the sulphuric smell of the estuary infiltrated the car; with a grimace he swallowed his nausea and focussed on the windscreen again.

Dishevelled trees brushed against the Mercedes. Thorny branches scratched at its roof. The car jolted and shuddered as it picked its way over potholes, knocking Lee from side to side, Jan's reflection flickering like a trapped frame on a screen. Then, rising up before them, grey stone, rotted wood and cracked roof tiles were starkly illuminated by the headlights.

'Asterion House,' Lee whispered with awe.

Jan pulled up outside the double doors and cut the engine, enveloping them both in silence. He climbed out, came round to Lee's side and opened the passenger door. Lee clambered out, squinting at the house as he straightened.

Wrought-iron balustrades and wooden decking hung broken, twisted and askew. Windows were black, sightless eyes. Unintelligible graffiti scarred the brickwork and the neglected outbuildings around them.

Jan hurried toward the doors, fitted a key in the lock and turned it. 'So glad you could join us. Especially tonight of all nights!' He pushed, and the doors rumbled ominously open. 'January 27th. St Winebald's Day! The perfect time to screen *The Black Remote*, don't you think?' He turned and grinned at Lee before beckoning him in with a finger. 'You'll meet the rest of the house later, I promise. But first, let's enjoy the film, eh?'

Unanswered questions rippled through Lee's mind as he followed the man through the doorway into a cavernous hall. On rickety tables candles burned in glass jars. Skewed chandeliers oozed cobwebs. To their right a staircase curled away into darkness; without hesitation Jan ascended, his feet thudding down on the wooden treads as he climbed.

The stairs led to a darkened landing where an unpainted door awaited. 'In here,' Jan said, twisting and pushing the handle, 'is the theatre.' The door opened onto red swing seats and a whirring projector set behind a window in an adjacent wall. The room was only partially lit by the projector's pale-blue glow and a red EXIT sign buzzing on the wall opposite.

Lee felt too on edge to fully appreciate the cinema's dank and decayed charm, and so lingered in the darkness for a while, spellbound and silent.

'Take a pew,' Jan said, and Lee snapped from his reverie as Jan brushed past him to shuffle along the third row of seats from the front. Jan stopped, pulled open a chair and perched himself on the seat. Lee sat beside him, crushing his hands together in his lap as he looked up at the wall before them.

A pale screen suddenly filled that wall, crackling and hissing, and Asterion House appeared. Moments later shots of empty rooms flashed before Lee's eyes. He blinked and looked around curiously, scanning the room for others, but there was nobody here but them.

Grimacing, his eyes flicked back to the movie.

Out of the darkness the man in the black paper mask stepped toward the camera, *toward the viewer*, and Lee shuddered involuntarily.

The throat cutting was graphic and shocking, the girl's face suitably contorted as blood spurted from between her fingers; the thin-looking male and his dark-haired girlfriend squealed and shrieked as they were jabbed repeatedly with the spear; the plastic, vomit-clotted bag sucked in tight around the young lady's face as she fought futilely against her ties; the girl in the combat jacket pleaded convincingly for her life before the machete was plunged into her; finally, the middle-aged man in the glasses let out a harrowing scream as his belly was slashed, his innards slopping out of that cavity to land steaming by his feet.

Thoughts of snuff movies again surfaced, and Lee gripped the armrests to still his trembling hands.

It's not one of those, he told himself. *Just fucking good acting and effects.*

After the final kill, Jan stood abruptly and made his way toward the centre aisle, his seat swinging shut behind him.

Lee barely noticed, eyes still glued to the screen.

Will I be rewarded with an ending this time? he wondered with a frown. To his disappointment the movie blacked out and snow filled the screen, just like it had done on DVD. 'Where's my ending?' he whispered to himself, turning in his chair to look about him again.

The seats were empty; of his host there was no sign.

He left his seat, then hurried toward the door they'd entered by. Grabbed the handle and turned it.

Locked.

'Let me out!' he shouted, shaking the handle violently. 'Open the *fucking door!*'

No reply.

The projector whirred and the film suddenly restarted, exterior shots of Asterion House giving way to rooms thick with cobwebs, shadow and rot.

Tearing his gaze away, Lee ran toward the EXIT sign and found a small door beneath it. He grabbed the handle, throwing one last look over his shoulder as he turned it.

Someone was standing behind the window next to the projector – a tall, stooped silhouette with an elephantine head and torso.

Lee shuddered as he stumbled out of that grim auditorium, leaving the door open behind him. He was in a corridor now, which was narrow and oppressively dark. Slipping his mobile out of his pocket, he used its meagre light to see by.

In front of him were steps leading down into a deep damp vault.

The door slammed behind him.

He wheeled, and heard a key turn in the lock. 'Hey!' he shouted, grabbing the handle, rattling it. 'Let me out! Let me out, you *fuck!*

What the *fuck's* going on here, *eh?*' His voice echoed off stone walls and gradually faded to nothingness. Tears welled up and slid down his cheeks, and with a snort of self-loathing he rubbed his eyes and approached the stairs.

He placed one foot in front of the other, descending into a chamber lit by candles in small alcoves. Directly in front of him was a splintered door, hanging ajar as though ready to receive him.

He checked his phone again, considered calling the police. He could alert them to what was going on; direct them to Asterion House and the secret rooms inside it. But as he lifted his mobile, he swore under his breath – there was no signal here.

A low chuckle.

He spun to see something red flash in the gloom.

Rather than confront whoever was there, Lee snatched open the door and stumbled into the familiar confines of a cold, coffin-shaped room ...

More candles burned and dripped in the darkness, and shadows twitched and slithered across bare, filth-encrusted walls.

Before him, chalked in red on warped floorboards, was a five-pointed star, and around it – within the wide outer circle – were the six victims of *The Black Remote*.

They stood facing one another, frozen at the consummate moment; on the very brink of death.

In the far corner of the room, a group of robed figures whispered amongst themselves as Lee stepped forward. He ignored them, eyes locking upon the stars of *The Black Remote* instead.

The blonde girl grabbing at her throat.

The middle-aged guy bent over, his stomach eviscerated.

The boyfriend and girlfriend with their torn, ruptured flesh.

The woman with the plastic pulled tight around her face.

The girl with the machete embedded in her body.

They looked horribly lifelike – too authentic to be anything but ... *real.* 'My God.'

He had to at least try and phone the police, try to get help, and ripping his phone from his pocket he saw that he had a signal at last.

With trembling fingers, he hit 999, but then his mobile rang and from the lit-up screen he saw it was Tia. He raised the phone to his ear but in his panic it slipped from his grasp, skittering across the room to lie vibrating on the ground.

One of the robed figures stooped and snatched it up. Candlelight painted the face within a hood, and Lee caught sight of curly hair and a rounded, pockmarked face.

'He's here, with us. The Cult of the Infernal Abyss.' Curly-Top pressed the phone closer to his sneering lips. 'Thank you for all you've done. The boy, too.'

Lee's attention was snatched toward another figure – the black-masked man – who'd stepped out of an alcove and was now wielding a chainsaw in his hands. He was giggling and staring intently at something over Lee's left shoulder. 'Ready, Master?'

The masked man yanked the chainsaw's cord and Lee shrunk toward the door, then whirled when he heard hoof falls and the creaking of floorboards behind him.

There was that flashing again – a tiny red dot – and Lee realised he was looking straight into the lens of a video camera.

The operator lingered near the open door, and Lee saw fur-lined shins and cloven hooves.

He spun to face the chainsaw again, which had now gunned into life.

'Watch!' the masked man shouted as he raised the saw above his head. 'Watch and *marvel,* friend!' He nodded toward the half-dead things positioned around the star. 'Bywa!'

Those things instantly came to life, shrieking and squealing horrifically in their death throes.

'*Rewi!*'

The word stilled them, denying them death once more.

From those ragged eyeholes, the masked man glared around his whirring saw as he said, loudly, 'We're almost there. *Almost.* We've been searching for the right formula for *centuries.* Now it's just you … the last of the seven … and it has to be *simultaneous!* All of you at the same time. To bring this to an end – so that *many* can witness *The Black Remote* in its full and flagrant glory!'

The words barely registered as Lee suddenly recognised that deep, booming voice as Jan's. Furiously he shook the realisation off and looked around for an escape route, but an abrupt swipe from Jan's saw forced him between those half-dead things in the circle. With a cry he raised his arm in order to strike his assailant, but the saw cleaved through Lee's elbow, sending blood spraying and spurting in all directions across the room.

The robed figures in the corner laughed pitilessly at his plight.

Above the sound of his own screams, Lee heard Jan shout 'Bywa!' and immediately the other victims came to life, shuddering and shaking as they rushed inexorably toward oblivion.

The saw dropped slightly, ploughed into Lee's chest, sent him spinning to the ground in a heap before his attacker's feet.

Jan cut his saw and tore off his mask, his bearded face twitching with delight. 'The gate's opening.' He turned toward the misshapen figure behind him. Looked again at Lee and the red pentagram upon the floor. 'The Spawn of the Abyss will bring blessed insanity to all!' His voice quivered on the verge of hysteria.

Blood was erupting from Lee, and darkness was quickly stealing away his vision. The other victims collapsed like string-severed marionettes, their blood staining the floorboards, their mouths wide and grotesque Os.

The Master cantered forward, camera raised, filming the smoke that was beginning to billow and rise all around them. Suddenly Jan's eyes bulged, and he laughed and screamed all at the same time. The robed figures in the corner began to scream too, and raising their hands they clawed frantically at their faces until bubbling pools of crimson had replaced their eyes.

The Master continued shooting as Lee felt the presence of many begin to materialise around him. And as he tried to turn, to see them, total darkness descended before he could catch so much as a glimpse of his ending.

FINNED ANGELS, FISH-TAILED DEVILS

Every Sunday in the parish church overlooking the scenic little harbour in Zennor village on the northwest coast of Cornwall, a handsome young chorister, Matthew Trewhella, would sing so beautifully that God-fearing folk from miles around would abandon their own chapels just to come and hear him. As well as possessing an angelic voice, Trewhella was also said to be handsome, a hard worker and a good, clean-living man, and as such he was watched closely by all the matrons in Zennor whose daughters were approaching marrying age.

Unfortunately, he would also prove attractive to beings of a more malign disposition.

Students of Cornish lore will already have guessed where this popular 17th century fable is heading. There are various versions of it, some of which by the 19th century, an era wherein myths and legends were often softened for inclusion in nursery books, had become stories of 'happily ever after'. But the original source material is of a darker ilk.

For example, Trewhella would sing more lustily, it was noticed, whenever a mysterious but incredibly beautiful lady appeared at the back of the church. No-one knew her name or where she came from, but she attended more and more regularly. When other available young men attempted to stand close, hoping to catch her eye, something always dissuaded them, something they could never put words to – a coldness, a vague air of menace, though the lady was never openly hostile. She merely gazed fondly upon Trewhella, sighing with pleasure when he hit his highest notes.

Perhaps this is why, one particular Sunday, Trewhella was unable to resist her any longer.

That noon, as the service ended, he accompanied his beguiling admirer through the church door. The rest of the curious congregation hastened to follow, but once they were outside, neither of the twosome was anywhere to be seen. All that remained was a wet trail leading along the churchyard path, down the harbour steps, and into the sea.

Nothing was ever seen of Matthew Trewhella again, nor the mysterious woman, though he wasn't forgotten. Rumours began to circulate that during storms his singing could be heard over the rolling grey waves off Zennor Point. Several decades later, a kind of explanation was offered when a local fishing boat was hailed by a mermaid, who was furious that its anchor was resting upon the roof of her home. The mermaid, who fulfilled the classical description – her upper portions those of a handsome woman, her tail that of a fish – promised that if the anchor was removed she would release Matthew Trewhella, whose entertainment value had finally begun to wane. The boat sailed away, but Trewhella never reappeared – which surprised no-one, for mermaids, like many of the faerie folk inhabiting Cornish legend, were deemed to be devious and untrustworthy.

The story of the Zennor mermaid, which is commemorated in the town by a carved bench-end in the local church, not only comprises several near-Gothic horror elements, it also turns the mermaid tradition on its head. Throughout the ancient beliefs of the world, merfolk are seen as antagonistic to Man, and though romantic entanglements with humans are not unknown, mermaids are most often portrayed as predators who will themselves use seductive singing to lure their prey. On this occasion it was different, the huntress herself drawn ashore by the harmonious tones of a human, though the outcome was the same.

Endless scholarly explanations have been offered for the widespread belief (and more importantly perhaps, the desire to believe) in mermaids. They range from the pseudo-scientific – namely that sometime in the Ancient World a prehistoric strand of homo sapiens branched away and evolved in the sea rather than on land; to the purely metaphorical – in that mermaid superstition owes mostly to Man's aeons-long fascination with the carnal and sensual and all combinations thereof, and his ability to invent imaginary beings who fit with this obsession; to the inevitable – in that the great unknown, the uncharted depths of the ocean for example, is a hive of mysteries, and that it would be astonishing if misidentification of strange, half-glimpsed creatures did not occur.

Cornwall is not the only corner of the British Isles where mermaid lore is deeply entrenched. All around the British and Irish coasts there are similar tales, though the Merry Maid of Zennor is a particularly interesting and unusual example. Two more Cornish mermaid stories comprise more familiar aspects.

An account of the Padstow Mermaid comes to us from the late Middle Ages. At this time the River Camel, flowing down into the Padstow estuary on Cornwall's northern coast, created a natural deep-water anchorage for fishing craft and merchantmen. As such, Padstow and its surrounding communities, Rock and Polzeath, became prosperous. Did this attract the mermaid? One can only guess, but initially she arrived in a playful, even frolicsome mood. Villagers would gather along the quayside to watch as she looped and dived through the waves. For modern day sceptics thinking this must have been a dolphin or porpoise, the medieval chroniclers assure us that she was mostly human, her upper half quite lovely but her lower half finned and tailed. However, the cheerful story took an ugly turn one holiday morning, when a foreign vessel, armed for war because it feared pirates in the Irish Sea, was sailing out of Padstow harbour. The mermaid approached, intent upon teasing the sailors as she did the local fishing lads. Unused to her and alarmed, they unloaded their heavy portside crossbow, and she sank from sight, a cloud of green blood in her wake. To those watching on land this was a very bad thing. Some even claimed they'd heard the dying creature issue a curse, and very shortly afterwards the estuary began to silt up with sand and debris. Soon it was blocked by the famously named Doom Bar; the fishermen couldn't get out and the merchants couldn't get in. The local economy went to rack and ruin, and for centuries afterwards Padstow was desolated.

The third of the most famous Cornish mermaid tales is more traditional still, and tells of a beautiful girl who would sit singing and combing her lustrous hair on the sea-begirt rocks off Lamorna Cove near Penzance. Local seamen knew of her and would avoid her, but those who were new to the area would be drawn unresistingly to her enchanting voice. Their hulls would then be torn on unseen reefs and they'd be cast into the sea, whereupon, the maid, siren-like, would throw off her human guise and plunge in after them, a ghastly amphibious something that would drag them to the salty depths and there devour them at her leisure.

DRAGON PATH

Jacqueline Simpson

'God, I'm thirsty!' The young man flopped down in the shade of the rock, hauled off his backpack, and dug out a can of Coke. He flicked the ring-pull away, and drank.

'Hey, pick that thing up, Geoff!' said his companion sharply.

'Oh, for God's sake, what's the matter now? Am I polluting Holy Mother Earth? Am I annoying the pixies? Pick it up yourself, Mick, if it bothers you.'

'That,' said Mick in tones of elaborate patience, 'is the way that fires get started. When the moors are dry, you only need for the sun to catch on a bit of metal or glass –'

Geoff groaned, but didn't move. Neither did Mick, but he glared at Geoff and at the ring-pull. The two girls had also reached the rock by now and stood listening, one anxious, one amused. The anxious one picked up the ring-pull and slipped it into her pocket, glancing hopefully at Mick for approval; he gave her a nod, but his eyes were on Geoff, and on the other, prettier, girl, who had joined him in the patch of shade. Grinning, Geoff passed his can to her, and she drank with a casualness which hinted at other sharings, other intimacies.

'Boy, did I need that!' Then, licking her lips and flashing a brilliant smile at Mick, 'Well, here we are, and there's your Cheesewring, so tell us what it's all about. I can't wait to hear!'

An answering smile lit up Mick's tense features. 'This is a sacred landscape, Julia – one of the best, almost unspoilt. Over there –'

'Over *there*,' said Geoff, waving his hand grandly in the opposite direction, 'is a bloody great quarry. Disused, I grant you, but not sacred and unspoilt. Not virgin soil unploughed.'

'Shut up,' said Julia, stifling a giggle, 'I want to hear this.'

'So do I,' said the anxious girl, whose name was Anne. 'Mick knows such a lot about the earth.'

Mick's interrupted lecture resumed. 'Over there, as you see, is the

Cheesewring. Seven round slabs, perfectly balanced on top of each other, nothing else like it in the world. The scientists,' (there was acid scorn in the word) 'being scientists, will tell you it's natural, it just happened that way. But as Cornishmen, we've always known better. We knew there was power in the stones; we knew people had put them up there for a good reason, like Stonehenge. So we made up stories to pass on the message, stories which make sense to us, but not to you outsiders.'

Geoff gave a loud yawn. 'OK, do your Mystic Celt stuff if you must. But you're no more a Celt than I am. Yeah, I know your name's Trelawney, but it's over two hundred years since your revered Cornish ancestor came to London, as you told me yourself, so how many of his magical genes do you think you've got? Come to that, one of my great-grans was an Irish tweeny who hadn't brains enough to say no to the boss's son. Maybe if I had enough Guinness in me I'd see leprechauns.'

'I said, shut up!' said Julia, kicking him. 'I like Mick's stories.'

'OK, OK, it's listen-with-mother time, if that's how you want it. Sitting comfortably, pet?'

He slid his arm around her, but she pulled away, her eyes on Mick. Go on, tell us. What do they say about the Cheesewring?'

'It *moves*. That top stone there, it turns round three times when it hears the cock crow. Now, if you say that's just silly, it's you that's the fool, because stories like that are a code. The storytellers, they kept the secret knowledge alive, and now we've found out what it was. It's amazing, but it's been proved, over and over again. The Cheesewring is a powerhouse, like Stonehenge, like Avebury – there were hundreds of them, powerhouses built to store earth energies five thousand years ago, so the currents could flow along the leys – even now, any good dowser feels it – and you know what, Julia? Here, right here where we are sitting, we're on the biggest ley of all – St Michael's Line – the Dragon Path!'

He jumped up and began pointing at the horizon with his blackthorn stick, pacing up and down and talking faster and faster. 'It comes from St Michael's Mount, and all the churches it goes through are St Michael's too – he's the greatest of the angels, he's my patron of course – and here we have the Cheesewring, and the Hurlers, and then away it goes to the northeast, straight to Glastonbury Tor itself, and on to Avebury, and out across England, straight as a die, to Bury St Edmunds and the North Sea! It's just amazing, and such power!'

Anne went over to him and took his arm. As she moved, she thought she saw Julia and Geoff catch each other's eye, and certainly Geoff grinned. 'Come back over here, Mick,' she coaxed. 'We can't hear properly if you keep moving around. So, why is it called the Dragon Path?'

'Dragons are earth currents, they guard the power, the wisdom. The Chinese knew this, and where the dragons went, they called their paths the Dragon Lines. It's not true, you know, what the Church says, that Michael *killed* the dragon; they go together, like yin and yang – neither makes sense alone. And Druids worshipped snakes, and the avenues at Avebury made it a Serpent Temple.'

'I think all this is rather scary,' Anne said.

'That's because you don't understand it. Julia's beginning to see, aren't you, Julia?'

'I think it's absolutely *magic*,' she agreed at once. 'Of course I don't understand it the way you do, Mick, but you're so good at explaining, and I think I do sense the power of the ley, just a little. I'd like another story, please. Did the Druids have anything to do with the Cheesewring?'

Now why, thought Anne, were Geoff and Julia sitting closer than ever? Why did they look so eager? And had Geoff just winked slightly? But already Mick was talking, his eyes fixed on Julia, willing her to share his vision.

'There was a Druid who kept watch here. They say he always sat on the same rock, and it's still called the Druid's Chair, and if anybody –'

He stopped dead, his eyes fixed and his mouth half open. The others waited.

'Geoff,' said Mick in a voice quivering with excitement, 'what did you say the minute we got here? Do you remember what you said? I do.'

'Er ... Was it about wanting a Coke?'

'Yes! You said you were thirsty. It's amazing!'

'I was thirsty too,' said Julia. 'Just suddenly thirsty, don't know why.'

'It fits, it all fits. This Druid, if anybody came and said they were thirsty, he'd give them a drink in a gold cup which nobody could ever empty, which of course means he gave them enlightenment, and this went on for years and years till one day some man who was out hunting stole the cup and rode off with it, but his horse threw him and he broke his neck on the rocks. And he was buried over there in Rillaton Barrow, and the cup was buried with him. But of course we're still thirsty, we still need wisdom ...'

'I never heard such crap. Beats me how anyone with even half a brain can believe a word of it,' said Geoff.

'Well, that's where you're wrong, and I'll prove it. This is one case where the old tales *have* been proved true, and it's really wonderful what happened. For centuries everyone round here had known about this Druid's cup, and where it was buried, and then along came the archaeologists and opened up Rillaton Barrow, and bingo! A prehistoric gold cup! So even the high and mighty scientists – hey, what's up? What've I said? What's up, Julia?'

But Julia was laughing too much to answer, clutching Geoff's arm, burying her face in his shoulder, shrieking with giggles. Geoff was grinning from ear to ear.

'Listen to this, mate, and next time, do your homework before you go round boring the pants off everyone. What date was the dig at Rillaton Barrow?'

But Mick, struggling for words, could only stutter.

'I'll tell you when, 1818, that's when. And do you know when that fine tale you told us was first told. Do you? Do you?'

'It's a f-f-f-olktale, there's no f-f-f-irst time for f-folktales ...'

'Oh, but in this case there is, you f-f-f-olksy p-p-p-prat! Nobody ever mentioned it before 1899, when it popped up in a book by the Reverend Sabine Baring-Gould, and that means there was eighty years for the story to grow in *after* the wondrous cup was found. What's more, the Reverend gent could have helped it grow a bit himself – a little more padding for his umpteenth book, you know. So much for your ancient lore and its amazing confirmation. Don't believe me? Show him the Xerox, Julia.'

Still giggling, Julia scrambled to her feet and held out a sheet of paper: 'We found this really good book on British legends, and Geoff said –'

'God damn him to Hell, what do I care what Geoff said? But you, Julia, you said you were thirsty, you said you could sense the ley, so why are you siding with him? Why?'

It was Geoff who answered: 'You still don't get it, do you? We were winding you up, weren't we? We've had Celtic Mysteries and Celtic Magic and Celtic Mumbo-jumbo till it's coming out of our ears, and enough's enough. So we set you up good and proper, but it's for your own good, really. What you need, Mick, is not so many leys and a few more lays, know what I mean? But not with my Julia, if you don't mind, mate.'

Anne shrieked: 'Stop it, will you? Don't speak to him like that, it's not fair! You know he's been sick. You bitch, Julia, you absolute bitch! Just stop laughing, and *look* at him!'

For Mick was standing rigid, his hands clenched on his stick. Slowly, his lips drew back in a snarl and his eyes rolled up, showing the whites. He swayed, but did not fall.

Mist, white mist over Bodmin Moor. And circling figures, hooded, tall, blue-cloaked. Harps, deep-voiced choirs. No, not harps, drums. A weird chesty chant. Furs, masks, feather cloaks. Torches flaring. Come to me, come. I need your power. Stags looming through the mist, stags with human voices. Men with stags' heads. Stag-man, man-stag. I need your power.

Take the power, son. It is already yours. It runs in your blood. Show them the power and wisdom of a Druid.

Mick drew a deep, rasping breath, and his contorted face relaxed abruptly. 'Nice one, Geoff, nice one, Julia. Thanks for the fun. And thanks for your pity, Anne, but it's not needed. Now come over to the Cheesewring, where I'll show you something. Not tell you, show you.'

'I said we've had enough,' Geoff began, but Mick turned steady, cold eyes on him, and to his own utter bewilderment Geoff felt all words and laughter drain away, leaving just one thought: to obey Mick in everything. Meekly he headed for the rocks, walking a few paces behind Mick, the girls, similarly compelled, trailing behind him. As they drew nearer, the darkly looming pile seemed more unstable, more threatening. Mick vaulted onto one of the lower boulders, while the others lined up awkwardly below, silent, like prisoners before a judge.

'It would be very interesting, don't you agree, to know how many adders there are on Bodmin Moor? A piece of scientific, factual research, just up your street, Geoff. And yours, Julia – oh, silly me, I forgot you don't like snakes. Funny, isn't it, I've always liked them, in all my lives. And now I have this fancy to know how many there are on the Moor ... Well, say something, can't you, have you all swallowed your tongues?'

No answer. No movement.

Mick slid down from the boulder and walked round them, staring at each in turn. 'I take it you all agree. Now, this is how it's done. You see my stick? It's Irish blackthorn, same as St Patrick had, and we all know, don't we, how snakes feel about *that*. So if the three of you stand *quite* still – thank you – while I just draw a little circle round, like so, and leave the stick upright at the edge, like so, we can begin. There's nothing to it – I just whistle for them.'

In a flash he leaped back onto the Cheesewring, swinging up from rock to rock till he stood on the topmost slab. Putting two fingers in his mouth, he whistled, shrill notes that ran through strange discords till the human ear could no longer follow them, though the air shook with their power. Then, as abruptly, he folded his legs into a yogic pose, and sat motionless.

'You may talk while we're waiting,' said Mick.

Released from their mental bonds, they broke into a babble of questions and exclamations, dominated by Geoff's angry 'Waiting for what? I'm bloody well not waiting!' as he strode off – only to stumble backwards with a yelp of pain, as if he had walked headlong into a glass door. A moment later, Anne and Julia too struck the invisible barrier. Mick watched them running to and fro, until repeated experience forced them to accept the incredible fact that they were imprisoned within a nine-foot circle whose circumference was defined by the faintly glowing track left by Mick's stick. The stick itself stood sentinel, slightly vibrating, its tip barely piercing the soil.

'That's what's doing it! Pull it out!' cried Julia, as she and Geoff lunged simultaneously at the stick. Both screamed and recoiled, their arms cramping uncontrollably as fiery waves shot up from fingertips to armpit. The stick's oscillations, momentarily disturbed, resumed their rhythm.

'Earth energies, if you believe in such things, might do that,' commented Mick, while Julia collapsed on the ground in tears and Geoff swore. 'And now, take a good look round. Nature is so comforting, don't you think?'

'God damn it, man, don't be so bloody patronising. Drop your stupid game, can't you? You look like bloody Peter Pan, stuck up there on your heap of stones.'

'I said, look round. Look at the path, the grass, the heath. Look.'

Despite himself, Geoff obeyed. Anne was already pressing face and hands against the solid air at the circle's further edge, staring across the moor. Even Julia, still whimpering and nursing her burnt hand, lifted her head to look – and hastily scrambled to her feet, for a tuft of grass had parted to reveal the brownish, diamond-patterned head of a small viper barely a yard away. Anne too cried out, pointing up the path. There were two more snakes, no, three, rapidly twisting their way among the granite chips towards the circle, while further off there were glimpses of movement among rock slabs and scrubby heath.

Julia flung herself into Geoff's arms. 'Get me out of here, get me out! Snakes, oh Christ, I hate them, I can't stand it!'

'Don't panic, pet. It's hypnotism, that's all it is. There are no snakes here, I promise you. The bastard has hypnotised us, but he can't keep it up for ever. We'll break free, and then, by God, what I won't do to him!'

But even as he spoke, more vipers came gliding swiftly towards the circle, where they halted, pressing noses and flickering tongues against it, coiling and rearing up, hissing and striking at the line of power. The three humans clung together in the centre.

'If I were you,' Mick's voice cut through their outcry, 'I wouldn't be trying to break free. Believe me, you are safer inside than outside, for the moment.'

'Send them away, Mick,' pleaded Anne. 'You called them, you can send them back.'

There was no reply.

Julia fell to her knees. 'Oh Mick, we didn't mean anything, it was just a joke, we're sorry, look, I'm apologising,' she wailed. 'Go on, Geoff, say you're sorry too.'

'It's only hypnotism,' he muttered, but added reluctantly, 'Well, if that's what it takes to get us out … for your sake, pet … I'm sorry, Mick.'

Mick did not answer. There were many more vipers now, making an unbroken ring, and in places mounting each other in tangled heaps.

'Mick,' said Anne, struggling to sound calm, 'this can't go on, and you've proved your point. We believe in your power, in the Dragon

Path, the Druid's cup, everything. How much longer before you let us go?'

'By my reckoning,' came the cold voice, 'there are seventy-eight here so far. Now you will, I'm sure, agree that in an area like Bodmin Moor (how many square miles would you say it is?) there are more than seventy-eight adders, not to mention grass-snakes. I have summoned every serpent on the Moor, but it may take several hours for the distant ones to reach us. Luckily, summer days are long. It will probably still be daylight when the tally is complete.'

'And … and then?'

'Why, then I take down the barrier, obviously.'

Momentary relief, followed by incredulous horror, and wild protests. Time passed, and the wall of writhing, flickering reptile bodies grew higher. Julia, who had vomited violently, lay curled in a tight ball, shivering and moaning. Geoff's threats and oaths had given way to humble pleading, even tears; but in vain; now he sat helpless, head in hands. Anne stared, stony faced, at the sun-drenched moorland, where still light glistened, every now and then, on the scaly backs of yet more approaching serpents. Then abruptly she looked up once more at Mick's motionless figure.

'I can see why you want those two to die, but why me, Mick? I listened to you, I believed in you, I thought the world of you. I didn't know what they were planning – how could you ever imagine I'd want to make a fool of you, Mick? Let me out, please, please. Do what you like to them, but please … Oh Mick, can't you answer me? I'm your friend.'

'I know exactly how much of a friend you are, Anne. You had no part in the joke, that's true, but why? Because you think I'm 'sick'. 'Don't laugh at him, he's sick,' you said. 'Sick' means 'crazy' doesn't it, my dear friend, Anne? You thought I'm crazy, so now you must learn your lesson like the others.'

More time, more grass-snakes and vipers. They were piled up to the level of Anne's shoulders now; soon there would be nothing to look at but seething snakes, the sky, the looming Cheesewring, and Mick's silent, watchful form. No sound but Julia's moans, which Geoff's occasional murmurs of comfort could not quieten.

Suddenly Geoff raised his head. 'God, how stupid can one get? We must be bewitched, I think. Look here, Julia, Anne, this is a famous beauty spot, right? There are people around, walkers, climbers, picnickers, right? We shout, they come, and someone can do something – get rid of the snakes, if they're real, or knock Mick out, or shoot him, the raving maniac, or whatever. So let's shout, girls.'

'Well done,' came the mocking voice from the rocks, 'you've achieved a thought. Rather late in the day, but better late than never. Now for another. We've been here – what, two hours? Three? Time goes so fast when one has fun – So why has no-one seen or heard you yet? No ideas? Dear me, time for another little lesson.'

Even as he spoke the landscape faded, the air turned chill, and beyond the wall of snakes they saw a second wall of thick grey mist which swirled around them, blotting everything from their sight, though directly overhead the sky remained clear.

'That,' said Mick, 'is the famous Druidic mist. Everyone heading for the Cheesewring on this lovely sunny afternoon ran into it, and most turned back at once – these sudden changes of weather make the Moor so treacherous, you know. For the few hardy souls who did press on, I prepared a good strong stench of rotting sheep. No-one has come within half a mile of us, and no-one will, I guarantee. And anyway, what makes you think soundwaves would go through my barrier if I chose to stop them?'

He waited for an answer, but heard only incoherent sounds of terror and despair. The mist rolled back and dissolved, and once again his victims saw him, standing upright now, poised on the capstone, turning to scan the moors on every side.

'Two thousand, one hundred and forty-one are here, and no more in sight. Every serpent on Bodmin Moor has heard me. It is time to finish the game.'

As he stretched out his hand, the blackthorn stick uprooted itself amid a shower of greenish sparks and cartwheeled up the rocks into his grasp. Simultaneously the snakes surged forward. For a few moments there were screams, as three struggling, staggering forms tried to shake off the creatures which swarmed over them. Then they lay still and silent.

From his high perch Mick watched contentedly as the vipers began to glide away, abandoning the bodies and scattering over the moor.

Then, on the western skyline, his glance caught a distant but massive movement, as if the earth were rising and falling in great rounded waves; with it came a deep rhythmic pulse, felt in the bones rather than with the ear. Shielding his eyes from the sun, he saw at the centre of the disturbance something dark and narrow approaching rapidly, while to either side, bushes and boulders swayed like small yachts tossed in the wake of a speedboat. In a few moments he could see more; the thing was dark, yes, and tall; it was rising from the ground yet driving forward, cutting through it, like a periscope through waves, like a swan's neck, like …

With an exultant cry he stretched his arms towards it: 'Dragon! Dragon of the Ley! Earth Shaker, Guardian of the Wisdom! Did you too hear my summons? Truly, my power is greater than I knew. Yet I should have known, for I am Michael – we belong together, you and I – Earth Dragon and Druid Lord!'

With unaltered speed it hurtled towards him, then at the foot of the Cheesewring it stopped dead. Coil upon glistening coil, it drew itself up until the swaying head was level with Mick's face, its scales shimmering in iridescent patterns of darkest blue and green. Cold eyes, moon pale. A purple, flickering tongue. Mick gazed, entranced.

Then the jaws opened, and hissing breath enveloped him, filling his lungs with sulphurous fumes. The head drew back, then lunged, striking obliquely at the topmost slab of rock, so that it spun with dizzying speed and sent Mick hurtling to the ground. Lying broken-backed across a boulder, racked by the choking of his seared lungs he did not see the Dragon whip its huge form back into the earth, though he felt the tremor of its going. The Druid mist closed over him, bringing mocking voices:

Power we gave you, for a while – wisdom we could not give.

He did not die till dawn.

JAMAICA INN

In 1936, Daphne du Maurier's fourth novel, Jamaica Inn, *was published. It was set a century earlier and told the tale of a rundown inn which was also a front for a gang of wreckers who would lure cargo ships onto coastal rocks through the use of false lights, slaughter any survivors, and pillage all those goods that were washed ashore. It was a deeply eerie and suspenseful story, which drew heavily on 19th century rumours that Cornwall was the land of wrecking.*

In actual fact, though impoverished Cornish communities were well known for pursuing foundering ships in the hope they could benefit from the flotsam, there is little evidence that they indulged in organised wrecking. So, from the outset, du Maurier's now legendary tale is a work of fiction. However, the Jamaica Inn she used as her central location – a mysterious stone edifice at the misty heart of Bodmin Moor – was a real place (and still is), and stood in exactly the location where the mistress of the British thriller said it did, on an isolated stretch of the Launceston/Bodmin road. Moreover, it was well known – at least in its early days – as a genuine den of thieves.

First opened as a coaching inn by the wealthy Trelawney family in the mid-18th century, it acquired its notable name because two of its owners had previously served as Governors of Jamaica. The original reason for its establishment had been innocent enough: the provision of rest and shelter for weary travellers. But Bodmin Moor in those days was a wild, bleak region regarded as a no-go zone for Cornwall's fledgling and disorganised law-enforcers. As such, Jamaica Inn became the regular haunt of highwaymen, smugglers and other felons. This was a reputation that was widely known about, so ordinary honest folk steered well clear until long into the 19th century, when organised policing finally found its feet. By this time the inn had degenerated physically, to the point where it was a decrepit relic of a lost age. With all the criminals fled, its ongoing air of menace was now put down to the presence of ghosts. Jamaica Inn certainly looked as though it was haunted, and with such a history it was easy to believe that a constant presence of bad men had eventually attracted bad spirits.

What's more, this particular legend persists into modern times.

As mentioned previously, Jamaica Inn still stands, now a fine pub and restaurant, and is hugely popular with tourists, but regular ghost hunts are also held there, and several different spirits have allegedly been identified. The most regularly recorded appears to be that of a young and forlorn looking sailor, who supposedly sits on the wall outside, watching new-arrivals. According to the tale, in life this young man was in conversation at the inn with an unidentified person, who suddenly asked him to step outside. The following day, the sailor was found murdered on nearby grassland. The murderer was never apprehended.

Many of the staples of psychic investigation are present at Jamaica Inn. Orbs have been filmed, and dramatic temperature falls recorded by investigators. But more traditional aspects of haunting are also said to be prevalent. Footfalls have been heard on stairs and upstairs landings when nobody was there, doors have opened and closed on their own, and disembodied knocking sounds have been reported from all over the building. One of the bedrooms, no. 5, is reputedly a hub of such activity, though as a sure sign that travellers to Cornwall are a different breed these days, it is enormously popular with visitors for this very same reason.

All that said, Jamaica Inn still occupies a lonesome spot in the midst of rugged moorland. When night falls and the mist comes down, it is easy to imagine oneself back in the days when killers and robbers roamed this region, and when the only structure one could find sanctuary in was a brooding pile of dilapidated stone notorious for the tormented spirits awaiting you inside.

THE OLD TRADITIONS ARE BEST

Paul Finch

Scott walked into the pub, checked the two fivers in the pants pocket of his new shell-suit, then marched up to the bar and ordered a pint of lager.

The landlord was someone he thought of as a typical Cornishman: huge and well-built; red-haired and apple-cheeked; grinning from ear to ear. His rolled-back shirt sleeves revealed immense, beefy forearms complete with naval tattoos. His smart tie bore a crest and a coat of arms. He gazed jovially down at the newcomer.

'And how old are you, son?' he asked.

Scott, who was sixteen, but small and skinny for his age, immediately realised the game was up, even on a day of celebration like this. He dropped his false smile, became surly. Rotten teeth showed between his curled lips. 'It's probably piss-water anyway.'

The landlord chuckled. '*You* won't be finding out, that's for sure.'

There were amused sniggers from his bar-stooled regulars.

'I'll send some firm round here!' Scott warned him.

Still grinning, the landlord pointed at the hostelry door. 'So long as they're over eighteen, that's fine with me. Now go out and watch Obby Oss.'

Furious, but sensing a different breed from the weary, apathetic Mancunians he was more used to dealing with, Scott backtracked towards the door. He'd only been in Cornwall two days and already he hated it.

'We call them hobby-horses where I come from,' he retorted. 'And you know what, they're like ... fucking kids' stuff!'

'Out you go, son.'

'Wanker!' Scott spat, to gales of scornful laughter from the men in the pub.

Outside, he was irritated to be confronted by the Kidwells. How the hell had they found him so quickly in this whirling mass of revelry?

'Where've you been, Scott?' Russ Kidwell demanded, taking his pipe out, but looking more concerned than angry. Mary, Russ's wife, seemed equally anxious. Scott wanted to hoot with laughter. He'd been missing, what – five minutes, and they were already worried about him. About *him*. Not about what he might get up to while he was out of their supervision. Typical airhead probation officers.

'I was looking for you,' he said, pulling his usual stunt, which was to pass the onus of blame back onto the person who was accusing him.

'Oh.' Russ puffed on his pipe again, and gazed at his charge thoughtfully.

Russ was a tall, lean man – in good condition for someone of his age, which was probably fifty or so – but he had a genial disposition and seemed incapable of thinking the worst of anyone. His shock of white hair, and taste for canvas pants, deck shoes and roll-neck jumpers, gave him a sort of 'eccentric uncle' look. His wife, Mary, who was twenty years younger at least, but more rounded, in fact dumpy, which contrasted oddly with her bobbed fair hair and very pretty face, was even more of a pushover.

'We thought you'd done a bunk,' she said, in a tone that was more apologetic than reproachful.

Scott merely shrugged. 'Where to in this shit-hole?'

He turned and began walking, elbowing his way through the cheering, dancing crowd. Russ glanced at his wife, rolled his eyes, and set off after him.

There was no way Padstow could truthfully be described as a 'shit-hole'.

Granted, it was more a town than a village these days, but it still had to be regarded as one of the quintessential Cornish holiday resorts. First built as a fishing hamlet on the western corner of scenic Padstow Bay – a vast and winding estuary of the beautiful River Camel – it had steadily expanded throughout the twentieth century, but had never quite lost its nautical character. Its quaint cottages, which seemed to tumble over each other down the narrow, zigzagging streets to the waterside, were exclusively built from local granite, but were also whitewashed and permanently bedecked with flowers, even in winter-time because the climate was so benign. Many gardens were filled with sub-tropical vegetation, while rumour held that some of the ancient oaks in the nearby deer-park were evergreens.

The harbours themselves, of which there were several, each contained their individual quota of fishing boats (the local oyster-beds, in particular, were still very busy, as were the pilchard grounds), but greater by far were the numbers of yachts, dinghies, and other leisure craft. The quaysides were gaggles of shops, restaurants and atmospheric pubs but, though endlessly thronging with visitors and tourists, the mood down there was unfailingly friendly.

It was no real surprise, perhaps, that such a charming and picturesque little backwater should still play host to the weird and wonderful tradition of 'Obby Oss', as the locals referred to it.

When the Kidwells and their reluctant responsibility arrived at the next set of crossroads, the creature in question was again close at hand, now spinning madly around its 'teaser', a guy dressed as Punch, armed with a balloon on a stick. The procession of May Day celebrants still dashed and jumped on all sides of it, hurling blossoms and confetti, singing and shouting at the tops of their voices.

The Oss itself bore no actual resemblance to a horse, being essentially a long and heavy-looking oval of black-painted wood, with a hole cut in the centre so that it could be worn on the shoulders. Whoever had the job of wearing it was clearly robust, judging by the speed with which he was cavorting. He'd stuck his head up through the hole, though his own features were hidden from view by the preponderance of red and black streamers flowing down from his conical hat (to render him even more indistinct, his face had also been painted, one half black, the other red).

His body was concealed too, in this case by heavy skirts attached around the rim of the oval and hanging to the floor. The tail was a chunky length of rope, but the creature's most alarming feature was its head, which was fixed at the front but jutted up and outwards at a predatory angle. It was handsomely carved and polished, but was again painted red and black, and had a fearsome countenance. It was almost demonic, more dragon-like than equine. Its lower jaw, inlaid with a full set of gleaming white teeth, was articulated and would *clack* up and down loudly, no doubt operated by some internal device.

Every part of the bizarre effigy was adorned with bells and ribbons, the purpose presumably being that no-one, however uninterested in the ancient customs, could ignore the thing when it came prancing along their street, looking for donations.

Despite Scott's natural antipathy to anything he didn't understand, he was momentarily fascinated enough by the weird sight to wonder what it was actually supposed to represent. 'What the hell's all this about, anyway?'

'I suspect an old fertility rite,' Russ replied, still puffing on his pipe. 'You know … a hangover from the Celtic days.'

And indeed, Scott did now notice that it was mainly girls – all dressed to the nines in colourful rural regalia – who, while seeming reluctant to make physical contact with the Oss, would dart forwards to pluck at its ribbons, then scurry away again, squealing and giggling as it chased them.

''Scuse me sir,' someone said, 'but that's not strictly right.'

It was one of the musicians who'd been accompanying the Oss. He was a Morris dancer type, with bells adorning his knees and elbows, and bunches of leaves fastened to his bowler hat. Again, he struck Scott as a typical Cornishman, being large and red-haired, with a bushy red beard. He had a heavy accordion slung down over his corpulent stomach; he'd broken off playing in order to sink a pint of chilled cider. A second passed as he finished the drink, wiped his mouth, then handed the glass back to a girl, who'd just come out of a pub with a tray.

He looked at Scott and Russ again. 'There *is* a fertility reference in the old story, that's true. But the Padstow Oss has a much more aggressive role than that. That's why Peace Oss was brought in to moderate it.'

'Peace Oss?' Russ said.

The accordion man continued. 'Obby Oss has a combined role these days. As well as being a fertility symbol, he's used by Padstow folk to repel thieves and raiders. Story is he was granted diabolic powers for this very purpose. So what do you think of that, young fella?' And he prodded Scott's shoulder.

Scott was bewildered by the gesture, but also frightened, and because he was frightened, angry. 'I dunno, why you asking *me*?'

'Because,' said the man, who prodded Scott again, 'you look like someone who needs to know.'

Scott usually tried to avoid violence. His long list of criminal offences mainly comprised house burglaries, carried out during the day when the householders were absent. This wasn't because he didn't like confrontation, but because if he indulged in it, he was usually the one who came off worse. But, like any trapped rat, he *could* fight if he had to.

As now.

He'd already spat on the accordion man's sissy costume and was about to kick the bastard in the shins, when Russ and Mary dragged him away.

'You pair of tossers … you said no-one would know,' he snarled as they hustled him through the crowds.

'No-one *does* know,' Russ tried to reassure him.

'You said you wouldn't tell anyone!'

'It'd be more than our job's worth to tell someone.'

'You said …'

'For God's sake, Scott, give it a rest!' Mary hissed. 'You're drawing even more attention to yourself.'

And it was true. Even in the midst of such noise and gaiety, Scott saw that several people were directing curious stares at him. More than a couple of their smiles had faded.

Half an hour later, the three of them were seated around a table on an outdoor terrace, waiting for their lunch to be served.

Mary pushed an open packet of crisps across the tabletop to Scott. He took a few out but didn't bother to thank her. The terrace was attached to a pub-restaurant called *The Old God's Rest,* and gave startling views over the estuary. It was early May, but the sun was now high and very warm. Seagulls dipped and looped over the rippling blue inlet. The windowboxes to either side of the pub's rear door were a riot of colourful late-spring blooms. A decorative cartwheel, painted a vivid green, was fixed on the pub wall, just under the triangular apex of the roof.

'According to this,' Russ said, reading from a guidebook, '"the Obby Oss celebration, while not unique to Padstow, has some unique Padstow modifications."' He glanced over at Scott. 'It's true what that bloke said, it *does* have something to do with raids on the town.'

Scott said nothing. He was barely listening.

'Check this out.' Russ read a selected passage. '"In 1346, during the Hundred Years War, England's king, Edward III, commenced a lengthy siege of the port of Calais. The French fleet was unable to break it, and thus launched a series of tit-for-tat raids on English coastal towns. One such was Padstow in north Cornwall, which was assaulted in the April of 1347. The town, denuded of defenders as the bulk of its male population was involved at Calais, could only offer resistance by carrying its traditional spring-time symbol, the Hobby-Horse – or Obby Oss – down to the harbour, and threatening to invoke demonic forces with it.

'"The French scoffed at this, but legend holds that, when they landed, the Obby Oss did indeed come to life and attack them. Several Frenchmen were borne away into the sea by it, before their comrades fled."'

Scott still wasn't listening. He was too preoccupied with the incident earlier, and what, if anything, it might signify.

As far as he understood, the 'Safari Programme', as the popular press scornfully termed it, was designed to provide short holidays for young offenders as an aid to their rehabilitation. It was supposed to be good for everyone: ease up pressure on the prison system, and show the offender that a different and more rewarding lifestyle was possible.

But surely the people who actually lived in the place the offender was being taken to weren't supposed to know about it? Surely the whole thing would be carried out as secretly as possible? This had worried Scott from the outset. Thoughts of mob vengeance were never far from a young criminal's mind. Back in Manchester, he knew of one lad who'd been tied to a lamp-post and had paint poured over him. Another had been locked in a shed with a savage dog, and had almost died from his injuries.

Russ read on. '"Owing to the infernal forces that allegedly worked through it on that long-ago spring day, the Padstow Oss has developed a reputation for defending the town aggressively, even cruelly. This is not entirely out of keeping with other hobby-horse legends. Scholars have suggested that the name itself, 'hobby-horse', derives from the old English word 'Hobb', which means 'Devil', though in the case of Padstow events have clearly gone a little farther than most. Even now, in modern times, the Padstow Oss has a disquieting appearance, and in a grim reversal of the role commonly played by fertility gods, is said to draw its power from violence rather than love."'

'Didn't know this place was so interesting,' Mary said, taking a sip of lemonade.

Russ looked again at Scott, who hadn't touched his own drink. 'Just shows though, doesn't it, Scott. You thought that bloke was having a go at you, but all he was doing was telling you about the history of the place.'

Scott grunted. He wasn't convinced. Or satisfied. Even if it was true that the strange conversation had been a coincidence, he wasn't having some carrot-crunching yokel pushing him round, making fun of him. He came from the inner city, from a concrete jungle where he'd had to fight and scratch for everything he got, while these fat, lazy slobs down here sat in the sun all day and danced around painted animals. He'd show them. He'd break their cosy little world in half.

Russ quoted the guidebook again. '"In fact, Obby Oss's reputation grew so fearsome over the years that Peace Oss was introduced to counteract it."'

'That Morris man mentioned something about a "Peace Oss", didn't he?' Mary put in, concerned by Scott's sullen indifference and trying to generate some interest in him. 'What's that then, Russ? Tell us about it.'

Russ shrugged, flipped a couple of pages. 'We haven't seen it yet because apparently it dances its way in from the other side of the town.' He read more. '"Peace Oss, which was introduced after the bloodshed of the First World War, is the spiritual opposite of Obby Oss. It is blue and white instead of red and black, and is noticeably of a less mischievous and frolicsome disposition. It was brought into the festivities not to arrest Obby Oss's behaviour as such, but to moderate it, to reduce it to an acceptable level.

'"However, as the two sides of Nature, the negative and the positive, are deemed indivisible from one another, Padstow's two horses must inevitably meet. The May Day celebrations in the town thus culminate when the two creatures, having paraded through different neighbourhoods, drawing ever larger crowds behind them, finally unite and perform a ritual dance, their numerous supporters capering around them. This in itself is a raucous occasion and may touch off a rowdy, drunken party that could well go on all night."'

Russ laid the book down and grinned. 'All's well that ends well, then.'

Scott stood up.

The Kidwells watched him.

'Need a leak,' he said. 'Fancy coming giving me a hand, Mary?'

'Don't be long,' she replied in a patient tone. 'Your pie and chips is coming.'

He sidled away into the pub, and as soon as he was out of sight nipped through the front door and out into the street. It was still a chaotic scene in the town, every road and avenue thronging with merry-makers. He wondered what they'd all do if it suddenly started pouring with rain, but, though it would give him a certain malicious pleasure to see their celebrations dampened, he decided he preferred it this way, warm and sunny, with everyone out of doors – and their houses undefended.

First off, of course, he'd have to put as much distance as he could between himself and *The Old God's Rest*.

On realising that he'd eluded them again, the Kidwells would initially search by themselves. Because of the embarrassment it would cause, they wouldn't want to alert the coppers until they were absolutely sure he was up to no good. But by then he'd have had plenty time to wreak havoc.

As he slipped down a side street, and found the crowds dwindling, Scott felt a tremor of excitement. He was on the job again, and there was no better feeling. He'd had it with playing stupid games: watching fancy-dress parades; sitting in beer-gardens, drinking lemonade for Christ's sake! What next, sandcastles on the beach? Fuck all that.

He walked for several minutes, doing his best to look nonchalant but already casing properties for possible weak points. He didn't have any tools with him, of course, but then he'd never got into the habit of using tools, owing to the way the police up in Manchester were quick to nab you for 'going equipped'. Nevertheless, things looked good. He was now descending towards the waterfront, but was still in a residential district, and the potential for break-ins seemed promising.

The houses round here, though small and often terraced, were quality. They were uniformly whitewashed – probably a local by-law or something – and were all in good nick. Again, profusions of flowers poured from their windowboxes, front doorsteps were scrubbed, woodwork was brightly painted. At the rear, they nearly all had gardens, tiny but well kept.

If there was any drawback, it was that the neighbourhood was a little cluttered. The streets were narrow, labyrinthine, and had the tendency to turn suddenly into flights of steps between different levels; you were never quite sure if someone was overlooking you or not.

A couple of times, Scott almost ran into trouble because of this. On the first occasion, he found a car parked up with its front-passenger window wound down, and a handbag in full view on a seat. He loitered for a second, glancing around, but only at the last minute did he look up and, directly overhead, see an elderly lady leaning from a window, watching him.

A few moments later he was wandering along another alley when he spotted a rear-gate standing ajar, and on the other side of that a window that had been propped open. Beside it, on the step, a row of uncollected milk bottles suggested the occupants were away. Again Scott dallied, considering – but then spotted a child in the next-door garden. Only its head was visible – it was probably on top of a climbing-frame or something – but it was gazing at him curiously. Scott gave the child the finger, and stalked on.

Neither of these incidents worried him unduly. At least, not as much as the sudden wooden *clack* he heard a few minutes later.

He came to an abrupt halt. Paused. Listened.

He stared to the front and back, but saw nothing and no-one. The alley was still deserted. All he could hear now was a distant cheering from the town centre. But that *clack* – it had been sharp, abrupt. Like a gunshot echoing in the narrow streets. Anything could have made it, but Scott had the odd feeling that it had been for his benefit.

That was ridiculous, of course. But even so, when he moved on he moved cautiously, ears attuned. He ventured thirty yards to the next junction, looking warily both ways before crossing it. Leftwards, the passage ran up to a parked car and a closed garage door. Rightwards, it bent out of sight under a whitewashed brick arch. As Scott peered down that way, he heard another, very distinctive *clack*.

He tensed, wondering.

Had the noise come from down there, beyond the arch?

But even if it had done, what the hell? There was probably a perfectly logical explanation for it.

Not that he could think of one.

Scott decided he wasn't going to hang around to find out. He pressed on quickly, feeling as though someone was watching him. He was quite close to the sea-front, he told himself. Once down there, he'd be among other people again. He could take a rain-check on the whole situation.

But suddenly, the sea-front wasn't easily to be found.

Gulls called overhead, he could smell salt in the gentle breeze, but every passage he now took seemed to switch back on itself and send him uphill again.

He glanced though the gaps between houses, but instead of masts and blue sky, and the low, distant woods of the estuary's eastern shore, he saw only more houses. What was worse, now it seemed there was nobody around to ask. Ten minutes ago, the knowledge that every front door and window was firmly closed because there was nobody at home would have encouraged him. Now, it disconcerted him. Surely the festival wouldn't empty the residential neighbourhoods this completely? Surely people had other things to do?

He started violently – having just heard hooves.

At least, they'd sounded like hooves.

On concrete.

His ears strained.

Had it been hooves, that eerie but fleeting *clip-clop-clip* from somewhere close behind? He glanced backwards, but again saw no-one. However, as before, the alley curved quickly out of sight, so someone could be close by and remain concealed.

But why should they be? And anyway, it couldn't have been hooves. They wouldn't have stopped after two or three beats. He'd have heard them fading off into the distance.

CLACK!

Much louder, much nearer.

Unable to stop himself, Scott began to run. He hared down the nearest passageway, taking pot luck rather than trusting to his sense of direction, and this time, ironically, shooting straight out onto the harbour-side esplanade, almost knocking over a couple of teenage girls as they walked cheerfully past, chomping on pasties.

He slid to a halt, aware that he was red-faced and dishevelled, acutely conscious that he'd drawn several querying glances from the numerous people dotted here and there.

One old boy seemed particularly interested; he was seated on a mooring-pillar, smoking a clay pipe. He had a grizzled, leathery face and white mutton-chop whiskers, and over the top of both he wore a faded seaman's cap. He was typical of the sort Scott would expect to find on a Cornish dockside: a living, breathing cliché, probably sat here every day bemoaning the fact that he no longer had regular access to his shipmates' arseholes. Still, the old git had clearly spotted Scott and was no doubt wondering who he was and what he was up to. The young hoodlum realised he'd already muddied these waters too much to continue trawling them.

He strolled across the esplanade to the edge of the dock, and gazed down at the green wavelets lapping the pilings. Striations of oil were visible on their surface, but ducks were bobbing about on them, and healthy fronds waved back and forth just underneath.

It was a pleasant enough scene, but Scott wasn't taking it in; he was thinking. He glanced right. Beyond the old guy on the mooring-pillar – who was still watching him – he saw jetties, a forest of masts and, on the far side of those, shops and arcades. In the other direction, however, the buildings ran out fairly quickly. A stone quay jutted into the estuary, with a miniature lighthouse on the end of it, and beyond that there was nothing but sand-flats running steadily northwards.

Not sure why, but thinking this was worth investigating, Scott strode off in that vague direction. When he reached the quay he walked a few yards along it, and glanced northwards again. What he'd thought were sand-flats he now saw were an extension of beach; the tide was so low that much more of it was exposed than usual. With the sun at its zenith, it would normally be heaving with visitors, but, thanks to the festivities in the town, there was currently no-one out there at all.

And then he saw something else.

Which pleased him no end.

Perhaps half a mile away, at the far end of the beach, there was a headland, and on that headland a cluster of four or five white bungalows.

Holiday homes, almost certainly. They had to be, out in a favourable position like that. Which likely meant that many of their occupants, if not all, would be up in the town, enjoying the fun. Add to that the headland's isolated position – it was probably only linked to the town by a narrow country lane, which would slow down the police response – and you had a handful of burglaries just waiting to happen.

Scott trotted down a flight of steps onto the sand and, with his hands thrust into his pockets, commenced an idle and apparently leisurely stroll north.

It wasn't the first time he'd visited the seaside and found his visual perceptions distorted.

After twenty minutes at least, the headland still seemed a good half-mile away, though Scott had now left the environs of the town well behind.

To his left, there were high, rolling dunes crowned with tussocky marram grass, and beyond those were wooded hills. To his right lay the estuary, the glittering waterline of which suddenly seemed substantially closer. The sand, though flat and rippled, as it tended to be on quiet beaches, had dried out in the sun and was becoming crumbly, difficult to walk on.

He'd already taken his trainers off to avoid leaving identifiable sole-prints, but he soon had to put them on again; fragments of shells, crab-casing and small twists of black, hardened seaweed were littered everywhere, and cut like glass. On top of this, to increase his discomfort, the sea breeze was stiffening and freshening, and Scott was wearing nothing beneath his flimsy shell-suit jacket.

He shrugged, strode on determinedly. Hell, it wasn't as if he wasn't used to the cold. He'd absconded from custody numerous times, spending whole winter nights dossing in subways or under motorway flyovers.

By the same token, though, he wasn't as fit as someone of his age should be. For one thing, he was undernourished: by choice, he spent most of his money on booze, cigs and drugs rather than food, while these, in their turn, had further damaged his health.

Even after twenty minutes he was tired and footsore, having trouble getting his breath. Still, who gave a shit? If he finished today with a pocket full of someone else's jewellery, he'd be perfectly happy for a week or so.

He carried on walking, only for it to then strike him that, out here alone on this huge expanse of sand, he made a conspicuous figure. Anyone currently in residence on the headland would spot him easily.

It might have made more sense to approach along the road, where he could have kept a lower profile. But it was too late to do anything about that now. And, in any case, Scott didn't really expect to get away with what he was doing here. Okay, they'd send him back to the clink, but they were going to do that come what may.

The main purpose of today, rather than make a major score that he could retire on, was to grab a bit of extra cash; that, and to get his own back on these fucking hicks who thought they were so cool taking the piss out of him.

But still the headland was no nearer. And now Scott had noticed something else. It wasn't a clear stroll to it. A line of rocks had appeared in front of him, extending all the way down to the sea. He'd have to scramble over those before he got anywhere near the headland, and they weren't small; they were more like outcrops than loose boulders. He'd probably be able to thread his way through them, but it wouldn't be easy. It might also mean there'd be people around; youngsters and their grandparents investigating rock-pools and such.

'Shit,' he muttered.

This wasn't running exactly to plan, but he'd keep going. If nothing else, he would give the Kidwells a good run-around for half a day. That should teach the do-gooding bastards a lesson.

So he plodded on defiantly, progressively narrowing the distance between himself and the rocks, which grew taller and taller, until soon they were towering over his head.

By this time his view of the headland had been blotted out. It was as though the last trace of fellow human life had been extinguished. That was an outlandish but nonetheless discomforting thought, rather like his experience down in the harbour-side neighbourhood, when he'd suddenly found himself eerily alone.

Scott stopped for a moment, breathing hard, his abused lungs working overtime. He glanced towards the water; the estuary had noticeably widened and its far shore was barely visible. Ahead, the rocks weren't just tall, they'd adopted curious shapes; all jagged peaks and crooked spires, no doubt carved by the weather and the sea, but reminiscent of an alien planet rather than the Cornish coast.

And then – his thief's sixth sense began to tingle.

He tensed, unsure what it meant. Was someone close by? If so, where? A moment passed, during which he scanned his immediate vicinity, seeing and hearing nothing. And then, slowly, he turned and stared behind him.

He couldn't believe his eyes; but that didn't make any difference to what he was seeing.

A large object – a large, red and black object – was in pursuit of him. It seemed to have come from the town, and it was approaching fast along the beach, unnaturally fast.

It was still well over a hundred yards away but he could clearly see the jutting, dragon-like head, the great oval body, the fluttering ribbons and streamers. And now he could hear it jingling, the bells on it, the harness.

At first Scott was bemused rather than frightened. How the hell could one man carry such a bulky costume, at such speed, over such a distance? And where were all the others who were with him? Where were the revellers, where was the 'teaser' dressed as Punch?

Scott tried to scoff, tried to laugh at the ridiculous, garish object, though it didn't look quite so ridiculous any more.

It was still awkward, clumsy, but it was also large and powerful, and even over this distance he could hear the ferocious, repeated *clacking* as its jaws snapped open and shut. And the question begged again, how could one man move like that under such an encumbrance?

If it *was* one man.

But then it *had* to be? Whoever he was, the guy's head was in place in the middle of the hobby-horse's broad back. The conical hat gave it away, but with all the paint and ribbons adorning it, it melded so comfortably into the rest of the creature's livery that, in truth, it wasn't really distinguishable.

And still the thing was coming.

Scott now fancied he could hear the thunder of galloping feet.

No – not *galloping*. That was ludicrous. Humans didn't *gallop*.

All right, the thunder of *pounding* feet. But more than one pair.

And still it was coming. Now it was less than a hundred yards away, much less. Unquestionably, there was no human who could move that fast, or show such endurance.

By sheer instinct, Scott started to retreat.

He reached the rocks in record time, and hurriedly began to clamber among them.

As he'd hoped, there were many clefts and crannies that he could follow, some of which were narrow, their side-surfaces slick with weed or serrated with barnacles; not ideal avenues for something as large as Obby Oss.

Yet somehow Scott didn't think this would pose a problem for it. And indeed, less than a minute later, he heard the jingle of its bells and harness again, the thumping and clopping – yes, the *clopping* – of its feet, as it came racing into the rocky enclave.

'This is not … happening,' he wheezed. 'Not … happening …'

He found himself at the head of a narrow defile shaped like an inverted triangle. It was cluttered with boulders and pebbles, and slippery with weed.

He tottered down it, falling at least twice, gashing his arms, ripping holes in his shell-suit. But none of that mattered because he had to get away, and he *would* get away. He was Scott Sinclair, and he'd done jobs all over Manchester. He'd evaded some of the toughest cops in the whole of Great Britain. Of course, his options now weren't quite as wide as when running for broke through the benighted sprawl of the city.

At the end of the defile, for example, he had to scale a sheer rock-face, skinning his fingertips, spraining his wrists. On the other side of that, he dropped downwards again. He didn't mean to drop so quickly, but gravity took over and he found himself sliding on his arse over another near-vertical face, slashing yet more holes in his clothing and flesh.

The next thing he knew he was on sand again but, though it was easier to land on than rugged rock, it was problematic for different reasons. He'd alighted in a natural cove, with no obvious way out –

other than the sea.

The walls hemming him in on all sides were probably not unclimbable, but they were hugely steep, and Scott was now exhausted. He hobbled forwards, tripping and falling onto his knees.

Immediately, there was a scraping and clattering of what sounded like wood and – yes, hooves – behind him. He turned. Like some immense, armoured insect, Obby Oss had appeared over the parapet behind, and was now perched on the incline just below it, at an angle that was surely impossible.

Briefly it was still, the sun embossing its brilliant but demonic colours, glinting greasily from its thick whorls of oil paint, from its flashing crimson eyes and clamped white teeth.

Scott crab-crawled backwards, rose, turned, tried to run, and tripped and fell again.

He heard it start to descend. He glanced back; unbelievably, it was climbing down the rock-face head first, bulky and clumsy, swaying from side to side, but negotiating the perilous footing with astounding ease.

With no other options, he jumped to his feet and ran towards the water – but he'd never been a confident swimmer. Beyond the line of surf, it deepened quickly, and the first wave to hit his legs bowled him over. He plunged beneath the surface, and for seconds was in a frantic, twilit world of swirling, salty bubbles and lashing strips of kelp. Even then, he might have tried to make progress, might have risked everything to swim out farther – had he not suddenly spotted certain *things* beneath him.

When he re-emerged he was coughing and gasping. He threw himself back onto the shore, drenched but shivering more with horror than with cold. When he managed to regain his feet, he stumbled backwards, retreating from the waterline but staring down at it all the same.

He'd have liked to think that the ivory ribs, broken teeth and multiple fragments of skull scattered across the shifting sands down there were all that remained of the French pirates who'd come here in 1347. But deep inside, he knew the real truth: they represented raiders of a more recent vintage.

Instinctively, he glanced up at the rocky ridges encircling him. He wondered if he'd see Peace Oss at this point: smaller, slighter, and with gentler curves than its mean-spirited cousin; decked in blue and white, its polished wooden head a reminder of graceful carousel rides rather than brutish, pagan feasts.

But there was no sign of it. And why should there be? Peace Oss had not been introduced to halt Obby Oss's activities, merely to temper them, to moderate them, to restrain them – perhaps, just for the sake of argument, to once a year?

Scott nodded, smiled bitterly. And a jingle of harness alerted him to the presence now standing directly behind him.

It was a couple of hours later when Mary Kidwell finally looked at her husband, and said: 'Okay?'

Russ Kidwell nodded amiably. 'Absolutely fine.'

'I suppose I ought to inform the police that he's gone?'

Russ, who was puffing on his pipe at the far side of the table, shook his head. 'Give it another half-hour or so. Let's enjoy ourselves a little longer.'

The pub garden and all the adjacent streets were teeming with revellers. The noise, laughter and song was astonishing, the music of drums and flutes almost deafening. Mary took another sip of wine. 'It's a fun night on the town, that's for sure.'

Russ nodded again. 'It is *now*.'

'The old traditions are always the best,' she sighed.

Her husband smiled. 'That's why I like coming home now and then.'

GUARDIANS OF THE CASTLE

Of all the faerie beings that abound in Cornish legend, the one most associated with evil is the 'spriggan'. The word itself has sinister origins, deriving from the plural Cornish term 'spyryiyon', which means 'spirits', as in unearthly beings. Much has been written about the spriggans, folklore often intermingling with fiction to create a confusing picture. But to sum them up in simple terms, they are the bandits of the faerie world, a rough and treacherous breed with a liking for mischief and violence.

Very similar to the orcs in J R R Tolkien's writings, the spriggans are underground dwellers, but unlike the orcs, they can move around in daylight and are usually adept at magic. Female faeries, it was said, were rarely safe from them. The spriggans would seek to ravish and imprison these elfin maids almost as a matter of course; it is no wonder that certain myths describe high points of land in the wild west of Cornwall, often barrows or the relics of Iron Age hill-forts, becoming enchanted havens where female faeries could seek refuge from their rapacious foes. But the spriggans were not simply predators. They were also mercenaries, and regularly found work with the Cornish giants, whose treasure hoards they would guard and enemies they would hunt and kill.

If all this sounds a tad brutal for a faerie tale, it is important to remember that such stories were not passed down for the entertainment of children, but in medieval times and even later were regarded as historical fact and issued as warnings that if men transgressed against the other world, serious and bloody repercussions could follow.

Of course, the giants were also known as a dangerous race, so their relationship with the spriggans should come as no surprise.

Many of the stories concerning Cornwall's giants almost sound humorous. We hear about unusual landscape features being created by giants throwing gargantuan boulders at each other or indulging in games of quoits; or giants who were so dim that humans were easily able to dispatch them, the Giant of Dodman Point for example, who allowed a village doctor to bleed him to death when he was merely suffering from a cold. But the prevailing theory in the Middle Ages was that these hulking, cannibalistic brutes, who lived among the rocks on the high moors or in coastal caves, such as the Ogre of the Manacles near Land's End, were antagonistic to all men, and would murder and pillage at every opportunity. The story of Jack the Giant-Killer may be a relatively recent work of fiction – its first appearance in print was in 1711 – but it recycles age-old tales in which giants like Cormoran, Blunderbore and Galligantua were cold-blooded killers who would ravage farms and fishing villages, and slaughter any knights sent against them.

We know today, of course, that giants, if they existed at all, could only have done so in the earliest days of mankind. Archaeological excavations the world over uncover more and more evidence that gigantic species of primitive, apelike men thrived in prehistory. The existence of Gigantopithecus, a ten foot tall hominid that lived up to 100,000 years ago, is established scientific fact. However, no evidence has been discovered to suggest that such beings dwelled in Britain at any time in the last two millennia, though who is to say these eldritch tales aren't recollecting lost folk-memories of a period when they did?

Either way, the Cornish giant whose story most interconnects with that of the terrifying spriggans, was Trecrobben, another murderous brute, who after years of raiding and looting, stored his heap of ill-gotten treasure at Trencrom Castle just inland from St Ives, and set a troop of spriggans to protect it. In time, Trecrobben died – it was said that he pined away with remorse after killing his wife in a drunken rage – and once they were certain of this, the local villagers began searching for his wealth. Trencrom Castle, which was basically a well preserved hill-fort, had always seemed likely to provide treasure thanks to its very ancientness, but whenever the excavators' picks and shovels encountered hard surfaces beneath the sod, caskets maybe or the granite lintels to underground burial chambers, the spriggans would emerge: ghastly creatures formed from the very earth and armed with axes, swords and war-hammers with which they would attack the interlopers. Many treasure-seekers were said to have been slain, others dragged screaming into the underworld, from where they would never re-emerge.

This unsettling myth persisted well into the 20th century. In the period between the two world wars, a farm-labourer down on his luck made a lone night-time trip to Trencrom. Using maps and ancient documents, he was careful where he dug, and very quickly, it was said, he uncovered a buried chest – only for a mini-earthquake to commence, the ground shaking, the very air rumbling. The labourer backed away, frightened, especially when he noticed that only the high ground of the Castle seemed to be affected. He turned and ran, and looking back over his shoulder, saw manlike figures appearing on the crown of the hill, but distorted and twisted, and in addition to that, increasing in size. The last time he looked, an entire band of *enormous misshapen forms stood silhouetted against the moon. With horror, he realised that the rumbling he could hear was the sound of their voices as they swore and hurled profane threats after him.*

Needless to say, he never went back.

All we have here is a century-old verbal account provided by a farm-worker who wished to remain anonymous. It hardly constitutes proof. But stories endure that mysterious guardians still lurk in the vicinity of Trencrom Castle. Now owned by the National Trust, it has changed little in recent years, and if anything, is regarded as a local beauty spot rather than somewhere to avoid. That said, venturing up there alone, especially at night and equipped with a spade, would seem like an unwise policy.

THE UNCERTAINTY OF ALL EARTHLY THINGS

Mark Valentine

There are places set apart. Something about them suggests they are different. You stray there, to one of them, perhaps while out walking, or arrive by car while exploring narrow by-ways, and get out, and at once you are alert to it. It might be very quiet, or full of the long shadows of noon, not quite still. Or there's something in the slant of light that makes the place seem hazy. It might be even be just the glint from a window, or the solemn stark green of a cedar tree, or the way the wind ripples in the grasses. You are only aware that some sense you hardly knew you possessed is telling you that here there are secrets. And of course you want to find out more, while being unsure that you should.

I didn't at first have this impression about Sancreed. I suppose this was because I was busy settling in for the first few days I was there. Yes, it was tranquil and cloistered, and anyone could feel they had arrived at a spot that was out of the usual run of things. Yet it was only after I had been there a week or so that this deepened into that feeling of something else.

And then one late afternoon, in the approach of an autumn dusk, it came upon me with a certainty, that sense of utter difference. I looked about me to see if I could find out why, what had changed. All I could identify was a sort of inheld silence, a stillness that was not disturbed, but only made more brittle, by the scuttering of leaves and the sighing in the trees. The moment was only broken when I had to chase after a jester.

Every so often the colour supplements and online news pages of the papers do a feature on 'Britain's strangest museums'. This invariably includes the witchcraft museum and the artificial limb museum. The others vary a bit, but even these never include the one where I accepted a job as curator – and, as I soon learnt, caretaker, cleaner, all round factotum indeed. If the heading had been 'Britain's obscurest museums', it might have had some chance.

After I'd completed my Masters, the question of finding a job in the field became quite acute, and I knew it wouldn't be easy. There is never any shortage of candidates, but there's always a shortage of funds. Getting a placement as a volunteer was always possible: persuading someone to pay you, distinctly less so. But one of the lecturers had given me a common sense tip: don't waste time applying to the prestige museums, look out for little provincial ones. You could always build up a reputation there, then go on to the bigger names.

So that was why I applied for and, rather to my surprise, got what I then thought of as my 'first' curator post at the little museum devoted to the almost forgotten explorer and missionary 'Congo' Grenfell, in the far west of Cornwall. The trustees, all aged, kindly and rather vague, said they wanted to give a chance to a younger professional: the previous incumbent had been there over thirty years and only ill-health eventually led to their retirement.

The museum had one main advantage from the point of view of job security: it had been generously endowed in the late nineteenth century by Grenfell's friends, and by the Royal Geographic Society, and the missionary societies, and these funds had been well looked-after. I wouldn't be relying on admission fees, grants and donations. I had friends who spent almost all their time chasing funding, a frustrating and often disappointing business, which was not why they had gone into the museum service at all.

I had given the trustees the entirely sincere pitch I had rehearsed, about involving the local community more, reaching out to schools and societies, broadening the appeal of the museum, recognising the ambivalence of Grenfell's colonial role and the richness of the indigenous cultures he had encountered (which indeed he had recognised himself), and so on. I'm not sure how much of this they took in, but they nodded and smiled a lot. There was talk of a 'new broom' and 'fresh ideas'.

It wasn't all bluster. I had done some 'homework' and thought that even though Sancreed was a hidden sort of place, it had two potential opportunities. It was on the route from Penzance to Land's End, and it had a notable archaeological site at nearby Carn Euny which attracted a certain number of the more thoughtful visitors, those who weren't only after sun, sand and souvenirs. If I could link up Congo Grenfell's museum with these tranches of visitors, I would soon start to boost numbers, I thought.

I must have been convincing, and probably seemed touchingly ardent. And that's why, one autumn day, I found myself with a one-way ticket to Penzance and a single big bag containing most of my possessions. A friend sent on a box of books later.

I had decided to walk from the station, partly as a sort of pilgrimage, partly to get to know the place slowly on foot, and partly out of a sense of economy, as I was not sure what a taxi would cost. The salary was modest, because the trust also provided accommodation. I soon regretted the girth of my bag, but I was sounder in limb then, and it was a minor burden when there was so much to see on the walk. At first there was the esplanade and the chill breeze from the sea, welcome after the fug of the train. Then, I walked through suburbs full of guest houses, their signs swinging in the wind. But soon I took a road to the right, climbing steeply uphill, with a seaward-bound stream for company.

It was not long before I left the houses behind and followed a lonely stretch of road that undulated in little hollows and slopes: at the crest of each I thought I should get some wider view, but it was not until I reached the hamlet of Drift that I became more certain of my way. Here a black and white sign bore the, to me, thrilling and encouraging word *Sancreed*, and I took a narrow by-road hemmed in by thick hedges, full of bramble and old grey stones. This rose slowly and I strode on in a deepening silence, gazing ahead for the first glimpse of the village. At last I could see a flourish of autumn woods lying along the slopes of a hill, like a slumbering creature with a coat of scales of bronze and gold: and just discernible within this were the slate roofs of the church and the few houses around it.

I marched on more eagerly, descending into the woods and what I later learnt to call Church Town, though 'town' was distinctly optimistic: there was a post office but no pub or other shop. Following my directions, I went further on, to a junction by the chapel, then skirted around the breadth of the hill, and followed a green track until I came up to a pair of cottages standing apart. Here I stopped, put down my bag and enjoyed the moment, taking in the view, the seclusion and the quiet.

Grenfell had been born in Sancreed, the last inland parish in the tip of Cornwall. He had left it at the age of three when his parents moved to Birmingham, but often returned to stay with grandparents or later as an adult, when it seemed to be a bit of a retreat for him. The little granite cottage where he was born had been chosen for the museum because of his abiding love of the place and also, I suspected, because Birmingham already had quite enough eminent persons and any memorial place there would be quite lost.

It was kept unlocked. I turned the worn knob of the wooden door and went inside. All the rooms in his birthplace, apart from the 'usual offices', had been turned into exhibition spaces which, I soon saw, had not been changed for some years: the displays looked dusty and faded. There was an oak desk by the entrance, with a visitors' book: the last entry was some weeks ago. I explored the rooms, already beginning to think of how they could be made more vivid.

I remember standing in the museum on that first day there with a feeling of delight running through me. It was tinged, if I'm honest, with some melancholy too, an edge of loneliness as I realised that few of my university friends would find their way so far down here, and as yet I knew no-one else. But most of all I was just glad to have a place and a role, and was full of confidence at the opportunity to make things new.

The next door cottage, smaller, had been acquired for the curator to live in, and would now be my home. It was dark, the windows small, the furniture a bit shabby, and it was warmed only by a hearth fire which smoked a lot, but I liked it, and was proud of my appointment. I'd agreed with the trustees that I would spend the months of the autumn and winter seasons learning more about Grenfell and the neighbourhood, before relaunching the museum with fresh displays in time for the spring. I made some tea, ate a squashed cheese roll and a bar of chocolate acquired at the station, and began to read through some of the Grenfell papers.

I made a couple more visits to Penzance in the week that followed, to get in provisions, and I called in at the post office, and went over to Carn Euny, which was unstaffed and marked out with green information boards, much weathered. I nodded and exchanged a few words of greeting with people I passed, in that slightly wary way we do, willing to be civil but not sure we want to be drawn into anything more, just yet. I worked hard, I'd say, at the papers and exhibits, and saw a few ways to liven things up.

There were sketches and a few anecdotes about Jack, the donkey who accompanied Grenfell on his expeditions, and seemed to be a bit of a character: he resolutely declined to swim or wade rivers and had to be carried over, still protesting vociferously, in a litter. I thought the story would appeal to younger visitors and animal lovers, and started constructing a display about him. And the missionary, though resolutely bringing his own faith to the peoples he met, had also taken a keen interest in their own beliefs, if only so that he could reinterpret them in gospel form. A brief note he had made in the draft of an article for *The Geographer* made me look again at the dusty wooden carvings of animal and bird heads he had brought back, which sat solemnly, and vaguely labelled, in a glass case.

Sure enough, on inspection they proved to have minute incised symbols on them, the characters of a language which (as I later found) had never yet been deciphered. The idea of an unsolved code would also be attractive to visitors, and I began listing possible theories: the words could be prayers to the animals and bird spirits, messages from the giver of the gift to the recipient, commands from a king to his courtiers, or the marks of the maker. I spent some time, indeed, trying to make out patterns and parallels between the symbols, but they kept their mystery.

I took one of the heads, an ibis with a broken beak, outside, to see it in a better light, then sat on the doorstep to dust it and apply a light beeswax polish I had found in the cleaning cupboard. Although I wasn't an expert at restoration, I thought there would be little harm and a lot of good in giving the piece some gentle care. I enjoyed the feel of the air, and as I tilted the ibis head in my hands to work on all its hollows and angles, the little notched characters seemed to become clearer and bolder in the pale autumnal sunlight.

The story of Jack and the riddle of the mysterious characters seemed a good start to the relaunch I'd discussed with the trustees, but those moments on the doorstep reminded me I was getting a bit fusty alone in the museum and the quarters next door, and I decided to turn my attention next to the little community around about. So I walked to the church. It had several notable monuments itself: there were two stone crosses, and a holy well, reached down some shaky stone steps fringed with maidenhair ferns and a sarsenet of moss, which gave a sort of green luminescence to the little shrine. The water was dark, still and cold. A few rags had been hung on the bushes around.

It was after I had risen from visiting the narrow dank chamber, walked around the oval perimeter of the churchyard, and returned to stand by the gate that I experienced the strange sense that Sancreed was a place of secrets, perhaps a sanctuary, perhaps the opposite of that. The rustling of the leaves and the soaring of the breeze in the tall trees seemed to act like the chanting of a spell. I stood listening to them, and listening, also, to the deep silence that lay beneath them, vast and inviolable.

Then the church door clattered and a figure emerged, clutching a sheaf of papers. She wore a purple woollen beret and a swoop of shawls, and a long coat played about her. The wind seemed to rush at her as she emerged, making her clothes swirl like an embarrassment of wings. One hand darted to her hat to hold it on, the other clung to the pages she carried, while also trying to restrain the enthusiasm of her colourful robes.

And then one of the sheets freed itself and flew across the lichened gravestones, dancing among them as it if wanted to waken their residents. We both set off in pursuit, but it seemed to know we were after it, and always leapt several steps ahead, pausing briefly among the wan grasses or on the kerb of a tomb, before dashing off again. At last, with a lunge that also saw me sprawl on the damp ground, I got my fingers on it and held on carefully, trying not to crumple it too much.

I scrambled to my feet and handed it back to its owner. I was breathing quickly, laughing, and trying to brush mud from my trouser knees all at the same time. I had glanced quickly at the elusive paper before I gave it back, and saw a peculiar picture of a face with a jester's drooping hat, mixed in with the coils of a serpent.

'Thank you,' she said, still summoning her clothes to be more obedient about her. Then, probably noticing I had glimpsed what was on the page, she added, 'I've been sketching the screen. The rood screen. Inside – have you seen it?'

I shook my head.

'You must. It's marvellous. All sorts of faces and creatures.'

She riffled quickly through the other sheets she held, and I saw a swift parade of staring heads and swirling beasts, in dusky blurs of pencil and charcoal.

'They look wonderful,' I said.

We were at that point now where we would either murmur a hasty, awkward farewell and go on our way, or linger and start to exchange a few more words. I felt that it could teeter on the brink either way, and out of both a growing loneliness and a keen curiosity, I lunged onwards.

'I've just started at the museum,' I began, 'and thought I'd better find out about the other, um, historical things in the village.'

'Oh, have you? Yes, I think I know it. A little cottage, up by the mill? I must visit.'

'Yes, please do. I'm just changing things round a bit.'

There was a pause.

'I'm Leah,' she said, 'Leah Penrose.'

There was another quick awkward scrabble as a fresh gust of wind seized some of the other pictures from her hands, but these didn't get as far, and we soon had them gathered up.

After this little tumult, I gave her my name in return. Awkwardly, we shook hands. Then we walked slowly together to the little red wicket gate in the corner of the churchyard.

'Well, please do call in soon,' I was just able to say before we each went our way.

The next day, before the museum was due to open (the hours were more limited in the off-peak season), I went back to the church, telling myself it was only polite to follow up Leah's suggestion of looking at the rood screen, but also because, of course, I wondered if she might be there sketching again. The church was empty, but I soon saw what she had meant about the screen. The figures had been carved with a bold imaginative flourish. Some of them were so low down in the wooden panels that they would scarcely ever be seen in the daily usages of the church. Yet it was easy to see their creator had been proud of their craft, knew just what they wanted to depict, and had gone about it with a certain devil-may-care zest.

Most of the human heads were double-faced, Janus-like, but there was one Triple Headed King with three faces in one head, each like playing card kings, melancholy and majestic, with jagged crowns, heavy-lidded solemn eyes and beards like black spearheads. When I flicked through the guidebook, it said this was thought to be a 'signum triciput', a symbol of the Trinity, but even if that had been the official intention, I felt sure it wasn't what has been in the wood-carver's mind when he made the piece. It was too strange, too exotic. It struck me that it might just as well have been an image of the three Magi.

The other figures included two shaggier-bearded heads with antler-like helmets in bold curves and two with black hair braided together at the neck, and two stern-eyed queens with curling head-dresses. All had the same look of haughty certainty. They were accompanied by a menagerie of peculiar creatures, including a coiled serpent, a goat, lizard, owl, and some that had no obvious earthly counterpart. The carvings were full of vigour and confidence: whoever made them didn't really care how real they were in the natural world, they were real to him.

Simply the shape of the figures was enough to give them an uncanny life, but they were also vivified by the rich remains of the medieval paint upon them in scarlet and gold and green, like the jewelled illuminations made by monks in medieval manuscripts. I half-expected one of the sly, sharp-eyed beasts to slither out of the screen and make its way nonchalantly to the altar.

I stood in the nave gazing at the rood screen for some time before I realised I ought to get back to open up the museum, not that I expected much in the way of visitors. However, I was glad I was punctual, because very soon after I put up the 'Open' sign, Leah called in. I took her around the museum, explaining about my plans, telling the tales about Jack the donkey, and explaining about the unknown language on the African carvings. She looked at these very carefully, and even tried to copy out a few. When we came back to the entrance desk, I offered her a coffee and told her how impressed I had been by the figures on the wooden screen.

There was a pause which I soon realised was a hesitation about telling me something more. Then she said:

'I'm trying to make a sort of Sancreed Tarot of them.'

'I can just imagine it,' I responded, enthusiastically, 'Some of the carvings do look just like images from the cards. Those kings … if they are kings.'

'That's what I thought. And – well, I had a sort of hint too.'

'Something you discovered?'

'Yes, as I made my drawings. They seemed to fall into place. Different rules, and a different set to the original Tarot itself, of course. But the same sort of idea. A pack of omens, if you like. It must be my gypsy blood.'

She made this last remark with a sort of wan smile, slightly apprehensive, but it was too good a lead to miss.

'From these parts?' I asked.

'Yes. My great-aunt. Granny Anne, the locals called her. A real gypsy queen. She used to sell charms and potions, they tell me. There's a photo of her, smoking a clay pipe, with a saggy face, her mouth turned down and a grim look in her eyes.'

'Oh, well, you certainly didn't inherit any of that.'

Leah looked at me sideways, arrowing a dark eyebrow.

'Nice, but a bit cheesy,' she said.

It could have been an awkward moment, but we both laughed at the same time, and I tried to look contrite.

'And have your family been here ever since her time?'

'No. My mother married out, you see, and my parents moved away when I was small. But I keep coming back, and now I've rented a cottage over the winter, so I can work on the cards. You can get places quite cheap for a longish let in the off-season.'

'Oh, that's good,' I said, a bit too eagerly, and before the eyebrow could dart up again, I added quickly, 'It was the same with Grenfell. He couldn't keep away either. I mean, when he wasn't in Africa. That's why they chose here for the museum. And I already feel I sort of understand it. There's something …'

But I stopped, because I didn't know quite what it was.

'There is,' she said, putting down her coffee cup and standing up to go, 'there is, and I'm hoping to catch it somehow in my Tarot.'

I hovered at the door, wondering how to fix up another meeting without getting the devastating eyebrow again, but she solved that for me.

'Have you been up to the rocket shed?'

'Rocket shed?'

'Yes, up on the down above Grumbler.'

'Grumbler?'

'Terrible echo in this place. G-r-u-m-b-l-a. Easy walk along the lane from here.'

'No, I haven't. Worth seeing?'

'Well, have you ever seen a rocket shed before?'

'Now you come to mention it …'

'I'll call for you when you close at the end of the week. Four-ish?'

I was in the doorway staring out at the indigo light that had possessed the village all day, a sort of brooding colour made up from a light sheen of mist and deep, sombre skies. It was a while before four, but Leah ambled up the street and found me before I caught sight of her, as if she'd been hiding in the rays of that bluish, blackish light.

'Busy then,' she said. 'Got time for these?'

She went inside, reached into one of her incalculable number of pockets and, with a flourish, spread upon the desk an array of bright panels, richly coloured, and embellished with touches of silver and gilt.

'The cards!' I exclaimed.

'The same. The only Sancreed Tarot pack. Or at least my first mock-up of it. I've just pasted my designs on odd bits of card. There's cornflakes and cat food packets beneath the pictures. You might think you've drawn the king, but secretly you've just got the breakfast bowl.'

She scooped them up again and shuffled them and I saw in a blur all the figures and creatures from the screen beautifully recreated. Then she slammed the pack onto the table face down, and ordered: 'Cut and draw!'

I picked up a cluster of cards and slowly turned the last in my fingers to show the image. It was the jester.

'Come on! He must have got free again!' Leah called out, in high spirits. 'Let's look for him on the moors.'

We strode along a rough lane and then began to head upwards over wild grassland covered with gorse and bracken. As we climbed, glimpses of the sea came into view, far below, grey and shadowy, and there were views of the crouched grey cottages scattered over the terrain, with their roof slates sloping across them in the way soldiers once held their shields over their heads. Leah went surely on, and I began to see the outline of a rounded structure ahead. As we got nearer, it resolved itself into a curving span of tin, like half an oval. It had once been painted and had signs daubed upon it, but now there were just streaks and patches of scratched colours, as if an artist had been let loose with a full palette and a lively knife.

'The rocket shed,' said Leah. 'Where they used to keep flares and warning signals. The coastguard people. I don't know if they actually fired them from here though. It's high enough I suppose. I'm sorry if you were expecting to get to Mars or the Moon.'

'It's a work of art, though,' I said.

'I'm glad you think so. I've taken some of my colours from it. I thought it would be a sort of tribute. Hardly anyone ever comes here and I think it's all but forgotten. Look – you see that blotch of red there? I think it was some sort of explosives warning sign. Well, I thought our friend the jester ought to have some of that, and so ...'

She rummaged and produced the card, placing it next to the starburst of scarlet on the tin arch. For a moment it was almost lost, seemed to merge with the painted surface.

'Hold tight,' I said.

I turned to look at the view. That brittle indigo light had deepened now, and there was a veiling that seemed more than just the first onset of dusk. I let my gaze wander over the horizon, then draw back from the sea and follow the lanes and low-walled fields inland. In the darkly luminous haze, there was an odd sort of perspective, as if they were all converging on the lonely green dome where we stood. I looked back at Leah, to see if she had noticed the effect too. She had moved away slightly from the gaudy, rusty rocket shed and was staring at the card.

I tried to find the church tower among the trees, back in the direction we had come. It didn't seem to be there. I had been told it was sometimes hard to make out within the woods, but couldn't quite believe it. I peered more keenly. And then there was a sort of jolt in the air, and I found myself looking through a series of facets, all at the same time. I still saw the rare amethyst light of before but now it shone upon several scenes simultaneously. I was shocked into silence as I tried to work out what had happened. I tried shaking my head, passing my fingers over my eyes, taking a few cautious steps backwards and forwards. Nothing changed back. It was like standing in a hall of mirrors and seeing them all at once, and each one reflecting something utterly different.

I saw in one plane of vision, a constant serpentine coiling, as a great writhing form unfurled itself, around and around the hills and fields of Sancreed, and seemed to pulse also under its narrow roads and tracks, and enter its stones and send out filaments into its trees and streams. Animal and bird heads seemed to revolve in my vision too, some with human eyes, others with human limbs, a mingling of horns, snouts, jaws, claws, and tongues. And I knew too that in some different dimension I also saw there were high, lunging tongues of flame, each with a face or some elements of a face, but with eyes that did not stay in the same place. There were forms that seemed made of the same hard indigo that had hovered over the land, like blue shadows edged with light. And these things, the ones that I can recall, were perhaps only a tenth of the vistas that were opened out to me all at once, like a vast surge of images, a kaleidoscope of lambent forces and lithe figures.

I reached out with a fierce despair, and called out, 'Leah! Leah!'

There was the slightest touch of fingers, then they were no longer there, then I tried again, and I felt an intensity of touch I had never known before, as we faltered, then clutched, then locked our hands together. This was followed by a gentle pressure, and I knew I was being asked to stoop and to kneel. I closed my eyes and sank to the ground. When I opened them again, dimly next to me I saw Leah staring upwards. I followed the direction of her gaze. A wave of relief flew through me as I realised I was seeing straight again, seeing only in our usual dimensions. But above, in the blue-black quartz light of the hillside, I saw in one great flicker of form, the image of the Triple Headed King, and caught sight too, for one terrible instant, of the eyes, the haughty dark eyes of the Triple Headed King.

'Mars or the Moon would have been quite enough,' I said, as we sat staring into the hearth fire back at my cottage, watching the pale amber flames warily. 'But I suppose I already knew this was a place where things happen.'

We both laughed a bit wildly. We were still exhausted and, we would have to admit, exhilarated by our mad dash down the hillside, back along the track and into the Church Town lanes.

Then Leah looked at me more seriously. She was still holding her painted card of the figure of the king, the one she had quickly found and flourished wildly on the hillside, not knowing what it would bring.

'Where they are always happening, I think. Alongside us. There's a sort of Sancreed Beyond, as well as the Sancreed we see. Lots of people have glimpsed it: artists, wanderers, preachers, mystics who have been here. We just got a better look, I suppose.'

'But why? Because you let the jester dance?' I asked. I meant it a bit light-heartedly, but Leah seemed to take the idea seriously, staring at me.

'It might well be that, you know. Or it might be you, bringing those mysterious signs into the light. Or both. Who knows? But I think it's always there.'

She paused, and then continued:

'When I was sitting in the church, or sketching outside, I was thinking sometimes what it would be like to see things from those eyes. I don't just mean because there's three eyes in one head, though that would be strange enough. And it wasn't because those eyes in the carvings are so proud and serious. I just thought, these are really completely different beings to us. What world would they see?'

I nodded slowly,

Leah went on, almost murmuring to herself now, 'After all, we rely so much on our eyes and what our mind makes of what the eyes tell us, but really both are very limited instruments, aren't they? Have you heard how some people are said to have 'the sight'? Granny Anne was credited with it by the villagers here. That always means a completely different 'sight', doesn't it, to what our usual eyes see. I think what the image of the three kings, or the three magicians, tells us is that there are other ways of seeing, other ways of knowing. And I'm going to stop here, and make my Tarot, and find out more. What about you?'

I thought of the knowledge glimpsed in the sombre eyes of the kings on the hillside. But I never hesitated in my answer. Because there still seemed so many ways of knowing each other to explore too, just as perilous, just as chancy, just as mysterious.

THE HOOPER

Sennen Cove epitomises the Cornish coastal experience. A picturesque bay about a mile northwest from Land's End, it stretches between the A30 trunk road and Cape Cornwall, boasts a white sand beach, high, rolling waves, a quaint village comprising traditional granite cottages, and though exposed to the hot summer sun for most of the day, it is sheltered from the worst excesses of the Atlantic wind by the steep green hills that arc around it. It is a Mecca for tourists, especially the surfing crowd.

But few of those holidaymakers who annually enjoy Sennen Cove will have any clue that it was once famous for much more terrible reasons.

Thanks to Cornwall's Celtic Christian past, the folklore of this region is interwoven with tales of devils, demons and evil spirits. Witches, it was believed, could summon disastrous storms. Cornwall's legion of ancient saints spent more time dispelling the forces of darkness than they did praying. And the Hooper was a formless entity, hellish in origin, which was specifically sent to terrorise the inhabitants of Sennen Cove.

Puzzled? You may well be.

The story of the Hooper is as inexplicable now as it was in the 18th century, its heyday.

In that era, Sennen Cove was the sole realm of fisher-folk, but it seems that from a time before records were kept, the local population knew and feared the Hooper. It would appear without warning as an immense blot of roiling mist, usually hovering around Aire Point, but gradually expanding until it had completely cut the bay off from the ocean. One might think this some natural phenomenon misunderstood by uneducated people – a sea-fret maybe. But there were other aspects to it that were even more unexplainable. By night, the light of flickering, reddish flames could be seen in the Hooper's depths – to all intents and purposes burning on the surface of the sea, which in any ordinary circumstances would be impossible. In addition, it made curious 'hooping' sounds, hence its name.

The appearance of the Hooper usually preceded a storm, even if the weather looked to be fine, so no-one would risk taking a boat out when it swamped the entrance to the bay.

Instead, the villagers would tremble in their chapel, praying for deliverance from what they were certain was an evil spirit which was only kept off them by their devotions. And then, one day, a fisherman with no faith determined to challenge it. Laughing at his friends as superstitious fools, he and his son readied their boat. Arming themselves first, the bold pair then sailed out of view together, stabbing and slashing at the enshrouding mist, shouting defiance. A short time after they were lost to sight, their cries ceased. Nothing else happened that day, but in the evening the Hooper sank and a terrific storm broke. The villagers took shelter, confident that if the spirit hadn't claimed their irreverent friends, the tempest would. Sure enough, three days later, with the sea calm again, the wreckage of the missing fishing-boat was washed up, and with it the bodies of the two men, which had been battered and mutilated to a bewildering degree, their faces written with expressions of terror.

How much truth there is to this lurid tale is a matter of debate. Could it simply be that there was a tragic loss in a furious storm and that village gossips embroidered it for the interest of outsiders? If so, that doesn't explain the rash of other stories concerning the Hooper's unexpected and fearsome manifestations. Either way, it was never known to return after the mysterious double-deaths.

By the mid-19th century, locals had modified the tale, adopting the point of view that the Hooper – which they still believed in unreservedly – had indeed been a spirit, but a benign one, which called at Sennen Cove to warn the fishermen that foul weather was approaching. The proof of this, they said, was the affront it clearly felt when the blasphemous father and son launched an unprovoked attack upon it and basically drove it away.

These days, inhabitants of the scenic bay take the tale of the Hooper with a generous pinch of salt. It seems certain that something curious was happening in this region a couple of hundred years ago, but most researchers consider that it was some natural weather occurrence that was repeatedly misidentified; the two gruesome deaths could still have been caused by a terrible accident.

And yet Sennen Cove is not the only British resort to experience such an apparition. The Isle of Man hosts a similar entity in the mysterious shape of the Dooiney-Oi, and Mundesley beach in Norfolk has the Long Coastguardsman.

Would the occupants of all these coastal locations be so easily fooled by foul weather when they had lived there for so many generations and had seen and heard everything the sea and sky could throw at them? There is no easy answer.

HIS ANGER WAS KINDLED

Kate Farrell

September in Cornwall. A gentle month. The children back at school and the crowds home in Luton and Wolverhampton and Stockport and Colchester, leaving time and space for the older travellers to enjoy a little West Country warmth before the winter's chill. A perfect end to summer.

Penharrack was untroubled by tourists or trippers or sun seekers or surfers. Its principal source of local employment, the arsenic extraction works, had closed down after the Second World War. The village lacked the waves of Newquay, the art of St Ives or the colour-washed cottages of Cawsand. There were no fish and chip cafés, no cream teas, and no-tooth rotting, cavity-inducing sticks of rock. There was a post office-cum-general store, a pub, a bus stop and a church. St Michael's. St Michael the Archangel: God's enforcer, patron saint of mariners, police officers and the sick; the saint who saved Shadrach and his companions from the fiery furnace.

The Reverend Luke Prideaux, the vicar at St Michael's, crouched over his writing at the kitchen table in the rectory. It was a miserable space, untouched by a woman's hand for some years, though he felt he managed well enough. Apart from the bedroom and bathroom, he had long since abandoned the other rooms in the house. Many nights he fell asleep in an armchair near the Rayburn. The kitchen was his sanctuary and his office, and the table was strewn with ephemera, from magazines to newspapers to tracts. There was a battered leather-bound edition of the *King James Bible* too. And there was much correspondence, all opened, all read, all unanswered. He wrote in his journal, employing a good firm round hand despite his advancing years. Unlike his sermons, which were intended for an audience, this was for his eyes alone.

'No rain. No wind. No sun. No congregation,' he wrote.

Something must be done. Soon.

In the vestry he found a large folder that had been stored away. It contained all sorts of coloured stiffened paper, a relic from the days when there had been a kindergarten scripture class for the under fives. They always seemed to be producing collages of biblical characters, angels, prophets, nativities. Suffer the little children who no longer came unto him, he thought. He spared a moment remembering the Warrender boy, drowned at Carlyon not a year past. The lad's funeral was held at Probus, not here in Penharrack where his father and grandfather had worshipped.

Back in the kitchen, he set about his task with sheets of cardboard, old newspapers, wallpaper scissors, rolls of sellotape and some wax crayons. At his side was the pile of read but unanswered letters, near the dust-covered telephone that never rang.

Some weeks later in October, David Densham boarded the 10:06 train for Truro at Paddington station. The train was not busy as Cornwall was winding down after the summer season, so he made full use of the table in his First Class carriage. He spread out his papers, familiarising himself again with the proposed improvements to the site he was about to visit. Though not a salesman by nature, once researched and rehearsed he liked to think he could pitch it with the best of them. His office had pre-booked a hire car from Truro station and he would be at his destination, St Michael's church in Penharrack, by about half-past three. He confidently expected to tie up his business in no more than two hours. There was a hotel reservation for just the one night and had promised his wife he would be back in time for young Emily's gymnastic display the next afternoon. However, the truth was he would not feel unduly bereft if he missed it, should his return journey experience any delays. In fact, David was looking forward to a night's peace and quiet in the backwaters of Cornwall. The hotel he had selected had a reputation for fine dining and his employers, the Church Commissioners, were picking up the bill for the visit. All good so far. He was less kindly disposed however when his train arrived at Truro an hour late and the car he had expected was returned damaged; seething all the while, he had to wait as paperwork was completed for a substitute. Like so many city dwellers, he held the arrogant belief that nothing runs smoothly outside the metropolis. The hold-up meant there was no time to check in at the hotel first so he headed off to Penharrack, only six miles away but with small, winding country roads to navigate.

Just after five o'clock, much later than he would have liked, he parked his car outside St Michael's church. A dark evening, clouds had gathered and the grey masonry of the building blended into the pewter of the sky. It was typical of so many churches throughout Cornwall, according to his notes; although the site was historical, the Victorian building itself had little architectural significance. This one had a small porch, a nave with pews on both sides and an east window with stained glass that was in a terrible state of repair. Some light showed inside the church, though the rectory was in darkness. 'Bible black darkness,' he would write in his report and though unoriginal, he liked the sound of it.

He entered the church from the porch through heavy oak doors. What a grand entrance they would make to the new apartments when the building was redeveloped! There was no electric lighting and the only illumination was from a candelabrum beside the pulpit where stood the Reverend Luke Prideaux. He was clad in cassock and surplice, a tall, vigorous looking gentleman, dark haired, of an appearance that gave lie to his age of seventy-eight years. The evening service was about to start.

Bugger, thought David, another delay. Strange to find a midweek service, in what he and his superiors were led to believe was a parish that had been all but abandoned. The murmurings of discontent from the parochial council had grown into outright dissent over the years. Apparently the vicar went weeks without providing any form of pastoral care, then suddenly would blaze into a fit of activity and expect the congregation to attend. And the state of the church was a travesty: any attempts at fundraising to provide building maintenance had either been ignored by the Reverend Prideaux or rejected out of hand. He would brook no meddling. So fully expecting rows of empty pews, David Densham was surprised to see the backs of worshippers; there were not many but they were apparent in the shadows nonetheless, standing silent, attentive. Perhaps the elderly vicar had seen the sense outlined in the letters from the Church Commissioners, although neither David nor his employers had received a response to that effect. Yes, most likely he had mustered a small flock for a valedictory service or two. It didn't change anything; decisions had been reached and timescales approved. Money had changed hands. The parishioners could easily be accommodated elsewhere as there were other places of worship, some only a short drive away.

Keeping a respectful distance, he waited in the narthex, his view partially obscured by the fretwork screen. He would wait for the service to end, and observe but not participate. There was the blessing, then a recitation of the *Lord's Prayer*. Next the Reverend prefaced his sermon: the central theme was to be God's wrath and the destructive and cleansing powers of fire. All this was painfully familiar to David who was a regular churchgoer, for his job demanded it. Besides he had briefly flirted with the ministry while at university.

It was cold. He sat on a dusty chair, bided his time, listened awhile and then tried re-reading some of his paperwork, though this was nigh impossible in the penumbra. David Densham dozed it must be admitted, catching snatches of a homily that featured the story of Moses and the ungrateful Israelites; he had heard great and good sermons in the noble cathedrals of Ely, Exeter, Canterbury, and did not feel the need to dwell overlong on the ramblings of an elderly cleric in the backwoods of the west of England. The children of Israel's complaint that they had forsaken their rich diet to subsist on manna held little thrall for him, though it was a timely reminder of his own anticipated dinner. Despite his apparent disinterest, occasional phrases percolated through to him:

'And when the people complained it displeased the Lord; and the Lord heard it and His anger was kindled ...'

'And he called the name of the place Taberah because the fire of the Lord burned among them ...'

'Who shall give us flesh to eat?'

'Thou shalt see now whether my word shall come to pass unto thee or not ...'

Had David been more alert he might have heard the Reverend's final rallying cry when he called on the faithful to remember that the Lord their God was a jealous God, a consuming fire, but urged them to remember that despite His wrath the judgement would be ultimately purifying.

'Thy will be done,' Prideaux ended.

David was finally aroused from his torpor by the vicar's strong baritone as he performed a strange solo without the congregation and without an organ:

He who would valiant be, 'gainst all disaster
Let him in constancy follow the Master ...

The service over, as he began to assemble his paperwork, David looked up to see the Reverend Luke Prideaux looming in front of him. He hadn't heard his approach. Close up he could see the cassock was stained and threadbare, and it smelled of something strange, something unpleasant and organic. Rotting potatoes perhaps? It was hard to define.

'We have a visitor. Why didn't you enter the body of the church and swell our little congregation?'

'Apologies, Reverend. David Densham, from the Church Commissioners.' He extended his hand.

'The Church Commissioners? I am honoured,' said the vicar, without a trace of irony and ignoring the proffered hand.

'Mr Prideaux, surely this visit can come as no surprise. We have written several times. My superiors have asked me to come and meet you, sir, to talk things over and hopefully to allay any fears you might have. A letter confirmed my visit to you over a week ago.'

The vicar folded his arms.

David ploughed on, keen to deliver his message:

'Look, is there somewhere we could go, somewhere with a little light perhaps? I have brochures to show you of the projected plans for the church. They're based on previous conversions by the developers but give the general idea. And I have a prospectus of the charming place we have in mind for you. It's just the spot for a well-earned retirement. If you don't mind me saying.'

Without comment the Reverend Prideaux led the way down the nave while David Densham riffled through his papers until he found what he was looking for, not easy in the candlelight. For a brief moment he wondered why none of the faithful were leaving as the service was over but didn't dwell on it. He was intent on the job in hand: all he had to do was explain the Church Commissioners' plans to this old boy, then the evening was his to enjoy. Soon he would be in the Michelin-starred restaurant less than five miles away, and then having a peaceful night's sleep after a good dinner.

'The fact is, sir, we have written to you repeatedly; we have telephoned you but we understand there is no connection here now. How can that be? How can you conduct your day-to-day affairs without a telephone? Well, no matter. We wanted to offer the courtesy of including you in our plans as soon as possible but weeks – no *months* – have passed since we first wrote in March and now it's October. The bishop is looking for a happy outcome for all parties. The fact is, and it pains me to say this, your parish is no longer viable and the parochial council has written several letters of complaint about how dilapidated the church and the grounds now are. Action is well overdue.'

'I do the work of the Lord,' said Prideaux. 'I'm not interested in parish councils, them or their idiot notions of whist drives to raise money. The spirit of God is not confined to the Tabernacle, but like the wind, blows where He listeth. His work can be performed in a bomb shelter or an igloo; even a dilapidated old pile such as this.' He opened his arms to encompass the entire building.

David hoped he wasn't going to be bombarded with quasi-Biblical quotations. Best to be blunt. 'That's not the issue anymore; it's gone beyond that, which you'd know if you'd read our correspondence. The die is now cast, the decision is made and you will have one month to vacate this parish, sir. We've taken the liberty of reserving accommodation for you at St Clement's just outside Penzance. We think you'll like it. It's well established in a fine spot overlooking the sea, a home to retired clergy from all over Britain. You won't lack for company! There are excellent medical facilities, everything you could possibly want or need.'

'Young man, everything I could possibly *want* or *need* is here in this little church and this little churchyard. I have been here since 1954; I was a young curate here; I was married here; my wife, my beloved Sarah, lies buried in this churchyard, and like her, I will die here and be buried here also.'

In an attempt to mollify the old gentleman David Densham said, 'You may well be buried here; this could indeed be your final resting place, though you will not die here. The church is to be deconsecrated. We have sold the land that the church and the rectory stand on, though the graveyard beyond the walls will remain. Planning applications have been approved; Sundial Homes are to redevelop the plot, and in little over a year this will be converted into highly desirable lifestyle apartments. The architect's drawings show how some original features will be incorporated into ...'

'*NO! That will happen literally over my dead body!* There has been a church on this site since the thirteenth century. This has been a house of God for centuries and you expect me to surrender the keeping of it? No, no, and no again,' said the vicar.

David tried a different tack: 'Sir, you are nearly eighty. Don't you want to spend your remaining years in comfort and safety, with on-site help? There is nothing here.' With a flourish he indicated the shadowy nave, the dusty altar, the masonry in dire need of maintenance, obvious even in the chiaroscuro.

'And I tell you there is everything here!'

'With respect, Mr Prideaux, apart from perhaps tonight, you don't even have a congregation. You are a shepherd without a flock.' David nodded behind him in the direction of the silent worshippers. 'I'm gratified to see some parishioners here this evening, though the parochial council tells us there have been no attendees for at least three years.' He found a letter to substantiate his claim. This he thrust at the vicar, who refused to take it.

'It's out of my hands,' David sighed, more in sorrow than in anger. 'We're prepared to offer all help possible to relocate you. A month is more than adequate. Our relocation officer will be in touch to assist with your move to Penzance. Here is a final notice, requesting you to vacate the church and the rectory. Believe me, Mr Prideaux, we only have your best interests at heart.'

David handed the crucial document to the cleric, three sheets from the Church Commissioners, typed on the finest laid cream paper. To his horror, dismay and alarm, Reverend Prideaux tore up the pages without bothering to look at them and slowly began to stuff the pieces into his mouth. He chewed methodically and saliva trickled down his unshaven chin. At which point David Densham felt it was time to withdraw. He began to replace the unholy assortment of documentation into his briefcase while the vicar continued grinding the pieces of paper to pulp and even swallowed some. He locked David with his gaze, never wavering, while performing this bizarre action.

There was no reasoning with the man. David had done what was required of him. He had hoped to return to London with an agreement from the cleric that yes, his days were in fact numbered and yes, he would acquiesce and move on without further ado. But this was not to be. Like Pilate, David would wash his hands of the affair. As he was attempting to cram into his case the prospectus for St Clement's Rest Home for Retired Clergymen, he became aware of a rustling sound, like crumpled brown bags. He assumed it was from his own papers yet it continued after he had closed his briefcase, which he held across his body like a shield. There was the sound of bolts being drawn across wood. He turned and looked through the gloom down the nave and saw two figures throwing the bars across to close the mighty oak doors. They were shadowy, oddly formed figures but recognisable as men. Probably farming folk in their work wear.

However, enough was enough.

'Now stop that, and open those doors please,' he said. He was unsure of the layout of the church but understood that his immediate point of exit was now barred. 'Open those doors,' he repeated. 'I have to be somewhere.' He tried to sound important, and ignoring the vicar for a moment, approached the men. As he went down the nave towards the west door, he glanced to left and right at the other members of the congregation who had remained still and silent throughout his exchange with the reverend.

He looked.

He peered into the gloom.

The figures in the pews were stirring and he saw them for what they were: they were cardboard cut-outs, roughly executed, mainly male forms but some female. All were life size. Some appeared to have crudely drawn features, the artwork not much better than a child's. Some were blank. They began to move from the pews, maybe twenty, or thirty of them. The rustling grew, became a scratching sound as their stiff paper forms unfolded and they lurched into the nave towards David; others crossed behind and created a barrier between him and the altar. He now saw that the 'men' at the west door who had thrown the bolts were also cardboard figures. They too stumbled towards him on badly drawn and cut out feet.

He turned back towards the Reverend who had stopped chewing and was raising his arms, like Moses summoning the Children of Israel.

'What the fuck …?' David began, forgetting where he was. 'How the fuck …?'

He backed away from some of the shapes that staggered towards him. The nearest, a female figure, skirted and featureless, raised a hand. It was a mitten shaped blob and it caught against his cheek in a sharp downward motion, drawing blood. David knew it was sheer insanity but couldn't quite bring himself to lash back at the thing, besides he was still clutching his briefcase. He retreated even further and turned on Reverend Prideaux.

'Do something! I don't know what the hell's going on here, what sort of stunt you've pulled, how you've done it, but make it stop. Make them stop.'

'This church is mine. This congregation is mine. You make *them* stop.' Here Prideaux waved some half chewed pieces of the document, the notice to quit that David had presented him with.

'I can't. It's out of my hands,' he wailed. Hoping there might be an escape route through the vestry, which he reckoned should be to the side of the altar, David backed away from Prideaux, away from the shapes that came closer and closer; they were helpless yet sinister, like blind men in a fog. If he didn't do something quickly he would be surrounded. He tripped as his heels came into contact with the lowest step leading to the altar and he fell backwards, still holding his briefcase, which flew open as he crashed down. The candelabrum with its four large fat candles wobbled, teetered then toppled as he made contact with it. The falling candles caught some of the figures that were grouped near the altar, their cut-out feet soon ablaze as spears of orange sparked into flame and quickly travelled the length of them. The card curled in from the scorched edges making the arms appear to stretch out in supplication before they were completely consumed by the growing conflagration. A few did a short but ghastly dance of death while devoured by the flames, and a ring of fire was created then as it spread to all the others. The contents of David Densham's briefcase, the carefully worded letters from the Church Commissioners, the architect's drawings for the proposed apartments, all were soon consumed as flame fed flame. The altar cloth caught, the desiccated old fabric sending fireworks of gold and red heavenwards.

David was surrounded by other cardboard people in their mad spasms as they caught alight and tumbled around him; sparks landed on his clothes, tongues of fire crowned his head, and he saw through the flames that the Reverend Prideaux, standing beyond the circle with his arms raised aloft, appeared to be conducting them in their demented choreography. David's hair blazed, the thin outer layers of his skin began to fry and he screamed, trying to avoid the falling, charring figures. The church was now brightly lit and as he attempted to twist his body away from the blaze that threatened to envelope him, he saw in the stained glass window the vision of St Michael, sword aloft, defeating evil, in all his damaged and crackled glory.

But his last sight was of the radiance on the Reverend Luke Prideaux's face, turned up in thanks and veneration. The flames had caught his robes and begun the swift progress along his cassock, though he seemed unaware as they spread and licked upwards. His arms, no longer raised, were stretched out, Christ-like, in triumph, and his person had become like the wick in a candle as he bathed in the fire's awful embrace.

'This church is mine …'

THE BODMIN FETCH

There are few wilder, bleaker stretches of terrain in the southern half of Britain than Bodmin Moor in east Cornwall. Covering 80 square miles, comprised of rough, rolling pasture, towering granite tors and scattered Neolithic monuments, and frequently blanketed in mist or swept by wind and rain, it won't surprise anyone that ghostly tales are common in this desolate realm. But perhaps the most terrifying of all was first penned by a churchman, Matthew Paris, a Benedictine monk and famed English chronicler of the 13th century.

The tale of the Bodmin Fetch was oft repeated in medieval times, particularly in England's Southwest, where the fear it created is said to have reduced the number of travellers attempting to cross Bodmin Moor to virtually none, though it is largely unknown today, the central characters having long faded into history.

It concerns Robert of Mortain, who was the Second Earl of Cornwall, and though an impressive warrior, an intemperate character who was as much feared as respected.

A Norman knight and an original companion of William the Conqueror during the 1066 invasion, Mortain was reported to have fought particularly bravely at the battle of Hastings, and in all subsequent battles against the recalcitrant Saxon-English. In reward for this loyalty, the Conqueror lavished titles and estates upon him, an amazing total of 797 manors, which included almost all the Cornish peninsula. Mortain, now catapulted into the highest echelons of the Anglo/Norman baronage, maintained a strong castle at Launceston and wasted no time dominating the local population. Though on one hand he was said to be pious – he fought under the banner of St Michael, for example, and subsequently granted the monastery on St Michael's Mount to the Norman monastery on the Mont Saint-Michel – he was also said to be rapacious. He drove out the monks at the Abbey of St Petroc to make use of the land himself, and was notorious for his reckless drinking and wild hunting. However, more than anything, the writers of the medieval Church took against Mortain because of his close friendship with William Rufus, the third son of the Conqueror and a man suspected of all kinds of vices, including homosexuality (which was probably true), flamboyance and excess (which was definitely true), and 'irreligious worship', in other words he was a pagan (which is most likely untrue, though he was known to have had many disputes with the Church).

Rufus also shared Mortain's love of the feast and hunt, a status that wasn't diminished when he became King William II of England in 1087. In fact, far from it. If anything, Rufus's gross appetites were said to have worsened when he acquired unfettered power, along with his cruelty – his subjects soon lived in dread of him, with the exception of Mortain, who ruled like a mini-king himself from his fortified capital on the edge of Bodmin Moor.

This fearsome duo's relationship wasn't always cosy. Mortain rebelled in 1088, and though he was pardoned, he was never again the bosom companion of his ruler. It is all the more mystifying then that the following tale of horror centres around this once-heroic knight.

Some years after his rebellion, he was chasing a herd of red deer through the Glyn Valley region of Bodmin, which in the 11th century was thickly wooded. Furious wind and rain caused problems for the hunting party, dispersing them from each other. Mortain arrived alone on high ground, at which point he felt unaccountably afraid. This in itself was an event. Mortain was a man who commanded all he saw. Fear was a new emotion. It left him bewildered, disoriented. And then, through the drifting mist came the cause of it: the apparition of a huge black ram upon which was propped the naked, bloodied figure of a man. When it drew close, Mortain saw that the figure was pierced clean through by a single arrow. He also saw that it was the body of his former friend, William Rufus, King of England, and by the frozen anguish on the king's haggard face, it was clear that not only was he dead, but that he had died in agony.

Petrified, Mortain drew his sword, only for the ram to turn and – to his utmost horror – speak to him, advising him not to interfere as it was carrying his king, 'the tyrant,' to justice. Appalled, Mortain fled and eventually found his companions, stammering out the bizarre tale. None of them could explain this until several hours later, when they returned to their lodge and were given some shocking news: the real King William Rufus was also dead, slain by a huntsman's arrow in the New Forest about 150 miles to the east.

Mortain lived a changed life afterwards, feeling certain the ghastly vision had been a personal message for him, while the woodland paths of the Glyn Valley were shunned for decades, the local peasantry, who, if they'd feared their ill-tempered king in life, were utterly terrified of him in death.

So say the ancient chronicles. However, there is some confusion here.

King William II was indeed killed by a huntsman's arrow in the New

Forest, but that was in 1100, and Robert Mortain, Earl of Cornwall, had died ten years earlier in 1090. In one fell swoop this appears to demolish the story, to out it as a monastic fabrication with no other purpose than to demonise the memory of a king who was antagonistic to the Church.

However, it is not impossible that the chronicler, Matthew Paris, who was writing a whole century later, had made a simple mistake. It is feasible that Robert Mortain's son, William Mortain, was the Cornish earl in question. In terms of age, William Mortain was more William Rufus's contemporary, and in addition was said to have been of a much more turbulent disposition than his father; in fact he was described as an incorrigible rebel who was always on the warpath – until certain unspecified events intervened in his life in the early 1100s, which resulted in his renouncing the material world and ending his days as a Cluniac monk at Bermondsey Abbey.

Whatever caused this sea-change in character, it must have been quite something.

FOUR WINDOWS AND A DOOR

D P Watt

He had given the usual edicts – no laptops, no tablets, no texting endlessly on the phone, no this, no that. *We're going on a nice, relaxing family holiday,* he'd said, *where we can spend time together; walking, swimming, playing, picnics and beaches and the like.*

It didn't quite happen like that. It never does.

The first day had gone quite well. The kids were thrilled enough by the strangeness of Polperro. They enjoyed having to lug all their bags through the streets that were too narrow to get a car down. They liked their quaint cottage with views out across the harbour. They looked over at a small promontory and could see a little beach where some other children were playing. David was the first to get irritated though, when his tablet wouldn't connect to the wi-fi. Emily followed suit in the morning, when she couldn't play some online game on her mother's phone due to a poor signal.

Tom thought he'd need to be very proactive right from the off if he was to rescue the week from moaning and grumbling about computers and phones, so he planned a packed schedule of walks and visits to nearby attractions to keep them amused. Over a glass of wine he chatted with Sarah about how he couldn't understand it; when he was David's age he'd have adored a place like this, if his parents could have afforded to have taken them there.

Yes, but when you were ten, they'd just got the electric light in hadn't they, and a light bulb was entertainment for the whole family, Sarah joked with him. She was twelve years younger than him and his age, and grumpiness, had become a family joke. They had a lovely evening together. It really felt as though the holiday might bring them all back together.

Tom had been spending a lot of time away more recently, especially at conferences. He had been a computer programmer in the early '90s and had worked his way from company to company, with a bit of freelancing here and there, making quite a bit of money – enough to purchase most of the expensive house they lived in now in rural Oxfordshire. He certainly wouldn't be able to afford it these days. He'd settled into a more stable job in the early part of the new century, and then David had come along, and then Emily. He now worked for a large accountancy firm, maintaining databases and servers, and it frequently took him to London for long periods, and up to Glasgow where there were other company offices. One of its directors was an old university friend of Sarah's and he'd jumped at the job that now made him feel rather inadequate, as younger people arrived, more skilled and knowledgeable in a rapidly changing industry. To even keep up to date he'd had to start on the conference circuit, and even go to extra training sessions during some of his holiday periods. It had all become rather a bind now. But he had to keep up with it, for the sake of Sarah and the kids. It made him feel dull and uncreative – the responsible adult he'd always abhorred.

Sarah seemed quite the opposite – a real bundle of joy. She'd worked as a teaching assistant for years, at the local primary school, and loved every minute of it, even though the hours were long and the pay poor. Tom couldn't remember a time she'd ever moaned about work to him. She'd given it up when David was born but was intending to apply again as soon as Emily was at school. She was four now and in September she'd be going. Tom was torn by the sadness of another milestone in her childhood, but also relieved that the intensity of those toddler and nursery years would soon be behind them. She was that perfect age and Tom was desperate that this be the perfect family holiday.

On the second day they visited the Eden Project; David moped about complaining about the heat and that it was 'just a load of flowers'. Emily loved it. The Lost Gardens of Heligan were more popular with David as he pretended to be on the moon of Endor, racing about on a hover bike. Emily got very tired there though and had to be carried around most of it. Tom reflected that it had probably been a mistake to do two gardens on two consecutive days. The Wednesday was marked out to see the Minack Theatre and Lizard Point. That was quite a trek though and he had told everyone that they needed to be up very early and away with no messing about. But Emily woke with a tummy ache and most of the morning was spent looking after her and trying to get a decent signal on the television before David had a meltdown. At around 11am Emily suddenly declared herself better and wanted a walk around Polperro and to play sandcastles on the beach. Tom bristled that his agenda had been thrown out entirely and they'd be lucky to fit Minack and the Lizard into the rest of the week with the other things he had planned.

At the small beach there was a long stone wall that offered further protection for the vessels moored inside. There, on a large billboard chained to the jetty railings, was advertised a boating trip. Immediately Emily and David were grabbing at their Dad's sleeves begging to go on the trip, which went over to Fowey and claimed to 'almost guarantee' seeing some dolphins.

'Well, I don't know how you can have an '*almost* guarantee', either it's a guarantee, or it isn't. Sounds a bit dodgy to me,' Tom said. 'And it's £15 each; I mean how long is the trip? It'd need to be a good length to be worth that.'

'Oh, come on grumpy,' Sarah whispered to him. 'At least they want to do something like this for once. Look, the next trip is at 1pm. I'll ring them and book it – my treat!'

It was duly booked and rather than go back to the cottage for lunch they decided to eat in a packed pub at the edge of the harbour, *The Blue Peter Inn*. Despite the long wait it was worth it and they all enjoyed fish and chips, and Tom and Sarah had a couple of the ales from the vast selection. The kids enjoyed playing with the pub dog, Timmy, and Tom was beginning to feel it wasn't so bad that his plans had been scuppered for the day.

At one o'clock they jumped on a small boat with about ten other people and chugged out of Polperro as the sun got brighter and brighter. There were a few other children and David was enjoying talking with another boy; it was nice to see him being a bit more sociable, Tom thought.

The boat hugged the coast for a good ten minutes and then headed out into deeper waters, to avoid the perilous rocks near the shore the captain told them – many a smuggling boat had been sunk there in years gone by, apparently, one skippered by one of the captain's own ancestors, a Mr John Creedy, the scourge of the King's

Excise Men. Other tall tales came across the tannoy at regular intervals. The kids loved it.

'See, not so bad, eh?' Sarah said, huddling up to Tom on one of the padded seats for, despite the sun, it was quite cold out on the waves and none of them had brought particularly thick coats.

'Yeah, not so bad at all,' Tom said, smiling.

'Look, Dad,' shouted David. 'It's a haunted house.'

Tom looked over at the cliff where David was pointing, and saw a large house, almost silhouetted against the climbing sun. It was very imposing, but not in a grand way, quite the opposite.

Its plainness and size combined to force it upon the landscape in a way that seemed crude and vulgar. The windows and door had been bricked up with grey breezeblocks. It was oppressive.

'It's where the pirate ghosts go at night, Emily,' David said, teasing his sister. 'And then, when they've drunk all their ghost rum they go out looking for little girls to eat! Ha! Ha!'

'Don't say things like that, David,' Sarah said. 'You'll scare her.'

Tom looked over at Emily, who was sat on the middle row of seats opposite them. She didn't look scared. She didn't look like anything at all. Her face was blank. Her eyes fixed on the building David was pointing at.

'Are you okay, dear?' Tom said, reaching out and putting his hand on hers. It was very cold.

'It's just a house, David,' she said, quietly. 'It's just a house like any house … like *every* house.'

'Come here and cuddle up with Daddy, you're cold,' Tom said, lifting her over onto his lap and rubbing her hands.

The boat swung round and made its way into Fowey. Emily turned and watched the cliff house intently, as it disappeared from view.

They had a good afternoon, browsing round the gift shops and enjoying an ice cream in the town square. Tom found a little bookshop that specialised in Daphne du Maurier and got chatting with the owner. She had discovered a lost story of du Maurier's from the 1930s, *The Doll* and had helped get it republished recently. Tom bought a copy of the collection and had the proprietor sign it to him. He didn't get much time to read these days but hoped he might be able to enjoy the story that evening. He turned to leave to find the children at the window, making faces at him to hurry up, pointing over the road to a toyshop with a window full of wooden boats. After purchasing a small sailing boat for each of them, blue for David and red for Emily, there was just time to look around the church and its beautiful grounds before catching the boat back at 5pm.

On the way back the waters got a bit choppier and just as they came out of the shelter of Fowey they really began to get quite rough. Tom felt queasy, but the kids loved it as the spray washed over them. A dolphin joined them and followed the boat, diving in and out of the water just ahead of the bow. It was covered in long grey scars and had notches across its fin and flippers from numerous battles.

As they came past the abandoned house Emily stopped her excited calling to the dolphin – now named 'Dolly' – and stood staring up at it as though it were a stern headmaster admonishing her for minor misdeeds. Tom nudged Sarah to look at her and they both cast worried glances back at each other.

The rest of the trip back – twenty minutes, or so – Emily seemed self-absorbed and didn't acknowledge Dolly at all, and barely spoke to her parents, or brother. As soon as she stepped off the boat she returned to her old self again and wanted a Knickerbocker Glory in the teashop on the way back to the cottage. They indulged her, relieved to see her strange reaction to the cliff house disappear.

The Thursday was spent in Looe, round the shops and amusement arcades. Despite it being rather less edifying than he'd hoped, Tom was pleased to see the kids enjoying themselves. Emily was delighted to have found a boxed set of *Mr Men* stories in a remainder bookshop, and a bumper pack of crayons and A3 sketchpad, which she bought with her pocket money.

As was their tradition their last full day of a holiday was always spent relaxing in their holiday home, reading, dozing and playing games. Emily made up *Mr Men* stories about Mr Dolly, the dolphin man and got into an argument with David, who said that the *Mr Men* weren't animals. Tom retreated to the kitchen and not having got to the du Maurier tale on the Wednesday evening, he read it that afternoon.

'Any good?' Sarah asked, after he'd put the book down.

'Er, well … it's certainly not what I was expecting,' Tom said, feeling rather unnerved by the oddness of the short tale. 'I think I'll stick to the novels.'

After a few minutes of reflection he decided to prepare dinner to take his mind off the image of the weird doll, Julio, in the story.

On their final morning, as everyone busied themselves with packing, Emily just wanted to sit at the breakfast table and do some drawing. So they left her too it as the bags piled up in the hallway, and rooms were checked and rechecked for stray belongings. It came time to leave and Tom went over to get Emily to tidy the crayons and paper away.

She seemed sad, and oddly contemplative; precociously thoughtful and troubled.

She had drawn a picture of the sea, with a small cliff and a large distorted building atop it. Four windows, of the childish cross-frame variety, looked out from it. It was more a symbol of a house than a depiction of a real one. But it was clearly meant to be the place they had seen from the boat.

'Well that's a really good picture, darling,' he said. 'But, with four windows and no door how on earth are people meant to get in?'

She thought for a moment and nodded her head solemnly.

'Yes, Daddy, I see what you mean,' she said, slowly. 'But the real question is ... how do you *get out*?'

Tom couldn't get those words out of his head for the whole journey home.

It was later that year, in October, when it happened. And, *when it happened*, Tom was in Hull listening to poster presentations and participating in a 'working group' on archive resilience and backup retrieval. During the late afternoon coffee break he looked at his phone and saw a list of missed calls from Sarah and five answerphone messages.

He rang back, wondering what on earth the problem could be. It was 5pm.

'Where the bloody hell are you?' Sarah yelled at him. 'And where's Emily?'

'What do you mean?' he replied. 'I'm at this conference in Hull.'

'What? But you were meant to pick her up from school this afternoon,' Sarah said.

'No ... I wasn't ...' Tom stuttered. 'Wait, I'll come home now. I'll be there in three hours.'

They talked for most of the journey back, Tom weaving in and out of the traffic, two speed cameras flashing him on the M1.

Sarah had gone round to the school and checked and Miss Hargreaves (her best friend, Susan) had said that Tom had collected Emily at around three o'clock. Arguments ensued and finally Tom put the phone down on Sarah in case he had an accident.

He finally got in at about 9pm to find two police officers, and Susan Hargreaves, in their front room.

Susan seemed to need more calming down than Sarah. She was distraught and kept breaking down in tears. Questions came from all possible angles and the police were making many notes.

Something terrible struck Tom as Susan explained Emily's behaviour as though it had been waiting for him somehow.

'Well, she seemed so preoccupied throughout the whole morning,' she said, cautiously. 'I asked her what was wrong and she said she hoped the new windows and door would be fixed in time for her to play later. I asked if you were having new double glazing fitted and she said no. She said that Mr Mann was putting in new windows and a door to your seaside house so you could all look out at the waves. I assumed you'd bought a holiday cottage and was going to ask Sarah about it when we were going to the concert on Friday.'

Tom looked at Sarah but she did not look back, she just stared straight at the empty blackness of the television screen and hugged Susan as she sobbed.

Everything began to fall apart.

Lines of enquiry were opened. Alibis were checked. There were hours and hours of questioning and re-questioning as the investigating officers tried to trip them up and find any weakness in their statements. Amidst it all Sarah and Tom were increasingly perplexed. Sarah blamed Tom for never telling her he was going away and for forgetting it was his turn to pick Emily up.

The real horror started early the following week when Tom was called into the police station to watch the CCTV footage. Sarah had also been asked to come along but they were asked to view it separately.

The officer assigned to the case, Detective Sergeant Lyle, asked Tom to look at the footage and see whether he could notice anyone on the edges of the film that he recognised, or who seemed even vaguely familiar.

Tom watched the black and white silent footage. Miss Hargreaves tidied her classroom and the last few children waited in the reading area for their parents. Emily played happily with them and seemed to chat on occasion with Susan, who turned then and greeted someone slightly off camera. Emily turned and ran to whoever it was. The detective was watching Tom carefully.

After a short exchange, they were gone. The view changed to a camera in the main corridor. Emily was alone and heading for the doors. There was nobody else to be seen. As Emily walked excitedly to the doors she seemed, to Tom, to be talking to someone, turning her head up and nodding in the way she would normally, pouring out the excitement of the day to her mother or father. But there was nobody there. Nobody at all.

The scene cut to the playground, and then the front gates. Other parents were milling around, doing up coats, packing up bags – the usual scene. Emily walked along, arm in the air, and then she was gone from shot.

Tom asked to view it all again. The detective played it again; and again; and again.

'Do you see how she's walking,' Tom said. 'She's holding someone's hand.'

The detective played the tape again and looked puzzled.

'Do you recognise *anyone else*, Mr Flanagan?' he asked. 'Or do you see *anyone* you do not recognise as a member of school staff, or another parent?'

'It looks as though she's holding someone's hand as she leaves the building,' Tom muttered to himself.

'Look, I know the footage is poor ...' the detective said.

'Have you been looking into this *Mr Mann*, and the things that Susan said about?' Tom asked urgently.

'We've been looking at everything, Mr Flanagan, *everything*,' Lyle said. 'It's difficult because we have a sworn statement from Miss Hargreaves that you picked Emily up – corroborated by the children in the classroom and two parents in the playground. But we have statements from all those you were working with at this conference in Hull that you were nearly two hundred miles away at the time. That leaves us in a very tricky position, especially with no other leads at the moment.'

'Can I go now?' Tom asked.

The detective nodded.

On the drive home, Tom kept on about how Emily seemed to be talking to someone and holding their hand. Sarah said she hadn't really noticed Emily's hand raised in the footage; all she could think of was what was going through Emily's mind – but she kept that to herself, and it would haunt her.

As the desperate days crawled by into weeks, and the weeks crumbled into months, Tom and Sarah saw less of each other at home, and when they were there together they seldom spoke.

Susan Hargreaves had a nervous breakdown as the guilt and remorse overwhelmed her. Sarah saw her often, they seemed to offer each other some strange consolation.

The divorce came through about a year later, among the hollow grief of the anniversary of Emily's disappearance. The house was sold by Christmas and Sarah and David moved in with her parents in Manchester.

Tom stumbled on for six months, going through the motions of his job, renting a little flat in Aylesbury. But his thoughts returned constantly to Susan's words; to Mr Mann, the abandoned house, Emily's drawings, the boat trip and her sad, serious expression, and a terrible sense that without being there – in Polperro, without searching *there*, he would never feel that he had done all he could to solve the mystery of her vanishing.

With his share of the money from the house, and the few investments remaining to him, he managed to secure a bedsit in Looe, from where he could try to set his mind to rest.

Just before Tom moved they pulled the old cliff house down. It was hazardous, apparently. Some local boys had tried to get in and one broke his arm on the back door they'd jemmied open after smashing out some of the bricks in front of it. It was a practical response to a practical problem; it would have collapsed into the sea anyway, eventually. For Tom, and for Tom alone, it answered a question – a terrible, unbearable question – with another question; a cryptic place became a cryptic space.

This land is strange: the craggy coasts and windy roads; the little, half-deserted villages and lonely houses that grow, fungus-like from the sides of hills. The daylight is so bright and vivid, as though it actually sheds colour into things rather than simply illuminates what lies within. And the nights are so dark, as though it sucks the daytime bounty back out in some unending cosmic trade.

The stars – the billions and billions and billions of galaxies, each with their billions and billions of suns, planets and moons – sparkle with a brightness you cannot find anywhere else in the country. They mock us with their flickering hope of life – that somewhere out *there*, there are *others*, billions and billions of *others*; all dying; all losing; all crying; all laughing at the pointless madness of the universe.

Tom walks along those crumbling cliffs towards Fowey every morning, and every evening, searching for his answer; wandering by that patch of rubble strewn ground, looking for somewhere called home.

Every house has a door and *every* door has a key; *every* key unlocks another secret, and once you are *in* be very sure you can get *out*.

OWLMAN

Of all the mythical monsters said to inhabit Cornwall, one of the strangest is the mysterious Owlman. It is also one of the creepiest, primarily because this weird tale doesn't date from the mists of antiquity, but from relatively modern times – the end of the last century in fact.

It all began on a bright spring day in 1976, when a family on holiday from Lancashire were visiting the pretty south Cornish parish of Mawnan, only to be confronted by a bizarre apparition. In broad daylight, the family's youngest daughters were following a woodland path towards Mawnan Church, when they were distracted by the sight of a figure apparently hovering above the tower. They looked more closely, and were astounded and horrified to behold what seemed to be a winged man, covered in feathers, sporting demonic claws, and apparently flying. They were so terrified that their father cancelled what remained of the family holiday and refused to speak about it to the press. The story eventually leaked out courtesy of Tony 'Doc' Shiels, a paranormalist showman who would later go on to be a well-known figure in Cornwall, partly as a hoaxer. However, other researchers also obtained details of the event and published them that same year.

The next incident occurred only a couple of months later, when two older girls who were camping close to Mawnan Church were disturbed by a foul stench and a harsh hissing sound outside their tent. When they emerged to investigate, they spotted the hybrid form of the Owlman, as he had already become known, only a few feet away. Almost immediately the eerie vision ascended, wings beating, and flew off over the tops of the trees. The descriptions the girls gave were much more detailed than those offered by the two children, mentioning red eyes, pointed ears and rough silver-grey feathers. Separately from each other, they drew pictures, both of which turned out to be astonishingly similar, though investigators still felt that such evidence was of limited value.

What was really needed was a photograph, but such a prize proved elusive, even though the Owlman reappeared again and again over the next few years, always briefly and always to lone individuals or small groups in close proximity to Mawnan Church. By this time, the terrifying creature had earned itself a secure place in the catalogue of British cryptids, though nobody had a clue what it actually might be. The two most recent sightings occurred in 1989 and 1995, the latter a particularly impressive event, when an American holidaymaker – with no prior connections to Cornwall or Cornish myth – returned home to Chicago and immediately sent a letter to the 'Western Morning News' in Truro, describing how she had been confronted by a 'man-bird with a ghastly face, a wide mouth, glowing eyes and pointed ears'. It isn't impossible that the woman already knew the story in advance of her visiting the UK and was merely looking to contribute to the legend, but if so, she'd gone to a considerable amount of trouble and for no apparent gain.

There have been many suggestions as to what the Owlman might actually be. These have ranged from supernatural explanations concerning Mawnan Church, which is located in an ancient and mythical place, a prehistoric religious site where unknown gods were once worshipped, to much more prosaic theories concerning escaped rare birds such as eagle owls, which can grow to over two feet in height and boast wingspans of about six feet. This latter explanation was strongly supported by the respected cryptozoologist Karl Shuker, who drew significant comparisons between the mysterious creature described by witnesses and the largest of Europe's native owl species.

As yet, the Cornish Owlman hasn't taken on the near-metaphysical status of a much more famous winged spectre, the West Virginia Mothman, whose appearances since the mid-1960s have been regarded as portents of disaster, and who has now become something of an emblem for that district. This may owe to the plethora of fabled monsters and devils that already people the histories and traditions of Britain, and Cornwall in particular – in other words it has got lost in the crowd. Alternatively, the combination of unlikeliness surrounding the existence of such a beast (a bizarre mixture of man and bird!) and the natural scepticism that runs in the British character might simply have relegated it to the rank of improbable footnote.

It doesn't help the legend that no sightings have been reported in the 21st century, or that Tony Shiels, not the most reliable character in the eyes of some, was involved in the original story. However, nobody had heard about the Owlman prior to 1976, and it only took one sighting to create an atmosphere of frenzy and fear. There is absolutely no reason why the same thing could not happen again.

CLAWS

Steve Jordan

That horrible sound – the screech of metal scraping metal. As the arcade's security shutters rolled up, Sonia's heart sank. Dust, stagnant air and yesterday's weed smoke attacked her senses in waves. Rows of imposing claw and fruit machines loomed back-to-back in the dark. The passageways between them were shadowy and narrow, labyrinthine.

'Just another day in paradise,' Ron said. Rather than chucking it out onto the street, he made a point of stubbing out his cigarette on the Coke-stained carpet (Sonia hoped it was Coke) with the heel of his trainer.

'I can't even laugh at this shit anymore,' Sonia said.

At least when summer was still in full swing, the weather would help her start the day with some kind of optimism. But summer was dead and autumn was digging its heels in. The holiday season was over. The plus side was that the arcade's perpetual lack of business was less embarrassing out of season. Even when the sun was shining and the streets were full of holidaymakers and surfers, Pirates Bounty Arcade was bereft of life, and yes, the arcade's name was also bereft of a much-needed apostrophe.

The Bounty was an inglorious waste of prime retail space on Newquay Harbour's doorstep – on a quaint street that hosted two rustic gastropubs, no fewer than seven beach and surf gear shops and other stores that hosted the usual tourist-bait tat. You know the sort, a blue shell with 'Newquay' written on it, £5.99. Sonia liked it – the harbour, the boat tours, the high street, even some of the other arcades. While Fistral Beach was the main draw of the town for families, the harbour had more charm to it. That was, until the Bounty dropped anchor. The size of at least three restaurants, the arcade must have cost a fortune to set up so close to the seafront. Jared must have thought he was onto a winner.

'I'm doing you a favour,' he'd sneered when he'd hired her. 'This place will be here for years. We're building a *dynasty*.' Sonia was fairly certain Jared didn't know what dynasty meant.

'Cheer up kid,' Ron said, pleading. 'I can't take your bad mood along with mine.'

At eighteen, Ron was only a year older than Sonia, but he seemed much older than that. He was a laid-back, kind bloke, with aesthetically awkward long, shaggy hair, bad stubble and a lanky frame. He was the second person she'd met back in July when she'd started at the Bounty, and within one conversation he'd lent her two *Guns N' Roses* albums. He was okay. While she sympathised with him, she didn't have the energy to show it. Not today.

'Let's just get everything up and running before *he* turns up,' she said, head down.

'Yeah. We wouldn't want to disappoint our glorious Führer.' He slowly goose-stepped down the row of game machines like Basil Fawlty, before hitting the switch for the main lights.

Jared's dictator-like management style had been a running gag among the staff since the first time he had fired someone for accidentally spilling coffee on the floor. A few months in, the joke was wearing thin.

The arcade floor was a sorry sight. It would have been passé when Sonia's mum was her age. Faded game and fruit machines lined the first couple of aisles – all with discoloured symbols and ancient theming. Sonia's least favourite was the *Coronation Street*-themed, shit-brown monstrosity near the front, with the hideous caricature of Ken Morley on it (they googled his name – just type in 'Coronation Street red glasses', he's the first hit). The newest machine was a *Deal or No Deal* machine from 2006. The arcade had only been open for six months. Where on earth all these clapped out, run-down pieces of nightmarish nostalgia came from was a mystery; Jared must have good contacts in the 'old shite' trade.

When Noel Edmonds' face is the most culturally relevant presence in a place of entertainment, you know something has gone unfathomably, hideously wrong.

What added to the misery was that the Bounty, despite being the newest arcade in town, was unfavourably compared to Silverfoil Amusements, which was just around the corner. Where Silverfoil featured *Batmobile* driving simulators and claw machines laden with cuddly dinosaurs from *Jurassic World*, the Bounty's claw machines were full of nondescript, undead-looking bears with mournful faces, stuffed with God only knew; probably used tissues.

Sonia had been working there for three months, and the bears' mournful expressions were infectious – Sonia, Ron and all the others that had come and gone, who couldn't get jobs anywhere else, were counting the days until college started. A pay cheque and freedom were coming.

As Ron checked into the office and started counting last night's take, Sonia hit the main switch hub. A jerky cover-version of what she assumed was a popular Disney tune beat out from one of the claw machines out there, somewhere in the void.

'we'll dance the sh-shade, we'll spring up at n-night…'

The dull yellow and red lights of the machines transformed the dark corridors into something vaguely less sinister, except …

'Ken Morley's bit the dust!'

She massaged her temples, contemplating what another broken machine might mean for her eardrums – whoever was around when a machine developed a fault got a pasting from Jared. There had been a lot of them. As the summer wore on, it seemed like 'ghosts in the machines' were a daily occurrence.

Ron shambled back from the office, but before he reached her, he stopped in his tracks.

'Oh God,' he said, and grimaced, pointing at the Bounty's one, sad, blue and red pool table (and in some parts black; there were a couple of dried stains that looked suspiciously like blood).

Someone had broken the pool cue in half, and stuffed the pieces into two of the pockets.

'Who did that?'

'Who d'ya think?' Ron said.

As Ron surveyed the damage, Sonia noticed some brown smudges on the floor, like tiny muddy footprints.

'Look, someone's cat got locked in again.'

'So you think the cat did it?' he said, rolling his eyes. 'We need to check this place more thoroughly before we leave.' He bent over to check the side of the table, and let out a mirthless laugh. 'All the balls are gone too. Fuck this – we need to move the broken fruity out back.'

'Is there any room for more? We've got so many deceased

machines back there it's beginning to look like a ghost-town version of our main floor.'

Ron shook his head.

'There's room for one more. Quickly, before Jared appears.'

'*Too late, mate!*'

Sonia winced and closed her eyes. Trust him to be early for once.

'Someone's broken the pool cue,' Ron said. Sonia wished he hadn't.

'*I can fucking see that.*'

Jared was a man who thought a pastel blue suit and hair grease were the height of fashion, and smelt like an odd mix of Brut aftershave and a corpse's final fart. He stood before them – hands on hips, gut thrust-out triumphantly like a Tesco value Henry VIII, eyeing them suspiciously.

'What have you done?'

'Nothing Ja … Mr Talshoy,' Sonia muttered. He hated it when his staff were 'too familiar'.

'I'm not talking to you, Sonia. You're clearly too weak to break the cue. I'm talking to *Iron Maiden* here.'

'Because I have long hair. I get it.'

'Why are you doing this to me? Why are you breaking my assets?' Jared said, just getting warmed up. 'Don't I pay you an honest wage? Don't I treat you well?'

Sonia and Ron shot each other a glance of suppressed amazement. Jared's beady eyes narrowed with anger. A single bead of sweat running down his left side-burn. His legendary rage had arrived in record-time – it was frightening.

'We didn't do anything Mr Talshoy. We only just arrived and found it like this.'

'So, what are you telling me? The *Coronation Street* machine just broke, did it?'

'Machines break,' Sonia said.

'And I suppose pool cues just snap in two overnight, do they?' he bellowed. 'What a pair of utter idiots. Don't think this isn't coming out of your pay at the end of the summer.'

Ron mustered a defiant smirk as Jared stormed off towards the toilets, punching the front window of a claw machine on his way. The plastic rattled in its frame.

'What a prick,' Ron said. Catchphrase of the summer.

'Just two more weeks,' Sonia said, closing her eyes as though in prayer. 'Just two more weeks.'

Another thunderous, furious scream. Ron's smile morphed into a look of quiet dread as Jared appeared, sweating with rage, and pointed back to the Gents.

'You little pricks get in that toilet and fish those balls out of there right now!'

'I can't get rid of the smell of that toilet,' Sonia said, with a shudder.

Sam offered her a cigarette. 'Might help,' he said.

'No thanks.'

It was lunchtime. The alley behind the building doubled as the bin area and the employees' staff room and canteen. Though Sonia didn't smoke, she pretended to just to get more time out of the arcade. Hanging out by some bins was preferable – the cold sea air was a welcome respite from the dank recesses of Jared's gaudy hell.

The back door slammed open – it was Ron. He ripped the rubber gloves from his hands and threw them on the floor in a weak display of frustration.

'Alright, Ron?'

'Fuck off, Sam.'

Sam looked at Sonia, wide-eyed and innocent.

'What have I done?' Sam said.

'Why is it whenever you *get your own back* against the old tit, it's always someone else who has to clean up after you?'

'It's because Jared's scared of me, innit?'

Sam was the third and final member of the Bounty's skeleton staff. He fancied himself as a tough guy, but Sonia had only ever seen him display spite and indifference. His stringy physique didn't help his 'image', nor did the fact that he had the face and teeth of a meth-addicted rat. If they hadn't been united against a common enemy, Sonia wouldn't have given Sam the time of day.

'Jared's not scared, he's just pissed,' Ron said. 'I mean, *breaking* the fucking *pool cues*? Do you want us all to suffer?'

'That wasn't me,' Sam said. 'The thing with the stuffed toy … that was me. Nothing else has been.'

'Rubbish,' Ron said.

Two weeks ago, Jared had fired a girl named Holly, a seventeen-year-old gymnast that Sam had taken a particular liking to. Sam had quickly decided it was time for revenge. He took a cuddly toy from one of the claw machines, emptied the stuffing, and replaced it with shit he scooped out of the dog bin outside Newquay golf club. He put it back in the machine, right next to the prize drop. Of course, the hapless child who wandered in and played it the next day got the easy win. The claw only had to nudge it over the edge to win the prize – a nice cuddle with a turd. The girl's parents gave Jared the grilling of a lifetime, and threatened to sue. Jared, defiant to the last, blamed it on the child.

'If it wasn't you Sam, who was it?' Sonia asked.

'I dunno, do I?' Sam said, and took a long draw on his cig.

'Did you see anyone around last night?'

'Around here?' he said and laughed. 'Quiet as the grave. Like always.'

'So you think the cue broke itself?'

'Yup. I think the pool cue had e-fucking-nuff and topped itself in a fit of rage and despair.'

No-one laughed.

'It's not funny anymore,' Sonia said.

'No, it's not,' Ron added, lighting up a cigarette of his own.

'It wasn't me,' Sam said again, with slightly more conviction. 'I'm at a point where if I pull anything, it's going to be legendary. Permanent too.'

Sonia didn't know what he meant, but then again neither did Sam. Despite his shady demeanour, she was inclined to believe Sam this time. If he was responsible, he would admit it – it would appeal to his ego. Someone else was to blame.

'A few machines breaking down was bound to happen. But fourteen?' Sonia asked. 'In the space of three months? Along with the broken pool cues, fuses blowing every other day, chewed up wiring …'

'Weird, innit?' Ron added.

'Perhaps this kid did it,' Sam said, pointing behind them.

A child with a beast's face, covered in pus-leaking sores with bloodstained lips.

'Bloody hell, Billy,' Sonia said, pushing him away. 'Where on earth did you get that?'

Billy took off his zombie mask, to reveal a guilty grin.

'Sorry Sonia,' he said.

'On first name terms with the adults are we?' Ron asked Billy.

'Yes, Ron.'

Billy was one of the few regular customers the arcade had – a ten-year-old, he lived with his dad above one of the tourist shops on the high street. None of the staff really liked having him around, but they grudgingly tolerated him because he had nowhere else to go either. He was socially awkward and not at all bright. He spent most of his time pretending to play the arcade machines because he never had any money.

'I saw Jared shouting at you,' Billy said to Sonia.

'Did you?'

He shrugged.

'Do you know what happened? With the pool cues?' Billy asked.

'Have you come to own up?' Ron replied.

'No, it wasn't me. Do you think it was me?'

Ron gave Billy a playful nudge.

'No, you idiot. You couldn't pick up a pool cue, let alone break it.'

'You see anything weird in there?' Billy asked, peering behind them through the staff door and into the arcade.

'Apart from you?' Sam asked. 'Just piss off kid.'

'Oi!' Ron said, flicking his cig at Sam. Sam slapped it out of mid-air and laughed.

'I saw little footprints,' Billy said.

'Probably a cat or something.' Ron said.

'Or your muddy trainers!' Sam chipped in.

'Haven't seen any cats, but I saw something. Like Piskies.'

'Piskies?' Sam asked.

'I did an essay at school about them,' Billy said enthusiastically. 'Cornish Piskies, little old tricksters that dressed like *Game of Thrones*.'

Their image was seemingly everywhere. Piskies were a local joke – twisted remnants of pagan religion that the local tourist board used to sell brochures.

'Mystery solved then,' Rob said, smiling. 'Hang on, how do you know about *Game of Thrones*?'

'I'm going to do the claws,' Billy said, and ran in through the staff door before Ron could tell him not to.

'Oi! Customers are not allowed through the staff door!'

Jared appeared in the doorway, glowering. 'That's enough

smoking, indoors and get those carpets hoovered.'

'I only just came out,' Ron said, but defeatedly shuffled back inside.

Sonia started to follow before she felt a tug on her shirt.

'Stay back a minute.'

Sam ushered her towards the other side of the bins, out of earshot.

'You're the brainy one. We got to get Jared back, right?'

'Still sore over Holly?' Sonia said, with a mocking grin.

'Sod that. I reckon it's Jared setting this shit up so he can fire us without paying us.'

Sonia raised an eyebrow.

'That seems pretty elaborate.'

'I reckon we should do something. Something *elaborate*, to make a point.'

'Just leave me out of it, Sam. Do what you like.'

Sonia didn't want to even entertain anything that might escalate the problem. Just two more weeks …

'I can't do it on my own.'

'Inside! Now!' yelled Jared's bulbous face as it re-emerged at the door.

'We're coming!' Sam said.

Jared gave them both a contemptuous stare as they drifted back inside. Moving slowly was the only real resistance they could get away with. It was like being back at secondary school, but with shorter breaks.

As Sonia stepped back inside, Billy came running up to them.

He looked pale. Disturbed.

Sonia crouched and placed a reassuring hand on his shoulder.

'What is it?'

Billy pointed towards the pool tables.

'What the fuck now?' Jared said, storming round the corner, flanked by Sam and Sonia.

Ron was sitting motionless on the floor, hunched forward awkwardly. The vacuum cleaner leaned against a smouldering plug socket in the wall, a black scorch mark around it. A light smoke hung in the air.

Holly rushed to check his pulse, before realising – she couldn't touch him, unless she wanted to risk her own safety.

'Get up you fool,' Jared said, shaking his head.

'Fuck me. Look at his arm,' Sam said, covering his mouth.

His arm was scorched red, and was peppered with skin burnt black. There was a collective in-take of breath.

'This vacuum cleaner was new at the beginning of the summer, look at it now!' Jared said, reaching out to pick it up.

'Don't touch it!' As limited as Sonia's knowledge was regarding the dangers of electricity, she felt she had to be the voice of reason.

He picked it up anyway and pulled on the cord – the wire's jacket and insulation had clearly come away at the plug end.

'Turn off the power and call an ambulance.'

Jared looked at her as if she'd just urinated in the Vatican's holy water. 'Who the hell do you think you're talking to, young lady?'

'Sam, turn off the building's power now.'

'Right,' he said.

Jared grabbed him. 'You'll do no such thing! You take orders from me, not her!'

'I don't take orders from anyone, you prick!' Sam said, trying to wrestle out of Jared's grip. Despite Jared being mostly composed of fat and struggling arteries, his grip on Sam's scrawny shoulder was vice-like.

'If you want your pay then you'll show me some fucking respect!'

Jared pushed him up against the fruit machine, so hard that the machine and Sam tipped over. There was an almighty thud as *Lucky 7* slammed to the floor. Thankfully, Sam rode the fall out and leapt straight back to his feet. He ran for the back office.

'Another machine you idiots have cost me!' Jared said, slamming his fists on the fallen machine.

The lights and sounds of the arcade died.

'Power's off,' Sam called back.

Sonia couldn't take the suspense – she placed two fingers on Ron's throat, feeling for a pulse.

'Call an ambulance right now!' Sonia called to Sam, who took his mobile out of his pocket and ran outside. Jared crouched down to Sonia, pointing at her accusingly.

'You lot have cost me enough money this summer! I'm not having another lawsuit on my hands over some exaggerated nonsense about a killer vacuum cleaner!'

As Ron lay dead on the floor and Jared hurled abuse at her, Sonia filled with quiet rage, building so quickly. In those seconds, she wanted to kill him. But then she caught sight of Billy, standing next to the pool table, quietly sobbing, watching the chaos unfold. The rage was replaced by sympathy. *Poor kid. Poor Ron. Poor us.*

'It's okay,' she said.

'No it's not – the claw machine's not working.' he said, pointing and sobbing.

He had to pay.

As night descended, the weather echoed the mood. A torrent of rain had been falling since eight, filling the dips in the roads with black pools. The beach in the harbour was wide and imposing as the sea receded. With the last of the nightclubs closed and the streets deserted, the only sounds were the distant roar of the ocean and the rain drops that fell like bullets. They watched the dark, wet bedlam.

'Can we get on with this now?' Sonia asked.

'Yeah, fuck it,' Sam said, before turning on the driver's seat to face Sonia. 'Sure you're ready?'

Sonia nodded. She'd never been more ready for anything.

Two in the morning. Sonia and Sam exited the car and ran across the road, hoods up.

Ron had stopped breathing, but Sonia had performed CPR while Jared hovered, mumbling about it being Ron's own fault. The paramedics had managed to get Ron's heart started while he was still on the floor. While Jared watched them, cursing and thumping any inanimate object in reach – Sonia had snatched the spare front door keys from the office, unnoticed. She figured that Jared would assume they were still in Ron's pocket and been taken to the hospital with him. Seemed she was right.

The police should have been called along with the ambulance. Someone had clearly tampered with the socket that had nearly killed Ron. On the other hand, no Jared meant no pay, for her or for Ron. Jared had a canny habit of deflecting blame; he had assured the paramedics that he'd seen Ron messing about with the wiring earlier. The chance of the boss suffering any sort of reprimand from the local police didn't seem good.

She opened the security shutters. For the first time, the noise didn't fill her with dread. Instead, she was grimly excited.

'He's going to wish he'd replaced that faulty alarm,' Sam said, with a cackle.

Sonia closed the shutters behind them, and they quickly got to work. They'd planned a short and sweet revenge plan – they were going to steal what little money Jared had left. They'd agreed to give half the money to Ron, so he could convalesce in comfort without having to worry about being out of work, and with the satisfaction of knowing that Jared was paying for it.

They worked by torchlight. Sam snatched the machine keys from the office, and started opening them one by one, emptying the coins and notes into his backpack. Sonia kept a lookout at the main entrance, just in case.

She heard him make his way back to the end of the arcade, filling his bag up, until the sound of cascading coins abruptly stopped when he was out of sight on the other side of the arcade floor. She shone her torch down the narrow spaces between the old fruit machines.

'Sam?'

She saw something.

Movement, something small. She thought she saw a shape in the darkness, scuttling across the floor between the *Deal or No Deal* machine and one of the smaller claw machines that wasn't 'nice' enough to go front-of-house. Sonia ran toward where she thought she'd seen it – but there was nothing, except clumps of mud on the carpet that Sam had walked in.

Sonia kept running, abandoning her lookout post entirely.

'Sam! Where are you?' she hissed into the dark. Only the eerily cheerful, faded faces of the characters on the looming machines greeted her.

Another shape in the distance, a shadow moving across the spot by the door that she had just left. She couldn't get her torch beam onto it in time. The only sound was rain hitting the roof above and her blood pumping in her ears – until someone hissed her name.

'*Sonia.*'

She let out a tiny squeak and turned.

'Where the fuck were you?' Sonia replied, irate and embarrassed. 'I was calling you!'

'I had to stay quiet for a sec, I thought I heard something moving,' Sam said.

'Yeah, *me,* you dick.' Sonia grabbed one of the bags from Sam's shoulders. It felt like it was full of bricks.

'How much did you take?'

'A fucking lot,' he grinned.

They ran back past Noel Edmonds, the rigged quiz machines, the ancient casino games, the knackered air-hockey, the mournful bears … in a few moments she'd never have to see any of them ever again. Good riddance.

They reached the shutters. Mission accomplished.

Sonia twisted the key and lifted. The shutters stayed put.

'Come on, hurry up!' Sam barked.

'I'm trying!'

Sam tried to lift the shutters with her. It was budging.

'You need to unlock the master too,' Sam said, sighing. 'There are two locks.'

'I haven't got the master, just the little key for the shutters. We only use that to lock up usually.'

'Then how did you lock the shutters behind us?' Sam asked.

'Oh God … the back door,' Sonia said. 'Come on.'

'You mean *you didn't?*'

They ran, but as they went, Sonia spotted another small shape between the machines. It was so fast, it was a blur.

'Wait, I saw something,' she whispered.

'What?'

Sonia put a finger to her lips for a moment. She crept toward to the adjacent row of machines, sprinting around the corner to find the culprit.

'Billy! You little git,' Sonia said, pulling the zombie mask from his face.

'How the hell did you get in here?' Sam asked.

'I'm sorry. I hid under the pool table at closing.'

'You're going to be in such much trouble,' Sonia said.

'I saw something when I was here, wanted to find it,' Billy said, pleading. 'After Jared killed Ron.'

'Ron's not dead, Billy,' Sonia said.

'Oh. Well, I saw them. The little guys I said about before.'

'Fuck this noise – we need to leave right now!' Sam hissed. 'And bring the idiot. Someone must have double-locked those shutters, what if Jared …'

'Too late mate.'

Sonia felt the grip of a hand on her shoulder. She screamed as she and Sam were pushed to the carpet with such force she twisted her knee on impact.

Sam was the first to be picked up off the floor and have his hands tied behind his back.

'I was a whizz at knots in Scouts,' Jared said, pulling on the coarse mooring rope, so tightly that Sam winced. 'A fine organisation it is. They would have instilled some duty and order into your lives – stop you from robbing good, hard-working citizens.'

Sonia tried to find words to protest, but what could she say? The next few hours were playing out in Sonia's mind as he pulled her up: the machines breaking, the pool cues, the balls in the toilet, Ron's electrocution – they would be blamed for everything.

'You forced us to it you old bastard! What you did to Ron was evil!' Sam yelled.

'Me? *Me*? You must think … I know it was you swines who rigged that plug socket to blow. Thought you could top the old coot as well as ruining his livelihood? You scum. I bet you didn't think one of your own would get it. Serves you right.'

He ushered them over to the pool tables, next to where Ron had had his 'accident'.

'I've finally got you where I want you,' Jared said, with a wide-grin, showing off his discoloured, plaque-encrusted teeth. There was a desperate look in his eyes.

He took a foot-long, heavy-looking wrench from the inside of his jacket.

'Time to learn you something,' he said, and grinned.

He moved closer.

The lights and sounds of the arcade came to life.

A tune from the claw machines skipped and stuttered, repeating the same lyric over and over – *we'll dance the sh-shade, we'll spring up at n-night, our claws will tear, our t-teeth will bite… we'll dance the sh-shade, we'll spring up at n-night…*

Jared turned one-eighty degrees, facing into the arcade. There was a curious whistling sound, like something shooting through the air at horrific pace. Then a piercing, grating squeak and a strange squelch.

'What was that?' Sam asked.

Jared exhaled slowly. He seemed to be looking for someone out amongst the machines, but then he fell back.

Two prongs of a cuddly toy machine claw were lodged in his eye-sockets. The third prong was lodged under his chin, the tip protruding visibly in his open mouth. Blood seeped from the wounds. He tried to cry out and speak, but only managed a wheeze as he struggled for air.

Sonia couldn't speak or move as Jared struggled to his feet. He tried to pull the metal claws from his face. He pulled on it with both hands and made such a terrible, pained cry. It wouldn't budge.

Panicked by the pain, he stumbled hard into the cuddly toy machine cabinet. The plastic buckled under the weight, and he fell face-first into the laps of the bears. He stopped moving.

'What the fuck just happened?' Sam said.

Sonia surveyed the room. Every claw machine around them was claw-less.

'Billy?' Sonia called out, tearing her eyes from Jared to inspect the corridors between the machines, now fully lit.

Billy ran into view from behind the furthest pool, wearing his zombie mask, only to let out a murmur of fright when he saw Jared's body amongst the old teddy bears.

'Did *he* do that?' Sam said.

'From over *there*?' Sonia yelled.

'It wasn't me, it was the little guys!' Billy said. 'The ones I've been chasing! Little piskies!'

Sonia knelt in front of him so they were face-to-face.

'Calm down Billy, look at me and tell me what you saw.'

'I told you already!' he said, defiant.

As the kid untied them, Sam continued to stare at the blood seeping from Jared's eyes.

'Do you think we should call an ambulance?'

Sonia checked Jared's pulse.

'We need to leave,' she said, her voice breaking slightly. 'Right now.'

Sonia searched Jared's pockets for the master key, and found it.

As the three of them ran, the machines around them flickered on and off.

The jarring tunes of the machines spluttered and mewed like dying animals.

The ceiling lights above them fell dark as the light bulbs shattered, one by one.

The way ahead was blocked. The arcade machines had been moved, the layout had been changed.

'Keep going!'

She heard quiet murmurs all around, like voices – chanting.

Sonia halted and turned to face the darkness, as the machines and lights dimmed around her.

Sam and Billy were gone. She was alone, as the chanting stopped. She screamed their names. No answers came. The only sound was the rain and Sonia's heavy breathing.

She took the torch from her pocket and turned it towards the darkness.

Small, fast shapes circled her, ducking and diving between the machines.

A cackle of laughter bounced around her, until it seemed to come from everywhere. The air became thick with a horrid, metallic smell.

'Come out!' she called.

And they did. There were so many of them, sharp metal claws and tools in their paws, humourless grins on their stained fur faces and pupil-less, black eyes.

Sonia moved her torch-light left and right. She caught sight of one of them holding the two ends of the pool cues up, and banging them on the floor to the rhythm of a war march. Another stripped some of the electrical wire from the wall, and gnawed into it viscously. A second later, it had burst into flames. Its comrades laughed.

While the chaos unfolded, the horde of stuffed bears pushed forward, circling, advancing toward her. Her back hit one of the machines. She was cornered.

She pleaded as they came closer, the ring-leader swinging a claw from a machine by its chain, ready to let it fly at any moment.

Her torch-light failed.

She felt them claw at her ankles, her legs, her arms.

They scraped at her skin with the cold, sharp metal.

They stabbed when she screamed, and then started to chew.

THE CURSING PSALM

It might be a surprise, but one of the world's most fearsome curses comes not from the annals of dark literature or even from a book of witchcraft, but from Psalm 109 in the Holy Bible. *Of course, it's all a matter of interpretation. The 'Book of Psalms' is a poetic and philosophical text, often seen as an advisory guide for the progress of mankind even today. But Psalm 109 contains several passages which it wouldn't require a twisted mind to consider dangerous.*

For example, the phrase 'let his children be fatherless and his wife a widow' is a fairly pointed one. In a religious context, it sounds like more than just a threat, and it is perhaps no surprise that Psalm 109 eventually became known as the 'Cursing Psalm'. It is equally unsurprising that, in former centuries, belief in this menacing utterance rooted itself in the God-fearing southwest of England. It makes its first literary appearance in Thomas Hardy's 1886 novel, The Mayor of Casterbridge, *which is set in Dorset, but it is Cornwall where it is first recorded as having been used in real life – and to devastating effect.*

In the 17ᵗʰ century, Sir Cloudesley Shovell was England's most celebrated naval man. A veteran of many fierce actions, including the battles of Solebay, Texel, Bantry Bay, Barfleur and, most successfully of all, the capture of Gibraltar in 1704, he had, by 1707, been promoted to Admiral of the Fleet, the highest possible rank in the Royal Navy. However, Shovell had not become a hero of the seas because of his sweet and retiring nature. A hard man and a strict disciplinarian, he was as feared by his own men as he was by the enemy. That year, having made a significant attack on the base of the French fleet at Toulon, he was heading home with a number of warships. Approaching England from the southwest, stormy weather drove Shovell close to the Scilly Isles. This alarmed a Scilly native, a young seaman on board Shovell's flagship, HMS Association. He warned the admiral that they were headed for the dangerous Gilstone Reef. Shovell was so outraged to be upbraided in this way that he sentenced the hapless sailor to death for mutiny. As the noose was placed around the stunned young man's neck, he was given the opportunity to speak his last words – instead, he recited Psalm 109, all the while staring his commander full in the face.

Shovell is not said to have reacted well to this, nor to the fact that the body of the hanged man was later wrapped in his hammock, weighted with shot and thrown overboard, only to re-emerge in the storm and apparently follow the Association, tossing unnaturally from wave to wave in the vessel's wake.

A short while later, Shovell's flagship and four of the other warships in the flotilla ran aground on the reef. The wild seas then dashed them to pieces. A fortunate few made it ashore, but at least 2,000 men died, which still makes it the worst disaster in British maritime history. Ironically, Shovell was washed up alive at Porthellick Cove on the shore of St Mary's Isle, but here his luck really ran out. He was found by an elderly woman – a reviled hag suspected by her fellow islanders of being a witch and a wrecker. Gleefully, she ignored the injured man's pleas, and chopped his fingers off to get at his rings, before burying him alive on the beach. His body was discovered a few days later, but the alleged cause of his death was only made public some 30 years afterwards, when the old woman confessed to her crime while lying on her own deathbed.

Naturally, the enquiry following the catastrophe gave no credence to the alleged use of the Cursing Psalm, choosing to blame a navigational error instead. They likewise ignored any stories about murderous old women, deciding that Shovell drowned while attempting to get ashore in a lifeboat, which was wrecked before he made it to safety.

As is often the case, we can draw no firm conclusions. Shovell was told that he was about to die, and die he duly did. But the dispute in the first place had concerned the course his ship was taking, and if the 'mutinous' seaman had feared they were sailing towards disaster, that was exactly the outcome without there being any necessity for magic or mystery.

A BEAST BY ANY OTHER NAME

Adrian Cole

Where there's a mine or a hole in the ground
That's where I'm heading for that's where I'm bound

Taken from the song 'Cousin Jack'
written by Steve Knightley
And recorded by Show of Hands

Amanda Beresford-Ellis allowed the teapot to simmer and, satisfied that the brew would be exactly as she and Derrick liked it, lifted the tray with her best china tea cups, milk jug and sugar dish, and walked steadily through the French windows and out on to the terrace. She set the tray down on the wrought iron table, brushed a stray wisp of hair back behind her ear and looked across at the immaculate gardens that dropped away from the splendid house in waves of precisely cut green lawns between the hydrangeas and dwarf rhododendrons. It was, she reflected, a beautiful day.

Across the deeply wooded valley she could see a dozen chimney stacks and old mine workings, the nearest of them towering over the forest, others receding into the distance to the upward sweep of Bodmin Moor, dotting its slopes in the unique beauty that characterised the county. There were few sounds to disturb the humid air, the bulk of the village being over a mile away and its one main road cut off from the house by the massed, protective ranks of the trees.

Amanda smiled wryly. Derrick was, as usual, immersed in the gardening. They had a gardener, befitting their status. Their considerable wealth allowed them to indulge themselves in whatever they desired in life. Derrick and his colleagues were successful on a global scale, ironically in a field that had once prospered here, but which was now so colourfully represented by those derelict stacks – mining. Of course, Amanda knew, Derrick could have retired fully years ago, but he liked to keep his hand in. However, he gave himself time to pander to his other love – his gardens.

Another wry smile. Yes, his other love was his gardens. Oh, she was a part of his life, as she had been for the twenty-five years they'd been married, with a significant inheritance of her own, but at forty-eight she had long since abandoned any illusions about their relationship. She liked to think she was still an attractive woman – and she'd had a few admiring glances – but Derrick's work took him to the far end of the world. She couldn't compete with the temptations his success undoubtedly put in front of him. Still, their way of life suited them and they yet maintained a few of their little rituals. Tea on the terrace was one of them.

She went to the edge of the paved area and shielded her eyes from the almost overpowering sunlight, looking down into the various patches of dappled light among the trees. Derrick wasn't in view, so she called him a few times. It normally brought him puffing up the slope, grinning and perspiring, his hands soiled. He did like digging in the ground, whether it was with his hands or supervising the machinery that had built his empire.

'Where on earth are you?' she called.

She made her way carefully down the paved steps. A rush of wings startled her, but it was only a disturbed pigeon, making for distant branches. In the shadows it was no less humid, the air almost stifling. Amanda reached a second, narrower terrace. From here the land dropped a little more dramatically down to the border with the forest and the river, where she rarely ventured. It was too much of a test for her knees. There was still no sign of Derrick. She did, however, see one or two of his implements, a fork and a pair of shears. They were lying in the grass.

She called again, her voice muffled by the verdant barrier. She went to the tools and saw, not far away, his old pullover. It was full of holes and should have been thrown out for the dustmen ages ago, but it was his gardening uniform, so she indulged him and let him wear it. Obviously he had found it too hot today.

Something about the way it had been tossed aside disturbed her.

She picked it up. Part of it was shredded, as if he'd caught it on barbed wire. There was none hereabouts, though – the borders were all dry stone walls. Curious. She moved on towards the boundary. There were sounds in the forest, but she didn't recognise them. Animals, perhaps. She knew there were deer hereabouts.

Beside the low wall she saw – surely not – a shoe. She went to it and drew back with a gasp, as if the air was suddenly too much for her. It was an old, laced brogue, one of Derrick's. He always wore the pair for garden work, as with his pullover. The lace had been pulled out of it, the leather torn, neatly sliced down the back to the heel, as if, God forbid, by a knife, or something very sharp.

She leaned on the wall, not daring to touch the shoe.

Her hand felt suddenly sticky. Recoiling, she stared at her fingers. Even in the shadow, she knew it was blood. It had spilled on top of the wall like paint. Derrick must have had an accident. She called out again, her voice more desperate. She wanted to climb over the wall, but she wasn't nimble enough. She put her hands on it, avoiding the smears of blood, some of them horrifyingly thick, and leaned as far out as she could.

The wall dropped a few feet further on the other side, down into a well of congealed leaves. There was something there. It must be a small branch, she thought. The forest floor was a jumble of them, poking up like the broken spars of ships, hung with moss and ivy. As she studied the object, she knew it was no branch. She could smell more blood. An animal had died here, possibly having been attacked – savaged – by foxes. They were common here, the curse of the farmers, who counted their losses in chickens.

As Amanda studied the carcass, light shifted among the trees and splotched the foot of the wall. As it did, it revealed more of the branch-like object. It was an arm, badly cut, dark with blood. Amanda wanted to scream but her throat constricted and she staggered back, dragging air into her lungs.

She had found her husband, or at least a part of him.

Cranlow hunched over his pint, watching the rain daubing the pub window, blurring the view of the moorland in the middle distance. It had been a forgettable summer, with so many wet days and so few dry, hot ones. Last summer's heat wave was long forgotten, a time when, on reflection, the sunshine seemed endless. Cranlow felt clammy, the air turgid, building to another thunderstorm. Much more of this and he might even throw in the towel and go back to London. He wasn't getting far with the project anyway. Nothing new to add to the records that could make his proposed book stand out from the others already written on his subject.

The Black Beast Killing.

Good enough title. Good enough subject, but it would need a new twist to make it sell well. Cummings and that other hack, Swarton, had already capitalised on the incidents of two years ago, culminating in the death of Derrick Treskellion. The first – and probably last – victim of the huge cat known as the Beast of Bodmin.

A figure emerged out of the pub's grey atmosphere and stood opposite him. It was a tall man with a thick mop of black hair and the swarthy face of someone who spent most of the year outdoors. His clothes were coarse, those of a man who worked the land, a farmer maybe, the hands tanned and scarred.

'Mr Cranlow?' he said, his voice low, almost an animal growl. 'I'm Jack Harrower.' His expression may have been a smile. 'I know why you're here. Treskellion's death. You're the third writer who's been here since he died. I see they turned their research into books.' He had an accent, but it was very mild, as if he were not necessarily a Cornishman.

'You've read them?'

'Sure. They were mining for sensationalism. I expect their readers wanted it. As far as they were concerned, the big cat was responsible and they made the most of it. Sold a lot of books, I think.'

'They did.'

'So why write a new one?' Harrower's oddly crystalline eyes fixed on Cranlow, a hawk studying movement in long grass.

'I've written about nature's … *anomalies* before. It's a sort of series. My publisher thinks there's still some mileage in the Beast. Is there?'

'Depends whether you can take the truth.'

Cranlow was puzzled, vaguely excited by the words. Was this the new angle he was looking for? 'I don't follow you.'

'Suppose I told you the Beast didn't kill Treskellion? Suppose he was murdered.'

Cranlow sat back, sipping his beer thoughtfully, wondering if this guy was a crank. Some of the locals weren't so daft that they couldn't try to capitalise on the legends and folklore of the area.

'The police looked long and hard at the case,' said Cranlow. 'They concluded that Treskellion was killed by a panther, the one they subsequently trapped in a mine and killed. They found enough bits of Treskellion inside its gut to convince them it was the killer. The last thing anyone wanted to admit was that a big cat had got loose and killed someone. The evidence stacked up, though. They were relieved to catch it quickly.'

Harrower nodded. 'The experts – naturalists and the like – said a big cat could have done it.'

'Just now you suggested the man was murdered.'

Harrower pulled an envelope out of his pocket and slid a news cutting from it. He pushed it across the table to Cranlow. It was an extract from a local paper, the *Western Morning News*, dated several months after the Beast had been killed. The article concerned a sea captain called Manolo Herrera, a Brazilian. He'd been knifed in a brawl in the nearby port of Falmouth, where his ship had been berthed. Apparently it was a regular haunt of the captain, where he unloaded and loaded various cargoes. The death had been a leading item in the media for over a month, even making the national news, but the killer had never been convicted.

'I remember it,' said Cranlow. 'The police assumed it was either one of Herrera's crew, or a rival ship. There were none docked at the time. And all Herrera's men had alibis, most of them not in Falmouth that night.'

'It was an outside job,' said Harrower, with confident finality. 'Very professional. Far too slick for the authorities.'

'So what's this got to do with the Beast?'

'Herrera made his money through trafficking. Not white slavery. He acquired animals. You're aware that there's a big black market trade in wildlife of one kind or another.'

'Sure.'

'He was commissioned to bring in something very special. From his own native South America. Wouldn't have been difficult.' Harrower took the newspaper article and slipped it back into its envelope. 'His ship was registered under the ownership of the Treskellion Corporation. Herrera was not averse to doing a few dirty little jobs for his immediate boss, a man called Ransome. And Herrera brought him a black panther, fully grown. It would have been known to very few – the creature would have been drugged and crated. Strictly illegal to bring such a beast into the country.'

Cranlow felt a surge of excitement. This really was the meat of a potential story.

'Later,' Harrower went on, 'Herrera was killed, silenced. Ransome had some very dubious contacts and had risen in the ranks of Treskellion's mining empire. He could afford to arrange such a professional killing. Herrera's secret died with him. No one of any importance knew about the panther. Ransome kept it in an old mine, Wheal Mary, on land that Treskellion owned.'

Something about the name 'Ransome' was ringing a distant bell in Cranlow's mind. Hadn't he married Treskellion's widow? In one stroke he'd gone from being a minor employee to a major shareholder in the company, and enormously wealthy with it.

'So what happened?' said Cranlow.

'Ransome was ambitious. He wanted to re-open some of the Cornish mines. Reckoned he'd found some very big lodes that could be worked at a huge profit. It's an old Cornish dream. Treskellion wasn't persuaded and wouldn't put up the money. Why should he? He had a fabulous empire, worth millions. Ransome wouldn't let it go. It was his opportunity to make his own fortune.'

'So he had Treskellion killed? Using the panther?' It seemed a bit far-fetched, Cranlow thought. Maybe this guy was trying to sucker him in – there'd be a price.

'Indirectly. Treskellion was murdered, probably by Ransome himself. In Wheal Mary mine. Ransome had the death made to look like an animal killing. He fed some of the body to the panther. Created a highly plausible trail. Very clever. Everything pointed to the big cat. Looked like it had snatched Treskellion while he was gardening, tore bits off him and dragged him back to the mine. Ransome made sure the police found the trail – and the cat. It was trapped and killed. You know the rest. And Ransome followed it up by courting Amanda Treskellion. Once he'd married her, he became a partner in the company. He's made, of course. But he still wants to exploit the new lodes he's found. Greed rules him.'

Cranlow sat back, regarding the strange man opposite him. It was a good story, but if he tried to use it as it stood, he'd be risking his career. He had a couple of very good contacts at Scotland Yard, but he knew from previous experience he couldn't go to them without some kind of proof. It would be nigh on impossible to trace the illegal entry of the panther, much less demonstrate that Ransome had either killed Treskellion, or had had him killed. Cranlow's contacts wouldn't want sending on a wild goose chase, least of all down here in the middle of nowhere.

'You need to talk to Mrs Ransome, as she is now,' said Harrower. 'She and her new husband still live at the same house. She spoke to the other two writers. She believes her former husband was killed by the big cat. Judging by their books, the two writers swallowed the whole pack of lies. They made a meal of it.'

'As you rightly said, they wrote the version the public wanted.'

'So what version will you write?'

Cranlow grinned. 'I need something fresh. But I can't risk anything libellous.'

'You need to see Wheal Mary mine. Ransome has it well sealed off. No one gets in there. If you can do that, you might find the proof you need.' Harrower rose slowly, nodding, as if to indicate the meeting was at an end. Moments later he had left.

Cranlow finished his pint and fetched another. Maybe he would try and visit Amanda Treskellion. He had nothing else to work with.

It proved relatively easy to arrange a meeting with the former Mrs Treskellion. On the telephone she was surprisingly cooperative and invited Cranlow to the house a few days later. Apparently her husband was out of the county on business and she was happy to relieve some of the day-to-day monotony of her life.

Cranlow sat with her in the large sitting room, with its panoramic view of the gardens, forest and distant moorlands, although the rain continued to drive across it from the Celtic Sea lying to the north. It was a bleak, inhospitable terrain. Cranlow could perfectly understand how the big cat legends had arisen.

He found Amanda Ransome to be an attractive woman, very well spoken, although recent events in her life had not treated her kindly. She looked stressed, her voice occasionally quavering as she went back over the events of the past.

'I suppose you think it a little odd that I'm prepared to talk about what happened,' she said. 'I haven't said a word about it since I spoke to your colleagues. I read both their books. A bit lurid for my taste, and there were a few exaggerations. But it is what happened. Derrick was a victim of that big cat. No one really understood how it came to be here.'

'Yes, what was the theory?' said Cranlow, making a show of bafflement.

'Oh, that there are several such creatures around the Moor, and probably beyond it in the forests. They must have been here for generations. There used to be zoos and things. Popular in Victorian times – possibly before that. Animals occasionally escaped. They must have been breeding. God knows, Mr Cranlow, there may be more of them still out there. We still get reports of sightings and from time to time people make a concerted effort to find them. So far, that panther is the only one ever caught. In some ways it's a shame they killed it. There wouldn't have been any malice in it. Just killing for food. I know that sounds horrible.'

'No, I think you're right. Do you think your husband – Mr Ransome – would allow me to have a look at the mine where it was killed? I'd love to take some pictures for my book. My work covers the whole of the Southwest and as many sightings as I can fit in. It's a photographic study as much as a narrative one. A new angle.'

'I don't know. Wheal Mary is sealed up. It's a sort of tomb. It's, well, sacrosanct. I don't think –' She stopped, suddenly aware of something outside the room. 'Did I hear another car? That's unusual.' She got up and went slowly, almost cautiously to the door.

Cranlow rose, aware of his hostess's sudden unease. Maybe he'd prodded a nerve.

'Excuse me a moment,' she said and left him alone. He heard voices followed by a pause. After a prolonged and uneasy pause, the door swung open. Cranlow recognised the man who entered. Alec Ransome was tall and angular, his face pinched, his eyes narrow, giving his expression an unfortunately unfriendly mien. When those eyes lit on Cranlow, the man smiled, but Cranlow thought it mirthless, contrived.

'You must be the journalist,' said Ransome. He extended his hand and Cranlow shook it, though there was no warmth in the gesture. 'I'm Ransome. Sorry to interrupt your conversation with my wife, but I got back earlier than planned.'

'Not at all. She's been very helpful. I realise these things can be intrusive. You've been through this before.'

'She tells me you'd like to photograph the mine where Treskellion died?'

Cranlow nodded, realising now that Amanda wasn't going to return, his interview with her terminated. Ransome had evidently told her to make herself scarce. He walked over to the drinks cabinet and fiddled with a brandy bottle, pouring two generous hits.

'Drink? Go on, it won't kill you.' He pushed a glass at Cranlow, who took it with a muttered thanks.

'You want to go down into the mine?' said Ransome. 'It's dangerous. I've started work in several of the old workings, but Wheal Mary is worked out. Made sense to shut it off altogether.'

Ransome gestured for him to sit and they both did so. Cranlow drank the brandy and put the glass down on a small table. Ransome warmed his own glass in his hands, rolling it slowly before setting it down. Cranlow noticed that he hadn't actually taken a sip himself. He seemed to have put the drink from his mind.

'Did you see the panther?' Cranlow asked. 'Were there any pictures of it, apart from the ones in the press?'

'I saw its carcass, briefly. And no, there were no other pictures. What they found in the mine was very unpleasant.'

'I can imagine. I –' Cranlow felt a slight wave of dizziness and put a hand on the arm of the chair to steady himself.

'It works very quickly,' said Ransome. 'Quite painless.'

Cranlow frowned at the words. He stared at the empty brandy glass, feeling his muscles tightening, as if they were slowly freezing, locking rigid. Jesus, had he been *drugged*?

Ransome leaned forward. 'I have a few questions for you, Mr Cranlow. Tell me about your friends in London. What do they know?'

Cranlow felt the words burrow into his head like worms, and realised he was not going to be able to resist answering. 'I don't understand. I – I ... who do you mean?'

'I've long ears. I was tipped off that you'd inveigled your way to an interview with my wife. My early return is no accident. I've been doing some research of my own. I understand that you sometimes work with Scotland Yard. Digging through the dirt for them. You scratch their back, so to speak. You've done pretty well out of it. Given exclusive rights to some of their cases. Nice work if you can get it. So what do they know about Derrick Treskellion's death?

What have you told them?'

Cranlow tried to shake his head but the drug already had too strong a grip. 'Nothing. They don't know I'm here.'

'Well, that's good to know. And what do *you* know?'

Cranlow could feel the words being dragged out of him and fought hard to contain them, but the drug was far too strong for him. 'I – you – murdered Treskellion. Faked his killing. Made it look like the work of the panther –'

Ransome sat back, seemingly very calm, as if Cranlow's words were ridiculous. 'I see. That's a very rash statement. Have you shared it with anyone?'

'No. Only the fellow I met in the pub. Called himself Jack Harrower. Local man.'

Ransome scowled. 'Never heard of him. Describe him.' He took a small pad and a pen from inside his jacket and scribbled down a few notes as Cranlow blurted out the details of his meeting with Harrower.

Cranlow was finding it increasingly hard to keep his eyes open. His head slumped forward and he made a huge effort to lift it.

'Feeling sleepy?' said Ransome. 'Just let yourself go. You'll get your wish. I'll take you into that mine. But it is dangerous. I did warn you.'

Cranlow came awake as though he were bobbing up to the surface of a pool. He shook himself, his vision blurred, sensation gradually returning to his limbs. It took a few moments to realise he was sitting at the wheel of his car. Outside, it was pitch dark, thin rain spattering the windows. He peered around, but couldn't make out where he was. He appeared to be in a narrow lane, with tall hedgerows looming over him on both sides.

Behind him, something stirred on the back seat. He made to turn, but cold metal pushed into his neck. He realised, horrified, that it was a handgun.

'Nice and easy, Mr Cranlow,' growled a voice he didn't recognise, although the accent was Midland. He could only assume it was one of Ransome's thugs. 'You do the driving. Switch on and I'll direct you.'

'Where are we?'

'Mr Ransome said you wanted to visit a certain mine. My buddy and I will take you. Switch on and drive slowly. Or we can do this the hard way. In the end, it won't matter.'

Cranlow was frantically trying to weigh things up, but he knew he had little choice other than to do as he was instructed. He switched on the engine and eased the car into gear. Its headlights picked out the winding lane, descending into a valley. The rain intensified, a heavy shower, typical of this dire summer.

He drove for perhaps two miles, surrounded now by trees, the darkness smothering almost everything. The lane debouched into a small clearing. Cranlow pulled up. There was a tilted sign among the bushes, its legend, WHEAL MARY MINE, barely legible. He had no time to study the surroundings. Something stung his neck and he understood too late that a needle had been slipped into him.

When he came round he was in partial darkness. The air was thick, a stifling silence pressing down on him. His instincts warned him that he was underground. There were hurricane lamps near at hand, hung from thick beams. By their wavering glow he could see that he was in a mine, its walls supported by vertical wooden planks, its ceiling shored up by other, fat beams.

His hands were tied very tightly, securing him to one of the beams. He knew he had no chance of freeing himself. He thought of yelling for help, but he guessed that no one would be anywhere near. This mine would be miles from the beaten track.

'You're awake,' said a voice so close to his ear that he started.

He tried to speak, but his throat was clogged with fear.

Ransome stepped into view. 'You wanted to see the mine, Mr Cranlow. This is it. You're standing in the very place where they found the remains of Derrick Treskellion.'

'Why are you doing this?' Cranlow managed to blurt.

Ransome laughed. 'You think I want your police friends back here? No, it will be easier to dispose of you altogether. I've checked you out, Mr Cranlow. Bit of a loner, aren't you? Divorced, no kids, small circle of drinking buddies in London. Not much of a life. Who's going to miss you? They'll mourn you for a week or so. Sorry victim of a landslide. My men have been preparing it for you, down in the deeper shafts.

'Unfortunately I don't have another big cat to do the job for me. Besides, I rather think that two such killings would arouse suspicion. However, this is a dangerous mine. Anyone entering it would be taking a huge risk. This place is peppered with shafts. Where you're going, no one will find you. You have made it rather easy for me.'

'How do you mean?' Cranlow could feel a cold sweep of panic rushing along his veins, the welling of real terror.

'Well, the facts will be there for the police. Your insatiable curiosity brought you here. People in the local villages know that you've been snooping around. My wife knows that you were interested in visiting Wheal Mary. She warned you it was dangerous. As did I. Yet you persisted in coming here and breaking in. That's what it will look like. The police will find your car outside. Nothing to suggest that anyone was with you – my men are very thorough at tidying up, specialists. They won't have been seen, not at night. As for you, well, your probing about set off a cave-in. Thousands of tons of rock came down, closing off the mine forever. Any attempt to find your body will be doomed to failure. As I said, those shafts are very, very deep. And there are a lot of them. The authorities haven't the resources for detailed searches.'

'They'll want to talk to you. They'll know you spoke to me –'

Ransome shook his head. 'No. I'll be back in the Midlands in no time. No one will know I've been here. I've a dozen alibis up there.'

Cranlow knew the situation was hopeless. 'You don't have to do this. I can go back, forget about the whole thing.'

'I don't like loose ends, Mr Cranlow. I'm sorry.'

Ransome glanced at his watch, as though waiting for a given moment to begin his final act. As he did so, there was a shout from further up the mine. Torchlight probed the chamber and a figure emerged. Cranlow barely made out the form of a well-built man in dark clothing and assumed this was one of the thugs who'd brought him here.

'Crane, what's wrong?' said Ransome, his voice lifted above a whisper by the acoustics.

The man's face gleamed in the torch-glow. He looked uneasy. 'There's someone out there,' he said. 'Joe's dealing with it.'

Ransome swore crudely. 'You mean he's been seen?'

Before either of them could go back up the tunnel, another figure appeared. It looked to Cranlow to be a duplicate of the first. The man staggered, reaching out as if to steady himself on the nearest beam. He looked about ready to collapse.

'What the hell's going on?' snapped Ransome.

The man called Crane had slipped a gun from his jacket.

Ransome held him back. 'Don't use it!' he warned. 'Not down here. You'll bring the roof in.'

They both went over to the other man cautiously. He was on his knees. He raised his head, trying to speak. His clothes were torn, as if he had been in a fight. Cranlow could see by the garish light that the man's throat was dark with blood, bubbling as his breath escaped through a puncture.

'Who did this?' snarled Ransome.

The man fell forward and Crane bent down to him, trying to get him up. He didn't seem able to move him.

'Is he all right?' said Ransome, but he knew the fallen man was dead. He swore again and motioned for Crane to investigate the tunnel leading back to the surface. Crane paused briefly, gun aimed into the wavering darkness.

'Keep out of sight,' said Ransome. 'I'll see to Cranlow.' He went back into the chamber.

Cranlow was staring at him, his terror complete.

Ransome reached inside his jacket and slid out a syringe. He paused before slipping something else from his waistband. The light from the lamps flashed on it briefly, a knife, threat of pain and much worse. Ransome held back.

Cranlow knew that if he was killed now, Ransome would have to be certain of evading discovery. He needed Crane to deal with the interference before he dare use the knife.

Ransome turned. The tunnel was silent, dark. No torchlight – no light at all back there. 'Crane. Crane!' he called.

There were muffled sounds – something other than voices. The darkness seemed to deepen, black as pitch. The hurricane lamps in the chamber wavered as if a sudden strong draught of air had cuffed them.

Ransome gripped his knife tightly, sweat smearing his face. Someone was coming out of that coagulated darkness and it wasn't Crane.

Cranlow recognised the man as he stepped into the light. It was Jack Harrower. He carried no weapons of his own, hands held loosely at his side, his cool gaze taking in the scene in the chamber.

'What's going on out there?' snarled Ransome, holding out his knife uneasily. His face was bathed in sweat.

Harrower seemed unduly calm. 'All your deceits and twisted plans are coming to an end, Mr Ransome,' he said. 'This is a fitting place for that. This is where you killed Dennis Treskellion. You had a bullet put into his head. Then you dressed up his death and made it look like it was the panther. Got away with it, too. The Black Beast of Bodmin. Always cursed, always hunted. Nowadays, anyone as much as gets a glimpse of a black cat, however big or small, they raise the alarm. The creatures of the land aren't safe. Persecuted. Driven deeper into the forests and the mines. The legacy of your deceit.

'Same way the miners were pushed out, once the profits went elsewhere. You had this place closed up, Mr Ransome and no one was ever likely to want to re-open it. I knew that you wouldn't be able to resist bringing Mr Cranlow here, though, once you knew he was on to you. It was the only way I could lure you out.'

'You're the one who rang me about Cranlow meeting my wife –'

Harrower nodded. 'I'm sorry, Mr Cranlow, that I used you as bait.'

Ransome had been slowly moving back as Harrower spoke. He was no more than feet from Cranlow. 'You can't prove a damn thing,' he told Harrower. He held out the blade, inches from Cranlow's exposed neck. 'Now – I suggest you leave, if you want this man to survive. I mean it. I'll kill him.'

Around the walls of the chamber, a sudden, soft creaking, not unlike the sounds made by an old sailing ship at sea, stirred the timbers. Within the earth, something beat out a muffled, drum-like rhythm, as though someone further away was trying to communicate.

Ransome's head cocked as he listened.

'A warning from the tommyknockers,' said Harrower.

Cranlow knew the folklore, and how the spirits of the mine were supposed to warn miners of danger, or in some cases, work mischief.

Ransome grimaced. If he knew about such things, he was dismissive of them.

Something else shifted in the tunnel behind Harrower. There was a sound like low thunder. Ransome and Cranlow gasped simultaneously as they realised what it was: a growl, deep-throated and full of menace.

Harrower stepped easily aside. A shape padded into the chamber. Ransome's fingers went numb; both the knife and syringe dropped at his feet. He was staring in horror at the creature limned in the lamplight. Beside him, Cranlow felt his body gripped in similar terror. Only Harrower remained calm, as if the shape so close to his side represented no threat to him. It could have been a pet hound.

Coming towards Ransome, silent as mist, was a black beast, perhaps a panther, perhaps something more. It seemed to be composed of the darkness, though energy began to pulse within it, solidifying it, as though the rhythm of that strange knocking gave it substance. The eyes, a deep feral yellow, fixed on Ransome and the mouth opened to reveal rows of pointed teeth. The creature snarled as if giving voice to its anger, its hatred. Dust trickled from the roof, loosened by the noise. The underground knocking became more insistent.

Ransome backed away but the huge beast followed him with deliberate, silent steps, its claws extending. Harrower said something unintelligible and the beast jerked forward at speed, streaming like a black fog across the chamber, crashing into Ransome and driving him hard against the far wall. Everywhere shook ominously. The beast's snarls reverberated through the tunnel, their volume threatening to bring everything down. The creature began to rip and claw its bloody way into Ransome, drowning his screams of agony in its triumphant rending of his body.

Cranlow, shivering with terror, hardly noticed Harrower at his side, using the fallen knife to slash his bonds, freeing him. Cranlow couldn't move, simply slumping into Harrower's arms like a huge doll.

Harrower put an arm around him and helped him to the tunnel, ignoring the slaughter nearby. Cranlow's ashen face gazed up at his rescuer, as if trying to ask a dozen questions.

'It won't harm us,' said Harrower.

On their way up the tunnel, they passed Crane's body. Cranlow was thankful that he couldn't see its tattered ruin clearly. He almost blacked out more than once before Harrower got him outside. The rain drove down steadily, but for once Cranlow was glad of it.

Harrower got him to the car and opened the door to the driving seat. He bundled Cranlow inside.

'When you're ready, Mr Cranlow, drive yourself back to the village. Get a good night's sleep. Don't worry about the mine and what's in it. I'll see to that.'

'The beast –'

Harrower smiled. 'Beast? No, just a landslide, Mr Cranlow. In this weather, the mines tend to flood. Landslides happen all the time. No one's going to look for Ransome and his men. They're in the Midlands, aren't they?'

Cranlow slept until noon. He had a pot of coffee sent up to his room and set to work making notes on his laptop and checking out as many references to the old mines as he could digest in one sitting on the internet. By the time he sat down to his evening meal, he'd re-thought his whole strategy for the book. A novel, that's what he'd write. Give his imagination a run.

'Rain's let up at last,' said the waitress, smiling. 'Bad storm last night.'

He nodded, looking out at the distant moors. In the sunlight, they had an altogether different aspect, almost inviting.

Later he entered the pub where he'd first met Harrower. At the bar he ordered a beer.

'Hell of a night,' said the landlord, a former Londoner. 'Enough rain fell to last a month or two. It's played hell with trade this year.'

They exchanged a few anecdotes about the city, enjoying a shared past, familiar distant settings.

'Tell me,' said Cranlow, 'Do you know where I can find the guy I was talking to the other day? You probably saw me talking to him. He's called Jack Harrower. Local man.'

'I remember you sitting over there, by the window. You were on your own, though.'

'You didn't see anyone?'

'No, but I'll ask some of the regulars. Jack Harrower? Hang on.' The landlord spoke to some of the small groups in the bar. Cranlow went to the same table where he'd sat with Harrower. There were a number of photos on the wall, pictures of old mines, local scenery.

'No one saw your Jack Harrower,' said the landlord. 'But Caleb here knows something.'

The man beside him, a farmer by the look of him, nodded to Cranlow. 'You lookin' fer Jack Harrower? You'm a bit late, boy.'

Cranlow sensed something of a mystery here.

The man tapped one of the framed photos. 'We've not had any Harrowers in the village since the heyday of the mines. There's a family over the border, up near Launceston, but that's a fair ways off.'

Cranlow studied the photo. It was old and faded, but the faces of the group of miners it depicted were still clear. One in particular stood out. He felt a thrill of recognition – it was the man he'd met here in this pub.

'That's him,' Caleb said. 'Jack Harrower.'

There was no mistaking that crystalline gaze, which seemed to fix him from within the picture, almost alive.

Caleb and the landlord exchanged mildly amused glances. 'Well, no,' said Caleb. 'Not seen him hereabouts. Sorry I can't help.'

Cranlow shrugged. Maybe it was better that he let things lie. Wheal Mary Mine would be closed up again now, its secrets – its bodies – hidden where they'd never be found. Cranlow saw an inscription in the bottom right hand corner of the photo. It was the name of the mine, another of the local ones. And there was a date. He felt the echoes of that deep dread he'd suffered down in the bowels of the earth as the implications hit him.

1890.

OF THE DEMON, TREGEAGLE

One of the strangest legends of old Cornwall is that of the demon, Tregeagle, a powerful but cursed being whose howls and screams have been heard all along the peninsula from the wild, grassy ridges of Bodmin Moor to the secret, rocky coves at Land's End.

Tregeagle doesn't just lament, or so the folk-tales tell us; he also has the power to raise storms and wreck ships, and inland to manifest as a ghastly, ghostly being whose sole purpose appears to be to torment the local population in death as much as he did during life – because though there is no doubt that Tregeagle fully deserves his demonic classification, at one time he lived on Earth as a normal human being.

An ordinary man somehow morphing into a demon is a rare event in world mythology, let alone in Cornish, but to make this myth even more curious is the kernel of truth at its heart. Because, amazing though it may seem, Jan Tregeagle was a real historical person.

A noted landowner, magistrate and steward for the Duchy of Cornwall sometime in the early or mid-17th century, Tregeagle was notorious for his ruthless, treacherous and lustful nature. Stories often grow with the telling of course, and though many additional tales have now been added to the roster to paint him as one of the worst villains in history – a man who stole and cheated at every opportunity, who terrorised widows and orphans, who was thoroughly corrupt and open to all forms of bribery, who was a drunkard and a blasphemer, who hunted nubile village girls across the moors with a pack of hounds specially trained to sniff out virgins, and even who supposedly made a Faustian pact with the Devil in order to enjoy unlimited wealth – his main offence, at least the one that history actually records, is that he forged paperwork in order to secure himself extra tracts of farmland.

This may not be the worst crime a person could be accused of, but it was the only one Tregeagle was ever taken to court for. Ironically and bizarrely, the case was heard after his death – but even so, Tregeagle allegedly appeared to give evidence.

According to the written accounts, the recently departed landowner was summoned to a courtroom – which particular courtroom history doesn't specify – and despite wild laughter in the public gallery when his name was called, a terrible shape slowly manifested on the witness stand. It was indeed Jan Tregeagle, but a travesty of the hearty village squire he had once been: ragged, undernourished and chained, a sure sign that since death he had been a prisoner in Hell. Eager to make restitution, the desperate spirit confessed to all his sins and enabled the court to reach a fair judgement on the case in front of it. In return, the presiding magistrate, not wishing to despatch the doleful form back to the Inferno, refused to release Tregeagle and instead imposed a difficult duty that was likely to keep him busy on Earth until the end of time. He was instructed to empty Dozmary Pool on Bodmin Moor with a perforated limpet shell. The Pool, which was actually a lake, was believed to be bottomless, and so that was expected to be a never-ending task.

However, not all parties were happy with the arrangement.

According to the story, Satan, enraged at having been thwarted, sent a pack of hell-hounds to drag Tregeagle back, and though they could not touch him as long as he had duties to discharge, they kept a close eye on him. At the same time, Tregeagle himself – still a wily operator – looked for chances to escape. When, several decades later, a monstrous storm briefly emptied the lake, it was his opportunity to flee. By all accounts, this was a night of terror for Cornish folk, the demonic dogs pursuing the damned soul across the storm-wracked skies, their furious cries mingling with the shrieks of the wind. Tregeagle finally sought refuge in the chapel of St Michael in the village of Roche, but an evil spirit himself, he could not enter and was trapped half way through a window. The devilish pack then tore at him from behind, causing such a commotion that the entire neighbourhood fled and the church walls cracked. At length, a team of clerics gathered and, in a challenging ritual, re-bound Tregeagle and inflicted a new punishment on him. This time, he was despatched to the beach at Padstow, where he had to weave ropes from sand, another task expected to last him all eternity.

Again though, Tregeagle was able to outwit his captors. One particularly cold night, the sands froze and with a little straw and judicious applications of seawater brought from the shoreline in a kettle, he was able to create actual ropes. The chase was on once more, the evil soul battling with the hellish hounds all across Cornwall's winter skies. This time, it took prayers to St Petroc to bring Tregeagle to heel, and for his next task he was ordered to transport all the sands from Berepper beach on the Lizard peninsula right across the Loe estuary to Porthleven. Again, it was impossible to complete this work, as the tide would constantly replace the sand, but a by-product of Tregeagle's herculean effort was the slow but steady emergence of the so-called Loe Bar, a sand and shingle bank which gradually separated the harbour from the sea. Local fishing-folk, seeing their livelihoods endangered, begged for the spirit to be banished back to Hell, but still the orders of the court were respected – at least a century after judgement, by now – and Tregeagle was this time exorcised to Land's End, where he still currently resides, endlessly shovelling the sands from Porthcurno Cove into Mill Bay.

His screams of rage can often be heard in the colossal storms that batter that remote headland, and allegedly, on particularly fearsome nights, a spectral form has been sighted digging along the sea's edge. But so isolated is this place that even Tregeagle's presence is at last deemed to be tolerable.

So goes the popular tale, and as earlier stated, it has grown considerably with the telling.

During the course of his many travails, his wild flights and furious battles with saints and devils alike, Tregeagle – soon regarded as a full-blown demon rather than the shade of an evil man – became the most well-known disturber of the peace in all of Cornish folklore. But he was as feared as he was reviled, especially in the districts with which he was closely associated, his wrath said to raise such tempests that all manner of destruction could result.

Modern interpretations hold that Tregeagle, though he actually existed in antiquity as a known felon, was later transformed through Christian fable into an embodiment of the elements that sweep the exposed lands of Cornwall, a living-dead incarnation of the intense Atlantic storm, a role once played by Celtic gods like Taranis and Mannan mac Lir.

Not bad company to be in, though Tregeagle, one suspects, would probably trade it for his freedom.

MOON BLOOD-RED, TIDE TURNING

Mark Samuels

Of course what took place back then wouldn't have seemed so disturbing had I not encountered her again just over two decades later. At that earlier time, you must realise, there was more of the farcical than the horrible in what transpired, or so I supposed.

I was only twenty-four, and when I think of myself as I was then, I realise how much of a stranger that younger man appears to me now. The memory of his hopes, his dreams, his view of life, all fill me with contempt. He would hate this future self, and regard me as a usurper.

But there are worse fates than regret.

And I believe I discovered one of them.

After a handful of jobs, none of which I particularly enjoyed and each lasting less than a year, I found myself employed at a small publishing house in Fitzrovia, close to its local landmark, the British Telecom Tower. The business specialised in what are termed 'acting editions', which are stage plays that are designed for the use of actors rather than the general reader. The only real difference is that these editions usually contain the likes of a furniture and property list, a lighting plot, and an effects plot, all printed after the play text itself and which are there to assist the director and the stage crew. My activities at this firm were in the department that licensed performance rights to companies who wished to mount productions of our titles, and for some reason (the job had little interest for me), I stayed on.

Perhaps I remained because the other staff were invariably interesting, coming from a theatrical background, and there was a high turnover of them. Aside from the board of directors, who had been there for decades, almost everyone else came and went within a few months. As you might imagine, a large proportion were 'resting' actors, and as soon as a new role came up they handed in their notice and disappeared. Some returned and then left again, some didn't, though I have to confess that only one or two out of the multitude ever achieved anything close to prominence in the theatrical world.

One of these 'resting' actors employed by the publishers was a young woman whom I shall call 'Celia Waters'. It is not her real name, naturally, but that detail is of no consequence.

We struck up an acquaintance of sorts. It was easy to do so, since the business was quite generous in subsidising its staff to see performances of new plays that might be suitable for its publishing list. Often too, of course, free tickets were provided to the firm by the playwright's agents. It was regarded as a staff perk I suppose, since their wages weren't exactly generous. I accompanied Celia Waters on two or three occasions to shows playing in London, sometimes just the two of us, sometimes with other staff members.

One time, after a long evening (a play I have forgotten and post-performance drinks at a pub I can't recall) I even ended up spending the night back at her flat in Shepherd's Bush. We didn't sleep together. I am not sure that either found the other sexually desirable. She was attractive in her own way, slim, petite, with long black hair and by no means without personal charm, but there was no chemistry between us.

And over breakfast at a nearby café the next morning she told me she was going to be leaving the publishing firm in a month to take up a part in a brief run of a new play being staged down in Cornwall.

She said it was being put on by a new repertory company run by a wealthy theatrical *auteur*.

I can't say that any of this was of great interest to me, and I asked in the spirit of polite enquiry, though I was genuinely curious, as to where it was going to be staged. There aren't exactly a large number of playhouses in Cornwall and the most likely venue had already suggested itself to me. I had a Cornish cousin with a cottage down in Sennen Cove whom I visited once or twice a year, located only a mile or so from Porthcurno, the site of the Minack Theatre. Moreover, I was due to visit him when Celia Waters would also be in the area.

'Is it the Minack Theatre?' I asked her.

'Why, yes it is,' she replied. 'Do you know it?'

This coincidence of our being in more or less exactly the same place at the same time gave an outside impetus to our continued association. Frankly, when she first told me she was leaving the publishing company I assumed our brief, unconsummated relationship would dissipate of its own accord, as they often tend to do with two people in their early to mid twenties, neither of whom wants commitment.

I promised that I would come and see her in the play while I was down there, and she was keen for me to do so, presumably with a view to the idea of its being reported on favourably and published by the firm. I didn't think there was much chance of that, since the business only really took on plays that benefited from a higher profile, but I didn't voice the thought.

Still, I asked her to tell me about it.

'Well,' she said, 'it's all rather a mystery really at this point. We have had some formulaic rehearsals for the last couple of weeks here in a space above a pub. It's all very ritualistic. But definitely cutting-edge and experimental.'

It sounded awful. Like something a group of students obsessed by Berkoff would try and put on.

Over the next few weeks I saw next to nothing of Celia Waters. We didn't work in the same department; she was in the showroom on the ground floor and I was up on the second floor in the licensing department anyway, but we exchanged pleasantries whenever our paths crossed. I felt as if we had already disengaged from one another.

One day she wasn't there at all. A director told me she had quit a week earlier than planned and had already gone down to Cornwall.

'Actresses, eh?' he said.

Back then even female actors themselves used the term.

I will admit that I didn't really feel anything much about her having left early and without telling me. My only worry was whether or not I was still obliged to keep my promise to go and see her in that play at the Minack. I knew she was primarily interested in my being there for her own reasons, to the benefit of the play itself, but I decided to delay the decision until I was down in Cornwall myself.

Perhaps the most gruelling thing about deepest Cornwall, if you are travelling from London, is the train journey itself. For some reason – and I had never shaken it off, despite several trips there – I had the feeling that it always took longer than one might reasonably expect from looking at a map. After four hours one gets to Exeter in Devon and from there one soon crosses the Tamar into Cornwall and imagines it can only be another ten or twenty minutes more to Penzance. It's not, it's another hour. And it's this last hour that's the most trying, because it seems so unexpected, as if the region itself extends time to fox outsiders. Of course one recognises it's an illusion, but it's no less disconcerting even when one admits the fact. My cousin had an apposite phrase he would often use in jest and whose use he solemnly advised me marked out a true Cornishman. It was, when asked to do a thing, that a Cornishman would reply that it would be attended to 'dreckly' which means not attended to directly at all, but rather in one's own good time. I suppose, too, that this warping of time was brought to mind most noticeably when one returned to London from Cornwall, because it then seemed that everyone and everything in the metropolis rushed around insanely to no useful purpose.

After two days spent at the cottage in Sennen Cove, occupying my time with walks along the beach, cycling along sunken lanes to little villages like Sancreed and drinking in coastal pubs where Cornish fishermen still grumbled darkly into their cider about 'English settlers', my thoughts were turned again by an outside agency to Celia Waters.

It was while drinking in the local pub, *The Old Success Inn*, I noticed someone had posted up a flyer on its noticeboard which advertised a play and its performance dates at the Minack. The thing was shoddily produced, being a black and white photocopied sheet of A5 paper with what looked like a still from one of those 1920s silent German Expressionist films at its centre. It was bordered with Celtic latticework. The cast were listed, amongst whom, was, of course, Celia Waters. And I now learnt the title of the play for the first time: *New Quests for Nothing*. The writer, director and producer was listed as one 'Doctor Prozess'.

The first night was this evening at 7:30 p.m.

I looked at my watch. It was just after five.

I ordered another scotch and soda, trying to make my mind up whether or not to honour my promise.

By 7:25 p.m. I was seated at the Minack Theatre, rather the worse for drink. I had stuck to scotch and soda, with only one beer in between, so as not to fill my bladder during the play and perhaps suffer the awkwardness of having to wander out mid-performance in search of the public conveniences. But I wasn't really used to drinking spirits and, one packet of crisps aside, the booze had worked on an empty stomach.

I had been to the Minack for the first time last year but the unique nature of it as the setting for a theatrical show impressed me just as much on this subsequent occasion. The venue is an amphitheatre carved into the side of a cliff with incredible views of the Atlantic stretching to the horizon. Huge gulls whirl and twist in the air currents, their cries echoing against the boom of the waves crashing on the rocks far below. And as the sun goes down one is hard pressed to keep one's attention on events on the platform stage right at the bottom of the tiered open seating.

I had plenty of room to myself, with only one other person on the same row, and he was some fifteen yards away. I counted around thirty people inside, dotted here and there, which made for an atmosphere very much like the venue being empty given its large capacity. There was no buzz of conversation from the patrons before the show began, no rustle of programmes being consulted, and no real sense of anticipation whatsoever.

The effects of the bracing sea air and the half hour walk to get from Sennen Cove to the Minack had finally begun to sober me up when the four actors entered the arena and began their performance.

They were all in formal black tie and tails, as if at a dinner party, both the two men and two women. It was very difficult to tell them apart. They were also all caked in white face-paint with dark circles marked around their eyes and with their scalps closely shaven. I only barely recognised Celia Waters.

When she had described the play to me as an experimental piece

I realised it had been an understatement. After some fifteen minutes of watching and listening to the actors I was still at a loss to know what was going on. Their dialogue was risible and incoherent, wandering from one subject to another with no definite purpose, and full of allusions and references that were never explained. They acted the piece in the stylised, melodramatic manner of the silent films of the 1920s with grand gestures and overwrought expressions. I wondered whether, quite deliberately, as with Brecht, the intention was to alienate the audience.

In my case, all I felt was a sense of profound depression and boredom. Eventually the dialogue even began to repeat itself, with one refrain in particular cropping up time and time again:

> *the fear of masks removed*
> *as black lightning illumines*
> *new quests for nothing*
> *the amnesiac thoughts*
> *of dying brains*
> *repeated but forgotten…*

Well, this same farrago went on for another hour and a half, without any interval and by now the sun had set and the moon had risen. Most of the audience had simply got up and left by this point, and were probably demanding refunds at the box office.

I would have left too, but for the natural, outside event that accompanied the play. I imagine that this performance had been carefully scheduled by the *auteur* behind *New Quests for Nothing* to coincide with the phenomenon. I hadn't known of it in advance, and indeed, I cannot say I saw the event reported in the press thereafter, but it certainly occurred. I am convinced I did not imagine it.

A lunar eclipse was taking place and gradually the moon turned blood-red as it passed through the Earth's shadow.

During this event the actors fell to their knees, arms raised aloft, and started chanting gibberish.

I watched for another five minutes and then left just as the eclipse began to finish. I had no idea whether or not the play continued, but I didn't want to see it through until the end. Nor did I want to have to run the risk, afterwards, of having to speak to Celia Waters about it. As I have said, there was scarcely anyone now left in the audience, and there was a chance she may have noticed me sitting there, having kept my promise to attend.

I returned to London the next day, having cut short my trip. My cousin in Sennen Cove advised me, some weeks later, that the play had been pulled after that one performance and had caused something of a rumpus locally as an obvious attempt at a publicity stunt. Eventually, the actors had to be physically removed from the stage by the management, for they carried on with the thing even when the theatre was completely empty.

Another play was hastily scheduled at short notice by the Minack to fill the gap; something by Alan Ayckbourn I believe.

I never heard anything further about *New Quests for Nothing* or 'Doctor Prozess' over the years. Though for some reason I half-expected it to turn up again at the Edinburgh Fringe Festival.

But I did encounter Celia Waters again, twenty years after the events I've already described.

By now I had long since left the play publishing business and taken up employment in another field altogether, working for a small property development agency situated in north London. One of our clients, who owned a number of derelict properties in Cornwall, but who lived in London, contacted us for a feasibility study on the erection of three new houses on a place about a mile or so from Sennen that had been, during the 1970s and 1980s, a 'surf village' called 'Skewjack'. People would bus over from it to the sandy beach at Sennen Cove. The place had been closed for decades, although a cottage on the site was still occupied and was rented out to a tenant who also acted as nominal caretaker for the grounds. No maintenance duties were required, but simply an on-site presence to keep the chalets and other buildings free from the likes of squatters or arsonists.

I hadn't been down to that part of Cornwall since that last trip, twenty years earlier. My cousin had emigrated to Australia six months after my visit, having met, fallen in love with, and hastily married a young woman from Sydney who had been on holiday in this country.

After arriving in Penzance (the last leg of the journey as interminable as I remembered it to be), I took a cab from the station in order to reach the remains of Skewjack surf village. We were almost at Land's End before it turned left off the A30 into a lane. One more left turn, then ahead for a few hundred yards and the vehicle parked at my destination. I told the driver to wait for me. I didn't think my business there would take more than twenty minutes at most to conclude. This was simply a preliminary evaluation.

I had telephoned ahead and the occupant of the cottage came out to meet me as soon as he heard the taxi pull up outside.

He was a man in his early thirties, quite tall, very thin, with long blond hair and a goatee. Back in the doorway of the cottage I could see his partner, a woman around a decade younger than he was. She was red-headed and looked like something out of a Rossetti painting. From the way they dressed, the two of them struck me as arts and crafts types, and I wouldn't have been surprised to learn they made a living selling pottery or jewellery to tourists at Penzance market.

'Brian Kelsey,' he said. 'Pleased to meet you.'

He stuck out a hand and I shook it.

'I won't keep you long,' I said. 'I just need a quick look around.'

'Redeveloping the old place are they? Been like this for ages now I reckon,' he said.

'Possibly. I imagine it wouldn't happen for another year, if ever,' I said.

'Don't bother me and my girlfriend if they do,' he said. 'We've off to St Ives in a few months. Make more money up that way we will, I daresay.'

'What do you do?'

'Sculptures, small ones. Heads mostly. Hand crafted. Want to see? Have a cup of tea beforehand?'

I shook my head.

'Wish I had the time, I really do. But as you can see I've got the taxi waiting and this is all a bit of a rush. Can you just show me around the grounds quickly?'

He looked at me steadily. It wasn't an unfriendly stare, but I could tell he didn't really like what I'd just said.

'Oh yes, I see, you're a busy man. Well, let's get on with it then.'

He set off and I followed.

What was left of Skewjack surf village only covered a few acres.

Its series of holiday cabins, shop, reception and bar/discotheque were all half-derelict and the pathways and grounds overgrown with weeds and brambles. Some of the roofs had collapsed into the cabins and mould had taken over the interiors. The drained, kidney-shaped swimming pool was choked with rubbish.

It seemed to me that the first thing would be to get a quote as to the cost of demolishing the buildings and clearing the whole area. I was making mental calculations when Brian Kelsey said: 'Got some tenants here, you know. In the cabin right just over there, behind the old reception building.'

'Tenants? What tenants?' I said.

He grinned sheepishly.

'Four old tramps. I warned them off at first, but they kept coming back.'

'You mean squatters?'

'Call them what you want. Anyway, they never did anyone any harm. They mind their own business so I ended up leaving them alone. Live and let live. Turns out all my predecessors did likewise the same as I did in the end,' he said.

I didn't reply.

'Let's go and take a peek. It's quite a show, believe me. Why not see if they're at home?' he said.

I followed him as he rounded the reception area building and onto a path beaten through the brambles.

After several yards we stood outside a lone cabin. Its exterior paintwork depicting multi-coloured sun-rays was peeling away. The entrance door hung off its hinges. There was a single dusty window, half-covered with a filthy curtain that was little more than a rag.

'Keep your voice down,' he whispered, putting a finger to his lips.

He crept up to the window, peered through it, turned and beckoned me after him.

When I got close enough, I could hear indistinct voices muttering to one another from inside the cabin. And then I looked through the window myself.

There were four people in there, huddled together in the semi-darkness. They were dressed in crumpled, torn dark suits. Their scalps were either bald or shaven, the dead-pale skin pockmarked by craters and sores.

Three of them had their backs to me but I could just make out the face of the fourth, a woman, much older now than when last I'd seen her. She was facing me but staring vacantly into the distance with black-rimmed eyes.

Celia Waters.

I heard a snatch of dialogue: 'The fear of masks removed …'

And then I turned away, and hurried back along the path, making straight for the taxi.

Kelsey was at my elbow.

'It's the same old thing all the time with them,' he said. 'Over and over again. Like the tide coming in and out.'

Dedicated to Reggie Oliver.

SLAUGHTER AT PENRYN

A very human horror story is said to have occurred at Bohelland Farm near Penryn on Cornwall's southwest tip, in or around the year 1618. It concerns hunger, desperation and brutal, premeditated murder.

Cornwall was not always the prosperous county it is today. In the ages before industrialisation and those easier modes of travel that would lead eventually to tourism, life was hard in this relatively bleak and distant region. Farming was never easy on the Cornish peninsula, confined mainly to the harsh, rocky moors lying inland, where it was a physically exhausting and often frustrating way of life. Tin mining was an exceptionally dangerous profession, but it was not extensive in any case. Other folk made their living from the sea, but this had long been a risky and uncertain trade, which caused many deaths.

It is probably no surprise that to some Cornish natives, crime was the only alternative to starvation.

The family who occupied Bohelland Farm, whose name was not given in the pamphlets wherein this story first appeared, were said to be in direr financial straits than most. The farmer and his wife had struggled through a succession of debt problems and were apparently at their wits' end. They had two grown-up children, but their daughter was married and lived in the next village, while their son, in whom they had invested so much hope when he was a strapping, adventurous youth, had gone away to sea and had not been seen or heard from for many years. In fact, he'd been gone for so long that his parents assumed he'd been lost. But it was on this errant child's return that tragedy really struck.

The son, who had made a success of his career as a merchant seaman, returned to Cornwall a wealthy man, and planned to spring a marvellous surprise on his mother and father. He thus called first at his sister's cottage. The girl did not initially recognise him as he'd grown and changed during his many years on the waves, but once reacquainted they hatched a mischievous scheme. The son would call at his parents' home, claim to be a simple traveller in need of lodging, and in the morning his sister would also call – together they would then reveal the truth, and advise their mother and father that all their money worries were over. A full family celebration would follow.

Initially, the jape went as planned. The son called at his home late that evening, where his aged, ailing parents, careworn to the point of irrationality, failed to recognise him. However, they agreed to give him a berth, mainly because they'd noted his fine clothes and bulging knapsacks. He clearly had plenty food and money. Almost by instinct, therefore, as he slept that night, delighted with the amusing joke he was playing, the son was attacked by his own mother and father. He awoke, struggling. The son was strong and healthy, and his parents were tired and weak, so he put up such a tremendous fight that they had to hit him with any tool they could get their hands on.

In the morning, his sister arrived to find a scene of carnage.

The interior of the farmhouse was destroyed and drenched with blood, while her brother lay dead and mutilated. Her parents, weary and wounded themselves, told her that the corpse belonged to a burglar who had attempted to rob them during the night – but she guessed the awful truth, and appalled, told them that they had slain their only son, and just at the moment when he was set to make all their fortunes. Driven mad with horror, the farmer and his wife committed suicide, though again the 17th century pamphlets give no specific details. The daughter somehow escaped the hangman's noose, an unusual event given that she was the sole survivor at a scene of gory slaughter, but she was deranged for the remainder of her short life.

This is a grim tale, but whether it happened exactly as the pamphleteers reported is difficult to ascertain. It is certainly true that the inhabitants of Penryn believed for centuries afterwards that these events had occurred on their doorstep. But very similar tales of mistaken identity and murder among family members were said to have happened in Leipzig (in the same year no less!), in 1649 at Thermels in Bohemia, and even as late as 1880 in Vienna. Of course, just because this story was stolen and retold elsewhere, that doesn't mean it didn't happen at Penryn first. In 1814, a very informed book of Cornish lore was published, in which the scene of the disaster was examined in detail and marked on a local map. The evidence, such as it is, suggests that this horrific event was real.

THE MEMORY OF STONE

Sarah Singleton

Six round white pebbles in a row.

The smallest was the size of a five pence piece, the largest like a hen's egg. They were ranged in ascending order on the stone sill outside the window.

He noticed the pebbles from the garden gate – the first clear detail he registered. The rest of the cottage, and its surroundings, existed in a kind of vague blur until the moment his eyes fixed on the stones, caught in a glimmer of sunlight, glowing white. The entire scene then came into focus – a low cottage hunched against the weather, a garden overgrown with coarse grass, tough old roses, an apple tree stooped over, branches almost touching the ground. Beyond the cottage, low Cornish hills folded over each other, and between them, a slice of the blue-slate Atlantic.

He picked up his bag, pushed his car keys into his coat pocket and walked up the narrow path to the door. The place was unlocked. His brother had left instructions. An iron key waited for him on the inside, a luggage label tied to it with the words 'Shrike Farm Cottage' written in faded ink. The door dragged on cracked flagstones when he pushed it open.

Inside, a dark room with a blackened fireplace and peeling wallpaper. The place smelled of damp and mould. To the right, a doorway without a door led into the second room – a kitchen with orange cupboards, perhaps from the '70s.

A couple of pictures from a magazine were pinned to the wall – three topless girls with bronzed skin. Michael dropped his bag on the floor and tore them down. The paper disintegrated in his hand. The girls were probably in their sixties now.

The staircase was hidden behind a latched door in the living room. At the top of the narrow stairs he found two rooms, one containing an iron bedstead without a mattress, the other a bathroom with an ancient wall-mounted gas boiler, a bath scattered with leaves. This puzzled him for an instant, till he looked up at the ivy growing across the ceiling.

Michael felt a plunging panic. He was alone, far from home. He took off his glasses and rubbed his eyes.

In the afternoon, an hour late, a delivery van reversed up the lane and dropped off a mattress, a cheap flat-pack table with two chairs, an armchair and a box of kitchen implements. The driver complained about the difficulty of finding the place, grabbed a signature, then drove off again. The boxes stood incongruously in the living room.

Michael placed the armchair in front of the empty fire and sat down. He hadn't the energy to sort out the rest.

He must have fallen sleep because it took a moment, as it always did now, to remember what had happened and where he was. The room was dim. In the kitchen, one small window provided a square of golden light from the westering sun, then that, too, faded. The light was different here, as far west as one could go on this Cornish promontory, surrounded by ocean.

Outside everything was still. In front of him, beyond the garden, hills mounted up to the moors. Behind the house, the land dropped away and away to the sea. No other houses in sight, no road. He glanced at his mobile. Some signal, no messages. He pressed the light switch without result. Distantly he thought he could hear the sea. Feeling vulnerable, he peered through the front window at an indifferent landscape. The front door gave a tiny rattle. Something dropped into the fireplace. A draught whispered.

A white face appeared at the window.

Michael made an involuntary sound. The face was low and small. It didn't seem to have drawn near – rather, it had appeared as an outline that filled in – pale, the suggestion of features, bead eyes. Michael pushed his hands towards the window, as though to fend it off, the face, whatever it was. He blinked.

The window was empty again.

He stared.

In a few minutes, darkness proper filled the eight small panes. He crept back, ashamed, to the armchair, curled up his legs and wrapped them with his arms, like a child.

Michael first saw her at the company seminar. He and a colleague had driven to the head office in Oxford, a converted industrial building developed by his company: exposed red brick, steel girders and expanses of glass. An award had been won and articles written in professional magazines. Michael's contribution had been minimal but it had been thought expedient to educate them, the older employees, on ways to maximise this and future successes through on-line media.

Michael was sitting at a large table sipping coffee, flicking through documents, when she walked in. He would never forget it, the moment his life began to unravel. She was young (later he would find out, twenty-two) and very slim with long brown hair tied up in a casual kind of bun, which allowed strands to slip around her face and neck. Her skin was the palest gold, her eyes bright blue. Little visible make-up. Her outfit was close-fitting but dark and featureless (even now he couldn't recall it exactly) but this seemed only, for him, to draw attention to the body it covered: waist, the curve of narrow hips, a flat stomach he instantly imagined his hand upon, the hinted swell of breasts, then above, most powerful of all, the expanse of exposed skin – smooth, glossy, clinging lovingly to collar bones, the tall pillar of her throat. The room, as in the worst kind of cliché, seemed to recede. An excruciating lust filled him. He couldn't move.

The rest of the day passed in a haze. She stood at the front of the room, introduced herself as Patrice, projected a Powerpoint on a screen and talked for an hour. Her words barely registered, though the sound of her voice seemed to stir electric currents in his veins. Everyone was captivated, it seemed to him, and when she smiled (perfect, white teeth) he started to tremble. She looked around the room as she spoke, engaging the audience. When her gaze rested momentarily upon him, it was like a spear in his chest. He wriggled uncomfortably in his chair. Had he felt like this before, this intensity, ever, in his long life, among the thousands of women he had encountered, the few he had loved in one way or another? He had moved into unknown territory.

During the coffee break he wandered to the table and collected his drink but it cooled untouched on the table in front of him. The colleague he had travelled with made conversation that Michael didn't hear, except for a passing comment (discreetly made, bloke-ish, that the girl was a fox) then another presentation by a man with one of those excessive beards that seemed all the rage with the young, and a group talk session that Michael didn't contribute to. Suddenly it was five o'clock and the day was over. They headed for a pub in town, a modern place with wooden floors and black and white portraits of film stars on the walls. She was with them, Patrice, laughing with the bearded man. Michael tried not to stare. He drank a couple of pints but declined the offer of a meal, claiming to be tired. He walked through the hot summer streets towards his hotel. Outside he felt different, the feeling of oppression lifted, and instead he felt a surge of elation. A pink sky lay over the spired city. People laughed and chatted on the pavements. The air smelt of heated asphalt and geraniums.

Alone in his hotel room, Michael pushed through the net curtains to open the window on a view of busy streets. Then he lay on his bed, almost hallucinating, blood surging through his body, until the light ebbed from his room.

The mobile vibrated in his pocket. Michael fumbled for it and the screen flared – a picture of his wife. The phone vibrated again but he put it down on the cabinet beside the bed. Later, under the covers, Patrice glowed in his imagination. He thought again of his hand pressing against her smooth belly, the column of her neck, the golden skin. He masturbated quickly, came in moments.

The second day was a kind of torture. She spoke again, briefly, and joined his breakaway group for more workshop discussions. Today she was wearing dark trousers and a pale rose-coloured shirt, buttoned at the collar, her hair in a loose plait. She smiled kindly at him when he spoke, but Michael was mortified by even her polite attention. Surely she must be aware of his feelings? Weren't they written all over him, sweating, almost panting? But she spoke to him as to the others, lightly, smiling. The day passed, and then he was driving home only partially listening to his colleague, who chatted inanely about the presentations, applications, a future holiday, football.

He woke in the morning, curled and cramped in the armchair. Seven o'clock. He remembered the pale face at the window, but dismissed it. Exhaustion, imagination? Cold and uncomfortable, Michael climbed out of the chair. He forced himself to function, fishing a kettle from the delivery boxes. It turned out the electricity was on, so presumably the lightbulbs needed replacing. He collected a box of meagre provisions from the car but on his return to the house he stopped in his tracks.

The white pebbles had gone.

Michael put his box on the ground and stepped to the window. He looked on the ground amongst the grass, pushed it aside with his foot. Nothing. He thought of the face in the window, the outline that had appeared to fill in. Kids playing around? He couldn't see any footprints or disturbance and what kids would come here in the night, in the middle of nowhere? Even Shrike's Farm was a mile and a half away. He fished for ideas. Birds? The wind?

After drinking a cup of tea, he drove through Sennen and up to Penzance. He had a list of stuff to buy, including cleaning materials, food, towels and bed linen. Pulling away from the cottage, his spirits lightened a little. The spare, granite landscape spread around him. Now and then he had a glimpse of the sea. Low cloud rolled across the sky. Stunted thorn trees, bent by the prevailing wind, like letters of a runic alphabet. In town he distracted himself with a coffee and list-writing, then set out to commandeer all the necessary supplies. He'd start cleaning the place when he got back, sort out the furniture, maybe light a fire if the chimney wasn't clogged with nests.

When he returned this moment of purpose melted away. The overwhelming sense of breakage returned, a reiteration of grief. Through this internal breach, memories flowed, vivid scenes of the life he had lost, fragments of the past he hadn't recalled in years – Amelia pregnant, times with the babies, beach holidays playing with his daughter, the children jumping through a spray of water from a hose on the lawn one summer. Those times had already long gone, but now they seemed lost to him in a manner he had never envisaged – as though the past had been taken away from him, as well as the present and his future.

He dumped his purchases inside the cottage and walked around the back, to a patch of long grass and a washing line from which hung several thin piece of fabric. Michael hadn't noticed them when he glanced through the window the day before. The rags blew in the wind from the sea, light and purely white. The line was high up, strung from two iron poles at either side of the once-lawn, raised in the middle in the old fashioned style with a long, cleft pole. Michael lifted the prop away so he could reach the washing. He clasped one long piece in his hand. It wasn't fastened with pegs but seemed to be wrapped around the line. Against his palm, it didn't feel like any fabric he knew – a kind of thin gauze, but slippery as silk. It had no particular form. The other pieces were the same, shiny-soft, of different lengths. When he held it to his face, the fabric smelt clean, though perfumed faintly of the sea. Salt and rock and water. Fine threads, like spider web, frayed at the ends. Pressing the fabric between his fingers, Michael thought again of the face at the window. He unwound the pieces from the line, folded them then laid them in a pile on the lawn in the sunshine, weighted with a stone. Reluctant to go inside, he headed out of the back garden through a broken gate, along a cliff path to the sea.

A blustery day. The cliffs dropped away in steps. The path was stony but easy enough, the sea in broad stripes of grey and blue as a procession of cloud and sunshine passed overhead. Waves heaved themselves onto the pebbles, white edged, blown up by the wind. Inevitably, the scene conjured up the past, his son hurrying down to the sea with a long stick in his hand, looking back, shouting at his dad. The colour of this historic moment (over saturated perhaps) flared in his mind, the sound of his young son's voice echoing from his memory.

He arrived in a little cove. Grey rocks, some with scooped tops, then smaller pebbles, a ribbon of sand, and more pebbles where the waves crashed. A cormorant, reptilian and prehistoric, stood on a stone pillar above the water and dried its wings. Michael sat on a warm rock. Something caught his eye.

Six white pebbles, lined in ascending size, on top of a flat piece of granite.

The same stones? How could they be? He picked one up, then another, then swept them off the rock, onto the beach. The only way to reach the cove was along the path from the house (unless you had a boat of course) so they had to be different stones. But he was disturbed. He felt the threat.

Night flooded the land from the sea. Michael couldn't be bothered to eat. He'd grown thin anyway, over the last three months and had lost the habit of hunger. He stood in the cottage and stared through the window, aware of the silence and emptiness.

When had he ever been so alone? He could be murdered here, and no-one would know. Under night's cover lay the moor. Wind whined in the chimney and pushed at the front door. What might be out there?

He felt a long-forgotten fear of the dark, something from childhood. The mind's instinctive questions – what was hiding in the dark, in the corners of the cottage, and outside of it? Monsters, or more corporally, lunatics and murderers. He closed down the questions but his body was alert – a sensitivity of the skin, his back, even the drums of his ears.

The light went out with a tiny ping. Michael's body twitched. A sound escaped his mouth, involuntary, and he pressed his hand over his face. He waited. One breath, two, three. Nothing happened. He moved to the kitchen door and tried the switch. The light came on, yellow and artificial. Only the bulb, then.

Stop it, he told himself. Don't do this to yourself.

A knocking at the door.

For a moment he wasn't inside the cottage but high above it, seeing his own, small face illuminated in the window of the stone box, an illusory protection, while all around spread the night and the Cornish moor and the ocean.

He saw a thin white creature creeping into the garden, silent, emerged from the sea, attracted to the heat and life of the man inside. It ran around to the cottage, pressing at the walls, peering into the windows, with long fingers. It knocked at the door.

The moment stretched, creating a tension, a tight thread, a long, plangent note that extended and reached a crescendo – a thread that snapped.

Michael ran to the door, unlocked it and threw it open.

Nothing. No-one there.

'Who is it?' he shouted. 'Who's there? Show yourself!'

He stepped out into the garden, shouting and blustering, making threatening sweeps with his arms.

When he turned back, pebbles were lined up on the windowsill. He went inside, locked the door and pushed the armchair against it.

That night, between new sheets on the new mattress on the creaking bedstead, Michael lay awake staring at the ceiling.

They came for him, the white children. They dragged him out of the house, like a rag doll. Rocks scored his skin and bruised his bones. At the edge of the sea, they peeled off his clothes and sank their hands through his pouched skin into his body, marvelling at his viscera, taking him to pieces, playfully. He lay on the strip of dark sand, ribs open, empty inside as they ran around him. He felt no pain, only a distant worry that something might be lost and he wouldn't be able to put himself together again.

Absurd infatuation. Mid-life crisis. Manopause.

Michael acknowledged the cliché and was still helpless against it. He hunted her down on the internet, found a few pictures and stored them in a file on his laptop. He sent her an email after the seminar (waited three days to send it). He drafted the message over and over again, framing a polite enquiry about the uses of Twitter. Patrice sent a brief, friendly and informative response.

He masturbated almost constantly, morning and night, sometimes in the toilet cubicles at his office, shamefully, sick of himself, but nothing offered relief.

He could hardly bear the touch of his wife, made excuses, stayed late at the office – then hated himself. He knew he was ridiculous and unreasonable and the victim of a delusion but he couldn't escape.

It had never been like this with Amelia. They'd met at university. A happy and intense friendship had deepened and blossomed over two years into a passionate relationship. She had seemed entirely beautiful to him, and knew him inside out. They were a golden couple, blessed, successful and fruitful. Marriage, two accomplished and good-looking children, his daughter now twenty seven and married herself. A harvest of happiness. They had ups and downs, of course. From time to time he had been attracted to other women (doubtless the same for Amelia) but he had never been seriously tempted. He had everything he needed. Amelia was still lovely. He had hardly noticed her ageing (until now, he noticed now).

Michael assessed himself frankly. He knew the score. He was fifty-two years old and probably hadn't worn as well as his wife. His hair had receded, grown white and wispy, so he kept it cropped close to his scalp. He was tall and heavy-boned, still imposing, but the flesh seemed to have slipped from him, from the once-muscular shoulders and arms, from the broad chest, sinking into a paunch, a spare tyre that he hadn't paid much attention to till now.

What should he do? Run away? Move house? Wait it out? Explain to his wife and go to some kind of counselling? The thought made him shudder. Why had this happened? Why now? It had to mean something.

He tried to dig beneath his feelings for an answer but found no logical explanation. He was tied up in all kinds of personal torture – and hardest of all, some part of him didn't want to escape. He didn't want the pain to stop, this needle he writhed upon. The slimmest, faintest glimmer of hope that this feverish desire for Patrice could be satisfied prolonged the agony.

Mortality, was that it? Some deep animal panic in the face of his advancing years? Perhaps. Because although he knew it was absurd, he felt, in every cell of his body, that if he didn't have her, he would die.

In the morning, the sky burned a clear, deep blue. Michael woke up late. He stepped out of the cottage and breathed deeply, tasting the sea-washed Atlantic air. Three pale shells waited on the doorstep. More white stones, in a spiral on the grass at the front. Streamers of seaweed and lengths of the odd white webbing hung from the washing line. In a broken, barnacled china pot, he found a dozen pieces of sea glass in opaque white and green and red, as well as several tarnished coins.

'Michael, come in.'

They were sitting behind the table, three of them, his fellow partners. Alone on the other side, Michael was outnumbered. He could see they were uneasy and embarrassed, the two men and one woman he had worked alongside for over a decade.

'What's all this about?' he tried to sound assertive, but recognised his tone was awkward and shrill. 'James – what's wrong?'

One of the men shifted in his chair. None of them would look into his eyes. At last, James seemed to gird himself and sat up straight.

'Let's get straight to the point,' he said. 'We've had a complaint.'

'A complaint?'

'Sexual harassment.'

The words hung on the air, as though painted there, visible for them all to see. The other two now looked at Michael too.

'What? What are you talking about?'

'A female employee from the Oxford office has lodged a formal complaint. Dozens of emails, phone calls,' he paused for a moment. 'Indecent photographs.'

The woman gave Michael a piercing glance.

James continued: 'Stalking. Both on-line and in real life. These incidents have been reported to the police. I understand you've been photographed waiting in your car outside her house on several occasions.'

Michael was shaking. He listened to the list as though the other people in the room were far away.

James sighed. His uneasiness had hardened into something more resolute – into distaste. He turned his large computer monitor around and flicked up onto the screen a series of photographs of Michael sitting inside his car in a dark street. He scrolled through a list of clearly identifiable emails.

No-one spoke. They were all staring. He was ripped open.

Around him, Michael sensed shattering and falling. His blood seemed to solidify.

Somehow it had always seemed – his on-line obsession – private and unreal, as though it had only happened inside of his head, in a secret space. The emails were not real, didn't exist. Even staring at her house from his car. He had never approached the house, spoken to her, or even stepped out of the vehicle. Absurdly, his activities had seemed contained, invisible to others.

Now his private world was breached. He was overwhelmed with shame. An agony of exposure.

'What were you thinking?' It wasn't James, but the other one, Martin. They'd often gone out for drinks together, socialised with wives in tow. 'I just can't believe it. Were you out of your mind?' Martin looked at him, incredulous.

'You will have to resign,' James interrupted. 'Clear your desk now and don't return to the office. We'll sort out the details later.'

Michael stood up very slowly. He walked straight to the toilets and threw up, leaning over the toilet bowl. With shaking hands he turned on a tap over the flat, steel sink and stared into the mirror. He could hardly hold himself upright. It felt as though his guts were spilling out, falling to the floor. The room blurred and he closed his eyes. One clear thought rang in his mind: 'What will I tell my wife?'

They came again the next night. Two of them, small white faces staring through the glass. They were genderless, with wisps of albino hair, tiny bead eyes, narrow shadows for nose and mouth.

They were waiting.

In the morning, in addition to the stones and shells he found dead things – a fish torn open to reveal the architecture of its white bones, and the wings of a seagull, grey and white feathered, ripped clean from its body.

He wasn't afraid anymore. It didn't make any sense. He had no explanation. It simply was. The exhausting resistance inside his body melted away. He could let go. He could surrender.

She was standing on the doorstep, fist raised to bang again. Alien here, angry-faced, in city clothes, red hair tinted and well cut.

When she saw him, her expression changed. She stared.

'My God what's happened to you?'

He tried to speak but he'd lost the knack.

'Look at you,' she said.

Michael swallowed. 'How did you find me?'

'I phoned everyone. I phoned Uncle Jack, and he told me, eventually.' She looked angry again. 'Look, are you going to let me in? I've been driving for hours. I got lost after Penzance. And no-one knew where this place was.' She emerged from the recollection of her own difficulties and glanced at him again. She lifted her hand to his arm and gave it a squeeze. 'Dad you look awful. You're really thin. You look a hundred years old. Can I come in?'

He stepped back and she pushed past.

'What a dump. How long have you been living here?'

'Jack bought it to do up,' Michael said. The conversation felt far away. He looked at his daughter with amazement and wonder, as though she were some kind of curiosity, the inhabitant of another world. His own flesh and blood.

'I'll make some coffee,' she said. 'Have you got any food here?' She went into the kitchen. He heard her outrage at the state of the place, then banging about as she looked for stuff. He waited, still standing, till she emerged and handed him a cup, glancing around the room.

'There's only one seat,' he apologised.

'Let's sit in the garden. It stinks in here anyway.'

Outside she glanced at the pebbles in the grass. She was silent for several minutes, staring into her mug, pressing and tapping it with her fingers. The subject hung over them. In the end she took a deep breath and said:

'What the hell, Dad. What were you doing? Were you insane?'

'Yes.'

'Mum's in pieces.'

'I know.' He stared over the cottage roof to the faraway curve of the headland.

'Jane,' he said, not looking at her. 'I'm sorry. I'm truly sorry.'

'How could you? D'you know how stupid you look? D'you have any idea how humiliated Mum feels? She's heartbroken. Fuck. *Fuck*.' Jane's anger bubbled up again, huge and volcanic. She took two quick, short breaths and glanced at him.

'You aren't eating. You look … derelict,' she said. 'You ruined everything.'

He paused. 'I ruined everything.' Then, 'Why are you here?'

She hesitated. 'I wanted to see you. I was worried,' and angrily, 'You're still my dad.' She noticed something in the undergrowth. 'There's a dead fish there. I can smell it. You've got foxes.'

He shrugged. They were silent for a while.

'I don't know what to say,' Jane said. 'Is it over – this craziness?'

How much had her mother told her? How many of the details did she know? He could hear the disgust in her voice, the taboo of a parent's lust, and the desires of the middle-aged and decaying for the perfect young.

'Yes,' he said. A vast lie that might, perhaps, appear to be true, even to himself. He'd bricked it away, the addiction and any possibility of its fulfilment. In doing so, he'd lost some vital part of himself – hope, longing.

'How's your brother?'

'He won't even say your name.' Then she added. 'He's okay.'

They talked for a long time. Jane said, reluctantly, she would stay the night and drive back the following day. She prepared a meal, nagged him to eat and urged him to return with her.

'Come back. Stay closer,' she said, 'where I can see you.'

He prepared to sleep in the armchair. He could hear the old bed creaking as Jane turned under the covers upstairs. Could he go back with her? To what? Might Amelia take him back? Even if she did, it would make no difference. He'd spoilt everything. It would never be the same. He'd wrecked their accumulation of years, the story of their marriage. The fact that he hadn't touched Patrice was a piece of sophistry. He'd have thrown over everything for her, given the chance. (Would he now, still?). Amelia would know she was second-choice, his fall-back option. He'd smashed it up.

Michael sank into the armchair and the familiar peace of the cottage. A light rain pattered onto the roof and window panes. He wondered if they would come tonight, with Jane here. They were more real than his in-pieces wife and his un-naming son.

Michael dozed. Some hours later he noticed the rain had stopped. He got up and wandered out into the garden, which smelt of damp soil. He couldn't see the white children or their gifts. Had they waited for him long enough?

He loitered in the garden, cold and stiff, and kicked around in the grass but the pebble spiral had gone, and the six from the windowsill. He left the garden through the back gate and headed down the stony path to the cove.

Dawn was not far away. He could make his way fairly easily. The sound of the sea was subdued. He could make out clouds massing on the Atlantic horizon. The wind lifted as he reached the cove but it was mild.

They were there – five or six of them, running along the edge of the sea. Sometimes they picked up objects from the waves. Thin, white as sea foam, their flat, tiny-featured faces turned as one, towards Michael. Some form of communication passed between them. They ran towards him, took his hands and pulled him to the ground.

Their hands were cold as ice, their fingers seeming to burn his skin as they rifled through his clothes and prodded his body. Vividly he recalled the dream, when they opened him up and ripped him to pieces, but he wasn't afraid. Warmth spread through him, and a distance from the proceedings happening on the beach. He could spectate from the high tower of his brain as his body was searched and manipulated. He acquiesced.

The children pulled him to his feet again. Two held his hands, the others crowded about. They looked from one to another. Sometimes their bead eyes stared up at his face. The wind played with their wisps of hair. They walked towards the sea.

He expected the water to be cold but it wasn't, not in the slightest. It was like stepping into a bath, the waves washing deliciously around his legs. The children grew more excited and made tiny squeaking noises, the first sounds he'd heard them make, like seals.

Michael waded to his knees and then his waist. Three seagulls flew overhead in the grey twilight before dawn. The moon emerged from a cloud to sink slowly behind the ring of cliffs. Seeing it, he hesitated for a moment but the children urged him on. He closed his eyes.

A seagull cried, breaking his trance. It called again, insistent, the sound scratching for his attention.

'Dad! Dad!' It wasn't a seagull. He turned his head. Jane – on the beach, scrambling over the rock and waving and shouting.

The white children whispered and cried and quickly dispersed into the water, letting go of his hand. Instantly the sea became cold, sucking the heat from his body.

'No!' he said, thrashing around in the waves, looking for them. 'Come back, come back. No, no!'

'Dad, Dad!' The aggravating, unwanted voice again, a chain dragging him. Jane lurched through the water, shouting and waving. Michael looked at the horizon, one last time, and then she was next to him, grabbing at him, pulling him back. He was freezing cold and the waves were larger.

'Get out of the water,' she cried. 'Get out now. Don't do this, how dare you? Come out. Come out.'

Salt water poured out of his clothes. He stood heavily in the shallows. Beside him, Jane was shivering and shouting. She kept hold of him, both hands gripping his arm. Then she hit him, slapped his shoulder.

'How dare you?' she repeated. 'You can't do that! Fuck you Dad. Fuck you! Yeah it's hard. It's hard for all of us. So you've lost your story. You'll just have to live with it. You just have to carry on. You don't just leave me. You don't get to give up.'

She began to cry then, shivering and shaking, keeping her hands around his arm.

Michael put his arm around her, his girl. Her body was shaking, her fingers pinched his skin. She was cursing and swearing at him, holding him tight. They stood for a long time, on the edge of the sea.

When she had cried herself out, Michael led her away to the cliff path.

He felt empty and tired. He put his hands into his pockets and emptied the pebbles onto the beach.

QUEEN OF THE WIND

Any discussion of English witchcraft is likely to be emotive. Still practised today, albeit discreetly, debate rages as to whether witchcraft is a force for evil in that it invokes dark and uncontrollable entities, a force for good in that it utilises benign magic, or a harmless eccentricity indulged in by those seeking a different route to spiritual enlightenment.

In antiquity of course, there were no such uncertainties. Witches were feared and hated across the British Isles, especially after the Protestant Reformation, which appeared to denude rural communities of the mystical powers the Catholic Church had seemed to wield in their defence. Even after the passing of the Witchcraft Act in 1735, which decriminalised the practise of the ancient arts, there was a strong belief in witchcraft and a deep suspicion of those involved in it. And it is from this era – essentially the mid-18th century – where most of the stories about wise-women and cunning men come down to us.

No longer in danger of persecution, many such practitioners stepped out of the shadows at this time and openly declared themselves. In fact, from this point on they quite often made a business out of their formerly secret talents. Take the Cornish wind-sellers, for example. Incredible though it may appear, numerous men and women claiming special influence would charge local seafarers for the certainty of calm winds. The vast majority of these were clearly frauds seeking to capitalise on an undeserved reputation they had skilfully manufactured. But people would believe what they wanted to believe, especially in small coastal villages where the success of local fishermen could be the difference between life and death.

Even as recently as the 1860s, there are reports of wind-sellers complaining that the advent of steam-shipping was ruining their income. However, if this seems amusing to us, there were other incidents back then which decidedly weren't. Much more sinister were those 18th century witch covens who used their new protection under the law to intimidate and terrorise. In this regard, look no further than the infamous St Levan Witches, the hub of whose activities was Tol-Pedn-Penwith, a suitably atmospheric spot on the toe of Cornwall, where crashing sea meets soaring cliffs and lush inland meadows intersperse with wild, tor-capped moors. The elemental nature of this place made it the perfect headquarters for a nefarious gang of whom the entire district lived in fear. Their leader was the charismatic Madgy Figgy, a woman who would sit enthroned among the high coastal rocks on a natural chair known variously as 'the Castle' or 'the Seat of Winds', and who from here, with hair and garments streaming dramatically, would throw curses at those passing vessels whose masters had refused to pay her toll. Many of these craft are said to have gone down in unnatural and colossal storms. Others, severely battered, returned quickly to harbour, where their skippers willingly paid Madgy's agents the price of a safer passage.

Just in case this wasn't an alarming enough concept for the superstitious to get their heads around, Madgy Figgy was also said to lead her followers on broomsticks across the Bristol Channel to South Wales, where they would gather ragwort and other noxious herbs for the production of wicked potions. It seemed there were lots of ways you could suffer if you opposed Madgy Figgy.

Whether there is truth in any of this, it is difficult to say. Very possibly, Madgy was another wind-seller who took advantage of Cornwall's furious seas to impose a reign of terror from which she could profit. Historians believe that she was a real person who also ran a smuggling ring, which her scary reputation would almost certainly have assisted with. But one particular story involving her, which again hints at the unknown rather than common criminality, is astonishingly detailed.

A Portuguese merchantman intending to round the tip of Cornwall had refused to succumb to her threats. Madgy thus took her usual seat and created such a tempest that the ship was driven into Perloe Cove, where it smashed on the rocks and skerries. Afterwards, Madgy led her followers down into the cove to gather what valuables they could from the dead and their broken cargo. However, among the corpses lay a handsome lady decked in finery and expensive jewels. The junior witches exulted in this, but Madgy, uncharacteristically afraid, forbade them to touch the woman. To evade accusations of wrecking, she later had all the corpses buried. The last and best grave was reserved for the handsome lady. At this point Madgy relented about the victim's jewellery, but claimed it all for herself, saying that it must be kept safe and in one place. She subsequently placed it in a chest in her moorland hovel at Raftra, and hid it in a secret compartment.

From this moment on, for many nights, a white form was seen to rise from the grave where the Portuguese woman lay, ascend via coastal paths, enter Madgy's cottage and sit itself in a nook by the fire. It had no distinguishing features, but the witches were certain that this was an angry spirit. Madgy alone refused to be cowed, saying simply that things would *resolve themselves in due course. A short while later, the spirit ceased its nightly visits, but a few days after that, a living person, a thin, sly-looking man who was said to be 'tainted of skin' (greenish, yellow, pockmarked? – nobody knows), knocked on Madgy's door and when she opened it, entered uninvited. She made no protest as he crossed the room, located the hidden chest, opened it to check that the treasure was all present and correct, and then tucking it under his arm, left without saying a word.*

Madgy's followers remonstrated with her that she'd simply stood by while a bold thief did his work. Madgy disagreed, with the curt reply: 'It takes one witch to know another.'

SHELTER FROM THE STORM

Ian Hunter

This was the last of their practise walks. Nine miles. Strenuous. Along part of the Cornish coast and into the hills and back again. A lot different from their very first walk, which had been a tiddler, not even two miles, starting from Camelford and back again. Over the months they had built up both the miles and the difficulty, walking around places like Tintagel and Padstow and King Arthur's Hall, all in preparation of next year's major walk from Land's End to Bude, nearly a hundred and fifty miles. They were making it as real as they could, with full rucksacks, and carrying their new lightweight trekking tents.

Yes, this was a lot different from those other walks.

'That's it!' cried Juggs, slamming down the barrier bag; it jingled slightly on the snow covered ground before settling on the slope. 'I've had enough.'

'Watch out, stupid!' Billy yelled behind him.

'Yeah,' agreed Murray. 'There's bottles of pear cider in there.'

Juggs screwed his face up in disgust, pulling his foot out of the hole in the ground, although the earth seemed reluctant to give it back, and only did so with a noisy *plop*. 'Look at the gunge on my leg,' he complained, glaring at the others.

'Black boot,' said Murray, laughing slightly at his friend. 'Usually fatal, it's probably eating into your brain already.

'Shut it!' growled Juggs, snatching the bag off the ground and digging inside for his litre-bottle of cider. He took a slug and wiped his mouth with the back of a glove crusted with a mixture of snow and mud.

'Do you have to do that,' Billy complained.

Juggs looked at him and then the bottle. 'Aye,' he said nodding.

'Isn't drinking in public against the law?' the smaller of the three Explorer Scouts asked.

255

'You're kidding, right?' Juggs said, spreading out his arms. 'Apart from us being underage. Where's the public, eh? Unless you count the sheep. Maybe the sheep are undercover cops. What a disguise. I give in, I confess, it was me and my cheap bottle of Snowblind that did it. Free the Scout Three.'

'You finished ranting?' Billy asked.

Juggs shrugged. 'Listen, I'd die to see another person right now, because that might mean we've finally reached Port Isaac. You know, the place where we started from? The place we should never have left.'

'It's probably over the next rise,' Murray told him.

'Rise?' Juggs shook his head. 'We should be heading downhill, towards the coast.' He looked round. Hills scarred by lines of snow surrounded them. 'I thought this was supposed to be a circular walk? Back where we started from?'

Billy made a vague gesture with his hands. 'It's more like a triangular walk, really, but it does take us back to Port Isaac again.'

'Put another record on, as my dad says,' Juggs told them, lifting the bottle to his lips again. 'I've been hearing that from both of you for the last hour or so. Where are we?'

'I'm not taking the map out in this weather,' Billy insisted. 'It'll get ruined. Don't worry, we're nearly there.' He looked over at Murray for support. Murray looked away.

'We're lost,' sighed Juggs. 'Admit it.'

Billy smiled. 'I'm telling you, Port Isaac is over the next hill.'

'Let's stop here,' Juggs suggested.

'What?' Billy said, almost stumbling in surprise. 'You're kidding, right?'

The other two scouts watched in disbelief as their friend took off his rucksack, swinging it onto the ground before crouching down beside it.

Murray sighed. 'Well, why not? I suppose we've got tents and my feet are killing me.'

Billy pointed. 'That's because you never broke in those new boots like I told you to do.'

'I'm breaking them in here,' Murray almost spat back at him. 'This isn't the big hike, is it? This is one of our practise ones.'

Juggs looked up. 'That's why we've got all the gear with us. Clothes, tents and booze. So are we camping or not?'

'We can't camp here, guys. Not in the hills, it's too cold.' Billy held out his hand, light rain splashed against his palm. 'This could turn to sleet, or even back to snow.'

Juggs ignored him, and took out a can of lager, which unleashed a white spray as he opened it. 'Brought some extra supplies,' he said, grinning, holding out a carrier bag. 'In case we run out.'

Murray accepted the plastic bag and fished around inside it.

'Look, this is stupid,' Billy told them. 'It's pissing down. We're too exposed here. We could all end up with hypothermia.'

'We could end up with it if Port Isaac isn't over the next hill,' Juggs said, saluting Billy with his lager can.

'Alcohol encourages heat loss,' Billy pointed out.

Murray smiled. 'We're not dead yet. We can get the stove going once we put the tent up.'

Rainwater poured off the top of Billy's hood. They couldn't stop here. They had to get to the hostel next to the coastal path. 'Come on, guys, don't give in. I'm sure Port Isaac is over the next ridge.'

'You promise?' Murray asked.

'Yes. Come on. Juggs, just the next hill, okay?'

Juggs gulped down some lager and sighed loudly. 'Okay, I'm a mug, but the next hill, and if there are no lights in the distance, then we get the tents out. Right?'

'Okay, okay.'

They walked on, heads down against the rain which was stronger now and, as predicted, turning into sloppy sleet, chilling everything, including them. Wearily they trudged to the top of the next rise, which Billy hoped would lead the way to other gentle rises, like a grassy rollercoaster riding the back of a huge green snake, eventually leading downhill to the little coastal village. Juggs stopped until the others caught up with him. The hill led down and up again, disappearing into the darkness.

'Let's get to the top of that rise,' Billy said, pointing

'Let's not,' Juggs replied. 'My idea is that we try and find somewhere to camp, a fallen tree, maybe a sheep shelter or something and pitch beside it.'

Murray peered down into the valley below, convinced that something was standing out against the dark and the long grass. 'Hey, look at that,' he said, pointing to the left.

Billy's eyes could just make out some ruined walls and the

remains of a taller structure.

'What the hell is that?'

'Salvation.'

'What?'

'A ruined church.'

'A church?' repeated Murray. 'Out here?'

'Come on,' said Billy, and he started to trot down the hill.

'What's the point of going to a church?' Juggs shouted after him.

Billy turned. 'It's shelter isn't it? We can pitch the tent beside the walls. Come on.'

Juggs gestured to the surrounding, snow covered hills. 'Who's in the congregation, fucking sheep?'

'We can fuck them later,' said Murray, marching past him.

Billy laughed and walked on, then hesitated slightly as he moved past the jagged ruins of what he guessed were cottages. Miner's cottages, perhaps. Could this be the remains of some old mining village in the hills? Were they that lost? As they approached the church, he eased himself past rounded lumps, which had to be headstones. There was more of the church left than he had thought. One wall had partially collapsed along with the roof, and pieces of stained glass clung to metal frames. The masonry was damp-looking, black and diseased and covered in thick, furry moss. For a second or two he thought of something lying at the bottom of the sea, and wouldn't have been surprised to see the moss moving slightly as the old building breathed in and out.

'Do you think Reverend Whatsit is at home?' Murray said behind him.

Juggs walked up to the doors and pushed one. It moved slightly. He pushed harder and it scraped open. 'Forget about pitching beside a wall, we can sleep inside. Give us a bit more shelter.' He looked at Billy. 'This is it, boss. End of the road for me tonight.'

'You want to sleep inside a church?' Murray said.

'It's not a church any more,' Juggs said simply, and forced the door open further with his shoulder.

Darkness greeted them, black as a pit, before the void slowly began losing some of its intensity and their eyes adjusted to the gloom. Juggs did a magic trick and produced another can of lager

'So much for shelter,' said Murray, looking at the way the roof had fallen into the church. It reminded him of a piano that had collapsed at one end, spilling its keys in a downward wave.

'Shhh,' Juggs told them. 'Listen.'

'It's only the shit weather against the roof.'

'No, listen,' Juggs insisted.

Things were moving about, as though aware of their presence.

Billy smiled. 'Rats.' He gulped down some of the lager that Juggs passed to him.

'Bats,' Juggs said.

Murray's heart jumped. He could almost feel the things flying above his head. Sharp claws ready to tangle in his hair. 'Get a torch out,' he hissed.

'Relax, they won't bother us,' Juggs announced. 'Not if we don't bother them.'

'I agree with Murray,' Billy said. 'I don't think we should stay here.'

'I never said that!'

'We're staying,' Juggs stated.

Billy stepped towards him. 'Listen, it's my hike. I'm in charge. We can't stay here. More of the roof might fall in on us, and a wall could collapse.'

'As if that's likely to happen,' Juggs replied. 'It's still dryer than outside and it's a lot better than stumbling around in the dark, listening to you tell us how close we are to Port bloody Isaac.'

'We could put the tent up in here,' Murray agreed. 'The floor seems damp enough to take the pegs, and the tent would be dry.'

'And we can drink our carry-out,' Juggs smiled. 'Inside our nice cosy tent. A lot better than trying to pitch outside in the sleet.'

Billy reached into the side pocket of his rucksack and took out his torch and shone it around the inside of the church. There were a few pews lying overturned on the floor, but no pulpit, unless it was under the collapsed part of the roof.

'Somebody left in a hurry,' Murray breathed, looking at the holes in the floor where the seats had been ripped up. He wiped his mouth with the back of his hand and nudged Billy with a bottle of pear cider. 'Finish it.'

Juggs shook out the tent, it flopped across the floor like a giant slug. 'You know what farmers are like,' he said. 'I'll bet anytime they needed some wood they just came here to get it.'

Then how come the doors are still here?, Billy thought, as he gulped down the cider. He trailed the torch beam across the walls. No crucifixes appeared, or even the board that showed the numbers of the hymns to be sung.

'Hey, what was that?' said Murray.

'Where?'

'Move the torch back a bit.'

The light illuminated streaks of falling sleet, and something he hadn't noticed, a plaque stuck to the wall.

'Let's have a look,' Murray said, moving forward.

'It's right under a hole in the roof,' Juggs complained. 'I'm wet enough.'

Billy and Murray stood beneath the opening, which wasn't too bad, like standing beneath a trickling shower.

'Is it gold?' Murray asked, running his gloved hand down the metal plate. His woollen fingers came away dirty.

'I don't think so,' Billy said, amused by the idea that there was gold lying forgotten in this ruin. He used the wet sleeve of his cagoule to wipe the sign clean.

Murray's face pressed closer to the words, trying to make out the thin spidery writing. It seemed as if someone had used a thin edged, red-hot chisel to carve delicate letters into the metal.

In the memory of champions of Tregeare Rounds: the Reverend Treeve Carveth, Pascoe Mylor, Kenver Gerrans, Jago Kliskey who stood against He who was bound in darkness and bound Him again.

'Crikey, talk about old Cornish names,' Billy whispered. 'We must be near the old hill-fort that was on the map.'

'What does that mean?' Murray asked.

We're a bit further inland than we should be.'

'So we're lost, aren't we?'

'What is it?' Juggs asked, holding a fresh can of lager in front of him as he walked closer. 'What have you ...?'

He didn't have time to yell as the floorboards opened up with a loud cracking sound and a dark hole tried to devour him. His legs kicked, turning pedals that weren't there as he dropped down.

The can disappeared. His fingers clawed the damp, rotten wood of the boards, and he felt them start to slide.

'Grab me!' he shouted.

Billy darted forward, stepping on his friend's hand. Juggs cried out as the darkness below swallowed him, his knee striking something on the way down, something that made a cracking noise; it hopefully wasn't his leg. He bounced away to the side and rolled over and held his knee, which felt like an erupting volcano, his hands doing their best to hold the bubbling lava inside.

The torchlight stung his eyes.

'Are you okay?'

'I've banged my knee on something,' he said, getting to his feet and grimacing as he tried to bend his leg. The pain throbbed on and on, and his kneecap made an ominous clicking noise when he moved.

The light moved off him and slid away to take in the rest of the cellar, empty, except for –

'Get me out of here!' Juggs cried. 'Get me out!'

Murray laughed. 'Hey, you're not scared are you? It's only some old coffin.'

And then the torch went out.

Juggs didn't notice that the pain in his knee had dwindled; he felt his skin pressing against his clothes as his body appeared to swell up, become super-sensitive. His eyes rolled around in their sockets, trying to see all of the darkness at the same time.

'Guys, this isn't funny, you know?' He listened, hearing only footsteps above him and the occasional sound of a bat. At least he hoped it was a bat. Not a rat, not down here … a whole nest of them, ready to pour out of the darkness on top of him. 'It's not fucking funny!'

Then there was a *whirring* round that made his skin crawl; coming closer. A giant snake, he thought; the tail of a rattlesnake vibrating, or the stinger of an equally large scorpion ready to jab forward out of the dark. He could imagine the pain in his chest and the dizzying numbness as the poison took hold. The sweat. The yellowish drool coming out of his mouth

The *whirring* sound got louder, closer, coming from above, bringing a light with it. Juggs let out a great sigh, tension deflating his body. He could see his friends standing beside the hole he had made, both of them turning the handle of a wind-up lantern.

'Get out of the way,' Billy told him. 'We've coming down beside you.'

'Wait,' Juggs said, not sure if that was a good idea, but it was too late. First Billy, and then Murray, lowered themselves down beside him, dangling from the floorboards above to drop the last few feet, Murray managing to hook the handle of his lantern onto a jagged end of broken floorboard above them.

'It *is* a coffin,' Murray said, wonder in his voice.

'Good thinking, you two,' gasped Juggs, as the pain flared up in his knee again. 'How are we supposed to get out if we're all down here?'

'We can drag the coffin right underneath the hole and climb on top of it,' Billy said simply, as if that was something they did every day. 'Once we see what's inside.'

Juggs started forward. 'I'll go up now.'

Billy grabbed his arm. 'We might as well have a look, seeing you went to the trouble of getting us down here.'

Juggs pulled himself free. 'This is a grave, thicko. Get it? You're talking about grave-robbing.'

'Come on, we don't even know if there's a body in there.'

'Maybe its Treeve Carveth,' Murray said.

'Who's he?'

'The local celebrity,' Billy said.

'Yeah,' nodded Murray, getting excited. 'Maybe he was buried with all sorts of things. Gold crosses, jewellery, a watch.'

Billy walked around the cellar, turning the handle of his wind-up lantern as he went. He stopped beside the far wall, and wrapped it with knuckles. 'Solid stone,' he told them. 'Look at this.' He turned the handle faster and faster, increasing the light from the lantern, illuminating several hooks on the wall from which chains and cutting implements hung. 'Now why do you need stuff like this in a church?'

'*Under* a church?' Murray reminded him.

Walking towards his friends, Billy's hopes of finding something interesting started to fade as soon as the lantern light revealed the coffin to be not much more than a poorly constructed wooden box with a jagged crack on the lid, probably caused by Juggs landing on it. He couldn't imagine a minister honoured by his parishioners being laid to rest in a crude coffin such as this? And placed beneath the church? It didn't make sense. There were no handles on the side, only a strong rope wrapped around the centre.

'What's the rope for?' Murray asked.

'To lower the coffin down, you dummy. Why else would it be there?' Billy reached into his pocket and took out his Swiss Army Knife.

'Wait,' Juggs said. 'I saw an old film like this once. The coffin was chained shut because there was a vampire inside, and some idiot broke the chains and let it out.'

'Well, this isn't a chain, and we're not idiots, and there are no such things as vampires.'

Famous last words, thought Murray, watching his friend begin to cut through the rope.

Juggs backed away, expecting the lid of the coffin to be lifted to reveal a cadaverous body with pasty-white skin, ruby-red lips, and –

'Hey, Juggs, take a look at this!'

His imagination had almost got it right. The body was perfectly preserved. Long and thin, an old man wearing faded, worn clothes who had straggly white hair, yellowish, wrinkled skin wrapped stretched across the jutting bones of his face and something stuffed in his mouth.

'What is that?' Billy croaked, making a face to accompany the bad taste in his mouth.

Murray bent down closer to the corpse's face. 'It looks like an old cloth.'

'Maybe its garlic,' Juggs suggested. 'As in clove of garlic, or bulb of garlic. You know, part of the old disposal-of-vampires routine.'

Billy laughed. The sound echoed upwards to disturb the bats in the remains of the church roof.

'I'm serious. The only sure way to kill a vampire is by driving a stake through the heart and cutting the head off, then you put garlic in its mouth and bury the body at a crossroads.'

Billy nodded. 'Sort of like leaving the bodies of suicides out in the hills so their spirits can't some back home.'

'And imagine how pissed off they would be if they did,' Juggs said.

'Well, his head is still attached to his body and this isn't garlic,' Murray pointed out, easing the piece of material out of the dead man's mouth. Juggs grabbed his arm, a little too late.

'Don't touch that, you might catch something.'

Murray shook the cloth, which opened enough to reveal several ominous-looking red stains. Screwing up his face in disgust, Murray opened his fingers and wiped his hand on the side of his wet jacket.

'Some vampire,' Billy said. 'There's no stake through his chest. Whoever buried him probably stuffed that rag into his mouth to swell the cheeks out.'

'But he's so lifelike,' Juggs whispered. 'He should be rotten, stinking, his flesh all gluey, the eyeballs fallen in. Covered in writhing maggots and –'

'We get the picture,' Billy told him.

'Maybe, it's the ground,' Murray said, looking round. 'Remember that school history project we did about the old American West? I read that they dug up Wild Bill Hickok to rebury him and his body was rock hard, looking as fresh as the day he was first buried.'

'Yeah, but this guy isn't buried in the ground, he's lying on top of it.'

'I was wondering...' Billy said.

'Yeah?' Murray replied

'We could look through his pockets, see if he was buried with something that tells us who he was.'

Juggs sniggered. 'What? Like a card that says do not resuscitate, or something?'

Billy glared at his friend. 'I meant maybe like a small Bible with his name in it.' He gestured above them. 'This is a church after all. He could have been a church elder or another minister or something.'

'I don't know,' Murray said hesitantly.

'I mean, we've broken the church floor, cracked a coffin lid, took the lid off to look at the corpse, how bad can things get?'

'Er, wouldn't this be a little thing called grave-robbing,' Juggs pointed out. 'We're supposed to be scouts.'

'I'm not talking about stealing his jewels or bars of gold or whatever he's got, just seeing if he has something on him. A Bible, a letter, a love letter, whatever, some clue to who he is.'

'Well,' said Murray, chewing his lip.

Juggs raised his eyebrows.

'Oh, for Pete's sake ... we'll be down here all night,' said Billy, moving forward, his fingers danced over the corpse's clothes, feeling the pockets. Nothing. He reached inside the jacket, pulling open the shirt to reveal the pale chest underneath.

'Look at this,' he said excitedly. 'There's something written on his skin.'

'What do you mean, written?' asked Juggs, curiosity aroused.

Murray peered over his friend's shoulder at a series of odd symbols.

'Shit,' said Juggs, backing away. 'He's caught some disease that killed him. That's why it's written on his chest, as a warning.'

'Rubbish, it's not a warning,' Billy told him. 'It's not even words, just symbols, like hieroglyphics, old stuff.'

Murray snapped his fingers together. 'I got it, he's a criminal and they branded the name of his crime on his chest.'

Juggs jabbed out his index finger in anger. 'Oh, yeah, who the fuck buries a criminal in a church?'

'How would I know?' Billy spat back at him. 'It's as crazy an idea as someone being buried with the name of a disease written on their chest. Some warning, Juggs. Who's going to read it down here?'

Murray moved away from the coffin. 'Maybe it's some magic shit. Black magic shit.'

Billy looked at his friend and back at Juggs. They both shook their heads slightly, and a smile crossed Billy's face as he tried hard not to tell Murray that was another stupid idea, like they would bury some evil sorcerer guy underneath a church. Despite their surroundings, he could feel a fit of the giggles starting up inside him.

Click!

'What's that?' Murray asked, cocking his head to the side.

'I didn't hear anything,' Billy said.

'I did.' Juggs pushed past him and moved closer to the coffin.

'His mouth just snapped shut, that's all,' Murray said, shrugging. 'That manky cloth must have been holding his jaws open.'

'But it shouldn't have closed like that,' Juggs whispered, staring at the corpse. 'Not after all these years.'

Billy moved closer again and stared at the body. The closed mouth had come together in something that looked like a satisfied smile, a knowing smugness on the face, which he didn't like. He glanced over his shoulder at the wind-up lantern hanging from the broken floorboard. Its light was starting to dim.

'Time to go, methinks, let's get the broken lid back on and tie this thing up again.'

Juggs stared up at the hole he had created, his eyes making out the shimmering drops of sleet that streaked down like miniature meteor showers through the holes in the broken roof. He tapped his foot, and looked over at Billy. 'Hurry up, will you?'

Suddenly Billy jerked forward, was flung back slightly and jerked forward again. 'It's got me!' he whined. 'Oh, Jesus, it's got me! Help! Help!'

Juggs swallowed. He couldn't move. Then he remembered something and his hand began to dig through all the crap he had in a soggy pocket for his own wind-up torch. He took it out and turned the handle, creating a *whirring* noise as it charged up. He stared at Murray. His friend looked frozen, rooted to the spot, like a small animal caught in the glare of a car's oncoming headlights.

Murray broke the spell and reached out to grab Billy's shoulder, pulling him back from the coffin.

Billy turned round, eyes wide and gleaming, full of glee. A grin split the bottom of his face. He looked mad, hair slick and wet and stuck to his head, making him resemble a malevolent ventriloquist dummy. He laughed, and pointed at them.

'Admit it, eh? That had you going. Turn around, Johnson, and let's see if that's really a chocolate stain on the seat of your trousers.'

'You dickhead!'

'Whatever you say,' Billy replied, and winced as a sharp pain lanced his ears.

'*Ohhh!*' Juggs moaned, holding up his right hand to his head and wiggling his finger inside his ear. 'What the hell was that?'

Before anyone could reply the sound of metal striking metal rang all around them, the hooks and chains dangling from the walls vibrating from side to side.

Juggs watched the metal links dance up and down as if shaken by something he could not see.

Murray now flinched, a shiver coursing through his body.

His hand was touching something wet and sticky; a moss-covered piece of the coffin, he thought, shying away from the source of his discomfort.

But it still touched him. In fact clutched him, squeezed him painfully. Tighter and tighter, the grip of someone pulling themselves back from the other side of the grave.

'*It's got me!*' he screamed.

Billy shook his head, and threw up his arms. 'Yeah, right. I've just done that one. Think up your own jokes.'

Murray looked at his hand and what was holding it and fainted clean away. His body slumped to the ground. Billy reached down towards his friend … as the corpse sat upright, rasping breath rattled in its body, struggling to reach collapsed lungs through thick layers of mucous.

Juggs bit back his own scream as he watched the shape grab Billy by the throat, and commence throttling the life out of him, The wind-up torch shook in his hand, turning the scene into a flickering horror film made at the beginning of the last century. Juggs reached up, straining towards the jagged pieces of floorboard above.

Even on his toes, the wood was too far away. He tensed to jump, almost weeping, as pain wrapped itself around his throbbing knee. He bit his bottom lip, face contorted, hands stretching. His fingers touched the sharp, broken edges. He could make it. He could, if that thing didn't get him first.

Take a long time dying, Billy, please. Do that one last favour for me.

He threw the torch up into the church and jumped, both hands clasping the broken floorboards. He kicked out, climbing on air. Swinging an arm round, he used his elbow to give some purchase on the floorboards and claw a way out of the nightmare. He pulled his other arm up, and wriggled forward inch by inch towards safety.

The wood bent beneath him.

Don't stop, he told himself. Keep moving, and he pushed on, ignoring the way the floor seemed to curve beneath his body. A sharp piece of wood pressed into him, stabbing his guts.

Move, Johnson. C'mon, move, Juggs told himself. *Move.* And he did. Downwards as the floorboards snapped.

He seemed to be falling through thick soup instead of darkness. He caught hold with his hand on the way down, and hung swaying in the fading light of the lantern. Then dropped again. Falling the last six feet gave him enough time to think how unlucky he had been. Just a few more inches and he would have made it. Typical. No luck. If he had been really lucky he would have landed on his head, knocking himself out, and not been aware of the thing that was now scuttling through the slices of darkness and light to get him.

THE VOICE IN THE TUNNELS

Visit St Agnes on the north Cornish coast today, and one could be forgiven for not realising that this was once a prominent industrial site. A picturesque village overlooking the Atlantic, a heritage area rightly proud of its beaches and coves, and a site of special archaeological and ancient historical significance, it attracts multitudes of summer-time visitors, apparently offering the all-round Cornish tourist experience. But in the 18th and 19th centuries, St Agnes, which sits half way along the road between Newquay and Redruth, flourished on the basis of its tin, copper and arsenic mines.

Even in the 21st century, 200 years after some of them were abandoned, relics of these small industrial outposts are visible all over Cornwall, their solitary chimneys and tall, gaunt engine-houses crowning isolated headlands or lowering at the ends of bleak moorland paths. But St Agnes was a real focal point of operations, the first mines opening there in pre-Roman and medieval times, expanding dramatically during the Industrial Revolution, and persisting well into the 20th century, only ceasing to function in 1941.

Yet this seemingly modern aspect to life in St Agnes does not mean that the town cannot share in Cornwall's esoteric reputation. Far from it.

All Cornish tin mines are haunted. That is a known fact among locals. The Knockers, for example, were mysterious invisible beings who would announce their presence in a mine by ceaselessly knocking on the other side of tunnel walls. Views about their nature varied from one pit to the next, some men seeing them as essentially benign – the souls of earlier miners killed in accidents and now offering warnings if disaster was again at hand, or even the remnants of deceased sinners (in one version those who stood by and allowed Jesus to be crucified!) seeking to atone by drawing the miners' attention to new undiscovered lodes. However, others believed they were faeries or gnomes, subterranean spirits who delighted in playing tricks on the human interlopers, and sometimes worse, stealing their lamps and tools, maybe even leading them into peril. In both cases, tin miners would often leave pasties in the lower galleries to try and appease this uncanny presence.

The St Agnes tin mines were no different, though one of these, the Polbreen mine, situated near to St Agnes Beacon, boasted its own unique and particularly unnerving story.

It was at Polbreen where a local woman committed suicide. The cause and date of this sad event are both unknown, but it was said that the woman's name was Dorcas, and that she lived in a nearby cottage. One day, in a fit of apparent mania – an unsubstantiated rumour holds that it was brought on by the death of her tin-miner fiancé – she threw herself down the deepest of the Polbreen shafts. A major excavation was undertaken to recover her body, which naturally was broken to pieces, but from this time on Dorcas's voice was heard singing, wailing or calling down the tunnels, often summoning miners who were working there by their actual names. No-one ever claimed to have seen the phantom, but a significant number of witnesses reported such events. Some said they were lured into deeper galleries in search of the source of the voice, and subsequently became lost, while others felt overwhelmingly frightened and fled back to the surface, a couple claiming that unseen hands had attempted to rend the shirts from their backs as they ran.

Despite this, most Polbreen tin miners claimed there was no feeling of evil in the pit, merely that they were distracted from their work, while at least one credited Dorcas with saving his life when she called him repeatedly until drawing him away from a gallery which a short time later was buried by falling rocks.

Very little remains of the Polbreen mine today, though the St Agnes area is still strewn with surface ruins. By all accounts, the spirit of Dorcas remained active underground until the pit was closed, and for some time afterwards an eerie presence could be detected at night along Polbreen Lane, the small road that once led out from the village to the disused mine.

LOSING ITS IDENTITY

Thana Niveau

Sole, Lundy, Fastnet, Irish Sea. South backing northeast 4 or 5, increasing 6 at times. Thundery showers. Moderate or good.

The waves moved like a carpet of restless bones, while above them, deep grey clouds writhed in the lowering sky. From somewhere out in the gathering shadows came a low growl of thunder. It made Miranda think of dangerous animals whose cages had just been sprung. They would bide their time, gathering strength. Then they would strike.

Sunny summers were a thing of rare beauty these days, and the nominal season seemed to get shorter every year. Gone were the long, languid stretches of warmth Miranda recalled from her childhood. In what amounted to fractions of seconds in geological time, the world had been transformed.

It had always been said that Britain had no climate, only weather. That was true now more than ever. Freak storms had become the rule rather than the exception. And much of their wrath was focussed on Cornwall.

The Cornish coastline was one of the most spectacular in the world. It was a wild, primordial place. Volcanic rock and Devonian slate mingled with fault-ridden limestone to form natural sculptures up and down the coast, and copper deposits gave the water its distinctive blue-green hue. Whitecaps surged and broke against the rocky cliffs, carving them into fantastical spires and pillars. For Miranda it had always seemed a place of ancient magic.

As a child, the seaside town of Tintagel had been her playground. She had swum in the turquoise waters, explored Merlin's Cave, clambered over the crumbling ruins of the castle, and wandered along the headland to gaze out across the Atlantic Ocean. A little further inland, the waterfall in St Nectan's Glen had provided sanctuary during turbulent times.

In her seventy-three years, she had lived as far north as Bude, as far south as Lizard, and as far inland as Launceston. But Porthkellis was the place she had finally called home. It was where she had met Will, the mirror to her soul.

Porthkellis itself was unremarkable. The tiny village was perched on the headland north of an equally tiny cove called Lost Moon. Most of the inhabitants of the village had gone, leaving empty homes they couldn't sell, shops they couldn't lease. Many coastal villages were similarly becoming ghost towns. But while Miranda might have been able to leave Porthkellis, she could never leave Lost Moon.

The cove was what kept her here. It was a picturesque little inlet with a beach that was difficult for even the most determined of tourists to get to. Once it had been a clothing-optional hotspot, and she and Will had spent many summer days basking in the sun, naked as Nature intended and free of all inhibitions. But the eroding coastline had destroyed the easy route down. Now only a set of steep, crumbling steps led to the beach, and the path grew more hazardous with each passing year.

Tressa was forever telling her to stop going down there, insisting that she was too old and forgetful. She wasn't as young as she once was. She could get hurt, lost, killed. Miranda had to wonder when her daughter had become her mother.

'I know that cove better than I know any place on this earth,' Miranda had told her, many times.

To which Tressa would shake her head with an exasperated sigh. Sometimes she would argue. Sometimes she would storm off in a huff. Their relationship was as full of cracks as the cliffs that made the landscape so dramatic.

There were exquisite places everywhere along the peninsula, but for Miranda, there was no place like Lost Moon. The inlet itself was only about the size of a football pitch, making it feel intimate, and the water was the magnificent blue of peacocks and kingfishers. Enormous stone formations crouched in the shallows like ancient guardians, while jagged cliffs soared upwards on either side of the rocky beach. High on the northernmost cliff, a derelict lighthouse was the only reminder of civilisation.

In low tide the cove was a place of eerie wonder, with the exposed seabed resembling an emerging causeway, a road to faraway places. The boulders closest to shore looked as though they might topple without the water to hold them up. Over the years, time and nature had wrought their changes, shearing off one of the legs of the formation known as the Charging Bull. His horns were looking weathered now, and it might not be long before they too fell into the water below.

The Dragon's Back was also in jeopardy. Most of the spiky protrusion along the southern cliff had already collapsed, with the remaining spines resembling the tail of a giant stegosaurus. It jutted upwards, piercing the low clouds.

The beach was littered with debris from the eroding cliffs and the pounding sea. When the tide rose, waves rushed into the cove, flooding the beach and smashing up against the curve of the rock wall, as they had done for thousands upon thousands of years. Violent storms were far more frequent now, and evidence of their fury was all around. Incredible to think that glaciers melting at the top of the earth could change the weather in places so far away, that smashing through the polar ice and permafrost could alter the climate of an entire world.

Lost Moon was no less beautiful for its deterioration, however, and Miranda marvelled that she so rarely encountered other people here. But then, as Tressa was constantly reminding her, there were other far more accessible places, with safer beaches. Places that didn't take so much effort to reach. Places that weren't such a deathtrap.

Will had never worried about her. The two of them were children of the land and they knew instinctively how to read its signs and avoid its traps. Will could always tell which bit of stone would crumble first, while Miranda knew without looking where to place her feet.

By contrast, Tressa had never felt at home near the wild sea, and she had fled to a comfortable life in the city as soon as she came of age. Miranda and Will had missed her, certainly, but it wasn't the traumatic, wrenching separation that other parents had experienced. Their daughter's leaving was more like the departing of a beloved, but nonetheless frustrating, minder. And with no one around any more to tell them off, Miranda and Will could climb all the treacherous cliffs they wanted to, and sleep out under the stars if they felt like it.

Tressa had actually been conceived on the beach one romantic evening, a fact that had only made the girl wrinkle her nose in distaste when they shared it with her many years ago.

'Too much information!' she had shrieked, a typical teenager who couldn't believe that her parents had ever been young. But now that Tressa was older she berated Miranda for not sharing *enough* information. Where was she going? When would she be back? When had she last eaten, and what? Was she *sure*?

That was the question that annoyed Miranda the most. *Was she sure?* 'Mum, are you *sure* you ate breakfast? Are you *sure* you took your pills?'

And no, Miranda *wasn't* always sure, but badgering her wasn't going to help her memory, now was it? The only thing that helped was Will. And he was in the cove.

'I'm sure of *you*, my love,' she said, her voice lost in the lapping waves.

The tide was out and the wet sand was riddled with the footprints of sea birds. They scurried between the rockpools in search of easy meals – trapped fish and crabs. Sometimes strange things washed up on the shore. Shoes, fishing nets, parts of ships, Lego bricks. Once Miranda had found the body of a dolphin. There were no obvious injuries, and she imagined the poor thing had beached itself. Its empty eyes had haunted her ever since.

Thunder grumbled overhead and Miranda noticed that the clouds had darkened and drawn nearer. The air was heavy with the threat of rain. All week the forecast had warned of nasty weather, but the warning was so familiar now that no one batted an eye any more. Brighton had been devastated by a hurricane the year before, and the Somerset Levels had drowned in horrific floods a few years before that. Tornados, blizzards and hailstorms were becoming commonplace all across the UK.

And Cornwall? Cornwall was sinking.

Rising sea levels were gradually nibbling away at all the world's coasts, reclaiming the land, but Cornwall's erosion was especially dramatic. A single violent storm now did the work of multiple smaller ones and it wasn't unusual to have several years' worth of damage in a single season. Conservationists could barely keep up as record levels of coastline vanished each year. There was no question that, in the battle between sea and land, the sea would emerge triumphant.

Miranda yelped as she trod on a shell and she glared at it reproachfully. It felt as though the sea were making a point. Making *Tressa's* point.

'Mum, you need to get out of here while you still can.'

The morning's row was still buzzing around in Miranda's head, nagging at her like a persistent fly. Or had it been yesterday? Oh, did it even matter? It was always the same, as though they were reading from a prepared script.

'You've left it too late to get anything for the cottage. You should just pack up your stuff and go. Bodmin isn't that far away, and Simon and I –'

'It's my home. And I'm not leaving.'

'What if you get hurt? Do you know how far away the nearest hospital is? An ambulance would never reach you in time.'

Miranda had heard that particular argument so many times it carried no weight at all. And she knew what Tressa was really afraid of. That her memory would get worse. That she'd forget something. Forget to take her meds or wander off and forget where – or even *who* – she was.

So she'd done it once. So what? Well, okay, maybe it was twice. But what the hell – everyone got a little confused once in a while.

Tressa had looked at her with intolerable pity. 'You really don't remember, do you?'

'I promise not to haunt you if I come to a bad end,' Miranda finally snapped.

'That's not funny! And it's not what I meant either.'

Miranda sighed. 'Listen, I know you think that every time you see me will be the last time –'

'I do not –'

'But I'm not going anywhere and you're not going to scare me away. This is my home and I'm not leaving.'

'You're not some bloody frontierswoman in the Old West! You're a –' Tressa had stopped herself there. She shook her head and looked down at the floor.

'I'm a what? Hmm? It's okay, dear, you can say it. I'm a feeble old woman who can't remember her own name, who doesn't have the sense to know what's good for her. Isn't that right?'

'Oh, for God's sake! I didn't say that. You know I didn't say that. And no, of course you're not that far gone. But it's only a matter of time. You have to face facts.'

'No, *you* have to face facts. This is my home, mine and Will's.'

'He's not here any more, Mum; he's dead!'

Miranda froze, staring at her daughter in shock. It wasn't the words so much as the vehemence behind them, the fury. For a moment she wasn't sure she even knew who the woman sitting across from her was. It couldn't possibly be her daughter. Her daughter would never say such a cruel thing.

Tressa seemed to know she'd gone too far. 'Mum, look, I'm sorry –'

But Miranda waved away her words as though they were a foul odour. 'I think you've said enough.'

'I didn't mean –'

'Please get out. Just go.'

To her credit, Tressa had managed to keep her temper under control as she left. She didn't slam the door this time, but Miranda had waited until she heard the car pull away before throwing Tressa's mug against the wall, showering the kitchen floor with tea and porcelain shards.

Twenty years ago, menopause had made her feel obsolete, as though, since she could no longer breed, Nature had no further use for her. But Will's passing had made her feel *invisible*, as if she no longer existed.

She'd stared at the broken mug through eyes blurred with tears, staring so long and hard that the mess became meaningless. Just a jumble of colours and textures, things that had no purpose. Like repeating a word until it meant nothing. Mug. Mug. Mug.

She didn't need reminding that she was alone. But she *liked* being alone. With no one else around, she could keep Will alive. He had been gone from her side physically for almost ten years, but she allowed herself to forget that. She still talked to him every day. In her solitary world, he still lived.

She had no idea how long she'd stood staring at the jagged shards and the pale brown puddle before coming back to herself. Then she had gone to Lost Moon.

The cove was where she came to be with Will. She had scattered his ashes here, and Lost Moon was where she heard his voice most clearly. She might confuse dates or forget appointments, but Will's presence was the one constant she could rely on.

'For whatever we lose (like a you or a me) it's always ourselves we find in the sea.'

Will had taught her that quote.

'By e e cummings,' Miranda said with a touch of pride. 'See? There's nothing wrong with my memory.'

But Will wasn't the one who needed to hear it.

```
Variable 7 becoming cyclonic later. Rough or very
rough. Squally showers. Poor, occasionally very
poor.
```

The sky was getting strange. It wasn't darkening so much as greying. And the water that reflected the steely colour was receding further and further, exposing more of the seabed by the minute.

Intrigued, Miranda ventured out into the empty cove. The wet sand squelched beneath her bare feet and between her toes. She had never seen the tide this far out before, never seen so much of what lay beneath it. It made her think of the land bridges that had existed millions of years ago, before the continents had broken apart and settled into their present arrangement. Her distant ancestors could have walked between Cornwall and Canada.

The water continued to trickle away, inch by gradual inch, as though beckoning her to follow. A chill wind teased the back of her neck and the words came instinctively.

'Will? Is that you?'

There was no response this time. The thundery sky had quietened and the only sound was the gentle slosh of the water as it receded.

In minutes the cove was completely laid bare. It was an astonishing sight, like a lake that had suddenly dried up. Miranda crept to the opening of the inlet, to where the cliffs stood aside like a gate. She had never been this far out from the beach before. At least she didn't think she had. She couldn't be sure. The high water marks on the headland looked very high indeed, and the muddy expanse stretched away to the horizon. The ocean had disappeared.

She hesitated before stepping out beyond the curve of Lost Moon, into an alien landscape. She was walking on the floor of the ocean. Fish flopped and gasped where they had been stranded, and Miranda felt a pang of sorrow for them. Their world and all they knew had been ripped away.

Was she dreaming? Had she fallen and hit her head? Or was she really just as confused as Tressa insisted she was?

The air was salty and sharp, the way it had smelled the day she'd scattered Will's ashes. She hadn't really known what to expect when she opened the urn. Her husband had not been reduced to powder, not entirely. The consistency was more like chalk, with small chunks of bone, like dead coral. How strange it was to hold those pieces in her hand, to clutch a fragment of what might have been an arm or a hip bone. Or even his skull.

From somewhere out in the boundless depths she had heard the calling of whales, so beautiful and yet so profoundly sad. On their honeymoon she and Will had gone on a whale-watching cruise. The magnificent animals had breached several times for them, putting on a spectacular display, soaring out of the water to become airborne for a moment before falling back into the embrace of the waves. That was when Will had told her to bury him at sea.

It had been difficult to let the pieces of him go. And in the end she had simply let them rest on her palm close to the water, where the frothy waves could kiss her hand and carry them away, out to where the whales were singing.

Now, as she stood on the empty beach, she couldn't help but wonder how many bones lay beneath her. Thousands of millions of years pulverised stone into sand. Was the entire seabed a muddy vista of bones?

Miranda had no idea where the water had gone, or when – if ever – it would return, but she felt compelled to keep walking. Crabs skittered out of her way as she passed. The wet sand sloped steeply downwards into a valley and she was soon very deep in the basin. The surface would be several metres over her head if the water were still here.

It looked like a desert of mud, but the empty ocean wasn't barren. There was debris all around her. Jagged shapes clawed at the sky, and one in particular caught her eye. It took her a while to realise it was the wreckage of a ship. It lay broken over several huge fingers of rock. Submerged, the rocks would have been invisible, lurking beneath the waves, a deadly threat to an unsuspecting craft.

As she moved closer she realised it must be the *Kilcarra*. The ship had been lost in a storm many years before, her whereabouts forever unknown. None of the fifty-eight people on board had ever been found. The ship was in several pieces, scattered across the open seabed like a child's toy dropped from a vast height.

It was one thing to dive into the ocean and explore a shipwreck beneath the waves, and quite another to simply walk up to one lying in pieces on the sludge of the exposed seabed. The world seemed to tilt beneath her feet. An eel squirmed free of the shattered vessel, twisting like an earthworm trapped on the pavement. The thought of what else might lie inside the wreckage made Miranda shudder and she turned away.

Something else caught her eye, something much further out into the sodden plain. A cluster of odd shapes. Her first thought was that it was another shipwreck, but it was far too large for a single craft. The shapes were squarish, suggestive of manmade structures. Even so, they didn't look at all modern.

As she drew nearer she could see that they were spaced at regular intervals along a curved, textured depression. Her breath caught in her throat. Now she knew she must be dreaming. This couldn't possibly be real. There was a road beneath her feet, with houses on either side. She was looking at a lost city.

Southwesterly severe gale 9, veering north and increasing storm 10.

'Oh, Will. Where are we?'

Her voice was barely a whisper, but it broke the unnerving silence.

She stood trembling at the edge of the road, staring, listening. The air was still, as though the sky were holding its breath. The only sounds came from the wriggling, dying fish and the steady drip of water from the rustic stone houses.

She stared in silent awe as she realised where she was.

'The Roscarrock drawings,' she whispered. 'It's all real.'

John Roscarrock was a thirteenth century woodcutter who had done a series of controversial maps and sketches of the area. They were generally dismissed as either whimsy or madness, showing, as they did, a completely different Cornwall than that seen on other maps of the period.

Will had always been fascinated by the drawings, in particular one that showed an island off the northern coast, a few miles out to sea from Tintagel. On it Roscarrock had drawn a small settlement.

The original village of Porthkellis.

Legend had it that the village had fallen into the sea and been rebuilt further inland many years later. But no one had ever found any evidence of a first settlement, and of course no one who lived in Porthkellis, not even the oldest residents, could verify whether there had been one.

She remembered it all now. At the time she had found the drawings charmingly fanciful, like those old shipping maps that showed dragons and sea monsters lurking in the oceans. Now she had to question whether the accusations of madness were true. Because if Roscarrock had been mad, then so was she.

It was all here, just as he had drawn. She could even see where the headland had once extended further out from the coast, curving like a crescent moon to form the cove. Time and the rising tide had submerged it completely, taking the village with it.

Centuries later, here it lay.

The houses had been flattened somewhat by the weight of the ocean, but there was no mistaking what they were. She had passed through into another place, another world. The air felt heavy, not with rain but with time. With voices. She heard whispering in the doorways and for a moment she was certain she saw movement in among the stone formations. She could imagine figures moving between the houses, going about their lives.

The largest dwelling stood at the end of the curving road and she hesitated before it, her heart pounding with exhilaration and fear. She was uneasy about entering the house. It felt like trespassing in a graveyard. For a moment she hung back, gazing through what had once been a window.

Curiosity finally got the best of her and she gave in to the urge to investigate. She had to duck to go beneath the crooked lintel but, once inside, she could stand upright. Naturally there were no furnishings or decorations. Just the crude skeletal structure of the stone walls.

Scattered across the floor were scores of stranded fish, gasping their last. Outside, many others had finally gone still. Like an inverted shipwreck, the walls had trapped the fish as the ocean bled away, leaving them to die in the open air. Would her own cottage look like this in time, laid bare and filled with dying creatures? Years from now, would someone stand in the ruins of it, wondering about the woman who had lived there?

As she gazed at the fish, their slick silvery bodies seemed to shimmer, to transform. She imagined people instead, the people who had lived here, who must have watched the ocean inching closer and closer every day.

What must it have been like to see the water creeping up to them, until the waves kissed the stone and slithered in through the doors and windows? It must have seemed like a living thing, a sentient creature seeking entry. Perhaps they worshipped it, made offerings to it.

The idea chilled her.

She turned away and left the house, continuing down the road. The water had washed away any trace of the actual road, but its path was obvious from the position of the houses. She followed it to the end.

For as far as she could see, there was only sand and silt, the exposed bottom of the ocean. The sodden ground on which she now stood had not touched the sky for hundreds of years.

High overhead the clouds were swirling, pale grey and yellow and green. Even the colours were alien. The wind was howling in the sky, but down in the lost city, all was calm and still. The storm was up there, circling, watching with a vast and empty eye. A sea change was coming. It had been coming for the last hundred years.

All at once she felt dizzy. She stumbled and lost her balance, falling to her knees. Her hands sank into the silt and she clutched at it helplessly. But she only drew away fistfuls of sludge. If the water never came back, the sun would eventually turn all the mud into sand. Then other things might emerge. There had been an entire village hidden beneath the water; what might be hiding beneath the sand?

Whatever we lose ...

Miranda's head was pounding, as though some memory was trying to reveal itself, some crucial understanding.

... like a you or a me ...

Her stomach plunged as it came to her. There was something she had forgotten. Something important. What was the word Tressa had used to describe the cove? Deathtrap. Yes. Oh yes, there was danger here.

Will was dead. And it was the sea that had taken him from her.

She had fought so hard to forget, to bury the memory, but now it flooded back to her like a wave. She saw herself kneeling on the beach, shaking him, calling his name, *screaming*. But the undertow had just been too strong that day. The sea they both adored had claimed him for itself.

Miranda had fed his bones to it, but the ocean would not give him back. It wasn't his voice she had been hearing in the waves all this time and it wasn't his voice she heard now.

There came a soft hiss, a susurration. The ocean had been holding its breath. Now it exhaled. The hissing built to a roar, a shriek, a banshee wail.

Out beyond the horizon Miranda could hear the waves gathering, meeting the storm in the sky and combining forces. The sea had swallowed the sky, just as it had swallowed ships, coastline, even villages. Just like it had swallowed Will. Because, like the polar ice, it too was cracked and broken. The ocean had lost its mind.

Ice melting. Chrysalis shattered. Metamorphosis complete. Imago rising.

Miranda turned and ran for the shore, but the sodden seabed sucked at her feet, slowing her down. Again and again she fell in the wet sand, her progress slow and hopeless.

'Will, help me!'

But Will was gone. She knew that now. There was only the voice of the sea, which was rising to a deafening scream. The shoreline was so far away.

The sky was bleached white and the icy wind stung her face. It was like trying to run through a blizzard. The lighthouse stood like a lone survivor on the cliff, a thin, pale guardian. Miranda kept her eyes fixed on it as she pushed herself onwards. Behind her she could hear the wave gathering, the waters swarming together into a monstrous shape.

And finally, she couldn't help it; she looked back.

She had never seen the Himalayas but she didn't imagine they could have looked any higher than the blue-grey mountain that rose behind her now. A scream caught in her throat and for a moment she stood transfixed, hypnotised by the deadly majesty of it. Only, unlike a mountain, this peak was neither solid nor still. It wavered as it rose and grew, climbing towards the sky, a living tempest.

At last it touched the sky and began to curve, forming a beautiful, hideous arch. Like a huge grasping hand, it reached for the shore, clutching with ghostly whitecap fingers.

And then the wave began to fall. Miranda could only crouch where she was and watch, spellbound and helpless. The wall of water descended with a roar and she saw animals swarming within it, trapped there in their thousands. Fish, turtles, dolphins, whales.

The ocean was alive. Every life form on earth depended on it for survival, and yet it was completely unaware of its importance. From the tiniest insects to the largest whales, to the most passionate human beings, it took no notice of any of them.

The great arm of water curved and fell, punching into the mud with phenomenal force. Spume exploded from the point of impact, a surge of blinding white. For a moment Miranda stood beneath the hellish blue arch of the pipeline, and then the wave closed around her.

Miranda felt the bones in her knees snap, but there was no pain. She was cut off from herself as the living liquid caught her and swept her inside. She flailed wildly, striking fish and other creatures as she struggled against the churning current. Her legs dangled uselessly but she continued to kick her thighs, instinctively fighting to reach the surface.

It all seemed to happen in slow motion. Her body was yanked in all directions by the surge as the wave pulled back, but she could feel herself moving upwards. At last she broke through to the air and she gasped for breath, gulping in as much air as she could.

She stayed afloat, pushed back into the sea as the wave gathered itself for another strike. It carried her up, all the way to its boiling crest. The world looked so tiny below, the way it did when seen from a plane. She must be thousands of feet up in the sky. Her ruined body was beginning to sing with agony now. She cried Will's name, merging her voice with that of the screaming wave. All she could do was go where it took her, and it was racing towards Lost Moon, towards the lighthouse and Porthkellis and all the other places sheltered by the land.

The monstrous wave began to curl high over the cliffs, all the indifferent madness of nature ready to fall on the flooded coastline below. And as the wave began to break, Miranda heard another voice. This time she was sure it was Will's.

```
Low Trafalgar 866 expected Lundy 993 by same time.
Losing its identity. Rain later. Good.
```

SOURCES

All of these stories are original to *Terror Tales of Cornwall*, with the exception of 'Dragon Path' by Jacqueline Simpson, which first appeared in *All Hallows* #30, 2002, and 'The Old Traditions Are Best' by Paul Finch, which first appeared in *Shades of Darkness*, 2008.

Other Telos Horror Titles

RAVEN DANE

ABSINTHE AND ARSENIC
DEATH'S DARK WINGS

CYRUS DARIAN SERIES (Forthcoming)
CYRUS DARIAN AND THE TECHNOMICRON
CYRUS DARIAN AND THE GHASTLY HORDE
CYRUS DARIAN AND THE DRAGON

SAM STONE

THE VAMPIRE GENE SERIES
1: KILLING KISS
2: FUTILE FLAME
3: DEMON DANCE
4: HATEFUL HEART
5: SILENT SAND
6: JADED JEWEL

KAT LIGHTFOOT MYSTERIES
1. ZOMBIES AT TIFFANY'S
2: KAT ON A HOT TIN AIRSHIP
3: WHAT'S DEAD PUSSYKAT
4: KAT OF GREEN TENTACLES
5. KAT AND THE PENDULUM
6. AND THEN THERE WAS KAT (Forthcoming)

JINX CHRONICLES
1. JINX TOWN
2: JINX MAGIC
3: JINX BOUND (Forthcoming)

THE DARKNESS WITHIN
Science Fiction Horror Short Novel

COLLECTIONS
ZOMBIES IN NEW YORK
CTHULHU AND OTHER MONSTERS